Where The Stars Are

Micah Flowers

To Black trans youth, adults, and elders alike—
The stars will always shine for you.

Acknowledgements

To say this book was a one-person effort would be a lie, as many individuals helped me throughout the journey of writing it.

Firstly, I would like to thank my sensitivity reader and first editor, Catalina Viator. Without them, it would have been impossible to write this book due to the absolute lack of available research regarding certain mental disorders. They aided so much in bringing my characters to life, as well as assisting me in avoiding harmful stereotypes and tropes. Thank you for the help!

Next, I would like to thank my second editor, Kisha Garcia, who has always been a mother to me. Thank you for taking the time out of your incredibly busy life to help me.

I'd also like to thank my partners, who have been my rocks during this entire process. We moved a grand total of four times in the last year, and I don't think I could've gotten this done without their constant encouragement. I love you guys so much!

I want to additionally thank my siblings, who sat with me during late nights while I worked on revision after revision for this novel. You guys fueled me with positive vibes and hilarious memes about my characters. You are all very near and dear to my heart.

And finally, thank you to every other friend, family member, or person who let me chat their ears off about the book; as well as all of my ARC recipients! You are all the best and I'm elated for the future of this series thanks to you!

CONTENT WARNINGS

Where The Stars Are contains explicit sexual content, violence, and other sensitive material. Please heed the following warnings before proceeding:

Heavy implications of child, religious, physical, and verbal abuse, animal death, attempted rape, discussion and implication of capital punishment, self-harm, racism, racially motivated violence/bullying, ableism, slurs (d*ke), mentions of police brutality, grooming, stalking, transmedicalism, forced feminization, implications of coercive sex, genital mutilation, SA/rape (in a dream, implied), suicide (in a dream), perinatal and postpartum depression (including thoughts of child harm), mentions of abortion

Worthy of Note: This book does not contain the traditional HEA/HFN found in romances. The main couple *does* find their HEA in the next book.

"However many years anyone may live,
let them enjoy them all.
But let them remember the days of darkness,
for there will be many.
Everything to come is meaningless."
-Ecclesiastes 11:8

Prologue

April 1978

Another evening in the forest, another limp-heavy stroll in store for Masika.

Snaking her way through troves of cypress trees, she was enlivened by newfound freedom. Her palms flapped animatedly against her torso. Only allotted an hour before curfew, she plotted a visit to her favorite river. The one oh-so-still yet teeming with fish, which she enjoyed watching kiss the surface of the water. Such sights comforted her after each laborious, mentally agonizing day of the week.

Struggling to walk yet again, she sighed in relief as the murky waters grew closer. Once at the threshold, she collapsed on the damp river bank as she always did. Dipping an arm into the tranquil pool, she was fascinated by the stinging that resulted. Blood droplets floated off the limb as she softly grinned. Her breathing slowed as the limited motion of the meander further captivated her, slipping into oblivion.

***

She didn't mean to fall asleep.

She stirred slowly at first, relaxed. Her cat naps usually ended quickly enough to scurry home five minutes before curfew. But sudden alarm set in, breaching her mind as she noticed the deep darkness around her. As her eyes adjusted, she sat up and shot away from the still, decaying water. She waited just long enough to process the combination of grass beneath her feet and a sense of direction.

Then she ran like a bat out of Hell.

Halfway through the mad dash, an abrupt trepidation locked her feet in place, freezing her to the spot. Her short breaths quickened at the reminder of how her grandfather reacted when he was awoken by *anyone*. Terrified at the prospect of unnecessary harm, she lowered herself onto the cold earth. Masika felt oddly calmed by the dark, pungent forest around her. She used it to distract from the panic, palms sinking into the soft underbrush.

Once she was composed enough to make a decision—explore the forest instead of daring to wake Kevin up—she stood. She brushed her hands off on her shorts, then reached into the left pocket. Brandishing a gold-plated lighter, she clicked off the top and brought fire to life. She used the tiny flame to open her field of vision.

Hours flew by as she trekked new paths in the comfort of night. She moved so silently that she spotted many deer during the journey treading as carefully as herself. Like them, she never lingered in an area for long; that was, until she came upon a large clearing.

The smokey heavens enticed her as she approached the center, blades of grass coming up to her calves. Nestled in a matted patch of foliage lay a stack of old, shabby blankets. Trash surrounded the makeshift bed and she briefly wondered if someone used to sleep here. As the lighter shut, killing the faint illumination, she took a seat.

At first, she nervously fidgeted with her hands. She tried to devise a plan to return to her room undetected. However, her focus wouldn't stay on the subject; she found herself staring up at the sky. A sky which gradually cleared, revealing a spatter of shining stars. She devoted her entire attention counting each and every one.

What felt like hours later, a *crunch* in the field startled Masika out of her task. She immediately sat up, feverishly scanning the tree line. Goosebumps raised on her arms as a familiar whistle filled her ears.

Kevin.

She lowered her form in an attempt to conceal herself. The whistling persisted as she began slithering through the unnaturally tall grass, trying to escape. To her dismay, the shrill death rattle only grew louder and louder. Each attempt to stifle her shuddering gasps simply made it harder to breathe. Making matters worse, her limbs threatened to give out, weakened from physical labor. Right as she reached a breaking point, the whistle cut off sharply. A nerve-wracking silence followed as she stilled, hands covering her mouth.

A man's voice shattered the quiet.

"Found you."

***

"Are you lost?"

Masika scrambled onto all fours like a frightened animal. She peered at the sight before her with a cautious glare, having been startled awake. A little Black girl with a red sundress and pigtails gazed at her with intrigue. The weariness gave way to neutrality, and Masika sat crisscrossed in the dirt, rubbing her face.

"No," she mumbled.

"Why ya out here then?" The girl pressed just as a woman's voice called out.

"*Bee?*"

Before Masika could fully wake up, another figure approached. This time, she recognized the woman as her next-door neighbor, Bethany. Kevin regularly voiced his disdain for her, but she had occasionally seen Bethany in passing. The woman came up behind the little girl and tousled her hair as she looked down.

"What do we have here? Ain't you Lina's grandbaby?"

"Yes," Masika answered.

"What are you doing out here by yourself?" Bethany noticed the wounds on her arms. "And you're hurt!"

She barely remembered the altercation with Kevin the previous night, yet she dared not look at the damage he caused. Had he really left her in the forest from evening until morning? What on Earth did he tell Gram? That she ran away? She bit her lip anxiously as Bethany continued.

"Why don't you come with us, dear? We're about to have lunch at my house, then we can get you back home safe."

Masika longed to tell Bethany she never wanted to go back. She didn't want to face Kevin's wrath over and over again. Last night had been brutal enough. Exhausted, she just nodded in acceptance.

Bethany and Bee led her out of the forest and to their quaint neighborhood. A chill raced down Masika's spine as she, still dazed from inner dialogue, espied Kevin's house down the block. She imagined him waiting in her room with the belt. Lost in a mixture of scenarios and memories, she ran into Bethany's backside following through the doorway. Profusely apologizing, Bethany gently hushed her.

"It's alright, dear. We all clumsy sometimes," she reassured, guiding Masika to walk in front of her. "Make yourself at home."

She nearly darted for the couch but stopped dead in her tracks when she realized the amount of filth on her body. "Can't sit or I'll dirty," was all that managed to escape her lips.

"A little grime won't hurt that old thing. I want you to be comfortable."

"Must be clean, must be!" Sensing Bethany's confusion, she proceeded with taught reasonings. "'Wash and make yourselves clean. Take your evil deeds out of my sight, stop doing wrong.' Is—"

"Isaiah 1:16," Bethany spoke in tandem. Masika rubbed her arm as she smiled softly. "How about I get you a few towels to sit on? That way you don't get the couch dirty?"

She agreed as Bethany vanished to retrieve the towels. She soon returned, spread them on the couch cushions, and implored Masika to sit down. She did so, feeling infinitely less guilty for relaxing. Bethany scrutinized her for a moment before speaking again, "Now, you want something to drink? Milk? Pop?"

"Have root beer?" Masika requested shyly.

"We sure do! That what you want?" Reinvigorated by Masika's nod, she gave a thumbs up before vanishing once more into the kitchen.

At first, Masika lounged alone in the living room. It was a cozy space; a well-loved plush couch centered before a yellow oval rug, rustic dollhouse sat atop. Various cabinets hung on the walls, holding porcelain baby miniatures. Spontaneously, Bee joined her with two crochet dolls.

"Wanna play while Mommy makes lunch?" she offered.

"Play?" Masika questioned back.

"Yeah!" She held up a doll adorned in overalls and copper pigtails. "This can be you 'cause you have orange hair."

She gently took the doll as it was handed to her. "Okay."

"This will be me, 'cause she's in a dress," Bee decided, admiring the doll that remained in her grasp. "What do you play?"

"Don't know what you mean," Masika admitted.

"Oh... that's okay! I can teach you," Bee briefly hugged her doll as she contemplated. "We can play hospital, house... I like playing grocery store, too."

Masika agreed upon grocery store. Bee brought a few more toys from her room: a basket, several felt-made foods, and various other dolls. She told Masika she could be the cashier while Bee bagged groceries for the customers. Masika didn't understand any of it, but Bee kindly explained everything to her; it was a game. Her patience warmed Masika's heart and, quickly falling into a groove, twenty minutes passed with ease. Bethany soon interrupted their game with two plates full of steaming hot grilled cheese. She set them down on the coffee table.

"You two eat. Then, Bee, I'd like you to go out to the garden. Check on the plants for me."

"Okay Mommy!"

Masika struggled, managing to consume only half a portion by the time Bee barreled out the back door. Bethany observed, trying not to make it obvious but failing miserably. Usually, Masika hated anyone gawking at her, but Bethany seemed genuinely concerned for her well-being.

"How'd you get those bruises and cuts? They're bad."

Masika had no response. She knew bringing Hell upon Kevin's head was a bad idea. Every time she wished poorly of him, God punished her accordingly, not him. She was the harbinger of Evil, a dirty liar, and she needed to be relentlessly reminded of that fact. God spoke to Kevin and told him that's as it should be. She couldn't speak of the yelling nor other things. It wouldn't be righteous, wouldn't be holy. Masika swallowed, cooking up a perfect lie to feed her.

"Fell out a tree."

"Ouch."

"Yeah..." Hoping that was enough to keep Bethany satisfied, Masika abruptly changed the subject. "Lived here long?"

"My whole life. I was born in this house. belonged to my granma, then to my mama, now to me."

"Are they dead?"

Bethany's expression twisted into deep confusion and apprehension. She carefully replied, "Yes... they've both passed on. You... you know what death is?" Masika nodded and she continued, "I take it someone close to you must have passed away?"

"My mom's gone," Masika explained, "that's why Daddy sent me here. Hates me now."

"I'm sure he doesn't hate you!" Bethany was quick to deny, "Does he plan on taking you back home soon?"

"Hope so. Don't wanna be here no more."

"I bet. Your grandfather seems like a mean man."

"Not mean; prophet, he is. God sent him to make sure I stay clean. Clean and good, he says..." Masika, once again cognizant of the befoulment covering her being, started to rub obsessively at her arms. Bethany gently took her wrists.

"All that muck is bothering you, isn't it? Why don't I get you a couple rags so you can wash up?" She lowered her voice, "Especially 'cause I don't want you getting in trouble."

Masika longed to tell the kind lady that she was already in trouble. Her mere existence smeared in sin, there was never a time she wasn't. She had to simply try her best to abide by the commandments laid out before her insufferable self. Any infringement would anger God's prophet; even this offer would be considered heretical. Reluctance aside, she couldn't resist Bethany's pleading eyes.

Masika was walked to the bathroom—a crowded two-by-two with faded blue wallpaper. Bethany took out a towel and multiple washcloths from the room's cabinet, setting them down on the toilet lid. She showed her how to turn the water knobs on and off.

"Don't worry about making a mess. I'll clean it up, okay?" Bethany assured her, "Just worry about taking care of yourself."

With that, she left. Masika plucked a rag from the pile, dousing it in scalding hot water. She scrubbed her arms first, then wrung out the rag in the tub, turning the water a rusty brown. She ignored the ache that came with any physical touch. Her face came next, followed by her exposed legs.

By the time she finished, only her shirt and shorts remained dirty. She could live with that. Her punishment would be lessened if it were only her clothes that were tainted.

As she stepped away from the tub, she happened to glance out of a tiny window above the bathroom sink; one with a direct view of Kevin's house. Her heart dropped when he rounded the back corner of the building, charging through the yard towards the front. She ducked away and crawled into the bathroom closet, sealing herself inside without a second thought.

Several heavy knocks rang out as she gritted her teeth, mind ridden with dread. Through the thin walls, she could make out the voices of Bethany and Kevin. He demanded to know if Masika was there. Bethany gave both an honest and vague answer. She offered to bring her home as soon as she finished.

Masika covered her ears, not wanting to hear any more of the conversation. She rocked herself, not noticing the front door slamming shut and footsteps growing closer. Bethany knocked on the bathroom door. Masika didn't respond and she verbally warned that she was coming in.

"Sweetheart? It's okay, you're safe. He left for now..." She eventually approached the closet, delicately opening it, "Oh, honey..."

"Don't make me go. K-Know I've been bad, but I hate him. Hate him, hate God, hate Gramma, hate that place! Please... please let me stay. Will be good, swear it! Be perfect, be a good kid..." She trembled, and the words that followed backtracked from her previous statement, "No. Evil, I am. Only God can save me, Him and only Him. Must repent, must be clean, must be good. 'Submit yourselves therefore to God. Resist the devil, and he will flee from you.' James 4:7. Know it's true... but still want to stay with you. So kind to me. Bee so nice, too. Makes me feel less unclean...makes me..."

She kept going, prompting Bethany to kneel before her. With sadness, she revealed the child couldn't stay. Masika broke down into further hysterics.

"Why?"

"Kevin's the kind of man who won't take no for an answer. If I keep you here, he'll hurt all of us," Bethany explained.

Masika's eyes wandered to a tiny red toothbrush sitting on the sink. "Don't want him hurting Bee."

"Yeah... Unfortunately, I wouldn't put it past him to do that. I'm so sorry, sweetheart. But tell you what," she brushed Masika's hair and smiled, "come over any time. You can play with Bee more, and I can make you whatever you want to eat. How does that sound?"

Teary-eyed, Masika conceded. She squeezed Bethany in a tight hug. Bethany squished back, picking her up and carrying her into the living room. She hesitated to let go, but Bethany didn't mind a bit, holding her until she finally asked to be put down. Masika then apologized, flustered and upset from craving physical affection. Bethany petted her head with a gentle grin.

"It's okay. We all need to be held sometimes, you know?" She paused and withdrew her hand. "Are you ready?"

Masika gulped, then nodded. They walked to the entryway, the once inviting oak door smelling like a freshly lit match. She couldn't help but wonder if Hell awaited her. She half-expected an arch of flames to appear as the doorway opened.

Following the path she knew would soon become charcoal, Bethany held her hand the entire trip down. Masika couldn't decipher her melancholic aura. She couldn't save her from God's wrath, after all.

Kevin sat on his porch in a rocking chair, shit-eating grin splitting his thin, uneven lips. Both hands held onto his belt, white knuckled. Masika thought to run, but instead she tightened her hold on Bethany. The two walked up the steps, standing in front of Kevin. He rose from the chair, wood creaking against rotting wood, arms unmoving.

"Hope the kid didn't cause you trouble," he practically sneered.

"Not at all," Bethany replied, "you have a good grandbaby, Kevin."

"Hmph. Well, come now, kid. Your gram's worried sick," he voiced sternly, taking Masika's free arm to pry her away. She unintentionally rooted her feet to the ground, not moving an inch despite faint stings along her forearm. His grip tightened. "Don't play stupid games you can't win."

With that, Masika released Bethany. She heard a weak 'goodbye' as Kevin hurried her into the house. A void of darkness greeted her as he shut the door behind him. Her breath hitched and her heartbeat pounded in her ears—Gram wasn't home.

"Your room. *Now.*"

Anxiety shot through Masika like a bullet. She robotically shuffled straight ahead to her bedroom. Turning the knob and pushing the door open, she tried not to panic at Kevin's presence behind her. Knowing exactly what to do, she went to the center of the room and lowered herself to her knees. She clasped her fingers in twine, closing her eyes and bringing them up to her trembling lips. As she quivered in terror, Kevin commanded with a single word:

"*Repent.*"

CHAPTER ONE

June 1993

R ainy days rarely visited Nevada. When they did, Aiden cherished them. On those occasions, he'd toast to long-lost nights, pondering over a familiar face.

Summer gifted him such a night in June. Precipitation pelleting against the windowpane woke him from a dead sleep. Despite it being almost two a.m., he peeled out of bed and broke out the champagne, nursing a tall glass while reflecting.

The last four years were admittedly quite comfortable. Switching identities with his twin proved to be cathartic. He remembered his apprehension, knowing she'd be on the run with a massive target on her head. A target she didn't earn, no less, but Abeje quelled that unease with occasional letters. She always used a code that Aiden would recognize. He heard from her every six months, more or less, so he rarely worried now. Instead, he spent his time alone enjoying manhood. No more shaving. No more pants without pockets. He wished the same for menstruation, but he would live.

Aiden's glass was empty by the time he entered the living room. A loud *bang* resounded outside the door on the opposing wall, causing him to nearly choke down his last sip. Alarmed was an understatement for the terror that coursed through his veins, pulse sitting in his throat with warming wine. Panic only worsened at the sound of several sharp knocks that followed. With gritted teeth, he retrieved a gun from the safe beneath his coffee table. After double-checking the chamber and safety, he cautiously approached his front door. The impatient knocking continued and Aiden feared who could be behind it.

He knocked back. Nobody answered for several seconds as Aiden grew restless. He tucked the gun into his waistband before cracking the entrance open an inch. Not bothering to lift his downturned eyes, the first thing he saw was a pair of limbs dressed in sleek black pumps. The stranger rubbed her feet together as Aiden allowed his gaze to travel up her drenched legs, going past her denim shorts and loose-fitting graphic tee. As they climbed, a wave of deja vu began to creep in. It only got worse when he saw her face.

Stepping back in shock, the door swung ajar. They stared at each other. She was no stranger at all, nothing close to it. Aiden invited her inside with a bow of his head and offered her a drink as she got cozy on the couch.

"Ah, no thanks. Don't drink no more," she declined.

Aiden didn't make eye contact, expression abating as memories washed over him. A palpable sense of anger began to strangle him the longer he relived that fateful sunrise. He remembered a dreadful morning, waking up to light beaming through wooden rafters, expecting to be in her arms. Instead, he found himself naked and alone. How awful the blanket felt against his skin, the betrayal burning in his stomach. *How could you fucking leave me?* He wanted to yell. As the question formed in his mind, he recollected whom he was supposed to be. Not his past self, but "Aiden."

So he attempted small talk instead, pushing down the bubbling thoughts. His voice shredded at the first try, hoarse from lack of use. He realized, much to his embarrassment, he sounded akin to a mumbling child; nothing like Abeje did. Voice being naturally much deeper than his, he struggled to drop the pitch that low.

The woman eyed him, saying nothing for the first two or three grunts of frustration. She stopped him at some point with a firm hand on his cheek. Aiden froze. Moving his hair to the side, she glanced behind his left ear.

Reddening, he knew instantly what she was searching for. Rising to his feet, he attempted to take a step away, but she mirrored his actions. He turned, mortified and hurt, not prepared to explain. Her voice called out to him.

"Know it's you. Abeje told me. Even if she didn't, could never forget that scar."

Touching the mostly healed over mark, he frowned. Aiden turned around to find her only inches away, looking down at him with heaviness. Without warning, before he thought to flee, she wrapped him in an embrace. Despite the momentary urge to push away, he melted against the warmth and familiarity of her body. She cradled his head and whispered to him.

"Missed you. I'm sorry. Probably wanna know why I left."

Nodding, he wanted to beg, *Of course I do*. After her disappearance, the heartache never left him. He thought her dead, or far, far worse. Aiden wished he could express all the emotions filling him at once—the relief, the anger, the confusion—but he just cried, droplets trailing down his cheeks. She moved and caught the tears with the tip of her thumb.

"Knew I couldn't be me down there in Alabama. Thought if I left, could find the real me. And, as ya see, I eventually did. Call myself Masika now."

What a stunning name. He left the room momentarily, only to return with a notebook and pen. She smiled, perhaps nostalgic at the sight. He scribbled down two questions: *Where did you go after that night? How did you find Abeje?*

"Went to Chicago first. Ended up traveling all over the U.S. for a job. Quit that job, stayed in Canada for a bit, where I ran into Abeje. Got her out of a real bad situation. To be fair, thought it was you. Learned otherwise. Told me everything, she did."

Aiden grimaced, taking a nasty fall down memory lane. He'd spent the past few years trying to forget he killed someone. Out of self-defense, sure, but murder was still murder. Repression was far more useful than regret, so he only thought about it whenever he thought about Abeje. Specifically, the night they fled Alabama and vowed to never be their former selves again. It had been the easiest, most effortless switch.

The murder was just convenient. Incidental. Now Abeje could be her authentic self and Aiden would never have to worry about the woes of identifying as a woman again. He didn't despise the identity itself, but the binary it existed in. The expectations of being a fertile womb and nothing else, subservient to men, always angered him. Abeje equally loathed the prospect of becoming one of those men. The trade was always meant to be, it seemed. Abeje didn't care if it meant she had to be on the run while Aiden worked an under-the-table job, keeping his head down. As far as Aiden was concerned, he had the perfect, most uneventful life. He wondered, though, if Masika approved of this change.

He took the notebook again. *Did it shock you?*

She glanced at the paper before shaking her head, "No. Have I shocked you?"

Aiden shook his head as well. Certain details of their complicated past weren't lost to him. He remembered practicing makeup on her, running red lipstick over her perfectly shaped lips. Giving her his razors that his mom forced him to buy. How she often talked low and hurt about her body, the eternal torment it dragged her through. She seemed far more confident now.

"Good. Like myself better this way. Look a lot more comfortable yourself." Sighing suddenly, she locked her hands together. "Need to be serious for a second, if you'll entertain me."

Aiden raised an eyebrow. He waited for her to continue as she leaned forward, gaze on the ground at his feet.

"Did the despicable to you, Aiden. Abandoned you. That was a mistake. Should have told you I wanted to run away. Could've ran together. You never would have—" she choked back a sob. "Doesn't matter. Came here to say I'm sorry. I'm so sorry. Not looking for forgiveness, either. Just.... just... needed to apologize. Deserved better, you did."

Aiden, shaken, simply stared at her as she began trailing towards the exit. When he realized she was leaving, he leapt for the notebook and pen. Running to her side, he tapped her shoulder right as her fingers brushed the doorknob. She watched as he wrote on the paper, tore it, and handed it to her.

Don't go. Please. Stay with me.

She stammered once she read the words. "Should *hate* me."

Aiden shook his head. It was embarrassing to be this desperate, but he couldn't bear to watch her walk away again. He set the notebook on the counter and held her hands pleadingly. She avoided his piercing gaze.

"On the run. Get involved and you'll be in danger," she explained.

He squeezed tighter. Aiden cared not what she ran from. Until today, he believed her to be gone forever. He refused to risk losing her once again. Masika's shoulders visibly relaxed.

"Okay. Gotta go to the hotel and get my stuff, but I'll be back. I promise."

Aiden, not chancing it, stuck out his pinkie. She accepted it, sealing their deal.

With that, she quietly bid him farewell and left the apartment. Overwhelmed from the surprising encounter, Aiden openly wept. Grabbing the notebook, he threw it on the floor and crumbled onto the carpet, attempting to steady his breathing. He collected himself and headed straight to the kitchen for another drink.

Aiden half expected her not to return. When a knock came thirty minutes later, he held his excitement by the tail. Nearly jumping into Masika's arms at the sight of her standing in his doorway, he welcomed her back into the apartment. She had changed her outfit to a flowing, hickory-colored skirt paired with a pitch-black turtleneck. Her orange locs were pulled into a ponytail, uncovering her cheeks and jawline.

He found himself admiring both her physique and the changes to her face as she carried her belongings to the guest bedroom. He could hardly remember how she used to look, just knew the differences were stark. It was in the best way. Masika was beautiful before, and she was unequivocally gorgeous now.

He stood in the doorway as she laid her luggage on the bed and turned to him. A smirk creeped onto her lips as she caught him peering at her chest. She grabbed both breasts and jiggled them playfully.

"Didn't expect them to get this big either," she commented.

Aiden's eyes widened as he tore his fixed look away. He hadn't meant to ogle. *God, I really am just a man.* She chuckled and let go before approaching him.

"It's okay. Don't mind if you stare." Her expression turned serious as she rubbed her arm. "Sure I can stay here?"

Aiden smiled softly, one that spoke a thousand words. She pulled him into a hug.

"Thank you."

***

It took a few weeks to grow accustomed to living with another person again. Aiden went to work like normal and returned to Masika cooking dinner regularly. He didn't ask her to do this. When questioned about it, she insisted she wasn't a freeloader.

"Same reason why you're getting rent money. Deserve help, least I can do."

Tonight, a hazy Saturday in July, he came home to the delectable smell of pot roast. It was a welcoming sensation, as the workday had been long and unbearable. Slipping inside the apartment undetected, he took a seat at the dining room table. She didn't notice, too preoccupied cleaning the countertops while wearing blaring headphones. Watching her dreamily, waves of relaxation crashed over him.

Glancing out the corner of her eye, she looked straight at him. An antsy expression crossed her face, and she quickly turned around, much to Aiden's hurt. He stood to tap her on the shoulder. She spun, hand clutched against her chest in fright. She covered up the reaction with a few steps towards the fridge. He leaned against the counter as she opened it with a shaky grin.

"Snuck up on me," she spoke nervously, acquiring a beer and orange juice. Joining him at the table, she slid the bottle over. "How was work?"

Aiden popped open the beer and gestured 'so-so' with a wave of his hand. The day started out fine, but a flare up crept in on him. He'd pushed himself too far the day before, creating a physical debt. He wasn't able to walk or move halfway through today's shift, so his boss assigned him to organize papers. He wouldn't tell Masika that, though.

"Aw, at least it wasn't terrible?" she tried.

He didn't answer, not wanting her to worry. They drank their beverages in silence. About ten minutes passed before a timer went off, causing her to hurry to the stove top. Once the pot was off the burner and the food was cool enough, she filled two plates full of roast. She gave Aiden his and returned with her own. Once sat, she took off her headphones.

"Let me know how you like it."

Eating in silence normally agonized him. When alone, Aiden often had the TV or music on. With her, the quiet felt tranquil. He scarfed down his pile, finding the meal far too good to take his time. She giggled at his indulgence.

"Taste alright?"

Aiden nodded with a mouthful of potatoes, covering his maw. Both found themselves blushing and tore their eyes away from each other.

Later, alone in bed, Aiden reminisced on former nights: cuddling up at Masika's side, smoking pot with her and Abeje after school, getting enough beatings to scare most people straight... He never once regretted any of it. He recalled how lonely the weekends felt without her, how the words they exchanged always occupied his thoughts. Those sweet things she told him, the things she promised.

One letter came to mind in particular. Aiden got up to search for it after a couple hours of tossing underneath his blankets. Turning on a lamp, he retrieved a tattered old shoe box from beneath his bed where he kept every single letter and note she had written. He pilfered through the stack of papers inside, knowing exactly where he had hidden it away. He stashed it at the very bottom of the box out of anger, out of hurt. Those emotions reached him all over again as he revisited her words.

Noticed something. Never get tired of you. Know I act like the touches and hand-holding mean little. If I told you that you meant the world to me, would you believe me? Dream of running away with you, I do. Dream of a world where you don't have to go home to tears and slamming doors. Wish you could come home to me instead. Can't help but wonder if you feel the same. Think I know the answer, though. Just too scared to admit it.

It was only two nights after getting the note that Aiden confessed his own feelings in the abandoned barn. No words were spoken; he didn't need to say a thing. All he had to do was kiss those soft lips, and Masika knew. He knew. Thus, he gave her his body and soul that night, even though he'd never dreamed of such things. Hell, he had never been attracted to anyone else at that point. The idea of sex typically revolted him.

At that moment, it didn't, not with her. The connection of flesh felt right with her, romantic like he secretly dreamed the act would be. Her breath against his ear replayed in his mind, and he found himself lost in the sensations all over again. Not wanting to release her from his grasp when she finished. Wishing to hold her there for eternity, to never return to reality.

He wished it had been enough to make her stay. The urge to weep overcame him suddenly, but he knew deep down he hadn't done anything wrong. She left out of necessity, for survival, yet he couldn't deny how much he blamed himself then and now. He could've gone with her. His life might have been entirely different. Would he be Aiden? Would Abeje still be carrying his legacy of murder? Would he have been able to witness Masika's blossoming firsthand? To support her?

Aiden put the letter away and chose not to dwell on it any longer. He left the shoe box on the nightstand, shut the lamp off, and crawled under the covers. Sleep found him soon after.

CHAPTER TWO

May 1978

A mere five days after her brush with Hell, Masika's kitchen cleaning was interrupted by a faint knock at the front door. Perplexed and aware Kevin nor Gram were due home anytime soon, she left the mop bucket and approached. Another knock rang out, just louder than the settling house and old pipes. Masika stood on her tippy toes to look through the peep hole. She saw Bethany adorned in a shawl, bearing a wooden basket with cloth strewn atop.

Not allowed company, she turned and crossed her arms. Standing there for mere seconds, Masika was convinced Bethany's arrival was a good thing. A guardian angel, perhaps, guiding her towards the light and away from sin. She spun back around and unlocked the door.

As it swung towards her, Bethany's posture straightened, "Good morning. Hope I ain't disturbing you." Masika didn't respond and she lifted the arm holding the basket, "I wanted to bring you a little something. May I come in?"

Masika nodded, inviting her inside. As Bethany took in the interior, she put the broom and dustpan away out of habit. Her visitor eventually set the basket down on the dining room table, taking a seat in one of the elderly oak chairs with a heavy sigh. She sat across from Bethany, eyes downcast upon her dirty hands.

Bethany spoke, "You know, I'm surprised you're here this time of day. Most kids your age are in school right about now."

"School?" Masika echoed, briefly leaving her chair to wash her hands.

Bethany blinked, "A place where kids learn all sorts of things. How to read, write... That's where Bee's at right now."

"Like how I learn from Kevin?"

"No. Nothing like that. I'm talking math, science."

"Oh..." Masika hesitated, fidgeting with her fingers as she returned. Going to ask if she was in trouble, Bethany was quick to comfort.

"That's okay, not everybody goes to school. I should have known 'cause I ain't ever seen you before. Only ever heard Lina mention you in passing. You're here all the time, ain't you?"

Close to shutting down from the questioning, Masika let out a sharp exhale. "Kevin don't let me leave. 'But if anyone does not provide for his relatives, and especially for members of his household, he has denied the faith and is worse than an unbeliever.' Timothy 5:8. Kevin works, leavin' me to clean. Clean and take care of Gram, I do. Says only place I can go is the trees. Must listen to Kevin; don't want to be Evil, don't want to be a sinner."

Neither person spoke for several minutes. Bethany resembled a kicked dog, how Masika imagined herself subjected to Kevin's wrath. Turning away, she fixated on one of the far walls as Bethany collected herself, staring right at her in return.

"You seem to know a lot of the bible, have you read it?" she asked.

Masika shook her head, "No. You? You read it?"

"Not *all* of it. It's a very, very big book, as I'm sure you've seen. You seem to know a lot of verses for someone who's never read it."

"Kevin taught me. That good? Am I good?"

"Sweetheart, you are good whether you know the bible or not. You know that?" Bethany told her, bringing the basket towards herself and moving the cloth aside.

Masika's mind reeled with protests. Bethany was certainly a kind woman, even when she lied to her face. Kevin would brand such nonsense as blasphemy, worthy of punishment and God's utmost disgust.

Yet the tiniest part of her, buried deep beneath fear of Hellfire and failure, believed. That part wanted to covet Bethany, to delve into the possibility of an existence beyond being a scripture machine. Would it be so shameful to stray away from God's grasp, to not suffocate beneath his mighty fist? Was there glory in knowledge beyond His word?

Lost in the turmoil, she didn't notice Bethany stand and walk to her side. She held something in front of her face. "Here," she offered, voice falling distorted and faint on the little girl's ears. "I made these for you."

Vision finally focused, she homed in on a gingerbread cookie. Near opaque tendrils of steam lifted into the air, delighting Masika's nostrils. She anxiously reached for it. "Mine?"

Bethany chuckled, "Yes." Passing off the treat, she returned to her spot, "Let me know how you like it."

Masika wasted no time inhaling the entire cookie, taking a good minute to thoroughly chew and swallow. Not quite tasting anything but enjoying the texture, she reached for the basket. "More please?"

Bethany pushed the basket towards her. "Have as many as you want."

The basket lay empty on the table ten minutes later. She wiped crumbs off the corners of her mouth as Bethany sat with her palms folded over her belly, grin of contentment across her face. She asked Masika a few more questions, most of which she didn't have answers for, leading to a lull. This didn't scare her, though. The quiet resembled a soft blanket, Bethany's warm gleam covering her the whole time.

When the sun began to sag towards the ground, she bid Masika farewell. "Kevin and Lina will be home soon and I don't want you to get in trouble."

"Come by again?" Masika requested instantly.

"Certainly, I can start coming over every Tuesday if you'd like. Neither of 'em come home early that day."

"Okay!"

She walked her to the door, watching Bethany tread across the yard and disappear into the neighboring house. Masika waited until she completely left her sight to head inside. She meticulously cleaned the table, chairs, and floor, lowering herself to check for any crumb or speck left. Once in the clear, she finished up the last of her tasks and returned to her room. Curled up in bed, she stared up at the ceiling.

***

For a little over a month, Bethany visited every Tuesday. Arriving at twelve p.m., she'd stay until the threat of sundown. Always accompanied by some sort of baked good or dessert, Masika devoured each and every one without hesitation.

Feeling safer and safer around Bethany with every interaction, Masika confided in her about Kevin's teachings and divulged in her collection of animal bones. Most of them had belonged to her late mother, her father having passed them onto her. In turn, Bethany shared tidbits of her own life, mostly stories about Bee's shenanigans and the cars she worked on.

Normally, she stayed on top of cleaning after visits. She cleansed any glassware used, swept and mopped the floors, leaving no trace of an extra presence. Kevin would come home drunk and oblivious, setting out to do his normal post-work tasks. Masika internally applauded her attention to detail every time, letting out a massive sigh of relief when he retreated straight to his bedroom. It was her little, well-kept secret.

Tonight, however, when the man stumbled inside, trouble brewed. He did his usual once-over as Masika sat on the living room couch, quietly watching him go through the doorway leading to the kitchen and dining room. At first, she felt no fear. That was until she noticed an empty glass of milk sitting on the dinner table. She stood right as he stopped in his tracks. His gaze locked on the glassware and he scoffed.

"What's this?" he questioned, glancing over his shoulder.

She rubbed her hands, "W-wanted a glass of milk."

"Liar," he accused, turning completely to face her. "You don't drink milk, only Lina drinks that shit! Who did you let into my fucking house?"

"No one!" She cried, face reddening as she backed up towards the couch. "Just me here, swear it!"

"'No one who practices deceit shall dwell in my house; no one who utters lies shall continue before my eyes.' Psalms 101:7. You *dare* to defy God's word? To lie to my very face, when I've done everything for you? Put a roof over your fuckin' head after your daddy dumped you off here? The *gall*," he snarled, stalking towards her like something bloodthirsty. "Speak the truth to me now. Do not lie, for God will know, and He will help me strike you down. Repent and you may be spared."

Masika could not bring herself to lie once more, nor speak the truth. So she said nothing, even as Kevin took a running start towards her.

***

Knock knock.

Masika, buried beneath a mountain of covers, groaned at the noise resounding from the front of the house. She knew exactly who stood behind the door and had been dreading this day for an entire week. Sluggishly, she tugged on her shoes and headed to the living room. Steeling herself for Bethany's arrival, she had prepared by choreographing an explanation.

As she opened the door, Bethany's bright smile shattered. A deep frown fell upon her lips before she covered her face. The corners of Masika's mouth also turned downward, head drooping in hopes of concealing some of the swelling. Bethany took a step towards her.

"Oh my God, what happened—"

"Stay away. Leave," Masika demanded coldly.

Bethany stopped, hand reaching mid-air for Masika. The hand fell flaccid to her side as sadness filled her eyes. "He found out, didn't he? I'm so sorry, I didn't mean to get you in trouble—"

"But you did. So please, go."

Right as Masika went to shut the door, a plead gave her pause. "May I give you this final gift?" Bethany inquired, gesturing to the basket over her arm. "I can retrieve the basket if you leave it on the porch, but what's within is yours."

Bending down, she set the basket on the porch's wooden panels. Masika let the door swing away from her. Bethany hugged herself, the two standing in shrill silence until she cautiously took the gift. Tears threatened to escape. She would sorely miss their conversations at the table and the purity of Bethany's heart—even if Kevin insisted it was worldly and wrong.

"Thank you."

"Of course," Bethany paused, fingers rising to her lips as she tried to conceal a quiver. "Once again, I'm sorry. I won't trouble you anymore, but please know I'll always be next door. If you ever need help, don't be a stranger, no matter what Kevin tells you."

Masika ran inside with the basket, not able to bear watching Bethany leave for good. She stifled her tears as she went to her room. Lifting off the signature plaid cloth from the lid, she opened it and peered inside. She expected cookies, heart leaping into her throat at the sight of what it actually contained.

Bones. Dozens of tiny animal bones, pristine and cleansed. Masika remembered Bethany promising to bring her some, since she liked collecting them so much. Removing each one until the basket sat empty on the bed, she then transferred the new prizes to her treasure box. Returning the basket to the porch as instructed, she prayed Bethany would collect it in a timely fashion. She didn't know if she could handle another punishment.

Trying to ease her anxieties, she tidied up the bathroom and performed her normal chores. Soon, she went to bed, emotionally and physically depleted. Her eyes drifted to her bedroom window. An eerie gut feeling convinced her this wouldn't be the last time she encountered Bethany, whether Kevin liked it or not.

Chapter Three

February 1981

For years, life was nothing but aching body, aching mind, aching heart. Animosity as the forefront emotion. Kevin's boot stayed on Masika's neck in every sense. Gram's compliance and willingness to watch her suffer fostered further resentment. It was only right, she would claim. Masika hated her for it.

Bethany remained on her mind as the years passed. The mother had kept her word, staying far away from Kevin's territory. Their exchanges were reduced to trading glances from each other's porches when Masika ventured to the woods each day. Neither spoke nor breathed near each other, fully understanding the potential consequences.

One positive change was the addition of occasional forest night trips. Over several months of learning Kevin and Gram's routine, she figured out the perfect time to slip away. Not daring to sneak off more than once a week, she always left her bed appearing occupied with several stuffed animals. She would return around two a.m. without fail. Masika kept Kevin placated with good behavior and frequent repentance, waning his suspicion.

On a particularly bleary night, she set out to her new favorite spot. The tiniest crook between land, tree and water existed deep within a creek. She liked to lay on the damp moss and daydream, often tracing the shapes wooden spires made sticking out of the swamp; counting to see if any had moved through the algae covering. She had been especially excited that night since her body burned in pain. Sprawling out, moisture soaking into her clothes, she shut her eyes.

Laying until the threat of dawn loomed, she had stayed longer than usual, yet wasn't concerned. She had a feeling she would come home to snores either way. As she dusted off her clothes, she began heading back, the night air wavering. When she rounded the corner of a tree, a menacing growl greeted her.

Masika froze. A battered yet threatening canine lingered amongst clustered trunks, snarling at her. She took a step only for it to lunge. A scream leapt from her throat as it attacked, jaws snapping. Falling, she was barely able to guard her face and body from the ambush of its claws and weight. She somehow managed to shove it off, sending it flying into the still water. She fled before it emerged once more.

It didn't follow her. She thought of the encounter for days, a horrid feeling pooling in her gut.

The next time she returned to the creek proved sour. As soon as she gazed upon the scene, she found a group of crows feasting upon a corpse. She briefly thought to interrupt their meal, having an inkling it was the beast. Instead, she felt compelled to watch.

Watched she did as the crows nibbled the creature's flesh, till there was nothing but bones. The group flew off one by one in search of another meal. Masika slowly approached the skeleton laid out delicately in the grass. She knelt before it.

She worried she may have caused its demise. She pushed it into the water, after all. It was just a poor animal; Masika a wretched beast, Evil and cruel as always. Sobbing into her sweater, her thoughts drifted to the morbid respect the crows had granted the creature; eating its remains so kindly as to leave no trace, no mess to clean. Surely, she could grant the same respect with its bones? She sat up, looking into empty eye sockets.

Masika kept the head and buried the rest a few yards away from the creek in a shallow grave. It was the best she could do. She cleansed the skull in the water, softly smiling. The empty eye sockets brightened, the unhinged jaw forming its own grin back.

The moment she returned home, she fetched her treasure box from beneath her bed. Nestling the skull atop the other bones crowding the interior, it brought it to capacity. Before putting the box away, she planted a kiss on its muzzle.

***

A mere three days later, tragedy struck.

It was another sleepless night. In the darkness of her bedroom, Masika lay on the floor. She stared up into nothingness, allowing her imagination to take the reins. The comb textured ceiling fizzled away, beige bursting into a black and purple void. Cosmos unfolded before her, stars dotting every inch of the ceiling. Sleep only threatened to take hold around three a.m., when a BANG shattered the outside ambience of cicadas.

She sat up, scrambling towards the window. Peeling back the curtain ever so slightly, she peered out into the front yard. At first, she saw nothing. Then, a sea of seven bodies appeared from the left side of the house. The group roamed down the gravel road, laughing and carrying on. She nearly returned to her spot, but hearing a shrill shriek from within the group made her stop dead in her tracks. She recognized the plea for mercy that followed.

Bethany.

Sure enough, when a couple of the boys moved aside, she could see her neighbor. The familiar figure was restrained, burlap sack concealing her face. Masika's heart wrenched at the sight of her thrashing form. A small part of her wondered if Kevin and Gram woke up from the ruckus.

She checked, cracking their door open as slowly as possible. The two snored soundly from their bed. Without much thought, she gathered up a few supplies before setting out. She made her way around the side of the house, clinging to the walls as she reached the front.

Following would've been significantly more difficult if it wasn't for blood drops littering the pebbles. Whose blood, it didn't matter. She hoped it wasn't Bethany's. Masika kept her distance the whole way out of the neighborhood and through an old, abandoned field. The teens were always several yards ahead, oblivious. Too busy celebrating their 'prize.'

When they entered the remains of an old mobile home, she tagged back, crouching as she searched the exterior for an alternate entrance. She decided a broken window on the right side of the structure would suffice.

She pushed in the hanging pieces of glass and vaulted over the windowsill. Remaining light on her feet, she crept closer to the explosion of voices in the living room. Scanning around a corner, she spotted Bethany amidst the crowd of teenage boys, fighting to keep her clothes on as appendages raked her body.

"Stop! Let me go!" she cried.

"Shut the fuck up, you aren't goin anywhere."

A recognizable voice rose from the swarm. It was Shelly, one of Kevin's employees at the brewery. He'd come over for a beer on the occasion. A mischievous simper formed on the edges of Masika's lips as she left her hiding spot, walking straight towards the crowd. At first nobody noticed, until Shelly happened to turn his head. He snickered.

"Well lookie here, fellas. We have a guest," Shelly said, "What, you wanna join?"

"Let her go," Masika deadpanned.

The mob erupted into laughter. It didn't last long when she charged Shelly, knife first. Jumping onto his torso, she latched on like an animal and drove the blade into his chest.

Panic ensued as the group fumbled over each other to try and grab her. Two of them foolishly released Bethany's limbs. She sprang to action, headbutting one assailant and throwing punches at another. Shelly successfully peeled Masika off and threw her across the room.

She recovered quickly, watching as the group tried to regain control. A moment later, Bethany joined her side, having beaten the two teenagers' unconscious. Masika handed her the pocketknife.

"Here," she insisted.

"What about you?"

"Have my hands."

Bethany accepted the weapon, ready to face the remaining boys head on. Shelly commanded the pair closest to attack. Turns out Bethany didn't need a knife. Easily incapacitating the scrawny kid near her with a heavy strike to the neck, Masika in turn dodged the other's sloppy punches. She eventually caught his wrist and twisted his arm behind his back. Slamming him into the ground, she advanced towards the remaining set of juveniles.

Bethany charged straight into one's stomach for a tackle as Masika threw an ambitious punch to the other's face. A few blows later and both writhed on the ground, wrapped up in their own limbs. Shelly dropped his makeshift weapon—a broken beer bottle—and backed into the corner, cowering.

"What's wrong? If you didn't want this, maybe you shouldn't be wearing those clothes." Bethany taunted in a sickly-sweet tone, head tilting. "Unless you don't follow your own word?"

"P-Please let me go! I'm sorry for taking ya, I am! Pl—"

Masika kicked him square in the groin, sending him bowlegged onto the vinyl floor, yowling. Just for good measure, she knocked him unconscious with a powerful backhand. Threat finally neutralized, she looked over at Bethany.

"What are you doing here?" Bethany asked, "Did you follow us?"

"Wasn't gonna let 'em hurt you," Masika replied, trying to catch her breath. She wiped sweat off her forehead, soaking it in blood. "You okay?"

"I am thanks to you," Bethany gestured vaguely to the pile of brutalized teenagers on the ground. "What should we do about this? Call the police?"

"Cops won't help you." Pausing, she remembered Kevin's lighter in her pocket. "Have a better idea. Trust me?"

Bethany nodded and Masika requested she step outside. Doing so, Masika wandered to one of the living room windows, an ugly tan curtain hanging half-way off the rod. Withdrawing the lighter from her pocket, she held it to the cloth as it began to spark. Flames slowly ate away the fabric and she walked over to Shelly, who was semi-conscious. She grinned ear to ear at him.

"Real funny you thought this was a good idea. Now you'll *burn*."

Kneeling down, she lit his shirt ablaze. She watched only a few seconds more before heading outside to check on Bethany, who shook with fear.

"What did you do?"

"The right thing," Masika whispered.

The home's barely standing infrastructure began to succumb to the inferno. Masika couldn't tear her eyes away and Bethany grabbed her hands. "Come on, we need to get out of here before someone notices."

Bethany led her through the field and down the gravel path, straight into her house—where the front door's lock was busted—to the dining room.

She anxiously paced while Masika sat at the table, vacant of emotion. She didn't understand why Bethany was so panicked. To her, the problem was solved. The world was seven white boys less, and Bethany was unscathed. However, it was obvious as Bethany's anxious jitters worsened that the problems had just begun.

"We better hope they all dead and nobody finds them. Otherwise, we in some serious trouble, you know that?" She sat across from her, expression muddled. "I mean, what if the cops show up?"

"Say it was me."

Bethany crossed her arms, "No way. This... this was my fault—"

"Was not. White boys cause nothin' but trouble."

"You're a child, and you've been through *enough*."

"Doesn't matter, even if I get locked up. Have Bee to look after, you do."

Bethany couldn't respond to that. The pair sat in stillness for five minutes, the tension oddly calming Masika. Bethany eventually got up with a long, heavy sigh.

"You're not gettin' locked up if we can avoid it. Come on, let's get you cleaned up and redressed." Bethany offered her shower, as well as obtained an outfit from her daughter's wardrobe. It was a pair of overalls with a flower-patterned shirt. "This is all I have. It'll have to do, just long 'nough for you to get home. I'm gonna burn your other clothes."

"Okay."

"Take a shower, get all that gore off—" Reaching for Masika's face caused her to instinctively flinch, but Bethany simply rubbed her thumb across her chin. "You got scratched pretty bad. I'll clean it up after, alright?"

"Ain't new—had that scratch a'while now. No way those boys touched me," she told Bethany with a slight smirk.

Sadness swirled within Bethany's eyes. The woman pat her shoulder and left her to her own devices. She took a cold shower, making sure to clean efficiently. After drying off, she tried on the clothes and was delighted to find they were her size. She twirled around in the mirror, admiring herself. Despite the earlier events, a wave of cool confidence washed over her. A knock on the door interrupted her mid catwalk. She straightened, brushing off her legs.

"You done?" Bethany called from the other side.

Masika turned the knob and Bethany stood in the doorway, miles more composed than fifteen minutes prior. Holding a palm-sized metal tin in hand, she moved to Masika's side.

"Are you hurt anywhere else?" she asked, setting the tin on the sink and removing the lid.

"Don't think so."

"Good."

She took out an ointment and a few alcohol wipes, treating the scratch on Masika's lips. Internally, she worried about what would happen next. Would Bethany take the sole blame? Not being surprised if she were to try, Masika promised herself then and there to turn herself in. All she had to do was confess to Kevin and he would bring her right to the station.

Once the wound had been tended to, Bethany instructed her to go home. She hugged her, much to the young girl's surprise, squeezing her tightly and sobbing quietly into her ear.

"Thank you for protecting me. You're a good kid," she tore away before she could grow more emotional. "Go. Say nothing to no one."

Masika bid her goodbye, taking leave and following the pathway to Kevin's. Finding the back door still unlocked, she carefully slid inside. Gleaming into the darkness, everything was perfectly still. She closed the door behind her quietly, waiting for her vision to adjust to the lack of light.

When it did, familiarity took over and she navigated to the hallway between bedrooms. Daring to check for Gram and Kevin's breathing, she aimed her ear towards the cracked door. When she heard their raspy snores, she retreated to her room.

For once, her body and mind were far too exhausted to keep her awake. She crawled into bed, not bothering to shed her clothes. Reminiscing on the scent of ash, slumber slowly overtook.

***

"Get the hell up."

Masika groaned at the sudden, rough wrenching of her arm. She didn't fully come to until Kevin was dragging her out of bed and onto the ground. Groggily breaking from his grasp, she landed flat on her butt. She leered up at him with half-lidded eyes. He glared down at her with pure hatred.

"I got a cop at my door asking for you. What did you do?!"

Last night was real? Masika thought it to be a long, endless dream. She met his glare with defiance.

"Dunno. What did I do?"

Moments after, she rubbed her stinging left cheek as she followed Kevin out into the living room. An officer stood in front of the television. Gram was on the couch, absolutely beside herself as she sobbed inconsolably. The officer snapped to attention when Masika and Kevin appeared.

"This is who you're looking for," Kevin declared, pushing her forward.

The cop, already impatient and agitated, told her to sit. He claimed to have questions. She knew she had answers. Wondering if he'd already spoken to Bethany, she sat, the older man crossing his arms above her.

"Where were you last night?" was the first question.

"Here, sleeping in bed."

"Oh yeah? 'Cause I got seven teenagers saying the opposite."

"What they saying?" Masika challenged.

"Shut it. I'm the one asking questions, so I'm gonna ask you again. Where were you last night?"

"Was sleeping in bed, but then I heard noise. Crying. Watched some boys drag our sweet neighbor Bethany away. Well, figured I'd follow. Made sure nothin' bad happened to her, I did."

"An eyewitness says you followed them to an abandoned home, where you assaulted the teenagers and set Shelly Dickinson ablaze. Is that your version of 'making sure nothing bad happened'?"

Kevin's blue glower seared into her from the other side of the room. Was there any point in lying? She wound up nodding.

"It is."

Chaos broke out as the officer placed her under arrest. Gram launched towards her, arms flailing in a desperate attempt to reach. Kevin swept in to move her away, wails resounding as Masika put her arms behind her back. The cuffs solidified her fate with a forceful click.

"Please no! Please don't take my grandbaby!" Gram begged.

"Shut it, Lina. There's no use," Kevin tightened his grip on her forearm. "Let it go."

Let it go she did as the officer escorted Masika outside, only to be greeted by a white sea. Hordes of people from the town, almost all of which she didn't recognize, gathered behind the patrol car. A few of the boys were there from the night before, accompanied by their parents. Said parents gripped them close, as if they would vanish if not held tight enough.

Upon stepping out, the crowd erupted into indecipherable chants of hatred. Masika ignored calls for her execution, finding them rather distasteful. She didn't kill anyone, did she? As far as she knew, the seven attackers got away largely unscathed. Besides, she wasn't the one who tried to hurt an innocent woman to begin with.

It mattered none. The officer shouted for the mob to move as he loaded Masika into the vehicle. She stared straight into their prying eyes as he walked around to enter the driver's seat. The bellows fell silent on her ears, along with whatever the cop uttered before turning the engine over.

***

"While I commend you for helping someone, I must ask; what the hell were you thinking setting that damn boy on fire?"

The question came during the grueling ride from the police station to Bethany's house. Her father Herb and Bethany sat up front while Masika occupied the middle seat in the back. Her nerves were ablaze.

Oddly enough, at the station, she had felt serene all alone in the small cell she was given. The officers ignored her and she had been at peace with the idea of staying there. She hadn't expected the two to scrounge up the bail in less than twenty-four hours, nor for Herb to make the drive to Louisiana to retrieve her.

"I need you to answer me, kid."

Masika adjusted her stance, trying to sit up straight but inadvertently slumping towards the other side.

"Wanted to protect Bethany. Hated hearing her cry."

Bethany sniffled, barely concealed by Herb's response, "You both beat the shit out of them. You could have left it at that."

"Wouldn't be enough. Whites never keep hands to themselves."

"What makes you say that?" he interrogated.

A pair of invisible claws clamped down on her shoulders. She sank into the seat, trying to relieve the pressure. Suffocated, she managed only one sentence.

"Kevin makes me say that."

Herb's jaw latched shut and the air turned sour. There was no conversation after that, not until he rolled up to Bethany's house. Everyone filed into the living room where the two adults stood while Masika occupied the couch. He asked Bethany if she had any beer. When she said yes, he helped himself to a can, downing it in a couple gulps. Herb wiped his mouth before looking sternly at Masika.

"This was brave of you, and Bethany is grateful, but now you've put yourself in quite the situation. You're gonna wind up in juvie, or worse."

Masika, largely unfazed, began to pick at her nail beds. Herb groaned in irritation and Bethany stepped towards him.

"I'll do my best to testify your child's innocence, Herb," Bethany vowed. "Don't you worry."

"I don't think that'll do much good since *someone* decided to plead guilty, but you can sure try. Lord knows I'll take anything other than my only child getting sentenced." He leaned forward and stared at Masika. "You listening, kid?"

She nodded as if she was, but she'd sank far into the recesses of her mind. She remained there for the rest of the conversation, not missing Herb's comment on her being too aloof to know what she did.

But Masika did know.

She tried to save Bethany, and by extension other women, from a handful of sick perverts. She failed. The mixed feelings that resulted were tough to chew on. A big part of her was grateful the boys weren't dead, another part feared they were destined to target another victim. The sole attempt to thwart Evil, Evil worse than her own, upended. She tried not to scold herself for the brash decision, but found it increasingly difficult.

All she could realistically do was wait and see.

Chapter Four

November 1993

Masika and Aiden easily fell into their respective and overlapping routines. He worked his Monday through Friday shifts before heading to bed. Usually, he would tidy up before turning in, but she rarely let him do so. She typically stayed at home meal-prepping, cleaning, or reading. Despite assuring her that he didn't need chores done for him, Masika insisted it helped her regulate. So, he let her, making sure to pitch in where he could.

The two's close relationship resumed as if no bump in the road existed prior. They frequently watched movies during Aiden's downtime and told each other stories from the past six years. She dazzled him with tales from all over the country, painting murals that the imagination couldn't do justice. Out of the dozens of conversations, however, something Masika never mentioned was the mysterious 'job' she vaguely noted the night she returned.

Feeling rather bold one night, Aiden decided to bite. She spun images of a Vancouver hostel over spaghetti while he figured out how to ask. On the notepad between their plates, he jotted down his question. Once she finished talking, she read it, tapping her nails against her leg. Aiden mirrored, trying to be patient in anticipation of the reply. It took Masika nearly a full minute to answer his inquiry.

"Want the truth or a fairy tale?" She didn't wait for him to write, snorting at the face of irritation made in response. "Okay, okay. Truth it is. May be... surprising, to say the least."

Aiden shrugged, inviting her to do her worst. She sighed.

"Was a hitwoman," she waited for his expression to change, but he remained stoic. "Probably have so many questions. Why that of all things? Well, didn't start off so straightforward. Met a lady named Everlee who offered me a place to stay. Asked me to help her with her 'mission.'"

Aiden did air quotes and raised his eyebrows in confusion. She continued, "Believed God wanted her to kill vile men. Fascinated me, admittedly, so I agreed. Started doing hits with her."

Aiden blinked, rubbing his feet together restlessly. She was surprised by the lack of expression, not knowing he'd seen what she did to his high school bully. It was all those years ago, and he didn't know whether to feign shock or keep the secret to himself. Nevertheless, she kept on with her explanation.

"That went on for a while. But we nearly got caught. So she stopped, had me continue her mission without her help, merely her guidance on who to kill. Once again, agreed so easily," A low hoarseness appeared in her voice. He didn't bat an eye. "Killed a lot of people, Aiden. Almost always for no good reason. Ignored it at first, 'till I got a hit on someone like me... Started to unravel after that."

Uncharacteristic sadness twisted her expression. Requesting a drink from the fridge, Aiden grabbed it for her. Idly staring as she chugged the entire bottle, Masika wiped her mouth and leaned in close.

"Oddly calm about this. Just told you I've killed many, many people; yet no fear in your eyes."

Aiden placed a palm on top of hers, locking their fingers together. Gazes met and for a moment, he swore she might kiss him. She didn't, though. Instead, her pupils flickered with sudden understanding. She reached for his cheek, cupping it.

"Not the same. Killed in self-defense, you did," the hand fell limp at her side while she studied his neutral expression. She shook her head and stood from the couch, "Getting late. Gonna head to bed, goodnight Aiden."

She tousled his hair and smiled weakly. With that, she left. Perplexed, Aiden stared off into space for a long while. Sinking a few hours into watching TV, he eventually retired to his room for the night.

***

A recurring nightmare frequently disrupted Aiden's slumber. The first few times he had it sent him into a spiral. After a couple years, he stopped caring as much. Having a glass of wine before rushing to bed usually ended the troubles there. Recently though, as winter droned on, the effects of the dream had significantly worsened. He couldn't go back to sleep no matter how hard he tried. Small details shifted each time, leaving him increasingly frantic upon awakening.

The dreams always began with a cornfield infinitely spread across the horizon. He would run deeper and deeper into the stalks, half naked and bloody. Every muscle burned yet he did not stop, could not stop. Something chased him. He didn't know what, never daring to turn and see. Why bother? It would catch him and surely kill him, he knew that much. He would reach the end of the cornfield, only to be met with a sheer drop. In every instance, he'd throw himself from that cliff edge.

In recent iterations, the monster caught him mid-jump, hauling him to the surface. Flashes of blue greeted him, face sandpaper-smooth besides an ungodly grin. What followed lasted far too long, felt far too real. Violated was an understatement for how he felt upon awakening, usually mid-scream and fighting the comforter. Wine no longer helped, neither did distracting himself with a shower or book. He'd stare at the ceiling until slumber took him near dawn.

One evening, the demented actions of the creature reached a new height. He awoke to the stench of urine, accompanying a thick film of sweat. Angrily stripping down both himself and the sheets, he collapsed onto the carpet. He cried there until a knock rang out on the bedroom door.

"Aiden? Heard a loud crash, you alright?"

Using the bed to get to his feet, he headed for the door, cracking it open. Peeking through the gap revealed Masika's exposed neck and collarbone, glowing underneath faint candlelight. He pushed the door further, uncovering her entire face. Holding a single tealight close to her chest, she stared down at him, her expression hardened.

"Everything good in there?" She sniffed the air, "What's that smell?"

Aiden's cheeks lit up in embarrassment. He went to close the door, but she stuck her foot out.

"Hey! Worried about you, is all. Sure you're alright?" with that, Aiden violently shook his head. Offering help, he put up a hand and she sighed. "Don't have to be alone, you know."

She slipped from the doorway and back into the halls. Waiting to hear her door shut before stepping out completely, he absorbed the silence. Shaken and naked, he made his way to the bathroom.

A scalding shower brought enough comfort to lull Aiden into a neutral state. He changed his sheets and pillowcase, humming quietly. As he did, Masika's collarbones flashed into his mind. He pictured the piercing in the middle of her bottom lip, perfectly aligned with her tooth gap. If he kissed her, would he taste the metal or her chapstick first? Bringing a pillow to his face, he released a screech into it.

These sudden sexual desires startled him. For the longest time, following the horrendous event leading up to him switching places with Abeje, his relationship with sex was unsound. Disgusting, abysmal scenarios constantly infiltrated his brain and plagued him with conflicting emotions. The primary one was arousal, which fueled his self-hatred. It became so unbearable, he forced himself to ignore it—well, tried to anyway. The thoughts persisted, much to his frustration, but he could at least semi-distract himself by the time Masika showed up.

Now that she was here, the distressing thoughts weren't as oppressive. The despicable images lessened, and he daydreamed of her in place. He had no reason to complain other than the fact he felt confused. How was he falling back into his feelings so easily after Masika abandoned him?

Even with the bewilderment, he wound up in front of her door after throwing the sheets in the wash and putting fresh pajamas on. Fist hovering, it opened as soon as he knocked, as if she expected him. He rubbed his arm as he gazed past her. A corner of her mouth lifted.

"Come on in," she stepped aside as he entered. "Sorry if it's messy, been going through my stuff."

It wasn't messy at all besides a giant pile of various clothes, books and other objects in the corner of the room. Aiden sat on the bed. Masika watched him as she closed the door.

"Everything okay?" She said, joining him.

There was little reason to lie, so he shook his head no. She retrieved a notebook and pen from her nightstand and motioned for him.

"Here, if you wanna talk about it. If you don't, that's alright too."

Details of the nightmare were written down and she frowned deeply, reading over his shoulder. Her body language violently shifted; relaxed muscles tensed as she clenched her fists in her lap. Aiden paused, remembering her earlier comment: *Killed in self-defense, you did.* His stomach tightened; she knew the nightmares were echoes of his reality. Her breathing steadied before she spoke again.

"Fucking hate that pig," she whispered at first, rubbing her knuckles together. She read the words with eyes full of contempt, "Glad he's dead. Wish it never happened, wish you could sleep in peace. Deserve that and more, you do. There a way I can help?"

Gaze lifting as Aiden thought, he found the answer in her arms. After scratching out the paragraph, he wrote a question. *Can you hold me?*

"Of course."

Masika cast the notebook aside, scooting closer to him and draping an arm around his shoulder. She rubbed it for several seconds before speaking.

"Safe here. Pig is dead and can't hurt you anymore. If he somehow rose from the grave, I'd get rid of him, promise you that."

Aiden melted into her embrace, Masika stroking his hair and cradling his head.

"You're safe," she reaffirmed.

The digits slipping through his coils relaxed him enough to fall asleep. He briefly rose thirty minutes later to find himself tucked in bed, laying on his side. Masika read a book under lamplight, nursing a glass of grape juice. She briefly closed the paperback and greeted his sleepy gaze with a grin.

"Go to sleep, Aiden."

He complied, allowing the tide of exhaustion to take him once more.

***

Sleeping in the same bed as her became a tradition after that. Aiden slept in his own only when he wanted total privacy, which wasn't much at all anymore. He obsessed over Masika's newfound presence in his life.

Even at work he found himself fumbling simple tasks, mind busy wrapped up in daydreams. Reveries, most often, of the near future: coming home to the delightful aromas of her cooking, the sight of her head bobbing to music. How concentrated she looked slicing and dicing, gutting peppers without a blink. Cold and calculated, until she noticed his return. The tilt of her head as she trained her eye on him, a slow smile stretching across her lips. The visions would always devolve into lustful fantasy, leaving him blushing and scolding himself as he scrubbed toilets.

He didn't tell her any of it. Things were already tense, and she seemed preoccupied with her own daydreams. Both were privy to long periods of dissociation. They were close enough to sleep in the same bed, but nowhere healed enough to completely open up. Aiden desperately wanted that to change, knowing she wasn't alright.

So Aiden made it his mission to check in more often, Masika beginning to do the same. Soon, bedtime conversation topics delved exclusively into bittersweet introspection where she often let him do the writing. Attempting to crack open her shell again and again to no avail, she insisted she had told him more than enough about her life. He was hitting a wall, touching an exposed nerve every time the topic of trauma was breached.

Aiden discovered her disheveled and worn one evening after work. Coming home later than usual, he decided last minute to grab ingredients for a new recipe. He planned to surprise her with breakfast sometime soon, and fluffy cinnamon roll pancakes sounded right up her alley. When he came home to a lightless and empty kitchen, he made haste to her room, leaving the groceries on the counter.

He found her sitting alone in the dark, door wide open. An uneasy feeling crept along his spine as he watched the stillness of her silhouette.

"Forgot about dinner. Lost track of time," she informed him. "Mind turning on the light?"

Doing so, he proceeded towards her. She flinched halfway through the stride and he paused, awaiting permission.

"It's fine. I'm..." she trailed off, staring at her palms as he cautiously sat beside her. "Head feels fuzzy, been zoning out all day. I'm sorry."

Aiden offered his hand to her. Hesitating at first, she soon slipped her fingers through his. He waited for her to speak once more but she didn't, eyes instead burning holes into the wall ahead for several minutes. Aiden didn't move a muscle, letting her process. The words that followed sent shears straight through his heart.

"Feels wrong being here. Taking care of you, being by your side again... Know I'm unworthy of you."

Aiden nudged her. Squeezing her clenched fist caused her expression to slip.

"Abandoned you, Aiden. Then had the nerve to come back. Should resent me."

He shook his head. Lifting her hand to his lips, he softly kissed her rough knuckles. Their gazes connected and she rested her head on his shoulder.

"Probably gonna keep apologizing for it. Hope that doesn't bother you?"

It didn't. It reassured him that no bad blood existed, and she regretted her decision. None of that mattered anyway with her head nestled against his clavicle. He was glad she was there, glad to share space with someone he admired. He hoped she would forgive herself. She deserved peace.

Maybe we deserve to be at peace together?

Masika peeled away as he reddened from the thought, getting up to stretch. Aiden unabashedly admired the muscles squirming in her arms before he was caught, slack jawed, and she threw him a smirk. Brushing out the wrinkles on her skirt, she walked around the bed towards the door, cracking it open.

"Gonna make dinner now, wanna help?"

Hip-to-hip they tackled dinner, bopping along to an old album they both adored. Masika sung underneath her breath as she chopped up steak, Aiden trying not to be too infatuated while he rinsed vegetables. Finished prepping dinner and putting it in the oven, they set out to the living room.

She zoned out the moment she got on the couch. Sensing her drift away, Aiden patted his empty lap. Brightening a little, she lowered her head onto his thighs. Brushing locs out of her face, he ran his touch up and down her right cheek for several minutes until her eyelids began to flutter. She drifted off effortlessly as he continued listening to the album. He watched her lips part in her sleep, a haziness washing over him.

The obnoxious shriek of the smoke alarm startled them out of their doze. Masika dashed for the kitchen, Aiden lagging behind. She opened the oven, then the kitchen window. Once the fumes cleared enough for him to see, he saw her outright defeated and slumped form in a chair.

"Messed it up," she mumbled, "failed again."

Aiden trekked up to her, fiddling with his hands in the process. When she wouldn't look up from the floor, he ever so gently took her face in his palms. Planting a kiss on her nose, he pressed their foreheads together. Masika cracked a smile.

"Go get something instead? Don't wanna try cooking again after that," she offered.

Aiden agreed, and the two waited for the smell to fade before venturing uptown on his bike. She didn't have any ideas on where to go, but he knew exactly the place. Driving to a shack on the outskirts of town, he craved nothing more than Jamaican food. Parking, she was the first to hop off and bound towards the building, squinting to read the sign.

"'Island Chick.' Kind of food they got?" she questioned, cursing under her breath only a moment after. "Fuck, forgot the notebook."

Aiden gave her a squeeze on the shoulder, signifying it was all good and leading her to the entryway. Once inside, the workers greeted Aiden with glee. He and Masika stood near the register as one ran up.

"Hey sweetheart! Been a minute since I've seen you. You've got a *gorgeous* friend with you, too!" the woman greeted, a wide grin stretched across her face.

Masika blushed, "Thank you."

"No problem honey," she looked to Aiden. "Want your usual lamb curry?"

Aiden nodded. After perusing the menu, Masika wound up ordering the same thing. The lady told them to wait at a booth and she would bring the food out. After choosing a corner, they gazed at one another. She said nothing, but he could tell by her posture she was doing significantly better than earlier.

After a thirty-minute chow-down, Aiden left a twenty-dollar tip on the table. She thanked him for the food on the way to the bike.

A short drive later, they were back at the apartment. On the way inside, Masika stopped to admire the setting sun; Aiden pausing halfway up the stairs to watch her. She noticed his captivation and chuckled.

"Sorry. Just thinking how pretty the stars must be here."

While his face stayed blank, he internally beamed with joy. As they hiked up the stairs, he made a mental note to take her to his favorite star-gazing spot.

CHAPTER FIVE

June 1981

Reality didn't sink in until two security guards twice Masika's height led her down a corridor. The men were escorting her to her new home for the next five years. She realized she knew nothing of the way prisons worked, nor the type of individuals in them (besides that they were 'Evil,' according to Kevin). She was diving head-first into the deep end.

The men skid to a stop in front of the last cell in the area. The thinner, balding one turned to her and gestured to the bars as his comrade fished out keys.

"Here we are. Home sweet home," the man grinned cruelly as the door swung open. "Roll call is at four-thirty, don't be late."

Shoved into the cell, door locking behind her, she simply sighed. At first, she thought she was alone, but the crinkle of bedsheets nearby alerted her to another presence. On the bottom bunk, a figure unfurled from beneath the covers, swinging their legs over the side of the bed. Masika was incredibly surprised to see a woman, not a man, greet her. The individual stood and stepped aside with a gesture to the mattress.

"Here, I'll sleep up top," she stated.

Masika stood rooted to her spot, observing the plain white bricks surrounding her, painted over and chipped. Small, square vents sat above a toilet built into the opposite wall, grungy sink right beside it. The whole room reeked of urine and body sweat. The woman looked her up and down as she absorbed her surroundings.

"I'm Teneca," she introduced herself, "and you must be my new cellmate."

Poofy, near-black hair eclipsed Teneca's shoulders, akin to a lion's mane. Dark circles encased her bold, golden-brown eyes. Her curved nose ended only a half-inch above small, thinly spread lips. Masika saw right through her contemptuous expression, detecting an underlying motherly energy. Teneca reached into her pocket and withdrew a small, wooden statuette.

"Tell me your name."

Masika's throat dried up, choking out her loathsome given name as Teneca squinted.

"That isn't your name, I can hear the disdain in your voice. Pick another one."

"M," she spoke it so fast she surprised herself. All she did was stop at the first initial of her given name, but it sounded right. Teneca bowed her head.

"Good to properly meet you, M. I'm shocked to see such a young person here. What have you done?"

Masika rubbed her wrists, pursing her lips before responding.

"White boys tried hurtin' my neighbor. Straightened them out, I did," she flashed a toothy grin. "Town was ravin' mad, wanted me lynched. Judge told 'em times ain't like that no more, sent me here instead. Cop that brought me here said I 'got lucky.'"

"This ain't nothing close to getting lucky. This is one of the worst men's prisons in the state. But you know that already, don't you?" she continued, thumbing the statuette. "I can tell you're smart, stick close to me and you'll do just fine."

"Why you care?"

Masika expected to be hit, a typical result of her sass. Instead, the woman rolled her shoulders back.

"You're a child. And you're certainly not invincible."

That night Teneca did not sleep, instead staying up to finish the owl that slowly formed in her hold. She told Masika not to worry, she hardly slept anymore. Closing her eyes, an abandoned structure drenched in flames reentered Masika's mind. The gentle crackle of the embers and reek of smog soothed her, consciousness drifting away.

***

Upon waking, her muscles and bones ached. Attempting to return to sleep, a pair of hands clapped nearby. She shot upward in the bed, clutching the sheets with a death grip. Teneca stood a few feet away by the sink, turning it on to wash her face.

"We got about ten minutes 'til roll call. You might want to wake up."

Masika groaned, rolling onto her side and covering her head with the sheet. "Ugh... what time is it?"

"Four-twenty a.m." Teneca answered.

"Stupid," she grumbled, not expecting Teneca to register it.

"I know, but you best get used to it."

She forced herself out of bed. Teneca finished washing her face and crossed her arms, inspecting Masika's posture.

"Do you want an idea of how everything's gonna go? Or would you rather find out yourself?"

Grateful for a choice, Masika opted to go in blind. The following five minutes were spent guessing what to expect of her first day. The only things she knew about prisons were learned from horror stories Gram taught her, and a handful of motion pictures. She envisioned lots of fighting, plenty of blood to fill at least four mop buckets. Well, at least she'd be entertained.

After being summoned to a rather short and painless roll call, it was time for breakfast. Teneca stayed by her side through the food line, all the way to an empty table. She wasted no time digging in, while Masika struggled to ignore the gawking. Having had enough after two or so minutes, she craned her neck ever so slightly.

"Don't acknowledge it," Teneca warned with a full mouth.

Masika resumed her original position. "What? Worst they do is kill me," she scoffed.

Teneca draped a hand over her lips as she finished chewing, eyebrows lifting ever so slightly.

"They can do and have done way worse than that," she asserted. Adjusting her seating position, she lowered both arms into her lap. "Let's not discuss such vile things, I want to know how long you're gonna be here."

"Till I'm eighteen."

"And you're how old?"

"Thirteen."

Teneca shook her head, disapproving. "You've no business being in this prison. You're a child."

"Ain't a child, miss."

Teneca tilted her head to the side, staring in confusion. "Come again?"

"Kids play. Wasn't allowed to play at Gram's, could only clean and go run 'round in the woods."

"What about the woods? Did you play there?"

Masika stiffened, not daring to look down at her hands where animal blood would surely be. Bones snapped in her thoughts and her pupils dropped to her shoes. Teneca realized she was drifting away and changed the subject.

"Well, I certainly don't think you'll be getting a new cellmate anytime soon."

"Why you say that?"

"I'm gonna be here much longer than you. Before this, I wasn't even allowed to have a cellmate."

"Why?"

"Because I'm a woman, my dear."

"Why you here then?"

The woman hesitated. Right as she went to respond, breakfast ended. As everyone got up, Teneca informed her of the rest of the day's schedule. After this, they were to work until lunch.

"Work?"

"We all have to work. Depends on the prisoner what job you get. I'm on janitorial, hopefully you will be too. I got a bad back and I do just fine."

As Teneca predicted, Masika was assigned janitorial. The wards instructed Teneca to teach her everything she needed to know. She spent two hours showing the child the ropes—where the supplies were, the focus areas, what to avoid—and learning about her in between tasks. Despite the constant questions, Masika never found her to be meddlesome. In fact, it felt good to be questioned about her interests. It reminded her a lot of Bethany's old visits. Eventually, Teneca asked if she could learn anything, what would it be.

"Ballet. Always wanted to be a ballerina," Masika admitted, feeling slightly foolish, "but can't be one. 'Cause... you know."

"Anyone can be a ballerina. Boys or girls, gender doesn't matter," she eyed her inquisitively. "Who told you otherwise?"

"Grandfather."

"Well, fuck him. You can do whatever you put your mind to, M." She stopped scrubbing, "Terrible men should never speak. Don't you agree?"

Masika did, but said nothing.

***

Days turned to months. Soon, two years flew by. Masika expected the worst, but she found herself tethered to Teneca's side. The older woman instinctively protected her.

Her routine went like this: roll call, breakfast, work, school, dinner, sleep. She usually skipped lunch to stay in her cell. Over the years, Masika gradually learned how to read and write, skills she never expected to possess. Teneca encouraged her where she struggled.

Her teacher existed as a marvel to Masika. She never outright queried why, as a woman, Teneca had to be in Ashgate Penitentiary. Having an inkling was plenty, leaving the rest to her imagination until Teneca felt comfortable enough to voice it herself.

It happened on a Sunday evening as the two settled down for bed. Normally, Teneca would meditate and read. That night, she paced in the cramped cell, rubbing her knuckles until they bled. She tried to hide it whenever Masika peeked up from her textbook. When questioned, she politely told Masika she was perfectly fine.

Masika knew better. Eventually, Teneca wound up in front of the mirror, staring intently at her reflection, trembling. At first, she couldn't tell what she was looking at. Soon, she noticed a pattern. Reach lingered on the sides of her face, fingertips glossing over the stubble forming on her jaw.

Over the following week, Masika stole a plastic knife from the cafeteria, sharpening it into a shiv while Teneca slept each night. Monday morning, she approached the woman.

"Teneca."

Masika twirled the shiv behind Teneca, who was gaze deep in her reflection. Not moving from her position, she reiterated. After another moment, Teneca sighed in acknowledgment.

"Yes?"

"Let me help."

Teneca turned with amusement on her face, puffy red eyes confirming Masika's concerns.

"With what? Do you plan to stab me? End my suffering?"

"Course not. When you have face hair, seem upset. Made a little razor of sorts."

Teneca scoffed, "Could've made it myself and saved you the time."

Masika frowned. Teneca bounced back almost immediately as she sat on the bottom bunk.

"I'm sorry, I'm bad at accepting help." Teneca sucked a sharp breath through her teeth, "I would usually shave myself, but it's been a rough week."

"Let me do it."

"Long as you promise not to cut me up."

The two wound up in front of the mirror, where Masika carefully shaved Teneca's face. Starting with her thick sideburns, she worked down her jawline. When she got to her chin, she asked a question.

"There a way to stop facial hair from growing?"

"Yes and no."

"Explain," she pressed.

"I used to be on a chemical called estrogen, it's a hormone. Exists in everyone, but I was born with a low amount. Started taking a pill every day to increase how much existed in my body. It doesn't fully stop hair growth, but it helps. Does that make sense?"

"It does," she finished one side of Teneca's face and switched to another. "How you get it?"

"Heh, a friend of a friend of another friend. In other words, illegally and off-market. You gotta know the right people," she gave Masika a curious look. "Why?"

She took in a deep breath, "Feel a lot like you."

Teneca, impressed with the meticulous job, ran her palms over her mostly smooth cheeks. Masika returned to her bunk, fetching her textbook from the depths of the blanket. As she began to read, Teneca thanked her.

"No problem. Do the same for me if I get any?" Masika requested.

"Promise."

Chapter Six

March 25th, 1985

"Happy birthday, M."

Masika accepted the congratulations with a humble smile. Teneca and she were walking side-by-side towards the cafeteria, breakfast awaiting them. She could hardly believe she was seventeen and, by extension, only had a year remaining in her prison sentence.

The past years were peaceful. Teneca passed on more knowledge than the prison could ever offer. Masika learned about transsexuals and two-spirits, tales from Choctaw legend and, most importantly, how to cope with dysphoria.

The mask had peeled away around Teneca to the point where Masika finally admitted she hadn't enjoyed being socialized as a boy. She wished for so long she could have a more prominent chest, less facial hair... When she was able to face this, Teneca had been expecting her to say as much. Masika asked if there was one set way to womanhood, and Teneca told her no such thing existed. Her body, her rules. The 'rules' society created weren't real.

Along with debunking made-up gender laws, Teneca taught her of America's brutal origins. Masika had known nothing about slavery, nor the indigenous tribes the whites brutalized. Teneca deconstructed it all in sizable bites, fearful she may choke in terror. She couldn't shake the anger or heartache for her and Teneca's ancestors.

Now, on the cusp of adulthood, she knew a lot more than she had coming into prison—having mostly Teneca to thank for that. Masika couldn't confess to her cellmate, but she loved her like a mother. She endeavored to not let her feelings get out of hand, knowing Teneca had a blood-related son waiting for her out of prison. There was no room for her, no family to be had. Already lost her chance, or so she thought until today.

Once the duo finished breakfast, Teneca passed her a carved fox sculpture. She took it curiously, admiring the fine details in the wood.

"What this?" she questioned.

"Your birthday gift," Teneca replied with a tender grin, "been working on it for a while."

"Why fox?"

"You remind me of 'em," when Masika pulled a sour face, she cracked up. "In a good way. You're swift, light on your feet."

Masika relaxed, putting the sculpture close to her chest. She allowed a smile, ending up keeping it in her pocket throughout the rest of the day. While she typically disliked birthdays, Teneca had made her last few tolerable.

Even better, she had received a card from Herb. This surprised her, as he had been late by a couple days the other years. When she opened it, her heart sank with regret as she read: *Miss you, kid. Working my ass off so we have somewhere to go next year. I'm gonna make sure this card gets to you on time. Stay safe and have a happy birthday!*

Between the gift and the card, Masika rode on cloud nine. During shower time, she looked forward to a night of reading and meditation with Teneca. What she didn't expect was Larry to pick a fight with her.

Larry, a sex offender with several charges against him, avoided Masika and Teneca most of the time. He had a habit of cornering and attacking prisoners he found inadequate. Teneca told her he tried to lay her out once and embarrassed himself in front of everyone. After that, crickets.

Crickets until today, apparently, the one-time Teneca wasn't accompanying her. They were the only two there currently, Masika finding this odd as privacy, even to this degree, was a rare luxury. She ignored his presence, hoping to spot Teneca. Trying to keep calm, she washed herself quickly. It took a mere five minutes for Larry to open his mouth.

"Where's ya friend?"

Masika didn't answer. Finishing up and turning to leave, he cut her off and backed her towards a wall. Panic soaring, heart racing, she prepared to strike. Remembered claws reaching outwards and then...

Nothing.

When she came to, water poured and fell to the ground in dense spurts. Two hands held her arms as her vision cleared, the first sight being Larry's still body face-down. Blood collected on the shower floor around his head, only to be washed down the drain.

"M? Are you listening?" Teneca's voice echoed.

She nodded, though she couldn't comprehend what had happened. She vaguely registered the elder instructing her to wash the blood off her hands. In a blink, she was in her cell, being lit up with questions as she tried to orient herself.

"M, are you okay?"

She didn't know what happened, nor if she was okay. Maybe he hadn't attacked her, but Teneca instead. Having trouble recalling if the two were alone or if Teneca had been there the whole time, she shrugged, only heightening Teneca's anxiety. There was one thing for certain—Larry was fucking dead and Masika was pretty sure she killed him.

"Don't worry, I'm not gonna let anyone blame you for this. Everyone will know I did it," Teneca stated.

Masika shot right back, "Why the hell would you say you did it?"

Confusion crossed Teneca's face, "What?"

"Killed him, I did. So why say it was you?"

Teneca processed her words with an uncertain expression. The next line she spoke was careful and calculated.

"To protect you."

"From what? Spending more time?"

"Yes, M. Believe it or not, your life doesn't end when you're seventeen. You have so much to see and do outside of this place."

"So do you!"

Teneca fell silent. Leaning against the wall, resigned, she shook her head, "No I don't. This is my resting place."

She scoffed, "What the hell you talking about?"

"I'm on death row."

Masika's mouth froze before she could respond again. Her chest and jaw tightened, the suffocatingly dire sensation causing a few tears to slip down her face.

"Were you gonna tell me?"

"Oh, save it. I'm not obligated to tell you shit, I'm really not."

Masika covered her mouth, stifling a sob. Collecting herself, she wiped her tears and hissed, "So what? Was gonna let me go the rest of my life thinking you're still alive here, that maybe you made it out?"

"I didn't know how to tell you. You were thirteen when you came here. Was it supposed to come with the introduction?" Teneca trembled, "I've even been lying to myself! Trying to convince myself this ain't the end for me; denial blinds us. I think I was waiting to give you hope, give you a better answer. I'm sorry, M, I really am."

She deflated onto her bed, burying her face into the sheets. As she wept, Teneca joined her side, waiting for her shoulders to stop shaking.

"M, please look at me." Teneca brushed a thumb across her baby hairs. "I know you're upset with me, I shouldn't have kept that from you. Will you forgive me?"

"Want to be there." Masika said.

Teneca exhaled through her nose. "M…"

"Can I be there?"

"Probably, the only one I know for certain attending is Mahpiya. I just… are you sure you want to see that?"

Masika nodded, gaze falling to her hands. She placed them flat on her lap, tear drops speckling her palms.

"Watched my mom die when I was three, think I'll be alright."

Teneca stiffened, "You never told me about that."

"Not exactly good for small talk," Masika half-joked.

"I don't mind listening, but it's up to you if you wanna talk about it."

Most people can't recall their toddler years, yet Masika could remember that entire day. The most vivid instance of her childhood, when she got out of the playpen and crawled to Mommy. Mommy said nothing, not a word, her cheek and body pressed to the tile. In the present, she held herself.

"Had stroke while cooking and watching me. Didn't know… didn't know she was dead. Pops' scream was unforgettable. Must've killed him to see his own kid playing with his wife's corpse, splashing in her blood. Sobbed and sobbed and couldn't look at me, didn't even pick me up. All he could do was wail, why he dropped me off with Kevin. Kevin says I'm infected, infected with the Devil. Neighbors all say the same… all the same… so I belong here…" she trailed off. "Like her, you are."

"Is that why you don't want me to die?"

Masika nodded, her face twitching as she withheld tears. Teneca tightly hugged her and she completely froze. The older woman stroked her hair carefully, smile faint. Masika melted and began to cry.

"I'm sorry, M. I owed you an explanation much sooner than this. I'm here right now, though. You're not alone."

With that, Masika's muscles relaxed against Teneca's chest. Crying and crying until, with one final breath, exhaustion swept her away.

***

"Rise and shineeee!"

Masika awoke in the cell with a couple annoyed guards explaining she missed roll call and breakfast. Ignoring the commentary, she asked about Teneca.

"She's up doing what she's supposed to. Now get the hell to work."

Glaring at him, she said nothing. He tried to threaten her again to no avail as she got up, making her way to janitorial.

She was relieved to see Teneca mopping the halls, the feeling fading when she didn't notice her right away. When she did, Teneca dragged Masika off to a secluded area.

"They found Larry. Fucker was still alive," she informed her.

"Shit..."

"It's okay, I think we scared him straight. I don't think he's gonna blab," she placed a hand on Masika's shoulder. "You okay? I'm sorry I didn't wake you. Figured you needed the rest and vouched for you at roll call."

"Appreciate it."

"Are you doing okay?"

The answer was more than complicated. How was she supposed to be okay after learning the news on her birthday of all times? After she foolishly attacked Larry and apparently didn't have the guts to finish him off? Not only did she fuck up, she could do absolutely nothing about Teneca's impending doom. Before she realized, she was crying again.

"C'mere," Teneca opened her arms.

Masika threw herself into the embrace.

Chapter Seven

March 1986

Teneca spent the next year trying to alleviate Masika's worries. There was no use as Masika began to spiral at startling speed. She feared herself, the life that awaited her outside of prison, and Teneca's absence. All of which inched closer and closer the more time she lost to dissociation.

She verbally attacked Teneca on several occasions, a result of feeling constantly cornered. Teneca would give her ample space, apologies always followed. Her guardian assumed fear of the unknown ate away at Masika just as it did her; she was right. Masika knew nothing about the real world, nothing outside of prison walls. Even Kevin's prison shed no light on what to expect following her inevitable release. She tried finding answers in everything, starting with the Bible. The verses he seared into her mind meant nothing now, replaced with Teneca's soft words and stories.

Soothing her, if only temporarily, until it made her realize she still felt small. Still felt like a frightened child with no one to help her. No one could but Teneca: her savior, her guardian, her dear friend. Nobody could replace her even if they tried. She didn't want them to either, but she yearned to find new companionship upon release. She was kidding herself, knowing reality wouldn't allow it. After all, what could a sick, twisted, Evil thing like herself have to offer anyone? The only reason Teneca tolerated her was out of pity, nothing more. Which is exactly why she questioned

Teneca at every possible turn, accused her of keeping company with the Devil. *1 Corinthians 15:33: Do not be misled: "Bad company corrupts good character."*

Teneca told Masika she knew what she was going through. This threw her into another downward spiral; how *dare* she deny her love for Teneca and accuse her of frolicking with Evil. Masika wanted nothing more than to believe her words. The words that resonated with her far more than anything Kevin spewed out during the nine years of her stay. The whiplash from doubt to faith, and back to unearthing the terror of adulthood, completely overwhelmed her. Tranquility remained scarce, leaving a shell of a human in its wake.

Worst of all, she wasn't impervious to Teneca's own struggles. Despite her instability, Masika could tell she feared her final day. She spent significantly more time in her cell, in isolation. When asked why, she claimed she needed to think.

"I've spent all these years telling myself this wasn't the end. That I would walk away, hug my son again. Now that I know that's not true... I have to find closure. I refuse to die without some kind of peace, so I need to do a lot of thinking. Hope you understand."

Masika did, but that didn't stop her mind from flipping between belief and disbelief. She lied to herself the same way her cellmate lied much of her sentence. Every day, despite Teneca's insistence, she told herself Teneca wouldn't die. She wouldn't die and, moreover, she would be freed.

The girl could run from it no longer. The dissociation that plagued the last year of her life lifted, traded in for hyper-awareness as the clock struck midnight on March twenty-fifth, nineteen-eighty-six. She couldn't sleep, Teneca couldn't either. The day marked a week before her lethal injection, mere hours before Masika's release. Teneca wordlessly joined her on the bottom bunk, a drooping smile on her face.

"Happy birthday, M. You made it. You're getting out," she said.

Despair pooled in the bottom of her stomach, "But not you."

The smile dropped. Teneca moved a couple locs out of Masika's face, deeply sighing.

"I know. If I could walk out today by your side, I would. I would do anything to leave with you, M, but I can't. We both know that," she caught a few of Masika's tears. "What I can do is spend these last few hours with you, happy instead of miserable. Okay?"

"Okay..."

"Good. Now, M," she began, shifting her weight slightly, "I want you to promise me a couple things. Can you do that?"

"Can try."

"Okay. First off, if you can, I want you to try and find Mahpiya. Befriend him. I've told him about you already, and he's very eager to meet you." She held up two fingers, "Second, I want you to live as yourself. Not as what Kevin wanted you to be, or what anyone else wants you to be. Be yourself and do not let a single soul suffocate you. Are those both feasible?"

"T-think so."

Teneca noticed the subtle shake of her hands, "Let's find a distraction, shall we?"

Climbing to the top bunk, Teneca reappeared with a deck of playing cards. The next hour, she taught her how to play Go Fish. At first, Masika found herself annoyed by such a simplistic distraction. But once she got into the game, she couldn't help but enjoy herself. She and Teneca were equally competitive, the two playfully challenging each other the entire time.

When five rounds of Teneca winning passed, she asked when Masika last heard a bedtime story.

"Dunno. Think when my mom was alive."

"Do you want to hear one I used to tell Mahpiya?"

She nodded eagerly. Teneca gestured for her to lay down and she did. The older woman took a couple minutes to collect her thoughts before beginning the story.

"One day, a panther stumbled across a starving possum. The panther, being enemy with deer, gifts him an offer he can't refuse—to trick the deer in exchange for a meal," Teneca smoothed out Masika's baby hairs. "The panther buried himself in a makeshift grave, rotten log sat atop to mimic a corpse. A group of deer fall for the trick, celebrating and chanting around the 'corpse.' The panther then leapt from his grave, slaughtering the big buck of the group."

"Does the panther kill the possum after?" Masika questioned.

"No, the panther keeps his word and the possum feasts upon the buck for a long time. He does so until he is startled by birds and grows fearful of retaliation, stashing the buck's backbone in his basket and fleeing. The possum traveled until he came across a creek. He climbed up a tree over-looking a footlog and took the backbone out to nibble on.

A wolf comes along, crossing the footlog. In the water's reflection, he sees the backbone and jumps into the creek, finding nothing but mud and leaves. The possum tries to call out to him, but the wolf couldn't find the source of the voice. He kept searching for the bone until he grew discouraged. With a howl, he threw his head up, only to see the possum in the tree.

The possum repeated his earlier words unheard by the wolf; 'Open your mouth and I will throw into it something good to eat.' As soon as the wolf obeyed, the possum threw the backbone into his mouth. The bone gets stuck and the wolf chokes to death. The possum uses a sharp flint to decapitate the wolf, taking the head along for his travels."

Masika stared at her with wonder and curiosity, begging her to continue. Teneca did so with a tiny grin.

"The possum crosses the creek, meeting a gang of wolves. The wolves question him about his journey and soon leave him once he answers. Another patrolling wolf comes along and, many questions later, he no-tices the wolf head in the possum's basket." Teneca's expression darkened, reflecting the sense of danger in the story. "The wolf howls for the rest of the pack, and they return. The wolves tell the possum he must die, the leader allowing him to choose the quickest way. The possum says there is a lightwood knot over on the other side of the hill that will kill him the quickest. He tricks the wolf who ratted him out, too, saying another knot lies in the opposite direction. Once the wolves leave, the possum retrieves a rattlebox and a sharp thorn.

Scouting the area, the possum burrows into a sink hole. The pack returned soon after, aware of the possum's tricks. They find the sink hole but hear the possum shaking his rattlebox, mistaking the hiding spot for a rattlesnake hole.

One of the wolves suggests drenching whatever the creature is with water. As a wolf pours brine down the hole, it hits the possum's throat. Another wolf ran a paw down towards it, prompting the possum to strike the paw with the thorn. The wolf jerked his paw away and the pack fled, fully convinced there was only a rattlesnake and no possum."

Processing everything, Masika sat in silence for a few moments. She mindlessly played with her limbs before vocalizing. "Tricked all of them, he did."

"That's right."

Without giving Teneca a second to breathe, she tugged at her sleeve. "Another one, please?"

Teneca chuckled, "Alright."

After another tale spilled from Teneca's lips, Masika inadvertently fell asleep. She woke up every hour or so, startled, and Teneca would soothe her into slumber. She dreamed of an abyss, an absence of emotion and feeling. She felt like such when she woke up for good to keys jingling nearby.

Her and Teneca both rose from the bed, glancing warily at two guards standing in front of the cell. The eldest unlocked the door, stepping inside with irritation on his face. He didn't need to say a word for Masika to know he'd been sent to fetch her. She shook her head.

"Want more time," she bargained.

He tutted, "Too bad, kid. You know that's not how things work around here."

Lunging forward only for Teneca to pull her by the waist, she thrashed in her grip. She released her and Masika collapsed to the floor, a puddle of sobs and hiccups. Teneca slowly lowered herself.

"Can't go. Can't leave you," Masika reasoned tearfully.

"M. Look at me, sweetheart," she gently tilted up her chin. "This is not the end, I will see you that day."

"How do you know?"

"I just know."

Teneca hugged Masika and bid her goodbye. She collected herself just enough to let the guards escort her away.

She didn't click back into reality until she stood before Herb, box of belongings in hand, sun blinding at the prison exit. He ran forward and crushed her in his arms, making her drop the box.

"It's so good to see you," he pulled away to grasp her shoulders. "Happy birthday. How's it feel to be eighteen?"

"Terrible. Fucking terrible..."

"I hear ya. At least you don't gotta spend most of it in prison. C'mon, let's get breakfast, I'm starved."

Masika didn't bother taking in her surroundings, head hung as she picked up the box. Spotting the wooden fox inside, she sorely missed Teneca. Herb didn't speak much and she felt the guilt radiating off him, stifling her. She wondered when he would get the guts to speak again.

He didn't until the two were inside a shoddy, run-down diner blessed with decent staff. He ordered a cup of joe, Masika a glass of root beer. Languishing out the window, the sun's rays reflected off the packed parking lot, not a cloud in the sky. She looked away from the glare.

"So bright," she muttered, mostly to herself.

"They didn't let you go outside?" Herb finally asked.

"Maybe once every six months."

"I could act surprised, but I ain't. Did you have a cellmate?"

Masika stiffened, the hairs on her neck standing on end. Their server eventually appeared with a plate of eggs and bacon. Despite it being her first proper meal since prison, she could hardly stomach trying a bite. Instead, she answered Herb's question.

"Yeah. Name's Teneca. Helped me a lot..." she trailed off to focus on picking at her eggs. "Real nice woman."

Herb nodded, only to furrow his eyebrows, "Hold on, I think I'm confused. Isn't Ashgate a men's prison?"

"It is. Teneca's not a man, though. Ain't supposed to be there."

Herb eyed her curiously, "are you saying she's a transsexual?" When Masika nodded, he did as well. "I see. I'm glad you ended up with her and not some creep."

"Protected me the whole way through. Dying next week, she is."

"Death row?"

"Yes."

Herb grimaced, "Good lord..."

Masika worked up the nerve to ask Herb if she could go back and get a witness form. He listened as she told him a bit more about Teneca and her circumstances.

"Wanna be there if I can. Please."

Herb looked at her over his coffee mug as he took a swig. Wiping his mouth, the corners lifted in the smallest smile.

"Of course, I ain't gonna stop you from being there. She clearly means a lot to you."

***

A day before the scheduled execution, Masika received word of being approved to witness. When Herb told her the news, she was speechless.

This meant Teneca was really going to die. It wasn't a lie, wasn't a farce, and she was to watch it unfold firsthand.

She grew unwell rapidly, her mental state deteriorating as the hours ticked by. Herb did his best to comfort her, providing support, but she had shut down and let the void take her. Staying up all night staring at the ceiling, she projected memories of Teneca onto the popcorn texture. Reliving every moment, good or bad.

The next morning, guards escorted her through the prison, eyes stinging as if she hadn't blinked for an entire day. Having cried to the point of exhaustion the night before, she was ready to lose her composure at the drop of a dime. Unhelpful, the guards snidely remarked on her relationship with Teneca. It took all her might not to cut the journey short and backhand both men in the face. She didn't, caring much more about being there for Teneca than getting even with idiots.

An hour later, she veered off to the closest restroom, splashing her face with scalding hot water. Upon realizing the stalls were vacant, she cried. Cried until snot ran down her lips and chin, until the sobs turned to howls of rage. Winding up on the floor, she hugged herself. Maybe Teneca wasn't gone? Maybe it had all been a practical joke? A prank? Masika laughed at herself.

No, Teneca was dead. That goodbye was final. Forcing herself to grieve the loss until the door opened, she got up at once and scurried into a stall. That moment of seclusion wiped her mind blank, blank enough to leave and wait in the parking lot for Herb. As she stood in front of the building, time seemed to drone on. She searched for Herb's truck to no avail. Surely he would return soon, she hoped.

Ten minutes ticked by when another truck—a navy blue one, quite low to the ground—crawled by the drop off area. The passenger window rolled down and someone shouted to her from the driver's seat.

"Need a ride?" Masika shook her head. The stranger insisted, "May I at least speak with you? Please?"

Looking up then, she came face to face with Mahpiya for the first time. He wore a midnight blue button up and slacks. A near-black mane, just as wavy and long as Teneca's, sat nicely over his shoulders. Low-lidded and crestfallen eyes begged her for a chance to speak. Her fists curled into jean pockets as she reluctantly agreed.

He parked and she walked around, climbing in and avoiding his gaze to instead scan the interior. She choked up at photos of Teneca taped to the dashboard.

"You're M, aren't you?"

She slowly nodded, "Teneca tell you about me?"

"She did, thank you for being there today. I fully expected to be alone," he told her.

Masika didn't know what to say, still shackled to her own grief. She shrunk against the leather seat, crawling away from her reflection in the mirror.

"Heard a lot about you too," she gradually responded.

"I can imagine, please tell me she spared you from the embarrassing stuff."

"Yes. Mostly how you were getting your degree, want to be a doctor."

Teardrops flowed down their faces until Mahpiya had the courage to speak again, "She told me you tried to kill several white boys; that true?"

She choked out a laugh, "It is. Wouldn't have it any other way. Means I got to meet her, be with her until the end. Teneca was an amazing woman, Mahpiya."

"She was. She will be sorely missed. I wish I had visited more before medical school..." his unibrow furrowed as he mentally drifted away. Then, clarity swirled in the amber of his irises. "Do you have a place to go?"

"Uh, yeah. Gonna live with my old man for a while."

"How old are you?"

"Just turned eighteen."

"How long ago?"

"Uh, about a week ago."

Mahpiya visibly tensed, piecing together the timeline. Going quiet once again, Masika opted to change the subject, asking for his age.

"Twenty-seven. Real close to earning the "Doctor" in front of my name," he smiled thinly, pulling out a box of cigarettes from his center console. "Want one?"

"Sure."

Having never smoked a cigarette before, she couldn't help but feel curious. Mahpiya lit one as it sat tucked between her lips. Taking a couple puffs, she gagged like a cat ready to vomit. Mahpiya broke out into hysterical snorts before composing himself.

"First time?"

After coughing she answered, "Yeah, my bad." She took a couple more hits before getting back to the subject of his career, "So, you wanna be a doctor. Wanna work at a hospital?"

"Fuck no. Those places are underfunded, understaffed, and full of nothing short of pain and grief. I plan on traveling, offering my services to people who can't afford a hospital bill."

"Sounds real nice."

"Thank you. Mom thought so too."

In the distance, a vehicle honked. Masika looked over her shoulder, noticing Herb parked a few yards away, grumpy expression on his face.

"Who's that?"

"My old man, better get going."

"Here, I'll drive you up," Mahpiya offered.

Mahpiya circled the truck around until he was right behind Herb's. Masika bid him farewell, but he ushered a business card into her hand.

"Here, my landline number and address are on there. Feel free to reach out if you need anything, okay?"

"Thank you," she stuffed the card into her pocket and smiled as sincerely as she could. "Nice meeting you, Mahpiya."

"You too."

She hopped out of the truck and got into the passenger seat of Herb's. Looking quizzical, he grilled her. "Who was that?"

"Teneca's son, only other person to attend."

Herb then asked how she felt, the question falling unexpectedly on Masika's ears. She resolved herself.

"Feel fine," she lied.

"Do you think I was okay when your mom died?" Herb retorted. "Kid, you're allowed to grieve."

Her lip twitched. "Kevin wouldn't think so, would tell me to be a man 'bout it."

"He don't matter."

"Clearly he does. Sent me off to live with him, after all."

He cursed her name under his breath, "Fine. Let me know if you need to talk."

Masika didn't say another word. Not for the five-hour drive from Louisiana to Alabama, and not when Herb rolled up to their new home. It crushed her to ignore his obvious excitement and pride. Granted, she wished she could show more enthusiasm. She was grateful, but stuck in a putty of despair and mourning, she couldn't express much other than a scowl.

Herb showed her around the two-bedroom trailer, the only thing within his budget. She didn't absorb many details other than her room. When they got to it, she brightened at the sight of her mother's vanity next to an oak dresser.

"Phillis always put you in her lap whenever she got ready in the mornings. So... I figured you'd want her vanity. As a reminder," Herb explained, noticing the shift in her demeanor.

She broke her silence only to thank him. Finishing up the tour, Herb ended it by requesting she sit on the couch. Obeying, he sat next to her in his recliner. She anticipated a serious conversation based on his fidgeting limbs. Herb cleared his throat.

"We gotta talk about your sentence."

"What 'bout it? Did my time."

"Yeah, you did. But your sentence also requires you to complete at least a year of high school."

"Great," Masika mumbled, too emotionally exhausted to care. "Good thing schools are prisons too."

"Hopefully not, I signed you up for one already. Local, private, Christian. The other schools didn't accept on account of your record. You start in August. Until then, consider this your summer vacation. I want you to explore town, meet kids your age."

"No thanks, don't need friends."

"I beg to differ. C'mon, would it kill you—"

He halfway said her birth name before she cut him off, heart racing and unable to bear hearing it. Not after all that time spent only being known as 'M.' She scratched her arms as she tried to speak.

"S-Sorry. Didn't go by that in prison, went by a different name. Feels... wrong," she stammered, waiting to be scolded. "Sorry—"

"Hey it's alright, kid. What do I call you instead?"

"M."

"Just the letter?" he gleamed, "Easy peasy."

Masika let out a long exhale of relief. Perhaps this arrangement wasn't so terrible after all.

CHAPTER EIGHT

January 1994

"**A**iden."

Groggily rolling over, he rubbed his eyes. Upon sitting up, Aiden nearly fell off the bed at recognition of Masika's naked body. She giggled at his reaction and held him steady with a hand.

"Acting like you've never seen me naked before," she teased, running a thumb down his arm. "How cute."

Aiden's ears burned as he explored every sweat slicked muscle. Heart racing, he struggled to calm himself with labored breaths. How had he already gotten so worked up?

She dug her nails gently into his skin before planting a kiss on his lips. Relinquishing control, he kissed back passionately and let her fall on top of him. Ripping his boxers in half, she exposed him, tossing the item to the floor. In an instant, her tongue was on him, sending shockwaves throughout his entire body. He couldn't hold in the moan that followed. She said only two words...

"Good boy."

***

Aiden threw off the comforter as he awoke. Sitting up, he caught his breath upon realizing he was fully clothed. It had only been a dream. Ignoring the slick gathering in his boxers, he checked the alarm clock on the nightstand. It was half past nine a.m. He found Masika's side of the bed empty.

Gathering his mental and physical strength to stand up and retrieve a glass of water, he headed out of the room and towards the kitchen. On the way, he heard the shower running down the hall. Thankful she was still in the apartment, Aiden proceeded to the kitchen. Splashing his face in the sink with cold water before filling up a cup, he retracted back upstairs.

A few steps from the bathroom door, he swore he heard something other than steaming water. Putting his glass on the nightstand, he retraced his steps, timidly pressing an ear to the door. Suspicions confirmed, he quickly withdrew. He touched his chest, exhaling in shock. After a minute of processing, he returned to the wood separating him and Masika, lips parted as he listened.

Beneath the running water, soft moans could be heard. He bit back a gasp as several seconds ticked by. The longer he listened, the louder she got. Butterflies paraded about his gut, and he tried to force himself to move away. He couldn't, repeatedly getting ensnared in the memory of those same sounds from seven years ago. Closing his eyes, he allowed the coinciding experiences to envelop him.

The shower suddenly shut off. Tearing away from the door, he proceeded to fall straight on his ass. Without a second to think, he scrambled to his feet and made a beeline for the kitchen. Clumsily retrieving a coffee mug, he quickly turned on the tap and filled it with water. A moment later, Masika appeared in the room wearing only a towel.

"Heard a bang in the hallway... you alright?" she questioned him.

Choking down some water, he nodded, trying to evade the soft brown towel perfectly hugging her figure. She closed the gap and lifted his chin, moving his head around to inspect for marks or bruises. She let go with a peculiar sigh, finding none.

"Acting strange. Hear something?"

Aiden wanted to say *maybe*, picking up one of her hands and stroking each individual knuckle. She let the limb slip away, lingering for only a moment before vanishing down the hallway. Aiden longed to follow her and take her hand again. He leaned against the counter, holding his head instead.

A few days later, she offered to go grocery shopping. Taking it as the perfect opportunity to release some tension, Aiden agreed. After all, the shower encounter had been haunting him, along with flashbacks from the barn. She bid him farewell and he locked the door behind her.

Laying out on the couch, he surmised that he had more than enough time to handle his business. Kicking off his jeans and underwear, he got to work. He rarely masturbated and found himself incredibly sensitive to any form of touch, even his own. It took a mere three minutes to reach his first orgasm, expecting to be satiated—yet his lower half ached for more. Obliging, he guided himself through a second orgasm, then a third, until he started losing count.

Oblivious to the mess he was making, he wound up slipping a digit inside himself. He added another and another, until he couldn't keep quiet anymore. He bit down hard on his free wrist, keeping his moans at bay.

His thighs convulsed violently as he came for a final time, crying out. Taking out his fingers, he rolled onto his side. As he did, a small giggle resonated from the doorway and his eyes shot open.

Shit.

Aiden sat up to see Masika, a shit-eating grin on her face as she leaned against the doorframe. Still hazy from the pleasure, he didn't bother to conceal himself, only wondering how long she had been standing there.

"Sorry. Heard some... noises. Came to make sure you were okay," she commented smoothly. "Guess we're even."

He turned bright red and she vanished back into the kitchen.

***

Day by day, brick by brick, thread by thread. That's how Masika had to go about her new life with Aiden. Growing used to dissociating through the years, she was never really present unless absolutely necessary. Even then, the memories would slip away into a vault afterwards, rarely surfacing.

The genuine safety and lack of danger was terrifying. It shattered her, cracking her open in the best way possible. It felt good to be vulnerable with Aiden, but it also meant starting from nothing.

So she did, day by day, letting an old mentor's lingering touch fade from her mind. Tried to anyway, unable to shake the feeling of being watched. To battle the paranoia, to thwart Evil from entering her mind, she played a constant image of Teneca's smile on blast. She rebuilt her relationship with Aiden brick by brick, holding herself accountable and never lying to him. Thread by thread she glimpsed at herself, her flaws, and made peace with them.

The sluggish speed of recovery proved the most challenging. That, coupled with her undeniable love for him, made her constantly fear for his safety. It felt like only a matter of time before Everlee would show up. She believed that wholeheartedly, and she couldn't let Aiden suffer Everlee's acrimony. She would have to finish the bitch off for good this time, no backing down, but she feared she would fail. She would fail yet again and all the efforts to undo her Evil would be in vain; losing Aiden being the cherry on top.

She refused to let that happen. One night, she stayed up late counting her money while he slept. Deciding to depart the next morning, she would tell him everything before leaving for his own safety. Satisfied with her total, she packed her things as quietly as she could.

Around six a.m., while Aiden stirred in his sleep, Masika sat on the edge of their bed. Nails digging into her thighs, she contemplated a thousand ways to phrase her goodbye, crying silently. Arguing with herself until the sun broke past the horizon, she didn't hear Aiden get up.

Turning her head slightly, warmth bubbled around her shoulders as he nuzzled against her. Sleepily wrapping his arms around her waist, his lazy grin imprinted on her skin as she broke away from his hold. It took a few moments for him to process her actions, simply smiling and reaching out to her in response.

"Have to go," Masika articulated coldly.

Expression hardening, he too rose from the bed. Standing a couple of feet away, respecting her space despite his perturbation, he waited for an explanation. An explanation she'd been rehearsing all night, thankfully.

"Killed hundreds, I have. Yet you let me play housewife, pretend I won't pay for what I've done. Pretend that you won't be killed for getting too close to me. Why let me stay, Aiden?"

Trembling after the final bite of the question, she covered her mouth. Aiden drew closer and reached for the sides of her neck, Masika remained unflinching. To her surprise, she didn't even tense or jump when she felt his calloused palms. He caressed just beneath her temples, a wave of comfort overtaking her entire body. She knew what the warmth of his hands meant—the blood on hers were nothing in comparison. It meant nothing if they could be together, never again separated by a foolish choice. She embraced him and cradled his head, fingers sinking into his hair.

"Scared she'll come after us," she admitted, his head shifting as if to ask 'who?' She moved away and put her palms atop her thighs. He mirrored. "Everlee. The things she put me through... the blood on my hands, it's mostly 'cause of her. Taught me to kill, to fight, to... how to be a woman. A more palatable one."

His eyebrows furrowed at the last sentence as she continued. "Too masculine, she claimed. Shaved me head-to-toe. T-Tried doing my makeup but

I didn't let her. Memory with you was too precious," she gritted her teeth as tears formed. "Forced me into too tight dresses, said I was gonna need surgeries to be taken seriously. Told me being miserable went hand-in-hand with being pretty. Know better now, thankfully, that it's okay to be masculine *and* feminine. Cut her off and told her she best stay the fuck away from me. Should've killed her... should've..."

She trailed off after a couple incoherent words. When Aiden picked up her wrists, she stared at him. He held a neutral yet sympathetic expression and she scoffed.

"Never seem phased by anything I tell you," Masika stated flatly.

He shrugged, walking over to the desk and sitting down to write. She walked up behind him, looking over his shoulder at the notebook.

She's a fucked up person. I'm glad you got away from her and I won't let her hurt us. I'm not scared of garbage.

"Could blow you full of holes or... worse. Much worse..." she whispered the last part.

What do you mean?

"N-Nothing. Don't worry about it," she faked a reassuring smile despite Aiden not being able to see it. She ended up walking away and returning to bed, staring dead-on at her packed belongings against the closet door. Eventually coming to her side, he held out the notebook to where she could read it.

I have your back, you have mine. You know that. We're going to protect each other. Is she worth running away from happiness? Haven't we run enough?

Choked up reading the last line, she attempted to hide her tears. Aiden didn't allow it, tapping the paragraph with a loving smile. He wiped her face as she re-read it, taking the notebook into her lap. Masika melted into his arms as she stared at the page.

Chapter Nine

February 1994

Let's go somewhere.

Aiden's proposition arrived unexpectedly several nights after Masika's runaway attempt. It was a Friday evening and he had just arrived home from a late shift. Wasting no time, he ran up to her giddily, paper in hand ready to be shown. She gave him a playful look after she read the note.

"Right now?"

Nodding, he pulled his arms through a leather jacket before roaming the house in search of something. Masika stayed in the living room with the tips of two fingers between her front teeth. The past couple months played in her head, mixed with the suspense of the unknown plan Aiden had. When he showed up with two motorcycle helmets, she perked up with a sweet simper.

"Oh I see, taking me on a bike ride."

Grinning, he passed her a helmet, leading her outside and into the parking lot. A blue sheet was dramatically removed, revealing his motorcycle treated with new paint and a wash. He patted the seat affectionately. As Masika equipped her helmet and got on, he sat in front of her. The engine roared to life and she instinctively wrapped her arms around his stomach.

The drive was short, yet the sun had vanished by the time they reached their destination. A blanket of darkness covered the desert. Aiden had taken her to the outskirts of town, where there was little but sand, road, and the infinite sky.

Masika departed first, walking away from where he parked on the side of the asphalt. Soaking in the abyss of stars, she took off her helmet and placed it on the ground. Aiden joined her side, holding a flashlight. The edges of her eyes crinkled as she looked at him.

"This what you wanted to show me?"

Unexpectedly, he let his head fall against her shoulder with a nod. Their arms knotted together as Masika concentrated on the twinkling above. He guided her further into the desert, where he eventually took a seat on the sand. It was a windless evening, but quite chilly nonetheless.

Fishing a tube out of his pocket, the two shared a cherry-flavored blunt under the lights above. Vision growing hazier, their bodies drew closer. It was getting hard for her to breathe or think, senses overwhelmed with yearning. Aiden put the roach out, returning it to the tube. Reaching for Masika's hands, she pulled away, words lodged in her throat.

"Should have never left you," she finally proclaimed. "Saw parts of me I never let anyone else see. Knew I was a woman, you did. Knew me more than I knew myself. Let it scare me and made a foolish choice 'cause of it..."

Aiden's smile faded, palms scrunching up in his lap as she spoke. Guilt wracked her sharp features as she refused to meet his gaze— so, he gently took hold of her chin. He unsteadily ran his palm down her cheek to her collarbone. She shakily grabbed his wrist.

"Came here thinking you would despise me. That you would turn me away, but now we're here. Doesn't feel real. Feels like you're gonna blow away from me in the dust," she admitted.

He lowered his pointer finger to her thigh. There, he traced three words into her exposed flesh.

I'm right here.

She pulled him into a hug, held his head in her hand. The heartbeat in her ears surely sang of death, yet she was alive. The most alive she had felt since that night at the barn. Her palms wandered to his neck, moving away slightly just for their foreheads to glue together. Once again, she expected their lips to connect.

Instead, Aiden pecked the tip of her nose and got to his feet. He dusted the sand off his jeans as Masika tried to compose herself. On the walk back, she pictured those hands running down her body, his teeth on her neck. The crickets howling outside the barn, the deadness of the night; she barely registered getting onto the bike.

The whole ride home, their first time played on loop, making her uncomfortably hard against the bumping leather seat. When they got into the apartment, Aiden put up the helmets, yawning dramatically. Walking past Masika to the first stair step, she didn't allow him to get to the second one.

She pressed on top of him, two pairs of eyes locking. His twinkled with piqued interest as her own narrowed with primal urges. Breaths quickening, her hands trembled as they touched his right cheek. Aiden's gaze dipped downward. Aching with longing, heat rose to her face as her head dropped.

The fuck am I doing?

She almost receded before fingertips ghosted her waist. Daring to look at him again, a knowing smirk had broken out onto his face. Placing both palms on the back of her head, he delicately pushed their mouths together. Masika cradled his face in return.

As their lips met repeatedly, his touches moved to her hips, down the hem of her skirt. Sliding off her panties, she in turn tore away his jeans and boxers. Pushing his legs apart, she glanced upwards, awaiting approval. Halfway through his nod, she eagerly buried her face into his cunt. He whimpered as her warm tongue pressed against his dick. She hooked both arms around his thighs and dug in.

Masika realized how much she missed this–the shivering, his back arching with every swirl and stroke. Barely audible moans escaped Aiden's lips as slick trickled down to the stairs beneath them. Sucking hard and slow, a firm grip on her hair caused her to growl into him. His contained, calm demeanor shattered as he unashamedly cried out in pleasure. Easing him through an orgasm, a hot jolt rushed her core as cum doused her mouth and chin.

It dribbled as she pulled away, adorning a bragging smirk. Aiden stared down at her, bleary-eyed, their pants the only thing to break the quiet. Taking a handful of Masika's blouse, he drew her close. Briefly allowing him to fondle her, she soon pinned his wrists above his head.

The playful aggression didn't frighten Aiden. Providing a provocative grin, egging her on, she teased him with a single digit. Adding one, then another, until three knuckles were buried deep; he was so wet it didn't take much effort. The scent overpowering her senses strengthened with the pump of her fingers. Admiring his blissfully hazy expression, the grip holding his wrists melted away. He mumbled incoherently through his moans, walls starting to squeeze around her.

"Don't hold back. Cum again," she commanded in her smooth, tantalizing voice.

Jaw clenching as he climaxed once more, he earned a kiss from his lover. Moving her head and hands away, he whined timidly. She licked her fingers with satisfaction before the debauchery continued, frotting against him with newfound desperation. Precum dribbled from her tip, the mere warmth radiating from his hole somehow made her harder. Pressing her forehead against his with one hand, guiding herself into him with the other, they gasped in unison.

Aiden moaned as she lifted his leg and sank all the way inside. Slowly thrusting in and out, her own moans were restrained, struggling to keep control. He fit her like a glove; perfect, too perfect, leaving overwhelming warmth spreading across her body. Several emotions overtook her, reliving the first time while cherishing the current moment.

She showered his neck in kisses, hips rocking against hers, fingers pumping his dick. Her other hand dug into his waist as she fucked him, losing herself as Aiden grew wetter and wetter. Somewhere in the bliss, he unabashedly orgasmed, but Masika was only focused on his expression. It begged her to cum, to let go and release all the tension and years of anticipation.

So she did, a strained moan escaping her throat as cum coated Aiden's insides. She slowly pulled out and watched semen pour onto his thighs. The stairs beneath them were thoroughly coated. Unworried about the mess against her stomach, she leaned down. Tenderly kissing his cock, a hum of content left her throat.

They warmed the bed next, fighting against the harsh winter outside. The frostbite worthy temperatures were no match for their dance atop disheveled sheets. Even with the heat out, neither of them shivered.

Aiden splayed one palm between Masika's breasts, holding himself steady as he rode. She grasped onto the leather jacket, gripping him like they were back on his bike. His eyes closed in concentration, flickering with the gyration of their hips. Braids bouncing around his parted lips, he lowered down to her neck and bit.

The second tussle in their bed left the two with a heavy silence. He faced the ceiling, a film of lewd juices lathering his half-naked body. She consulted her stash box for joint supplies, making quick work of a roll as his mind roamed.

"You alright?" he let out a heavy sigh and she chuckled underneath her breath, "Hope you're not already regretting it."

His brows raised, turning to face her and shaking his head firmly. Catching her tongue dragging up and down against rolling paper, he blushed.

"Ah, understand now. More so surprised."

Masika brought the joint to life with a flick of a lighter. Taking a long draw, her head fell as smoke dispelled between her tooth gap, swirling into the air. A languid smirk spread across her lips as she passed it to him.

"Me too. It's a welcome surprise, though," she passed the joint to him. "When we were out with the stars, had a feeling."

Aiden's gaze dropped to her mouth. He filled his own with smoke and locked their lips together, sending the hit to her lungs.

***

"Run away with me for a little while."

The request came suddenly over dinner. Mashed potatoes escaped Aiden's mouth as his jaw dropped. Masika reached across the table, napkin in hand to wipe his face, her own expression unreadable. She drew back and stirred the contents of her platter.

"Sorry, been on my mind. Just think we could do better than this apartment. Besides, bet there's a lot you haven't seen."

She was right. As much as Aiden enjoyed routine, he needed to see more than the elementary school he worked at, more than the walls of their apartment. Youthful and wasting time by sticking to his ropes, he didn't have a clue where they would go.

"Shit, will pay six months of rent in advance for you. Think of all the places we could see."

He nodded in agreement, ascertaining from her surprised expression that she didn't expect a yes. Joy broke out on her features and she snatched him into a crushing hug, anxiously rubbing her palms together afterwards.

"Will your job fire you?"

Aiden shrugged, not knowing until he spoke to his boss.

***

Principal Ruby didn't so much as bat an eye when Aiden came bearing the news. He informed her of a family emergency, needing a few months leave, if not longer. He also recited Masika's offer to pay for a few months ahead, the notion immediately waved off.

"Do you plan on returning?" The answer being yes, she was satisfied and simply hummed beneath her breath. "Then don't worry about it. It'll be here when you get back."

Aiden tried to give her even a little bit of money, but she insisted she didn't need it. All she requested was for him to return in one piece. He apologized for leaving the job so abruptly and she simply chuckled.

"It's alright, Aiden. We're only a couple months away from summer anywho. I appreciate everything you've done for my little school."

A firm handshake and goodbye later, Aiden was in the parking lot. Masika waited by his motorcycle, beaming softly upon his return.

"How did it go?" He gave her a thumbs up and the smile widened, "Great. Pack tonight, leave tomorrow?"

Aiden nodded before strapping on his helmet, Masika hopping on behind him. Her arms squeezed around his midsection, holding steady and preparing him for whatever awaited the pair.

Chapter Ten

August 1986

Every week at Evergreen Academy was the same for much of Aiden's time attending; a singular day of peace, four filled with harassment. He thought twelfth grade would bring an end to these juvenile bullying tactics, yet nothing changed during senior year.

On Tuesday, en route to first period, he was ambushed by his usual tormentors. An unruly quartet led by Edmund "Eddie" Jones dragged him from the school entrance towards the nearest bathrooms. As the tardy bell rang, the group shoved him into the pavement. He landed on his behind, trying to recover before things escalated.

Unfortunately, being outnumbered, Aiden found himself unable to escape. Two of Eddie's friends—Rodney and Carter—pinned him to the ground with a foot each on his back. Aiden squirmed under their grip, glaring up at Eddie as he lit a cigarette. He lowered himself to Aiden's level, taking a long drag before blowing the smoke into his face. Coughing, Aiden attempted to catch his breath before letting out an ear-piercing scream. Eddie pressed the lit end into his neck, only increasing pressure as he thrashed.

He expected it to worsen when the clique took off running. Confused but grateful, Aiden's whole body relaxed, ignoring the burning pain on his flesh. He didn't move from his position on the ground, not until a pair of tennis shoes stepped into eye-line. Clutching the spot behind his ear, a voice spoke as he trembled.

"Let me see."

Who Aiden saw shocked him. It was the new kid who everybody whispered about on the first day. The one who, according to rumors, single handedly beat up a bunch of white boys. No wonder the bullies dipped.

She crouched to his level as he sat up and moved his hand away from the injury. A lone, calloused thumb pushed a couple hairs aside. He caught the stranger's eyes; swirls of umber carrying a quiet, almost concealed concern.

"That's bad. Want me to walk you to nurse's office?"

Aiden shook his head. The new kid helped him to his feet and he fully took in her appearance. She was completely out of dress code, instead wearing dark blue jeans with a large green hoodie ending at her thighs. Finding her features to be genderless, he couldn't tell and didn't want to assume based on what he heard around campus. Part of him swelled with envy, but he didn't know why as he stared at her chest absentmindedly. She tittered.

"Trying to figure something out?" Aiden blushed profusely and the stranger smirked. "Think we have Physics together. Your twin's in there too, right? Sits in the back and sleeps?"

Aiden nodded as the lunch bell rang out, signaling the end of break and the continuation of class. The new kid gave him a crooked grin.

"Call me M. See you around?"

Aiden couldn't contain the butterflies flipping in his stomach as she walked away, joining the bodies filling the halls.

***

"So, you talked to the new kid?"

Aiden paused his dish washing, turning his head in acknowledgment as his twin walked over. Throwing wine bottles into the garbage, she nudged his shoulder.

"What they like?"

Aiden hesitated, uncertain about her choice of words. Arching his eyebrows at 'they,' Abeje did the same, albeit mockingly.

"What? I can't tell what's going on there, neither can anybody else. The teachers and our peers call them one thing, but it's obvious they don't like it. At least... to me it is. That's why I've just been using 'they,'" Abeje rambled before looking off into space, longing yet melancholic. Aiden didn't understand. "But if they tell me to call them something else, I will."

The explanation itself made enough sense to him, so he decided to refer to the newcomer as 'they.' Abeje pivoted the conversation before he could finish his thought. "Anyways, I heard they're trouble. Figured I'd warn you," she earned a dramatic eye roll, pointing her index at him. "Hey! I'm lookin' out for you, y'know. I worry."

You don't need to worry about me, Aiden thought, racking up the remaining dishes and drying off his limbs. Shoving past his sister, he ducked towards the hallway and into their bedroom. Abeje trailed him indignantly.

"I just don't want you getting our house set on fire. Mom got plenty to deal with already."

Aiden almost laughed at that comment, taking out his Walkman and signaling Abeje to leave him be. She snorted, retreating into the hallway as Aiden flopped onto the bed face first. Music soon swept him away.

***

The next day in Physics, someone punched Aiden's shoulder lightly. Having little time to react, Kelsey, the girl who sat behind him, handed over a folded piece of paper. He glared at her before returning his gaze to the note. *What are we, five?* Opening it, he realized the note wasn't Kelsey's.

Wanna meet up? -M

Aiden searched for Masika, eventually spotting her on the opposite side of the room, silhouetted by windowsills. Greeting him with another wickedly striking smirk, she regarded the note in his grip.

To his shock, he found a grin of his own forming at the corners of his mouth. Scribbling a response, he passed it to Kelsey and waited patiently as the note traded hands. Inevitably landing in Masika's, she read the response with a neutral, cool expression. Unable to reply, teacher turning to face the class, their gazes locked on the clock.

On the way to next period, she approached Aiden. "Meet me at the track field in ten minutes," she told him, "don't get caught."

Winking, she brushed past him into the hallways.

Sneaking out with a bathroom pass five minutes later, Aiden went to the track field as instructed. Listening to the thud of his sneakers against concrete, he passed several wings. He tried to prepare himself for whatever shenanigans might ensue.

Crossing the threshold between building and track, Aiden kept an eye out for any staff. To his relief, the vast field was completely empty, seldom a single figure sitting alone on the bleachers. As he grew closer, he recognized Masika. Allowing a smile, he watched her mindlessly rip up a brown leaf. She stopped and eyed him as he walked up the stands, coming to a rest next to her.

"Hey, didn't think you'd show up."

Aiden squished his palms between his thighs and looked towards the sky. Nervousness and uncertainty created knots in his stomach, her eyes on him feeling wrong yet inviting. Bringing his gaze down, she brushed off her pants and stood up.

"C'mon, let's ditch this shit hole."

She didn't speak further as she led him off campus, ducking through a hole in the fence. His thoughts gnawed at him; he knew damn well he shouldn't be doing this, yet he craved a little adventure. When was the last time he wasn't home or at school anyway? The captivating guide was simply a bonus.

They walked a couple blocks until stumbling upon a convenience store. There, Masika fished a wallet from her hoodie pouch, heading towards the entrance.

"Hungry?"

Aiden almost lied, his stomach betraying him with an obnoxious growl. She chuckled and proceeded to the door. One step in tow and Aiden tumbled to the ground, his body giving out. He cursed internally as she crouched beside him.

"You okay?" she expressed her worry even as he nodded. Glancing through the store windows, she got up as he began to do the same. "Sit down, I'll grab everything."

He almost protested, but when he tried to stand, he fell once again. So, he resigned to sitting cross-legged on the sidewalk as Masika went inside.

Massaging his thighs, he tried to offset the pins and needles sensation. A few moments later she returned with arms full of various snacks, a root beer, and a pack of cigarettes. She sat down, passing him the food. He tore into a lemon-flavored mini cake.

"You smoke?" she broke out a cigarette and lighter when Aiden shook his head. "Good, shit's terrible. Take 'bout six hits and then toss it aside myself."

She did just that while Aiden stared, enraptured and perplexed. He had no response, yet she didn't seem to mind at all. She caught on quicker than most that he didn't and wouldn't speak. Additionally, she comprehended his intelligence. Despite everyone's perception, he understood English just fine, never had trouble reading or writing. It was speaking—anything beyond the occasional grunt of pain or unintelligible bellows of anger—that eluded him. Abeje learned to love and communicate with him anyway, but his mother, Dorothy Ann? She never let it go, never tried to find ways for the two to talk. His sister was the only one who would have drawn out conversations with him. And, now Masika, he supposed.

Her complacency regarding his silence paired with the simple, yet kind, act of feeding him? It made him fuzzy all over, a little light-headed too. He blamed the blaring August sun for the sweat, but deep down he knew that wasn't the only reason. Yam-orange locs cascaded down her shoulders, framing her crooked nose and plush lips. Breath hitching, he had to tear his gaze away from her.

"Wanna go back?" Aiden shook his head and Masika smirked. "Figured. There's a playground near here. Able to walk?"

He nodded and the pair strolled to a playground he had never seen before. Vibrant rainbow equipment stood out against the blue sky, rhythmic creaking of empty swings filled the air. Masika went straight for them, Aiden right on her heels. They each took a swing. He tried to avoid the disgusted gazes of two or three white people. Focusing on her shrugging off her backpack, he locked in on the notebook and pen she had splayed on her lap.

"Wanna learn about you. Talk this way?" she offered him the pen and paper. Aiden flushed faintly, nodding as she flipped to the first page. "Gonna ask some questions, you can answer on here," she prepared her initial query. "Were you born here?"

Simple enough.

He informed her that he'd been born in this town, never seen anything else. Back and forth they went, though he pondered why she was so willing to tolerate the lack of verbal responses. He told her several hobbies of his—sewing, baking, music—as she beamed with admiration. When he asked about hers, she said she recently started teaching herself ballet. Aiden pictured Masika's body lost in endless, fluid motions. He returned to reality and wrote his response:

You should dance for me one day.

She read the words under her breath and paused. Nerves spread throughout his entire body as she gazed straight into his eyes.

"Mean that?"

Aiden swallowed a frog threatening to burst from his throat, nodding. He barely caught her blush as she returned to the notebook. His heart swelled in his chest.

"Should probably head back before seventh period is over," she spoke.

Managing to sneak onto campus undetected, Masika parted ways with him behind the gymnasium. Aiden arrived at seventh period five minutes before dismissal.

He spent the subsequent bus ride in a daze. Back home, he adhered to his usual schedule—homework, cleaning, making dinner—but something felt off. Before he could detect what, Dorothy Ann approached him while he cleaned the kitchen. Turning around to greet her, he jumped.

Aiden wanted to run for the door. He always did when he saw the paddle clutched in her grip. Knowing what it entailed, he slinked towards a corner of the room. Abeje stood close by, eyes darting between her mother and sibling. Dorothy Ann stomped over and grabbed him by his wrist.

"Come here," she spat, expression laden with rage. "The school called. You skipped?!"

He sheepishly shrunk away, upset at his foolish belief the teacher wouldn't blab. Unlike a few of the other kids, Aiden never skipped. He was too much of a goody-two-shoes.

"Do you know how much I pay for you to go to that school? Waste of my damn money," she slurred the last part, rendering Aiden instantly cognizant of her drunken state. "All you do is waste my money!"

Abeje interjected, telling Dorothy Ann with a quaking voice that Aiden was in fact in class. Dorothy Ann released Aiden, who caught himself before falling face-first. He didn't move an inch as she staggered over to Abeje, lifting her chin.

"Swear to me that's the truth."

"It's the truth. I swear. We have seventh period together, *remember*?"

Dorothy Ann set the paddle down on the dining room table, taunting Aiden as she retreated to her comfort chair. He bolted out of the house and into the front yard, frantically sobbing. Sitting down, he began plucking blades of grass violently before Abeje stepped within vision. He scoffed as she joined him on the ground.

"You okay?" He buried his face into his knees as she pressed a palm against his shoulder. "I'm sorry I didn't step in sooner."

Aiden shrugged. She rocked her feet for a couple moments. The sun sagged at the bottom of the sky, preparing to give way to the moon within the hour. Abeje's touch never left her twin's back. He would normally swat it away, but the comfort was welcome for once.

"You were hanging out with that new kid again, weren't you?" She smirked, "You two are gonna be good friends, I can feel it."

Aiden's pessimism conquered his thoughts. *I doubt it. Why would anyone want to be around me?*

Abeje headed inside to take a bath while he remained on the lawn. Laying, he stared up at the heavens above. The stars hid as usual, overshadowed by thick clouds of pollution. Planting where he envisioned the glowing clusters might be, he preoccupied himself for another half-hour. He eventually got up to check on Dorothy Ann, making sure she didn't take anything out on Abeje.

Thankfully, she had dozed off watching her late-night soaps. Aiden did his ritual of retrieving a blanket from the linen closet and draping it over her. As the quilt settled, Dorothy Ann stirred and briefly rose from her slumber.

"Honey, I'm sorry for... sorry for accusing," she murmured, "I know you're a good... a good kid."

He ignored her and shut off the lights. She called out his name a couple times to no avail as he made a swift exit for his room.

****

Not even ten minutes into class, Masika moved to an empty seat next to Aiden. Connie, the desk's regular occupant, hadn't shown up in nearly a month. He didn't mind, needing to tell Masika that they couldn't skip ever again. Doing exactly that, he scrawled on the margin of his notebook and angled it so she could read. She acknowledged it with a slow nod.

"Get in trouble?" she whispered, barely audible over the teacher.

Yes, he wrote out to emphasize.

"Sorry. Don't have to go anywhere, but wanna spend lunch together tomorrow. That alright with you?"

Aiden stuck the eraser of his pencil between his teeth, thinking.

It's alright by me, he decided.

The next day, the two approached a table filled with what most students would refer to as outcasts. Aiden considered himself a part of those outcasts, and they treated him better than everyone else at the tiny Catholic school. Upon seeing Masika strut up alongside Aiden, all of them hurriedly gathered their lunch trays and scattered like roaches. Masika almost turned right back around, but Aiden encouraged her to take a seat.

"Hope those weren't friends. Didn't mean to scare them off."

Aiden shrugged. He hardly knew the individuals; it was simply the only table no one bothered him at. She raised her eyebrows with a huff and dug through her packed lunch. He picked at his tray of cafeteria food. Noticing his disgust, she split her ham sandwich. Staring blankly as she offered half, he pointed at himself questioningly.

"Yeah. See you're struggling with that... slop." She motioned both halves to him, "Have the whole if you'd like."

Placing it in front of him, Masika gave Aiden a nod of confirmation. Wondering when she would stop taking opportunities to feed him, he scarfed it down, not wanting to waste a single crumb of the gift. As he was swallowing the last bite of bread, his full cheeks burned at the sight of his sister.

He was rooked into a playful headlock. He quickly gulped down the last crumbs before Abeje could eject them from his throat. Grunting in annoyance, he tried to wiggle out of her grip. Masika watched with an inexplicable gaze.

"Hi there," Abeje greeted boldly, releasing Aiden and moving over to Masika's side, "You must be–"

"Go by M, not that," she stated firmly.

"Ah, I get it. Well, it's nice to meet you! I hope my sibling ain't driving you nuts."

Aiden buried his face into his palms as Abeje craned her neck to give Masika a once over. He desperately wanted her to leave. To his dismay, she instead plopped down between him and Masika, starting to run her mouth. He forced a couple deep breaths, trying to rationalize. Masika wouldn't abandon him, and on the flip side, Abeje wouldn't outright embarrass him. Self-soothing half-successful, he tuned out most of the conversation.

Masika's voice brought him back, "You okay there?"

He shot Abeje with a dagger of a glare. She blew a raspberry and got up with her arms in the air.

"Damn! My bad, didn't mean to interrupt your little date," she scoffed. "I'll leave you lovebirds alone."

She walked away and Masika repeated her question. He assured her with a polite nod. Upon hearing the dismissal bell, she requested to sit with him again tomorrow. He delightfully agreed.

Later, when Physics rolled around, Eddie threw an unexpected wrench. When Masika went to sit by Aiden, he flew across the room. His butt met the chair before she could even make it halfway. Approaching anyway, clear irritation on her face, Eddie glared up with a malicious smirk.

"Oh, sorry," the brunet shrugged, "this seat's already taken."

Aiden turned away. He should've known it wouldn't take long for Eddie to recognize his new companionship. Should've known that, like other kids who attempted to befriend him, the brat would chase Masika away. Or worse, Eddie would turn her against him. Either way, Aiden wished he had the courage to shove the bigot out of that goddamn chair before any damage could be done.

But he didn't. He moved his face into his hands, praying Masika would let it go. A resounding scoff was heard instead.

"That's alright, Eddie," she said in a sweet, milky voice. "Don't get too comfortable there, though."

Footsteps receded to the other side of the room while Eddie snickered to himself. Glancing over at Aiden still covering his face, he jabbed him in the shoulder right as Miss Vayn closed the classroom door.

"Eddie, knock it off. You know I don't tolerate nonsense," she snapped. "In fact, switch seats with Brooke. I'm not dealing with you today."

Eddie groaned and begrudgingly switched desks. Brooke wasn't much better, but she knew how to keep her hands to herself. Most of her bullying was the verbal variety, her favorite insult to hurl at Aiden being 'dyke.' Muttering the word the moment she connected with the chair, Aiden ignored it and took out his notebook.

Thirty minutes later, bodies piled excitedly out of the classroom. He stayed behind, finishing a doodle in his notes. Not noticing Masika bound up to him, she splayed a palm on his desk and interrupted his train of thought.

"That white boy bother you a lot?" she questioned, him answering without looking up. He drew beady little eyes on a spider, the finishing touch. She sighed at that, "Someone oughta put him in his place."

Aiden closed his notebook with a shrug. Everyone–besides Masika–knew Eddie was untouchable. His father was vice principal, his mom a cop. None of the staff acknowledged his cruel behavior because of that, especially with all of his victims being Black. The only time Eddie got punished was when he attacked another white boy during sophomore year. Any other time, nothing was done. The five or six Black students, seniors or not, suffered his racial epithets and fits of rage in silence. Worn from years of it, worn from lack of action.

One boy tried to pipe up, but he was turned away due to 'lack of evidence.' Eddie and his groupies ran him out of the academy a week later, never to be heard from again. Even though Aiden despised feigning complacency, he did it anyway. Dorothy Ann would kill him if he got into any kind of trouble.

Miss Vayn called the duo's names, instructing them to hurry on to seventh period. Masika, with permission, escorted him to his next class arm-in-arm. On the way, she noticed something. Rage burned momentarily in her eyes, only for her to quicken her pace. When the pair reached the classroom, she broke away from him.

"Gonna leave. School is pissing me off today," she said matter-of-factly. "Take care of yourself, okay?"

Affectionately pinching his cheek before vanishing down the hallway, Aiden reeled at the warmth of her touch long after she was gone.

CHAPTER ELEVEN

September 1986

Aiden always kept his prized possession close.

To outsiders, the hand-sized, tattered plush of a golden retriever looked insignificant and past its prime. To him, it meant the world, representing the pain and beauty of it captured within black, beady eyes. Dad had gifted it on his fourth birthday, told him it was his favorite childhood toy. He introduced the toy as Brawny, but its name could be changed to whatever Aiden wanted. He decided on Mr. Snuggles, based on how soft the faux fur felt against his tiny cheek when he squeezed. Unadulterated joy danced on Dad's face every time he saw the plushie being carried by him.

When Dad died a few months later, Aiden's bond with Mr. Snuggles remained solid. Bringing the stuffed animal everywhere, much to Dorothy Ann's annoyance, he often got in trouble at school for having it out. He resorted to keeping Mr. Snuggles in his backpack, still close but hidden away.

Nowadays, Mr. Snuggles rarely left his backpack outside of bedtime. He slept with it in his arms every night for over a decade and didn't plan on stopping anytime soon. This past weekend, however, it occurred to him

Mr. Snuggles needed a bath. Delicately washing it in the kitchen sink, he left it on the porch to dry overnight.

Aiden found the toy still damp the next morning. Distraught, he decided he was far too much of a nervous wreck to leave Mr. Snuggles at home. Not wanting to get his homework wet, he resigned to carrying it around. After all, one day out of his backpack wouldn't hurt.

At school he received the occasional odd glance, but nothing more. Happily stimming with Mr. Snuggles under his desk all day was worth the side eyes. At lunch, Masika showed great interest in the toy, noticing the moment Aiden put it on the table.

"Who's this little cutie?"

Over the past three weeks, despite Eddie's meddling, Masika and Aiden's friendship had grown strong. They sat at lunch together every day, occasionally in Physics whenever she would beat Eddie to the classroom. She even convinced him to smoke pot with her after school. Abeje would tease him for not inviting her along, to which he would only laugh. This closeness left Aiden feeling more than comfortable sharing about Mr. Snuggles, writing down its name on the notebook between them.

"Mr. Snuggles? That's adorable."

Masika picked up the toy, triggering Aiden to rapidly snatch it out of her grip. Recoiling in shock, he took a deep breath, waiting for the upset.

"Sorry, should've asked first." she simply said.

Aiden held Mr. Snuggles tight. It relieved him that she recognized how important the plush was. Not attempting to touch it again, she focused her energy on finishing her meal. A slight twinge of embarrassment left him staring at the floor.

"Hey, it's okay. Have stuff I would kill someone for touching," Masika spoke through a mouthful of food. She finished chewing and smiled. "No need to feel bad, love."

Love? Aiden blushed at the term of endearment. Curling around Mr. Snuggles further, his leg bounced at high speed. He tried not to stare too hard at Masika wiping her lips with a napkin, moving faster as he focused on her mouth. He wondered, for but a moment, what it might feel like to kiss her. He imagined it to be soft and welcoming, like being wrapped up in a warm towel after a typhoon.

Lunch ended much sooner than Aiden would've liked. Heading to fifth, Mr. Snuggles in hand, a foot haphazardly stuck out in front of him. Falling face-first onto the concrete, he wasn't down for long before multiple hands hoisted him off the ground. Recognizing Rodney and Carter's laughter, the henchmen held him steady as Eddie approached.

"Hey there, tomboy. How's it hanging?"

Aiden darted to Mr. Snuggles, crumpled on the ground only a foot from Eddie. He tried to escape as Rodney and Carter grabbed an arm each, pulling and pinning him. He attempted to untangle himself as Eddie snatched Mr. Snuggles up by a leg.

"Now what's this? Your only friend besides that other freak?" he snickered alongside Rodney and Carter.

Aiden couldn't contain the floodgate of tears as Carter and Rodney threw him to the ground. The bell tolled as the trio fled. He lay face-first on the concrete, ignoring the scrapes on his knees, palms, and face. Brain berating him for not putting up more of a fight, he didn't bother showing up to fifth period.

Instead, he retreated to the closest bathroom, tears managing to cease as he cleaned up and washed his face. The solution, he decided, would be to do his best to forget. To denounce his attachment to the plushie, to let it die off in his memories. Knowing damn well he wouldn't see it again, there was no use shedding tears. There was no use in letting Eddie see him broken.

Dissociating in the stall, the numbness didn't stop until the bell rang. The thought of seeing Masika made him bound out of the bathroom towards Physics class. Having beat him there, she guarded the seat next to her, questioning him the moment he sat down.

"Did someone hurt you?"

Aiden moved not an inch. She lightly poked him, receiving a swat in response. She shrunk away.

"Sorry. Worried, is all."

The tardy bell rang and Miss Vayn shushed the classroom. Aiden tried to ignore Eddie's glare burning into him. He knew engaging with him was a bad idea. Masika seemed to care not, staring the boy down at any given opportunity. Aiden enjoyed the way Eddie slumped at her sharp gaze.

Class ending, Eddie was the first to barrel out of the room. Masika and Aiden were close behind in the halls when she suddenly stopped; she saw Mr Snuggles' limb hanging out of the bully's backpack. Aiden tried to block her view, but she draped a protective arm over his shoulder. Taking hold of his chin and tilting it towards her, he bit his lip. A cooled, contained rage swirled in her pupils.

"Wanna know something? Karma doesn't always do the trick. Better to take things into your own hands."

She smirked and kissed Aiden's forehead before releasing him. Bidding him farewell, she marched down the hallway towards Eddie's direction. His fingers lingered on his forehead as he bobbed up and down, trying to see through the crowd of bodies. Unable to find her, he headed the rest of the way to his next class. Masika's final words danced in his mind, sending goosebumps down his arm. Focus left him for the rest of the afternoon.

***

That evening, Dorothy Ann threw another fit. This time, Abeje forgot to do her chores. Their warden was quick to retrieve that godawful lump of wood.

When it was all said and done, Abeje and Aiden sat in their shared room. Abeje did her best to conceal her cries from him, but it was futile. Attempting to comfort her multiple times only got him chewed out in return. Tired of the uncomfortable energy, he daydreamed. The park Masika took him to was at the forefront of his mind. Certainly the walk couldn't be that far?

When Dorothy Ann finished drinking herself into a stupor, he snuck away. Slipping out the front door quiet as a mouse, he began to walk towards his oasis. Thinking he knew nothing of the town's structure, he was proven wrong as he left the neighborhood and didn't immediately get lost.

Five minutes in, his confident saunter turned to slow, calculated steps. Deep, pulsating pains wracked his legs all the way to his toes. Managing to navigate past the school, he eventually made his way to the playground. The streets leading towards it were vacant and eerie. Seeing the gas station, he knew he must be close. When the park's entrance came into view, he crossed the threshold from gravel to sand.

Winding down the path, he continuously checked over his shoulder. The park came into view, desolate, and he caught himself beaming. He spent a while on the swing set, his mind as empty and quiet as his surroundings. His body sighed in relief, every muscle relaxing. When thoughts did pass, they all revolved around Masika. The way she spoke, the curve of her smile, her compassion; all of it tangible. He wished she was there with him.

The snapping of a twig startled him. He instinctively scrambled behind a tree towards the edge of the park, encroached by forest. The annoying, high-pitched chatter that followed was instantly recognizable. Eddie, Carter, Rodney, and Brooke frolicked on the night-cloaked playground, drunk by the sounds of their nonsensical gossip. Aiden's mind exploded with curses. Turning to leave, he caught wind of Masika's name in Brooke's mouth. Not 'M', but the designation she denied. Feet weighed to the ground with curiosity, he listened.

"What about that freak?" Eddie deadpanned.

Aiden squinted through the spherical jungle gym. A pale pink skirt marked Brooke, who stood between the three boys. She swayed as Rodney and Carter silently sipped beers, prompting her to speak. Eddie just glared, livid at the topic change.

"You pissed 'em off," she replied trepidly.

"Oh, did I now?" Eddie hooted, his pseudo-brothers joining in. "What makes ya say that?"

Though far away, Aiden could see Brooke's knees trembling in fright. He crawled to another tree, whose overgrown branches outstretched to the divide of sand. He got a clear view of the group as anticipation exploded with a sudden outburst from Eddie.

"Fuckin' spit it out already!" Eddie hissed.

Brooke cried out, hot tears of fear flowing. "You shouldn't have taken that stupid toy! Now... now we're gonna end up like them white boys–"

"Oh, shut it. That's just a stupid rumor," Rodney cut her off.

They all went back and forth debating on the validity of the rumor, discussing it in vivid detail. Aiden got to hear the story in full via unreliable, privileged mouths. The criminal had heard a neighbor yowlin' her head off, watched as a group of white teens dragged her away. She followed them to somewhere isolated—a farmhouse, or a cornfield, maybe even a junk-yard—and took 'em down with only a rusted pocketknife and bandaged fists. The place got torched after that, leaving them all for dead. One of them kids managed to slip away, banging on front doors until somebody called the police. Masika surrendered without a fight, did her time in juvie, and that was that. According to the wrecking crew, anyway.

"And that's exactly why we shouldn't be messing with that bastard," Brooke asserted. "How are y'all not scared?"

"Ya think we're scared of that freak? We ain't a pussy like you, Brooke."

"Yeah, Brooke! You're such a scaredy cat!"

The boys carried on, ignoring Brooke's increasingly pale face. Eddie trekked over to a pile of junk—a few backpacks strewn amongst other trash—pulling out a ragged object. Mr. Snuggles dangled from a hand as he held a lighter in the other.

"If you're so worried, maybe we should just burn it."

He flicked the lighter, drawing the flame within reach of the precious possession. Aiden nearly bolted from the safety of the trunk just as a figure emerged from the front of the playground. His classmates' laughter fell to shocked, low gasps. He dug his nails into bark as Masika sauntered up to the group with an expressionless face. Carter, Rodney, and Brooke all stepped backward; eyes befallen on an old baseball bat. Eddie lowered the lighter and glared.

"What the fuck are you doing here?"

The corner of Masika's mouth lifted, scanning the group. Bat dragging in the sand, grains swirled behind as she got closer.

"Brooke here was nice enough to tell me your plans for the night," she replied calmly.

Brooke fled right then, leaving the three boys on their own. Aiden watched her fly past him and through the tree line, not stopping once.

"W-What do you want?" Eddie asked, trying to sound brave.

"Know exactly what I want. No need to play dumb."

Eddie turned to his friends, only to find they too had abandoned him. Aiden half-expected him to run. He didn't. The fool stood his ground, puffing out his bony chest at Masika. He gripped the plush harder, holding it away.

"I wanna know why you care so much about that dy-"

She snatched him by the throat before the final word could escape it. Eddie whimpered, stuffed animal slipping from his grasp. She pulled him close, flashing her teeth in a menacing grin.

"Give me the toy, Eddie."

"Fuck you!" he managed to get out.

Masika threw him, sending him flying across a few feet. Landing on his stomach, he immediately curled up like a frightened snail. Eddie apologizing repeatedly, She closed the gap between them, bat gripped tightly. She stamped her shoe against his torso, pushing him onto his back. Lifting the bat above her head, the darkness in her eyes glowed against the playground lights.

"White boys like you never learn."

Crack. Aiden cringed away as the first blow echoed throughout the woods. He tried to steady his breathing, Eddie's bloodcurdling sobs keeping his heart rate quickened. Sneaking a glance, he saw Eddie helplessly try to cover his head with his forearms. Blood poured down the sides of his face, the dark liquid caking the sand into mud. Masika hit him again and again, Aiden expecting another bone to shatter any second. Instead, she tossed the bat aside in rage and wrestled with Eddie, pinning both arms to his side. Headbutting his split forehead, she stunned him enough for his body to go limp.

Once he stilled, she delivered several hard punches to his face. Crimson splattered everywhere, coating her own. Coloring Eddie's pallid skull with red, she shakily stood and stumbled. Mr. Snuggles stared up at her with beady buttons. Picking him up and dusting him off, Masika grimaced at notice of blood spotting the faux fur. Aiden took a step back, the crunch of a root underfoot echoing outwards. Not stopping to check if she saw him, he bolted into the forest.

He ran all the way home, through the ache of his joints and muscles, determined to flee to his bed. Too terrified to see if someone was following him, he scrambled to his bedroom window. Trying to open it, he found it locked and cursed under his breath. Tapping lightly on the pane, he prayed the one person he wished to hear was awake. *C'mon, c'mon!*

Abeje pulled back the curtains, opening the window in an instant. She offered an arm to pull him up. Heaving him into the room, both collapsed onto the ground. Aiden stood up as fast as he could and steadied himself. She crouched as she rubbed her head.

"What the fuck are you doi—"

Aiden shushed her before stepping over to his side of the room. Getting up and shutting the window, Abeje watched as he collapsed onto his bed. Smothering his face with a pillow, he squeezed it as she crossed her arms.

"You scared the shit out of me. I thought you ran away!"

Aiden let the pillow slide down his face. Surely this must be a dream. Any minute now he would wake up in the very same spot, covered in his own drool. Flashes of Eddie's pleas for mercy and the pool of blood beneath his unconscious body permeated his thoughts.

No, what he saw was undeniably real. Masika's earlier comments summoned a trail of goosebumps. Little did he know she would be the harbinger of justice. Initial fear and adrenaline residing, Aiden felt oddly comforted by the whole thing. For the first time in his life, someone other than his sister had his back.

"Are you alright?"

He waved her off and rolled over, not bothering to shed his clothes as he pulled the cover over his head. He heard Abeje sigh.

"Alright... just let me know if you wanna leave next time, okay?" she paused. "And... I'm sorry for being a bitch earlier."

Aiden ignored the apology, not having the energy to properly show he appreciated it. Abeje shut the lights off and climbed into bed on the opposite side of the room. He listened to her settle into the covers, tossing and turning for a couple minutes. The crinkling finally ceased and she let out a sigh right as he did, both chuckling under their breaths.

"Love you."

He leaked a smile at this. Riled brain finally at ease, he fell into a sleep filled with dark silhouettes and swing sets.

***

Right as Aiden stepped off the morning bus, Masika awaited. Details from the previous night crept into his mind as he approached, her arms hung behind her as she leaned against a wall.

"Morning," she inspected his tired face. "Seem exhausted."

He waved, unable to look up at her. The crack of Eddie's skull reverberated as she held out something in front of him: Mr. Snuggles.

Aiden accepted it, plush lingering near his face. He wondered if he would smell blood in place of Dad's Camel cigarettes. Reluctantly meeting Masika's gaze, a crooked grin sat on her lips.

"Look who I found. Washed him for you too," she rubbed her neck at the sight of his expression. "Seem... surprised."

He hugged her. Her arms lifted at first, soon wrapping around his back and staying that way for a good while. When Aiden finally pulled away, the chatter of students around the two had begun to fade. Realizing they needed to head to class, they walked side-by-side, reaching where their paths usually split.

"See you at lunch?" Masika confirmed.

Aiden nodded, already eager to see her again in the coming hours.

Chapter Twelve

February 1994

It was Aiden's first time ever riding a train, and it was not what he imagined. He initially pictured long, crowded bus rides, just with a different vehicle. The train car was dead, however, seldom maybe five people. Watching the scenery fly by as Masika nursed a root beer, workers frequently checked on the two's wellbeing. He was far too busy wondering where the train was taking them to interact with anyone. Other than her, that is.

Masika hadn't told him where they were going. In fact, she decided to leave the entire road trip a complete mystery. A part of him believed that she was winging the entire thing, but that didn't matter to him. When he would peer away from the window, his gaze always fell upon her. She was mesmerizing in a burgundy pea coat, locs tied up into a messy bun atop her head. They didn't make much conversation, but neither cared.

A few hours passed and somewhere along the line he fell asleep, not waking until the train stopped and passengers began to rush out. Masika patted his head, startling him out of a dream.

"Come on, sleepyhead. We're here."

One step off the platform thrusted him straight into a massive crowd of bodies. She held onto him tightly as they wedged their way through everyone, managing to find a nook of the building with significantly less outpour.

"It's a lot, know where we can be unseen," she said.

Winking, she guided him down a crowded sidewalk, dodging anyone who got too close. The smells and sounds sent Aiden's head into a fuzzy state, leaving him dissociated for most of the walk. So dissociated he hardly noticed the ache of his legs. Beginning to slow, they moved towards a shop window, away from the foot traffic. He was breathless and Masika stared at him with concern.

"Need to get you a cane." Shaking his head caused her to squint, "Don't be stubborn. Pretty sure it would help more than you think."

Several grueling blocks later, she found a hotel. Rushing him inside with a pep in her step, she told him to take a seat in the lobby while she paid for a stay. He spent the following few minutes people-watching until she returned. The pair rode the elevator to the eighth floor and eventually found their room.

"Got us a suite," she stated, unlocking it and letting the door swing open. With a sway of her hands, she gestured inside, "Go ahead."

Aiden wandered in and Masika headed straight for the bed. Laying down, she stretched out catlike as he awkwardly stood in the corner. Remembering the shoddy rooms he'd stayed in during his journey to Nevada, this suite was completely different. Smelling crisp and clean, no dirtiness or neglect present, it boasted all the utilities of a regular home.

"Come here. That was a long ride, need to relax." As he sat down, she moved behind him, palms hovered over his shoulders. "Can I rub your back?"

Aiden leaned into her touch as she worked her magic. Massaging, she acknowledged seven different straps underneath his shirt.

"Must be painful layering all those bras. Trying to bind your chest?" Defensive, he nearly jumped off the bed. She calmed him with a gentle touch of the shoulder and a charming smile. "Aiden, it's okay. Was just curious."

Caving, he informed her that, yes, he was trying to flatten his chest. In his head, he tried to write it off as an attempt to look more masculine after the switch. She saw right through him, as if she could read his thoughts.

"Been doing this since I've met you. Can tell you a less painful way to flatten yourself, if you'd like."

Aiden's scooted closer to her, giddily waiting for further explanation. Cracking a grin, she bopped his nose.

"So cute..." she shyly looked away. "Anyway, heard ace bandages might be a good way."

He tilted his head, as if asking how she knew. He'd never heard of anyone else wanting to flatten their breasts to disguise them, in fact, Dorothy Ann had always teased him for being ashamed of his chest. Telling him it was just a part of 'being a woman' and he was overreacting. She never once allowed him to process or understand that shame. Now that he knew other people had that very same shame—how could he not be curious?

"Met a lot of people like me between hits, Aiden. Want you to meet some of them during our journey, if you're okay with that. Have a contact here I think you'd like."

Aiden flushed, both terrified and intrigued at the prospect of meeting other people like Masika.

***

After a couple hours of snoozing together in bed, Masika and Aiden braved New York City once again. On the way to the bar Masika wanted to show him, she stopped at a fancy store and bought him a cane. It was rickety and old, but it relieved a little of his pain, enabling him to walk for much longer periods of time. She helped with an arm draped around his waist, leaving him blushing and fawning. It was so odd being taken care of after being alone for so long.

As they arrived at the bar, she took a moment at the entrance.

"Ever been to a bar before?" He shook his head and she smirked, "Well, this is a gay one."

His eyebrow raised, smirking back as she walked him up to security. The guard monotonously requested both their IDs and Masika held up a limb, notecard sat between two of her fingers.

"Sister of Briggs," she announced, flashing the front of the card at him, "my plus one."

"Go right on in," came his reply, letting them through.

She thanked him, quick to answer Aiden's confused glance as they approached the door, "Organization I'm in. Gets me free access to the VIP lounge and drinks half off."

As Masika pushed the door open, noise flooded Aiden's senses. Expertly guiding him through the crowd of bodies to the closest bar in sight, she helped him onto the seat before occupying the one beside it. He took in the scene with bated breath, never witnessing so many vibrant colors and energies. People of every race, every gender, every sexuality twirled and danced to techno music. A tall woman with dramatic makeup performed near the second bar, spotlight highlighting her rainbow dress and heels. People waved handfuls of cash at her. Taking it all in, he turned to see Masika admiring him.

"All good?" she asked.

Nodding, he put a firm hand on her thigh, and she blushed. Her starry stare strayed as the bartender grabbed a few bottles near them. At notice of new customers, they half-acknowledged Masika.

"Hey," they greeted, focused on a drink they were starting.

"Hey, Monet," she responded in kind.

Face lighting up, they nearly dropped the items in their grasp. They set everything down to give her a hug from across the bar.

"Masika! Oh my god, its been a minute." They pulled away before glancing to Aiden. "Who's this? Usually you travel alone."

"Aiden, my..." she trailed off, searching for an appropriate term. "My partner?"

She shrugged, predicting discomfort from him. Instead, he nodded before sticking his hand out. Monet firmly shook it.

"It's so nice to meet you, Aiden!" They let go and gestured to the various liquors stocked behind them, "What can I get for the two of you?"

"Ice water for me," Masika fiddled with her pocket, pulling out a tiny notepad and pen. Opening it, she set it in front of Aiden. Scribbling his response on the counter, she read with a smile, "Margarita for him."

"You got it, coming right up!"

"Doing good?" Masika asked Aiden as Monet pranced away.

Curious, he jotted a question down. *Are they like you too?*

"Yes, they are. Dear friend of mine. Came here a lot after jobs in the city, always made drinks perfect for me."

A sullen look crossed her face, but she dismissed it by fanning herself. Monet arrived with the drinks, bowing after the two of them nodded in thanks.

"Once I finish up, we've gotta chat!" Monet chimed.

"Will do," Masika agreed.

Aiden and Masika sipped on their glasses, both naturally falling into people-watching. She pointed out a pale-faced straight couple hiding in a corner while he showed her a few cuties. This went on for nearly ten minutes, at which point Monet returned.

"I got a couple minutes. Girl, tell me *everything!*" they urged Masika.

She looked at Aiden nervously. Getting an affirming smile and pat on the back, she started giving Monet details from the past few years. He admired the scene until his bladder ached and he excused himself, making a beeline for the men's room.

As expected, the bathroom appeared a war zone laden with litter, grime, and questionable substances. Once ensured he was alone, he headed into the sole stall. Squatting over the toilet, he was terrified of his bare skin touching the seat. Halfway through relieving himself, the bathroom door opened.

Shit.

Underneath the stall door, a pair of feet staggered forward. Following several seconds of stillness, they vanished towards the wall of urinals. Aiden finished as quickly as he could, wiping and standing up. Waiting until he heard the other man urinating to flush the toilet, he ran out and briskly washed his hands. Not bothering to use the paper towel dispenser, he instead opted to wipe his palms on his jeans after exiting.

To his dismay, the crowd had doubled in size since he entered the bathroom. A few men flew past him as he cautiously approached the horde of sweaty bodies swarming the dance floor. Aiden couldn't spot the bar Masika and him had been sitting at.

Tension skyrocketed at the sound of a masculine voice behind him. Not waiting to see who the man was, he threw himself straight into the crowd, wedging through bodies. Meeting a standstill when a close-knit group of queers wouldn't break apart to let him through, the stranger caught up to him. Aiden's heart leapt to his throat as a claw clamped down on his shoulder.

"Hey, slow down. Trying to get a good look at'cha," the stranger teased.

Aiden ripped his arm away, stumbling back and bumping into someone. The person, an Indian man slightly taller than him, apologized. Upon seeing Aiden's concerned, frightened look, he straightened up and glared down the pasty individual.

"Do you know this guy?" he asked, stepping forward towards the sleazeball. Aiden shook his head and the man puffed up, "Beat it. Unless you want your ass handed to you."

The creep put his hands up in surrender, slinking into the crowd. Aiden's savior suggested they move somewhere quieter, walking him over to a mostly empty corner near the DJ-booth.

"I'm sorry, even places like these have their fair share of weirdos. Are you okay?" he asked, stepping away to check on Aiden physically. He nodded as the man inched closer once again in a non-threatening way. "I'm Ashok. You got friends nearby?"

As if on cue, Masika's arms reached for him from the crowd. Being pulled into view, Aiden buried his face into her chest. She held his head as he sniffled.

"Thought something happened to you. Everything okay?"

"Some guy tried to haggle him," Ashok responded, "I took care of it."

"Aw, love, I'm sorry," she whispered to Aiden before directing her attention to Ashok. "Thank you."

"Of course. Dudes like that can be scary," he shifted on his feet. "Could I maybe buy you two a drink?"

Aiden shook his head, not moving away from Masika's body. She politely declined as well, and Ashok said it was no problem. As she thanked him, Aiden turned his head ever so slightly. His gaze fell upon Ashok's chest; specifically, the horizontal scars beneath his nipples. Before he could think about it further, she swept him away and out of the bar.

She had another plan, leading him in the opposite direction. She once again matched his slow, turtle-like pace with enthusiasm and contentment. This time they walked hand-in-hand, both individually absorbing the city scenery and blinding streetlights.

Chatter and music filled the air, sidewalks not as crammed as before but still populated. This time Aiden noticed a couple of stares, and Masika was always quick to snap her neck to glare back. He would giggle as blue eyes darted away from his direction; she'd squeeze his hand and hum underneath her breath at the sound of his laugh.

He didn't expect a bookstore, but that's where he found himself standing. *Deylin's Book Shop and Brewery,* a sign read in bold print. The lights were all off and closing hours had long passed. Masika fidgeted with her pager.

"Know it looks closed. Pretty sure he's still here, though."

She sent out a message then pocketed it. A few moments later a pudgy, doe-eyed gentleman emerged from the back of the store. He walked up to the door with an impressive ring of keys, opening it.

"You're lucky," he spoke, standing in the doorway. "I was just about to head home for the night."

"Lucky us, indeed."

Aiden and Masika followed him behind the counter, through an archway and down a staircase. The stairs creaked with each step as Deylin led them to a light pink door, taking out his keys once more. Aiden admired him from the penultimate step; his frizzy, large afro complimented his dark green eyes. Formally dressed in slacks and a yellow button up, he had nearly the same body type as him, only boasting a pudgier gut.

The doorknob twisted and the three entered his office; Aiden idled by the door as Deylin sat behind his desk, Masika in front. As Deylin turned to glance at his computer, he grew envious of the man's beard pattern. He subconsciously scratched his own.

"Sit down, love," Masika guided sweetly. He did and she redirected her attention to Deylin, "Partner has some questions for you."

Aiden snapped out of his trance. He looked at her in confusion, then at Deylin who sipped his wine. Smacking his lips, he set the glass down.

"Does he now? I'd be happy to help if I can," he told her.

Aiden didn't have a clue where she was going with this, staring at her until she continued.

"Binds, he does, but in ways that hurt badly. Wants to know if there's any other way, one that won't cause pain."

"Certainly. What's the current method?"

Masika looked at her partner for permission to answer, which he gave with a quick blink. "Six, seven, maybe eight bras on top of each other."

Deylin winced and brought his palm to his mouth briefly in horror, "Oh, you poor thing. That sounds dreadful. Thankfully, I know a couple ways to help. Give me a second."

As he briefly retreated to the office, Masika took Aiden's hand. Rubbing her thumb along his palm, she smiled at him.

"Like me, he is, but transitioned in a masculine way. Been binding for about thirty years."

The words felt wrong. He couldn't place why beyond Dorothy Ann's constant shriek in his head. Swallowing, he made a writing motion, urging her to action. The notepad was handed over, whereon he scribbled a sentence.

It can go both ways?

"Can go any way you want. Some people don't call themselves men or women; some are neither, both, or somewhere between. Maybe even somewhere beyond."

Deylin returned promptly, leaving Aiden's head spinning with questions from Masika's response. The way he grew up, there were two choices: accept the womanhood forced upon him or get snuffed out. Anyone who trodded the lines between man and woman was a criminal, a miscreant, or worse. Though something deep inside him roared in delight from recognition, he closed it up. Nothing he felt had to do with gender, the switch had nothing to do with any of that. This was simply a role to play.

Yet, as Deylin placed several varieties of sports tape on his desk, his heart stopped. It somehow kicked into overdrive when the man began unbuttoning his shirt. Pulling the garment off his shoulders, Aiden's mouth parted in shock. One of the very tapes Deylin put down had been used to bind his own chest. So incredibly well-done, he couldn't help but admire.

He let the curiosity take over and fired off several questions. Each met with delight, he learned just how incredibly common binding was, how long you could wear the tape, and more. Aiden could hardly believe his final question, yet it made its way onto the paper.

Can you teach me?

"Of course I can! I can even do the first round for you. Once we're done, I'll give you a couple rolls to take with you. How does that sound?" Deylin rounded the desk to join his side, "It might take some practice to get it right, but once you have it down, it's easy as cake. Just let me know whenever you're ready."

Aiden took a sharp breath. Looking over at Masika, he stood and began to remove his top. Once cast aside, he worked to remove the seven sports bras. Deylin grimaced at the deep red marks in his skin from the straps shifting around throughout the day. Aiden tried not to think about it, but it hurt a lot. By the time his chest was bare, his shoulders deflated in relief from the pressure.

"When was the last time you took those bras off?" Deylin asked, examining his bruised, slightly warped chest.

He looked away guiltily and bit his lip, wanting to sob already. The embarrassment seeped into his bones, yet Deylin placed a kind hand on his arm, avoiding the angry red skin.

"It's alright. This is going to feel a lot better, but you have to take it off every few days to change it. Okay?"

Watching and listening throughout, Aiden allowed Deylin to bind his chest. Masika observed, assumably so she could help him in the future if needed. Her friend recommended a few brands, oils, and lotion as he applied the tape. It took longer than Aiden would have liked, and he grew angrier at his body the more time ticked by. Deylin finished ten minutes later, at which point he could finally process... *relief.*

Relief in his lower back, shoulders, and chest itself. Glancing downward, he hummed in satisfaction as he ran a palm over his pecs. Deylin did a fantastic job flattening him, a grin forming on his face as more aftercare instructions were rattled off.

"If you start to itch, or get a burning sensation, remove the bandages immediately. Other than that, you should be all set!" Deylin sat on the edge of the desk, "Is there anything else the two of you needed?"

They looked at each other. Aiden shrugged as he put his shirt on, Masika responding to Deylin with a slight tilt of the head, "Don't think so."

"Well, you two are welcome to come by my place. We could have some drinks, maybe catch up?" Deylin suggested.

"Down for that. Aiden?"

He agreed.

With that, Deylin locked up shop and piled everyone into his car. From the back seat, Aiden watched the scenery fly by. When he wasn't gazing outside, he admired the muscles in Masika's arm that draped over the center console.

Within the span of a few hours, she'd once again flipped his world upside down; feeling like a newborn, fresh from the womb and full of life. Everything he once knew mattered less and less the longer he spent by her side. She'd exposed him to the glittery rainbow underbelly of the universe. Touching his flat chest, he rested his head against the foggy glass.

Chapter Thirteen

February 1994

A fifteen-minute drive later, Deylin rolled up to a massive apartment complex. Stopping at the gate to punch in the code, he waited for it to open before breezing through. As he navigated the crowded parking lot, Masika questioned him.

"No more house?"

"Nah, let my ex-wife keep it in the divorce. She was the breadwinner, after all. I moved further upstate instead."

"Still see your daughter?"

"Every other week. This one's my off week."

He snagged the closest parking spot to building two thousand. Seeing three flights of stairs caused Aiden to wince. Deylin chuckled as he opened the driver's door.

"Don't worry, there's an elevator."

The short walk to it proved difficult. Once inside, Aiden nearly collapsed to the floor. Masika steadied him, squinting at his empty hands.

"Cane?"

Aiden flushed red, having left it in the car on accident. She simply let out a soft sigh.

"Gonna grab it before we leave, don't want you walking without it."

Arriving at the third floor, the group spilled out and Deylin walked towards the closest door. Masika assisted Aiden it was unlocked, leading him into a decently decorated living room. She gently placed him onto the couch. Sinking into it, he exhaled as Deylin trailed to the kitchen, flicking on lights in the process.

"Do you guys want anything to drink? I have..." Deylin's voice faded as he opened the fridge, "juice. Lots of juice. Uhhh, water, alcohol—"

"What kind of juice?" She asked as she scooted closer to lay her head on Aiden's shoulder.

He wound up closing his eyes, not opening them until Deylin asked if he wanted anything. He answered on notepad, the response which she relayed. Arriving with drinks a couple moments later, Deylin set them in front of the couple before lounging on the second couch.

Masika and Deylin spent hours catching up; she told him what happened with Everlee, he spoke of his divorce and dreams of publication. Aiden spaced out for the majority of it, not purposefully. He kept getting distracted by their physical traits, albeit in different ways. The parts of Masika's legs that peaked out beneath her shorts allured him. On the other hand, Deylin's fantastic beard and hairy arms embittered him.

He enjoyed himself until a ball of anxiety formed in his abdomen. Excusing himself to the bathroom, a fiery storm of thoughts began to consume him. First, his brain chastised him for flattening his chest, claiming Deylin did a wretched job. It questioned if his own presence was unnecessary; after all, Deylin and Masika had been hitting it off with little to no issue. Why couldn't he do the same?

Frustration and confusion surfaced as he stared blankly at his reflection, battling internally. A light tap on the door startled him, and he opened it to see Masika.

Ecstatic to have a break from his thoughts, his arm was gently taken in hers. She eyed him knowingly, lips curled into a feline grin.

"What's up? Look flustered."

He was incredibly so, already having decided to avoid Deylin for the remainder of the visit. He *hated* feeling jealous, but how could he not be? Deylin had everything he desired. Incoherent mumbles caused her to lean forward.

"Aiden?"

He teared up and she offered her arms as an escape once again. Accepting, he allowed her to cradle his head with such tenderness it made him weep.

"Must be overwhelming for you. I'm so sorry, can go back to the hotel if you want. Deylin won't mind."

Aiden refused, he needed to stop running away from confusing emotions. Joining her in the living room, Deylin did a better job of including him in the conversation this time. He learned a little about the last few years of Aiden's life—the stuff that mattered to him, like the swap and working for Ruby—as well as a few gender woes of his. He fully voiced his disdain for his chest.

"Well, everyone is different. There's nothing wrong with disliking parts of yourself, though. Insecurity is common," Deylin leaned forward suddenly. "When did you start binding? Before or after switching places with your twin?"

Masika glanced over at Aiden who nodded, giving her permission to respond on his behalf. She turned to Deylin, "Before. Long before. Back when we first met in high school."

"I see... Interesting."

The hairs on Aiden's entire body stood. *Interesting?* What was he, some sort of freak science experiment? Thinking far from rationally, he started to scratch obsessively at his jeans. The scratches grew harsher as Deylin pressed further and further with inquiries.

Masika didn't answer for him, looking between him and the notepad. Deylin wanted to know what he *really* was; an answer Aiden found himself too terrified to confront. He wanted to lie to himself, say he was just playing a role, but the tiniest part of him questioned otherwise. The meddling grew infuriating and he broke down in tears.

Deylin didn't notice at first, too busy excitedly theorizing. When he did, he flushed and scratched his head. "Oh dear, did I cross a line?"

She held Aiden as he sobbed violently into her chest. "Too many questions for today, if had to guess," she answered.

"I see. I really am sorry, Aiden. I got carried away."

Not wanting to upset him further, Deylin opted to take the couple to their hotel. On the drive there, she held Aiden's hand ever-so-tightly, having joined him in the backseat this time. Comforted by her presence, he dozed off. When he came to, her and Deylin were talking in the parking lot.

"...I'll be in touch. Just let me know when a good time is—" Deylin declared before noticing Aiden was awake. "Hey there, we made it! You're probably ready to hit the hay."

Aiden nodded as Masika exited the vehicle. Following suit, he drowsily stumbled by her side as she rounded the car. Deylin rolled down his window.

"It was great to meet you, Aiden. I hope the tape works well for you," he said.

He left the parking lot, vanishing on the road shortly after. Aiden let everything blur until he set foot in the suite. When he did, he asked Masika if he could vent his frustrations on the notepad. She agreed and they laid down on the bed together, feelings being transcribed into words on paper.

I don't know who I am and it scares me. You and Deylin seem so sure. Here I am, twenty-six years old, having no idea what I am or what I'm here for. I don't know anything, Masika, and that scares me so fucking much.

She glanced up at him with a sad twinkle. "Aiden, took a long time to figure things out. Still figuring a lot out to this day. Allowed to be scared, okay? Very scary, it is."

Aiden trembled and hugged himself. His mind leapt to badgering as she planted a firm grip on his jaw. Tilting his face upward, she kissed him deeply and he kissed back. Face cupped with both of his palms, she pulled away just enough to breathe, leaving their foreheads pressed together.

"Love you no matter what you decide to be. Take time to figure it out, on nobody's but your own."

He offered another kiss, placing his hand over hers. The notepad still in her grasp crinkled beneath their overlapped fingers. Setting it aside, he pushed her towards the bed. Willingly falling onto the slightly disheveled sheets, he hovered above her. He pinned her wrists over her head and she looked up at him hazily.

"Someone's pent up," she teased.

Aiden steadied his breathing. Pent up was a gross understatement. He thought seldom about anything else, the night they shared a couple days prior only strengthening his urges. And oh, how Masika electrified him with a simple curl of the lip and a submissive gaze. Was he supposed to resist? He couldn't back in senior year, knees bruising as he prayed for his lust for her to vanish. There was no way he possibly could now. Succumbing, he dove towards her neck for a hasty bite. She gasped into his ear as his teeth snared her flesh.

Fingers dove for her shorts, unbuttoning them with ease. He effortlessly exposed her to him, grinning as she reached desperately. Pushing her wrists up again, he began to stroke her shaft. Whimpering, her hips lifted beneath him and his breath hitched.

Desiring control, something he had always lacked, Masika knew exactly what he was thinking. She urged him with needy, pleading eyes. Her hands wriggled in his grip as he decreased speed, reaching an agonizingly slow pace. Baiting with an amused yet mischievous expression, she let out a sharp breath.

"Please." he turned an ear towards her, eyebrow raised. Her voice pitched higher, "Aiden, give me more. *Please.*"

Obliging, the begging didn't stop as he released her and lowered himself between quaking thighs. Running his tongue up her length before taking it into his mouth, she shuddered in delight. She was no match for the wet heat enveloping. Taking hold of his hair as his head bobbed up and down, he watched the muscles in her thighs twitch, egging him on. He playfully groped at her ass, the combined sensations sending her over the brink as cum shot down his throat. It was swallowed without hesitation.

Moving away, she placed a palm over her mouth, the other hovered over her shaking thighs. He wiped his mouth and smirked down at her throbbing cock.

They cuddled naked while he played with her hair, eventually sitting up.

"Going to clean myself, wanna join me?" Masika asked.

Aiden thought to decline but recalled the waterproof bandages eclipsing his chest. Jumping to his feet, he nearly fainted the moment they touched the ground. Masika rushed to steady him as he struggled to fight fuzzy vision. She held him tightly.

"You okay?"

Guiding him to the bathroom slowly, they showered together. The two taking turns washing each other's bodies caused him to fall into a complete sense of safety. When she lathered his back with soap, she asked him a question.

"First time showering with someone else?" Aiden nodded and she continued hesitantly, "Wish could say the same for me. Was no showering alone in prison, didn't matter I was only thirteen. Showered with dozens of naked men, terrifying. Had a very caring, strong cellmate who protected me," she grazed a thumb over his jaw. "Would've loved you. Wish you two could have met."

The aura of the suite shifted drastically after the shower. The broody yet erotic energy grew tense and grief ridden. Masika didn't bother getting dressed into pajamas, instead standing motionless at the foot of the bed. Aiden tugged on a pair of boxers before gently touching her shoulder. No response. Tapping carefully, to which she startled, he glanced up at her full of concern.

"Sorry, got in my head."

Pointing to the bed, Aiden offered his best warm smile. The two proceeded to cuddle up under the covers, her remaining emotionally distant. He turned on the television, hoping it would help distract. It did no such thing as he watched her slip away into a void once more. After a while, he reached for her hand but she snatched it away. When he flinched, she bit her lip.

"Sorry. Sore 'cause brought something up I shouldn't have."

He grabbed the note pad and pen off the nightstand. *Your cellmate? You can talk about her if you want.*

"No!" she exclaimed, reading the note before rubbing her hands together nervously. "S-Sorry. Not used to people wanting to know. Or caring. Need to stop lashing out..."

Aiden nodded, twirling his fingers as she asked if she could move closer. Once they were hip-to-hip, she lamented.

"Teneca, she called herself. Choctaw woman sentenced to death for killing the man who orchestrated the destruction of her home. Didn't do it, but the courts don't care. Taught me everything I know. When to fight, when to back down, how to braid my hair, how to be a woman... Knew long before I did that I wasn't a boy. Remember shaving her beard every two weeks while she cried, told me I was the sweetest girl she'd ever met. Never forgot that. W-Watched her die, her son sitting next to me. Smiled at us, told us it would be okay..."

Guiding her head to his chest, he wrapped his arms around her shoulder. She collapsed into him and wailed. He didn't stop her, only continuing to hold her as tight as he could. Doing so until the cries slowly died off and he found her asleep in his arms.

Watching television for a few hours, skimming, he settled for a film channel. He shifted Masika onto the pillow beside his, tucking her in. The movie's pacing proved too fast for him to articulate the plot, not aided by jumping in half-way through the runtime. Half paying attention, he primarily absorbed the busy day bit-by-bit.

An on-screen distraction thwarted his thoughts, an actress appearing and created various shapes with her hands. At first, he had no idea what the shapes meant; when he realized she was doing sign language, he beamed. He admired ASL, wanting to study it during school but never having the chance.

Gears turned in his head. If they could learn ASL, there would be no more paper trail. Not that Aiden minded writing, paper just wasn't always readily available. After all, what if an emergency happened and he had nothing to communicate with? There needed to be some kind of backup, and learning ASL would be *perfect*.

***

Over cups of coffee at a small café the next morning, Aiden pitched his idea, suggesting the two find books on ASL during the remainder of their trip. Masika agreed wholeheartedly, showing excitement for a new form of communication.

"Maybe Deylin's shop has some," she suggested.

She seemed less stable since the previous night, but she did a damn good job of hiding it. Aiden listened to the gut feeling saying to wait before bringing it up, so the two consumed their drinks before heading into the bustling city. Not wanting to hurt him with a hefty walk, she called a cab.

Deylin stifled his laughter from behind the counter the minute the duo entered his establishment. "Couldn't get enough of me, huh?" he joked.

Masika walked up with a tiny smirk, "Damn right. Might also need some books."

"Sure thing, what kind?"

"Got anything on ASL?"

"Yup! Follow me." Deylin took them to the linguistics section of the bookstore, the eight-tier bookshelf stacked to the brim with language guides. He pointed to a cluster of books on the end of the third shelf, "Those should all be ASL. If you're learning for the first time, get beginner level guides."

"Thank you."

She had Aiden pick out as many books as he wanted. Winding up with a beginner's guide, a dictionary, and a workbook, he felt beyond satisfied leaving Deylin's shop. Her mood had lightened as well, based on her now-straightened posture. Out of the blue, she asked if he wanted to go clothes shopping.

Aiden shrugged in response, having no idea what buying his own clothes was like. Growing up, he only got hand-me-downs. For the last few years of adulthood, he'd been wearing a mix of handmade clothes and Abeje's old wardrobe. The prospect of shopping both tantalized and frightened him. Then again, this whole trip was supposed to be about breaking out of his comfort zone; so he retracted the shrug and exchanged it for a nod.

Masika took him to several different clothing stores—none of which carried his sizes. This created deep frustration and fostered his self-hatred. Noticing his growing agitation and disappointment, she promised after each time they wouldn't give up so easily.

The last boutique they visited started off promising. Aiden managed to acquire a decent pile of clothes, though he couldn't shake off the bug-eyed employees; older white ladies whispering amongst themselves at the front. Judgmental gazes followed him and Masika around the thrift store. She paid it no mind, but the longer it went on, the angrier he got.

The final straw came as they strolled up to the counter to pay. Aiden itched to complete the transaction as soon as possible. The cashier, a burgundy-and-blonde haired petite woman, scanned each item at an agonizingly slow pace. All the while, she muttered to herself. He didn't know what she was saying at first—not until he recognized a single word. The word so many people he loathed had constantly used to insult him.

Masika looked at him in confusion as he made a beeline for the door, leaving the items behind. He burst out onto the busy sidewalk, ducking into an alleyway. Right on his heels, Masika called out for him. He didn't hear, surroundings drowned out by the insult replaying in his head. She reached for him as he paced in circles, rapidly shaking his hands.

"Aiden—"

He slapped her arm away significantly harder than intended. Staring up with regret-ridden eyes, he didn't waste a second taking both of her hands into his.

"Wanna go back to the suite?" She asked.

He nodded, boiling over.

She said nothing the whole way as Aiden mentally tore himself to shreds. She tried doing something nice for him and he ruined it. He should have kept himself in check and ignored the treatment, let her buy the clothes. Inside the elevator, Aiden signed the only sign he knew.

"I'm sorry."

Masika exhaled deeply, "No worries. Vibes were definitely off, made the right call back there, Aiden."

She still held the part of her arm he struck. He pried at her digits until they fell away. Not a mark or bruise detected, it didn't make him feel any better.

"Don't feel bad. Used to getting beat up, seen all the scars yourself." Frowning, she lifted his chin, "Wrong thing to say. Promise it's okay. Know you didn't mean it. Were overwhelmed and anxious."

He stood on his toes to kiss her. After being around her again for so long, he still wasn't used to her endless understanding. The feeling of being known typically mortified him, yet she bathed him in saccharine light and always knelt before him in worship. Her devotion proved so powerful she had traveled the entire world alone and still felt incomplete without his presence. She came back for him after all that time, unsure if he'd even be capable of loving her like he had before.

Now she planned to take him around the states, all the while accepting every inch and flaw of his. Even during those rare moments of blind violence that drove Abeje and Dorothy Ann and everyone else away, she remained unaffected. Was this...peace?

She pulled away and captured his face in her hands. *Yes, this must be it,* he thought.

***

While Aiden slept that night, Masika returned to Deylin's. Waiting with a glass of grape juice, he scoured the details of fake passports with a magnifying glass, ensuring their validity. She daydreamed of Jamaican waters, blissfully blue and serene as her and Aiden waded through. Once he was satisfied with the results, Deylin slid the passports to her across his desk.

"How do those look?"

She inspected them, reading the printed names. *Masika Holt. Aiden Holt.* The tenseness in her shoulders melted.

"Gave us the same last name," she tried to say nonchalantly.

"Indeed. I tried to make it look like you were married. Is that okay?"

"Yes," she chimed, picturing Aiden in a tuxedo as she slipped a ring on his finger. She'd make it a reality eventually.

"Then you're all set."

Sliding out of his desk chair, he stood and gestured to the office door. Masika gathered her belongings, including the passports, and joined him as he returned to the bookshop. Approaching the front counter, Deylin stopped suddenly.

"Where are you two going?"

She stilled, those turquoise tides illuminating her thoughts once again. "Jamaica."

"That sounds beautiful, you'll have to write me and tell me how it is."

"Know I will."

Hugging goodbye, she made her way to the hotel. Back to her shimmering light in a world of darkness.

CHAPTER FOURTEEN

October 1986

Halfway through autumn, as leaves adorning trees began to sour and litter the ground, Dorothy Ann announced she'd be gone for a week. When she gave them the news, Aiden could see Abeje's barely contained excitement hidden behind a blank expression. Dorothy Ann implored the two to stay home whenever they weren't at school, even on the weekends. They both knew that rule wouldn't be adhered to.

"No funny business while I'm gone. I better come home to a sparklin' clean house and both of ya in bed, asleep. Is that understood?"

The twins nodded. Those first two requests would be ignored, the last was promised.

In their room, Abeje talked quietly of her plans for the week as Aiden listened. He scoffed at her ideas of staying over at Tiffany Morgan's (a girl she'd been pining over since third grade) and possibly throwing a party. After convincing herself the party was a bad idea on account of police frequently patrolling the neighborhood, she directed her attention to Aiden.

"You should see if M is doing anything, maybe you can finally spend time with them outside of school."

He flushed. Following the Eddie incident, life became a lot quieter and Masika filled the void with her consistent presence. The pair had fallen into a routine. In the morning, once the bus dropped him off, he'd sit with her behind the gymnasium; a halfway full notebook splayed out on the sidewalk. Chatting until the bell rang, he had grown quite comfortable using paper and pen to express himself, even when he could use a gesture of the head or hands instead.

They'd have their normal run-ins at lunch and Physics before the day would end, Masika walking him to the bus or home. Aiden found out she lived only a couple blocks over, a short fifteen-minute walk. He couldn't lie to himself that the temptation to visit wasn't already there.

At lunch the next day he asked her, feeling a bit more brazen than usual, if she could have company over. She choked on the sliced apples she was eating.

"Wanna come over?"

He nodded and she took a moment to chew properly.

"Don't reckon my old man would mind very much. Always tellin' me to make new friends," she raised her eyebrows. "Didn't think you were allowed to go anywhere?"

Aiden told her about Dorothy Ann's vacation, and Masika's entire face lit up in jubilation.

"Must be excited to have some space."

We are.

*****

The following Monday, a day after Dorothy Ann left, Aiden couldn't shake Masika from his thoughts. Her father gave permission to invite him over, and he found himself obsessing over the excursion. Excited to spend time with her outside of school, such a foreign feeling puzzled him as he often opted to be alone. Never wanting socialization or contact until now, everything was different with her.

After school, he headed to parent pick-up to meet with her. As he approached, he spotted her standing up against a pole, smoking as a few staff members eyed her. Aiden couldn't find anything wrong with her demeanor, besides the fact she seemed to be in her own world. Staring off into space until he was only a couple feet away, she straightened at his presence.

"Hey," Masika crushed him into a bear hug. He grinned into her shoulder before she pulled away, "Ready for a walk?"

A surprisingly short stroll followed, the duo reaching a fifty-five plus mobile community in less than fifteen minutes. The homes stood side to side, all suffocating each other, leaving *just* enough room for two vehicles to park at each. She led Aiden all the way to the last row of trailers. On the way, he saw elderly Black folks sitting on their porches, finding the sight refreshing. It was nothing like his neighborhood where only whites could be seen outside. In fact, now that he thought about it, his household could very well be the only nonwhite one in that immediate community. A shiver drove down his spine and he violently shook his limbs. Masika paused at the edge of her home.

"You okay?" she asked.

Aiden bit his nails, bowing his head in apology.

"Just making sure you're good."

She continued to the front door, taking a key from her hoodie. Unlocking it, she told him to go ahead. Neat brown carpet over wooden flooring greeted the pair, couch sat to their right along with a TV stand under a massive window. She walked further, passing the kitchen counter to reach the empty doorway beside the fridge. Aiden followed her, going down the hall and through the first opening on the left.

"Here's my room."

It led into a crowded ten-by-twelve, twin sized bed sat cozy between two full bookshelves. A vanity leaned up against the same wall a singular tiny window was affixed, rather large navy dresser stood adjacent. Aiden walked over to the vanity, staring at his reflection as Masika closed the door and chuckled.

"Nice, ain't it? Was my Mama's before she passed."

Diving head-first onto the bed, she let out a grand exhale. Aiden, nosier than usual, quietly opened the first drawer. At the bottom several makeup brushes, lipsticks, and eyeshadows rolled from disturbance. Wondering if these had also belonged to her mother, he halfway reached inside before a hand touched his wrist. Jumping at her sudden presence behind him, he studied her forlorn expression in the mirror. Watching as his own started to form, he didn't notice her fishing inside the drawer.

"Curious?" she hummed, "Didn't pin you as a makeup fan."

Wanting to apologize, Aiden didn't know what had come over him. Masika plucked a deep maroon lipstick from the collection, turning to face him as she twirled it in her fingers.

"This one's my favorite." Aiden tilted his head quizzically at her response. Still eyeing it, she tore her gaze away and cleared her throat, "To look at I-I mean. Y'know, the color's nice."

He pictured Masika applying the color onto her flawless lips, nose-to-nose with her reflection. Glancing downward as she returned the lipstick to its home, he left the drawer open as she nervously chuckled and moved to the bed.

"So, what you wanna do? Got a VCR. Old man ain't home till late, so we can do whatever."

Aiden gave her a thumbs up, joining her in the living room. As she stripped titles from the entertainment console, he watched with intrigue. That was until sharp pains bubbled beneath his abdomen and he winced. He covered his mouth, not wanting her to notice. When he looked up at her, she was already staring.

"You alright?"

Aiden folded over on the couch, hugging himself as Masika practically flew over to him. Hesitating a moment, she rubbed his shoulder blades. She kept on until he recklessly sat up. He forced a smile and she tutted.

"That's not gonna work on me. You sick? Eat something bad?"

Shaking his head, Aiden had a lurking suspicion which he didn't want to manifest into reality. Another surge of pain rippled throughout his lower half, stomach lurching. Covering his mouth, a wave of nausea subdued him as Masika stood.

"Gonna get you some water, okay?"

Masika hurried to the kitchen as he resigned himself to curling up on the couch. She came back and crouched by his side just as the nausea and stabbing sensations had him in tears. Requesting he sit up, she handed him the water, which he gulped down without a second thought. Watching pitifully from the floor, she took his hand. The warmth of her touch breached through the agony, sending shockwaves throughout Aiden's body. Closing his fingertips around her palm, he focused on her face.

"Worryin' me here," she said.

A small snort of laughter left Aiden's lips. Without thinking, he put the drink aside and rested his free hand on top of Masika's head. Patting her locs assuredly caused a deep red to pervade her cheeks. He captured her jaw with stubby digits. She rose at the touch, seating herself again as she mirrored him, stroking his cheek. Normally terrified of eye contact, he found it impossible to look anywhere else.

Aiden couldn't help but notice the patchy stubble on Masika's face as he ran over her jaw, finding several razor bumps. Not having time to pay it much mind, the two instinctively leaned in closer, noses nearly brushing together. She abruptly flew off the couch at the sound of the front door unlocking.

He barely had time to collect himself as a man entered the trailer, taller than the doorway he ducked under. He hobbled into the living room. A large, tattered pair of overalls hugged his brawny frame, contrasted by gray-white cornrows and sunken eyes. Aiden noticed Masika's change in posture and swallowed.

"Hey Pops," she greeted.

"Hey kid." He paused at Aiden, "This ya friend?"

"Yeah, it is."

"I recognize ya from church. You've got a... a twin, ain't ya? Always with your mama?"

Aiden nodded politely. He never paid a lick of attention in church, opting to stare off into space until the ruckus ended. Mass often grew rowdy with glee and prayers, many people apt to tears and songs and roars of faith. He hated it; always sweaty, crowded, and all-around way too much. He wouldn't have been able to remember a singular face even if he tried. The face in question introduced himself as Herbert.

"Or Herb fa'short. M been treatin' ya well," he asked loudly, "or been drivin' you crazy?"

Masika answered for him, "Can't talk."

"Ah, no worries," he yawned obnoxiously. "I'll leave y'all to it, I gotta get cleaned up. Behave, will you M?"

"Will do." As Herb left, she turned to him and spoke in a low voice, "Sorry if that was awkward. Not used to company and neither am I, really."

Aiden didn't hear, preoccupied with recalling the moment they had shared before the interruption. Cheeks probably still a little red, he remained shell shocked as they returned to Masika's room. He sat on her bed as she retrieved her school backpack.

"Didn't expect him home so soon. Might've got out early. Wanna do homework instead?"

The homework session ended up lasting for a couple hours. Aiden breezed through his objectives, leaving him to help Masika with much of her work. Struggling significantly with English, he noticed how much grief it caused her. Each time her frustration manifested, he expected to receive outward violence. But she resigned to quietly berate herself, every time Aiden writing a phrase of encouragement on the margins of the paper.

"Thank you," she spoke up at one point. "suck at reading. Didn't know how 'till after I got arrested."

Aiden told her it was more than okay, that everyone had their individual weaknesses and strengths. This soothed her, and the self-deprecating slowed to a lull.

When Herb announced food would be ready in thirty, Aiden took that as the perfect time to go home. Abeje would kill him if he left her alone to deal with dinner, so he planned to head out after using the bathroom.

As he sat on the toilet and pulled down his underwear, a mass of dull red caught his attention. Mouth opening in dismay at the sight of blood-soaked underwear, to his further embarrassment, it went through the skirt as well. Frantic, he temporarily put it back on and scoured the bathroom for any toiletries. Cabinet after cabinet he found nothing; right as he went to return to the toilet, another fit of cramps sent him straight to his knees. Groaning, his face pressed against the floor as he held beneath his stomach.

After not moving for several minutes, he heard a knock at the door. Half-expecting Herb, Masika's soft voice came from the other side instead, asking if everything was okay. He didn't respond and the handle turned. Not having the energy to react, she was witness to his writhing form. Groans of pain caused her to rush to his side.

"Hey! Hey, are you awake? Can you hear me—*oh*." Seeing the red, she quieted, "Shit, don't have anything for that. Let me tell Pops and he'll run to the store—"

Aiden's fingers dug into her arm. Kneading against it, she grabbed his back ever so gently.

"Look. Seem like you're in pain, don't think you want a mess on top of all that. So please, let us help."

He relented, allowing her to leave despite worrying he might die of embarrassment. Returning shortly after, she let him know she'd be going with Herb to the store.

"Love him, but he's clueless at times."

Aiden reached for Masika's limb and tugged in desperation. The last thing he wanted was to be completely alone in immense pain. Tears streaked down his face as she intellectualized his anxiety-laden expression.

"Okay. Pops," she shouted from the doorway, "gonna stay here!"

The front door closed in the distance and Masika moved in on Aiden's shuddering figure.

"Show me how to help." A lip curled as she flinched at her tone, "D-Don't know much about this, sorry."

He pat the ground beside him, Masika taking the hint and sitting down. Without thinking, Aiden crawled into her lap. It felt stupid, but the only thing he craved was human contact. Expecting her to shove him off, she didn't, accepting him into her arms and cradling his head instead. Briefly worried about getting blood on her, he wriggled away slightly. Reeling him back immediately, she ruffled his hair.

"Don't care about getting blood on me, promise you that."

Aiden, flustered again, scoffed. She proved masterful at reading his every expression and thought. Slumping against her body, he relaxed as much as he could with the pain. Her fingertips sent pricks of shock all over his body. They trailed from his head all the way down his arm, stopping at his wrists only to resume from the top of his head.

Remaining entangled until the slam of the front door rang out, Masika got up to greet Herb. When she returned, she held a box under each arm, tampons and pads respectively. Aiden, sat up against the toilet.

"Didn't know which you use, so I said grab both. Wash up in the shower if you want, towels in the closet. Gonna bring you a change of clothes, too."

Aiden took the box of tampons and waved her off, already overwhelmed and distraught at her involvement (or perhaps the intimacy). Vulnerability embarrassed him, he rarely needed anyone's help. Masika left him in the quiet bathroom as he cleaned up in the shower. Getting out and drying off, he found cargo shorts and boxers waiting for him.

Feeling better after getting dressed, he retreated into the hallway. Finding Masika in the laundry room, he caught a glimpse of her shoving a fitted sheet into the washing machine. Aiden attempted to conceal his mortified expression as she walked over and put a hand on his shoulder.

"C'mon, let's go to my room for a sec," she guided him there, where she closed the door. Inside, she spoke in a concerned voice, "You okay?"

Aiden crossed his arms, longing to lie and cease Masika's anxieties. Unable to deny how shitty he felt, both physically and mentally, his cycle always made him miserable the times he would get it. One day at thirteen, he started bleeding and didn't stop for a month. After that, it lasted in stretches bi-yearly. When he was sixteen, it didn't happen at all. It came back the next, though; he couldn't keep track so he didn't.

Usually he would be lucky enough to catch it before school, where he could stuff Midol and enough pads to fix five busted water pipes in his bag. He'd suffer silently, resigning to sneaking naps during classes. No such luck this time, and he had a dark, isolated, fifteen-minute walk home ahead of him. Huffing underneath his breath, Masika drummed her digits against her stomach, deep in thought.

"Could always stay the night. Have my bed and I can sleep on the couch," she suggested.

Aiden cringed, having never slept over at anyone else's house other than the rare trip to his grandparents. The thought of being away from Abeje frightened him. Pushing irrational fear aside enough to consider, he knew he could barely walk right now and probably wouldn't be able to later.

Would it hurt to stray away... just this once? Would it hurt to tell Masika she could sleep in the same bed as him?

No, it wouldn't hurt at all, he decided and agreed to her plan. On an index card, he told her they could share the bed, too. A timorous glint flashed in her eyes.

"Sure about that? Really don't have to if it makes you uncomfortable."

Aiden didn't know if it would or not, having never shared a bed with anyone other than his sister. It couldn't hurt to find out, especially with who he considered to be his best and only friend.

After dinner—which turned out to be leftovers night—Masika and Aiden retreated to the bedroom. The two stood in a swollen silence for nearly a minute, Aiden couldn't look away and neither could she.

"Uh, don't have any pajamas for you. Don't think cargo shorts would be very comfortable either."

Aiden discarded his school shirt and lended shorts, Masika spinning on her heel to face away without so much a second of hesitation. Laughing, he turned her around by the shoulders, showing he was in a tank top and boxers.

"Don't mind sleeping in that around me?" Aiden shook his head and she sighed in relief. "Okay if I sleep like that too?"

He nodded. Masika didn't break eye contact as she unbuckled her belt, his stare staying put until he heard the slacks softly fall to the floor. He glanced at dark green plaid boxers before meeting her gaze again. She broke the tension this time as she turned her head, rubbing her arm.

"Gonna turn the light off now."

Flipping the switch, she quietly walked to the bed, Aiden joining her. Laying on the naked mattress beneath a large quilt, at first she faced away from him towards the door. Aiden tried to relax but found it difficult with the cramps. He noisily breathed out his nose in irritation.

"Cutie," Masika commented groggily.

Soft snores filled the dark room soon after. After thirty minutes of empty thoughts, Aiden managed to slip into the abyss.

****

Breakfast aromas and music lured Aiden out of sleep the next morning. He had to shield his face from rays of sunlight pouring in through the window. Turning his head, he found the spot beside him vacant.

After changing his tampon and putting the lended shorts on, he headed down the trailer halls. Powerful masculine vocals filled the home alongside a jazzy instrumental. Aiden grinned, recognizing the artist as he sleepily walked to the kitchen.

Herb and Masika bustled about the room, each managing different tasks. Herb worked on eggs and bacon as Masika mixed several ingredients in a bowl. Both sang; his unabashedly loud, hers a soft hum. Aiden bobbed his head along and quietly sat at the dining room table. A brief spin towards the fridge made Masika's eyes fall on him.

"Good morning!" she cheered over the music, opening the fridge. Herb echoed the greeting as she carried bread to her workstation.

Waving even though neither saw, Aiden observed the twenty-minute-long cooking process. Masika made his plate first, Aiden wordlessly thanking her as he accepted it. Winking, she slid to get her own helping.

Herb lowered the volume on the record player right before he joined the table, last of the three. Aiden and Masika waited to touch their meals as he clasped his palms together.

"Let us pray."

Aiden let his lids close as Herb recited a lengthy prayer. Halfway through, he let them crack open a peep. Having a habit of doing so, Aiden only ever shut them at 'Amen.' Another set of eyes challenged his, Masika's burned with tedium, peering from across the table. A crooked grin flattened her lips as Aiden stifled a giggle.

"...and in Jesus' name we pray, Amen." Herb opened his eyes, the teens pretending to open theirs in turn.

"Amen," Masika prayed.

Everyone dug in. Herb told Aiden he was welcome over at any time. A surprising yet honored invitation, Aiden gave him a thumbs up with a genuine smile.

"Lord knows my kid needs a friend. You might honestly be the first one," Herb met Masika's glare with a small snort. "Hey, I'm just sayin' I'm glad you found somebody, M. I can tell he's good."

Aiden nearly choked on his eggs. Herb and Masika simultaneously watched as he struggled to recover.

"Ya alright?" Herb asked.

With a curt nod, he patted his chest, forcing an exaggerated smile. Never being referred to as a boy before, Aiden sped up his consumption pace to disguise his stagger.

Masika took a meager few bites before excusing herself, Herb doing the same after putting his dishes in the sink. The man was out the door as Masika returned with Aiden's clothes, looking dejected.

"Shit, didn't get to tell him bye..." she moved to Aiden's side, "It's alright. Here's your stuff, should probably get ready."

The trip to school proved burdensome with the continuous pangs. Aiden managed through it with Masika's flirting touches. Holding hands the whole way surprised Aiden in the best way possible. Too bad the moment they set foot on campus, Abeje bounded towards them, eyebrows raised in concern.

"Where the hell were you? I was worried," she said.

Masika smoothed out her hair, "Lost track of time, offered to stay the night."

"Is that true?" Aiden nodded and she sighed, "Alright, just... give me a call next time or something! Fuckin' hell."

Good thing Abeje forgave easily. By lunch, everything was perfectly ordinary, excluding Masika's rising impulsiveness.

"Do you guys wanna scope out a cool place I found?" she asked the twins.

Abeje's eyebrow raised in interest, "After school?"

"Yeah, about a forty-minute walk, it is. Have some green for when we get there."

Abeje accepted the invite instantly, Aiden feeling a little more uneasy. Masika gently nudged his shoulder.

"Can walk you two home instead if you want."

Aiden disagreed with a shake of his head, knowing deep down he needed to get away from that house while he held freedom. Mostly worried about Abeje (who was especially prone to mischief around non-kin) he couldn't let that stop him. As Masika beamed down, delighted by his agreement, he knew he made the right decision.

"Alright cool. Meet you guys by the busses."

Chapter Fifteen

October 1986

The stroll began as Masika led the twins into the east part of town. Suburbs and clustered buildings traded for copious fields and farmland. The trio only passed a couple sprawling properties every ten minutes. Aiden didn't know this part of town very well since it belonged to richer white folk. He gawked at every two or three-story mansion nestled amidst acres of grass. They reminded him of plantations. While Masika and Abeje chatted, he wondered if they had been such in the past.

It would be no surprise; Dorothy Ann had already told him the town's dark history. Plantations used to be everywhere, few demolished in recent years to free up land. Even then, things had hardly changed for Black folk. Painfully aware of the townspeople's continuous ambivalence, the fear in their eyes when they saw any Black person angered him. It angered his daddy too, when he was still alive.

Completely overtaken by his insight, Aiden crashed into his sibling. Both her and Masika had stopped at a tall, rusted metal gate. Beyond it a path winded through grass plains, leading to a skeleton of a house. Masika pushed the gate open and took a couple steps down the path. The twins followed, Abeje brimming with inquiries.

"So we're gonna smoke there?" Abeje asked, pointing at the home's exposed bones.

Masika shook her head, "Nope. Barn's a bit further into the property."

"How did you find this?"

"Do a lot of walking at night. Found the whole place empty 'cept some dying livestock."

"So it's recently abandoned."

"Correct."

Aiden's legs crumpled beneath him suddenly and he tumbled to the ground. Masika ran over and helped him to his feet. Wrapping an arm around his shoulder, she supported his weight as they traversed. Ankles caving once again as the farm building came into view, Masika told Abeje to go ahead.

"You okay?" she asked, redirecting her attention to Aiden.

He nodded deliriously. The world fuzzed around him, head spinning with dizziness. Masika, sitting crossed legged and sporting a thinly veiled look of concern, tilted her head to the side.

"Gonna carry you the rest of the way."

Aiden panicked, a voice in his head—which strangely sounded like Dorothy Ann's—told him it was impossible. Not wasting a second, Masika springily crouched and scooped him from the ground. Her warm arms held him protectively, easily as she practically skipped to the barn. Abeje watched with amusement from the entrance, Aiden shocked at how nice it felt to be carried. Typically despising physical contact, especially unexpected instances, Masika managed to literally sweep him off his feet. There was no complaint past the initial shock and he relaxed halfway there, Masika chuckling quietly.

"Got you always."

Aiden blushed, resting his head against her shoulder as they reached the massive doors. Masika pushed them open with minimal effort. As sunlight filled the interior, Abeje ran straight in.

Masika walked calmly through dusty whirlpools, beelining for several stacks of hay on the left side of the structure. Setting Aiden down on the straw, he immediately propped himself up and grabbed her wrist. Masika's movements stuttered before occupying the spot beside him, not letting the touch break. Eyelashes fluttered as she pried her gaze away from his.

"Way of saying thank you?" she asked, pressing her knees together. One foot shook, jittering.

Aiden smiled, providing his answer with a closed-eyed nod. Allowing his hand to creep to Masika's, she abruptly jerked her head away. Their fingers remained cozily tied together until Abeje obnoxiously cleared her throat. Both Masika and Aiden turned as she tutted, standing a couple feet away with crossed arms.

"You two done gettin' handsy? I thought we were comin' here to smoke," Abeje chided.

"Grab my backpack."

Masika rolled up like she had all the time in the world. The herb crumbled in her fingertips as she sprinkled it along a tobacco wrap. Abeje pilfered through her English textbook as Aiden watched Masika, entranced.

In the dimly lit barn, the three friends huddled in a circle, sharing a blunt that cast tendrils of smoke into the air. Abeje went on and on about town and school rumors as Masika provided occasional responses. Aiden also listened but found himself deeply distracted, too busy staring at Masika's chiseled arms and shoulders.

Having taken off her hoodie, a dirty wife beater clung to her torso, barely fitting onto her muscular frame. Repeatedly, Aiden combed each muscle, remembering how easily she'd carried him away. As Aiden exchanged the blunt with Abeje, his and Masika's eyes would meet. She'd crack an amused smirk, setting his stomach ablaze with desire.

Blunt reduced to a nub, Masika flicked it onto the ground. Thirty minutes were spent in nearly complete silence, all three adequately stoned and content. Abeje crafted a makeshift instrument with a grass blade while Masika and Aiden stared off into space, or at each other. Masika intermittently asked if he was okay, to which Aiden would give a thumbs up or some other acknowledgement. Right as Abeje finished her project, an obnoxious car horn nearby startled the group. Masika bolted out of the barn, returning a few minutes later exasperated.

"Sorry, it's my pops," she sighed, *"Shit."*

"What's up?" Abeje asked.

"Herb wants me home. Worried about me being out here, said he'd be back in ten."

"He's not gonna be mad?"

"Not really. Picking me up keeps me out of trouble, don't think he wants me in prison again."

Masika gathered her things as Aiden and Abeje traded a look of confusion. Abeje dared to bite.

"Prison?"

"Yes, prison. Think I went to the fucking mall?"

"N-No. It's just... everyone said you went to juvie."

"Should know better than to believe a bunch of crackers," she kicked a pebble on the ground. "Juvie, huh? Would've been a lot nicer."

Nobody spoke after that. Masika sat at the barn entrance alone, Abeje and Aiden tagged back, waiting for Herb to arrive.

"They've been through some shit, huh?" Abeje said suddenly.

Aiden held himself. He hadn't thought about it, really, but it was definitely true. Wondering how Masika could be resilient through it all, he knew it certainly couldn't be easy. More importantly, he pondered if she was really okay after the conversation. As if reading his mind, Abeje lightly punched him.

"You should be with them right now," she suggested softly. "They aren't saying it, but they need someone."

Aiden paced up to Masika, who stared out into the field blankly and anxiously rubbed her palms together. Not wanting to startle her, he sat down on the opposite side. A few minutes passed before Masika talked.

"Sorry for snapping," she apologized. "Don't like thinking about that place, you know?"

Aiden closed the gap between them until he was practically sitting in her lap. Wishing to be even closer, he took her arm and gently massaged it. Foreheads naturally met and Masika's lips trembled.

"Thank you."

A single horn honked in the distance and they sat up, Masika being the first to get to her feet. She helped Aiden get to his, gaze lingering only for a second before speaking again.

"C'mon, let's go."

The group set foot down the path once more. Masika offered to carry Aiden, but he felt much more energetic with a buzz still calming his usually pain ridden limbs. Barreling through the gates, the group scurried into Herb's vehicle. Twins taking the backseat, Masika got shotgun. Buckles clicking, Herb's stern voice startled everyone.

"M, what did I tell you about this place? What the hell were you doing?"

"Hanging with my friends."

"You were *trespassing* with your friends," he stated, lowering his voice. Starting the engine again, he made a three point turn, glancing into the rearview. "Ah, you didn't tell me you were friends with *both* the twins."

"None of your business."

"M! Goddammit... listen. I know you hate when I harp on ya, but y'all need to be careful. You're in the rich part of town, not a damn negro for miles. Do you hear me? One phone call and you got the Klan running up on you. And that's *not* an exaggeration. Not me nor anyone else can help you then."

"We'll be careful, promise," Masika told him. "Times ain't like that no more anyway."

"Like hell they ain't. Just because you don't see it doesn't mean it ain't happening." He redirected his attention to the twins, "Where's Dorothy

Ann? Did she give the two of you permission to be out this late on a school night?"

Aiden's heart accelerated, praying Abeje would give a solid excuse.

"She's out of town. Got no idea what we're doing, sir, but we're grown enough to take care of ourselves!" Abeje said.

So much for that. Aiden groaned into his palms. Thankfully, Herb once again requested the trio be careful and left it at that.

Fifteen minutes later, he pulled up to the twins' home. They left the vehicle, joining each other on the passenger side as Masika rolled down her window.

"Night Abeje. Night Aiden." Aiden's heart fluttered when she looked at him, "See you tomorrow."

"Goodnight!" Abeje called, "Nice meeting you, M's dad!"

"Nice meeting you too, young lady."

As the siblings embarked towards their house, Abeje squealed. Grabbing Aiden's arm, she shook it, "Did you hear that? He called me a young lady!"

Aiden wasn't sure if she found it funny, took genuine joy from it, or both. Her excitement died down as they entered the house and got ready for bed. Once Aiden bundled himself in the comforter, Abeje's voice echoed in the room.

"You know, M's totally into you..." Aiden shot right up and glared at her. Giggling maniacally, she turned on her lamp. "Oh please, Mom left and you got close *real quick.*"

Hiding beneath the covers, he hoped it would shield him from embarrassment. While he didn't want to admit it, the feelings he had for Masika were... more than complicated. Going back and forth in his brain, he ping-ponged possibilities and concerns. If this was love, was he ready for heartache? That's all he knew of any kind of love—a constant and persistent heartache—would he risk that again? There was no doubt the betrayal would send him into a downward spiral.

Oh, but there was Masika's smile, teasing as always behind his eyelids. If his heart was to break for anyone, he'd gladly break for her.

Chapter Sixteen

August 1994

Aiden had zero complaints about spending six months in Jamaica.

When the couple weren't perusing nature or dining, they taught themselves American Sign Language. Aiden grasped it quickly while Masika struggled, much to her frustration. Constant reassurance helped to put away her worries, and by week two they had memorized the alphabet along with key phrases: *'Good morning,' 'I love you,' 'Need help?' 'It's okay,'* and more.

By August, Aiden could communicate quite easily with his hands. Still finding joy in using paper and pen, he found himself eager to use ASL in addition. Switching methods frequently, Masika expertly adapted, benefitting from the dual languages as well. On low energy days, when she felt too mentally suffocated to verbalize, she signed everything and hardly spoke a word. Aiden couldn't help but think this was no such coincidence, instead a matter of fate.

On the final Friday of the trip, they braved a local lagoon. Guiding him down rocky ledges, water pouring and gushing at their feet, Masika's eyes trained on his wobbling legs. Aiden was terrified yet elated as they drew closer and closer to the river below.

"You ready?" she asked.

"Yes."

Diving into the water first, he followed Masika shortly after with a splash. The aqua was shallower than either of them had expected, only coming up to his shoulders. She fell backward, floating on the surface tension; Aiden's limbs danced underneath. Taking everything in filled him with elation as they both let go, enjoying the Caribbean warmth.

Masika glued their bodies together, his breath hitching as she cradled his head into her chest. Moments passed in time with her heartbeat, the basin embracing the pair in undulating swells. When Aiden pulled away, he signed.

"You're beautiful under the moonlight," he longed, filled with infatuation.

Brushing a stray hair with her index, a soft smile formed before moving her hands in front of her chest. "So are you, love," Masika signed back, matching his gaze with her low-lidded, besotted one.

"I love you."

"I love you too," Masika whispered.

The two fell into soft, hushed giggles, hugging each other tightly. The giggles stifled tears, then sobs, then laughter once more.

****

As they packed up for the next venture a couple days later, Aiden suggested Florida. When Masika asked why on Earth he would want to return to the South, he shrugged.

"That's where my dad was from," he told her, "he wanted to take me there."

Masika nodded in understanding. Not exactly liking the idea of going to that place, she would tolerate it for Aiden.

"If that's where you wanna go, we can," she responded.

He frowned, "What about you? Do you?"

"Not opposed to it. Just... afraid. Last time I was in the South, someone I loved died."

"Do you want to talk about it?"

Masika told him about Anuli; the first time speaking about them to anyone. Half-expecting Aiden to be disappointed or uninterested, instead he actively and patiently listened until she reached the end of her story.

"Everlee killed them. Should have never left them alone, maybe would still be here if it weren't for me."

"Do you think they would want you blaming yourself? I may not have known them, but based on what you're saying, I don't think that's what they would want."

"Know that. Hard not to, really feels like failure."

"It's not your fault. I know it feels that way, but it isn't," he tilted his head slightly to the side, eyebrows furrowed. "We don't have to go to Florida if you don't want to."

"No, think we'll be okay. Might need help rationalizing, is all."

"I don't mind, you know I'm always here for you."

Masika appreciated it more than he knew.

***

The plane ride to Florida proved to be the worst leg of the trip thus far. The couple wound up split between a particularly loud individual who kept goading Masika with nonsense. Opting not to entertain, Aiden put his headphones on as Masika iced him out with her normal flat expression.

Once landed in Clearwater, they took a taxi into the city, Masika entertaining herself with a tourist brochure. Having picked it up at the airport, she scanned through it only to wad it up in her hands.

"Funny how they leave out the scientology presence here," she joked to Aiden in the backseat.

"What's that?" Aiden asked.

Masika giggled before giving a brief spiel on scientology, the limited amount she knew about it anyway. She was met with ferocious laughter from her partner. The taxi driver glowering at them in the rearview only caused Masika to join in. A couple minutes later when they calmed, Masika told the driver to stop. Getting out first to retrieve their luggage, she helped Aiden out of the vehicle soon after.

Post hotel check in, Aiden took a quick shower as Masika browsed television channels. Once both of them were ready, they embarked to their first stop—the high school Aiden's father graduated at. Masika called another taxi, taking only five minutes to reach their destination. When it came into view, Aiden's eyes welled with tears.

Mostly demolished, only the track field and gymnasium remained standing. The taxi driver idled in front of the school, waiting for the pair to depart. Masika watched tears roll down his face and frowned.

"Can still look, can't we?" she tried.

He nodded, the two getting out of the vehicle and approaching the fence. Construction and no-trespassing signs littered every gap in the fencing. Aiden bit down hard on his thumb as he absorbed the school's carcass. Masika slid her hand into his.

"Know it hurts, love. Sorry."

He shook his head, telling her not to apologize. Taking his hand, he responded, "It's alright, not your fault. Was a long shot anyway. Used to be an all-black school," he paused, investigating the breadth of the perimeter. "Can we still walk it?"

"Course we can."

Aiden and Masika trotted along the sidewalk. The whole time, he shared stories about his father, cane tucked underneath his arm so he could sign.

He spun tales of a saxophone player who travelled the states for years. Years and years until Dorothy Ann caught his eye during a performance.

"After the show, she came up to him and told him how much she liked his music. Asked if he did private performances. You can probably guess what happened next," he snorted. "She started tagging along on his trips. Then, one day, she found out she was pregnant. He quit his band to raise me and Abeje, wish I could tell him how much I appreciated his sacrifice."

Masika swayed ever so slightly, "What happened to him?"

A pained expression broke out on Aiden's face. Stopping in his tracks, he took a couple shuddering breaths.

"Cop killed him. Beat him to death while I was in the backseat," Aiden explained, signing growing erratic as a flurry of emotions overtook. "Same cop who attacked me and tried to... tried..."

"Know what you mean," Masika assured, sensing the turmoil. "Didn't deserve that, neither of you did."

"Thank you," A teeny smile formed on Aiden's face, "Dad would've loved you."

Masika flushed.

Aiden managed three-fourths of the walk before his legs gave out. Despite his insistence on being fine, Masika forced him to stop. The two sat next to each other behind the property, watching cars pass by on the street. She suggested they go somewhere they could both sit.

That somewhere ended up being a queer bar. They got there pretty early and stayed until around eleven p.m. to catch a few drag performances. It proved largely a snooze fest. Unlike the place in New York City, hostility outweighed hospitality. Troves of men glared hard at the two as they entered and approached the bar, making it impossible to relax. Aiden knew he didn't want to stay long.

"Get a few drinks and head out?" Masika asked, as if she had read his mind.

"Sounds good."

Masika watched Aiden get buzzed—completely understandable after the retread down memory lane—and took a shot of rum herself on impulse. One shot wouldn't hurt. She noticed a guy across the room staring at her. Ignoring it, she waved the bartender over to close the tab. Expecting the stranger to stop gawking, he did no such thing and a flood of paranoia intercepted her thoughts. She briskly stood.

"C'mon. Let's get out of here," she told Aiden.

She guided him outside and onto the sidewalk. Asking if he wanted to go anywhere else, he suggested another bar.

"Want more to drink?"

"No, just want to find one with less assholes."

Chuckling, hand-in-hand, the couple traveled west. Passing restaurants and gift shops, she noticed contentment on Aiden's face and beamed. Liking how perceptive he was, never impervious to the hatred directed at her by strangers, it helped lessen her paranoia. Elation also filled her knowing he would enjoy himself regardless of what befell the pair.

The alleviation only lasted for a few blocks. For every footstep her and Aiden took, an offbeat one rang in her ears. Masika wrapped a protective arm around his waist, lowering her head to whisper into his ear.

"Being followed, we are."

Aiden nodded to confirm he understood as they maintained their leisurely pace. Masika was unsure if she wanted to alert the stalker just yet. Simply holding Aiden as tight as she could, she kept an ear out as they rounded a corner into an alleyway, hoping to lose him. The footsteps only grew louder and closer. She gritted her teeth, deciding on the count of three she would tell Aiden to run.

Not getting the chance, wiry claws clamped down on her shoulders. Spinning around, she found herself face-to-face with the lurker from the bar. She swung, fist connecting to his right cheek and sending him twisting towards the ground. He recovered quickly, taking a butterfly knife out of his pocket. Lurching forward, he managed a lengthy diagonal slice of

Masika's torso. Wincing in pain, the sensation of skin and flesh tearing temporarily stunned her.

She took a step forward and white flooded her vision.

When her surroundings cleared, her eyes instinctively fell to her hands. Crimson doused her palms and fingers. A shriek of horror caught in her throat at sight of the man's crumpled body resting below them. Turning to check on Aiden, seeing him hurriedly tuck something into his coat, she grabbed him.

"Have to go back to the room. Now."

***

Seventeen minutes later, Aiden rubbed his wrists as Masika paced the room. Had he made the wrong decision? In the moment, all that mattered to him was her life. He could tell she was shaken by the skirmish, at the spontaneity of it. The ease of it. Or, perhaps she was afraid of being caught, of finally losing her runaway streak. Abruptly stopping, she crashed onto the bed and covered her face briefly.

"Dragged you into my mess again," she seethed, stifling a sob. "Don't know why I kill, don't know why I can't spare anyone. Hands only know death. Only something truly Evil behaves this way. Something not of this world, something not human..."

As she continued, words jumbled and incoherent, he raised an eyebrow. Interrupting her with a single step in her direction, she fell quiet instantly, ferociously rubbing her appendages.

"Masika... I stabbed him. Not you," he argued.

"No! No, you didn't, look!" She desperately shoved her hands out to him, palms up, "Look at the blood. Me. It was me, Aiden. Killed him. Killed him like the Evil bitch I am, don't you understand?"

He inspected her trembling limbs, only to find them clean. By contrast, blood drops speckled his coat and button up. Going to argue her innocence once more, he stopped mid-sign. Terror, guilt, and anxiety flickered in her dilated pupils. Both feet jittered on the floor, her entire body shaking along with her hands. Internally, he battled his own confused thoughts. Had she not seen him stab the bastard? She'd watched him drive the knife into his chest, yet here she was, fully certain she ended his life. He carefully contemplated his next response.

"Hey," he joined her on the bed, "it's alright. We are safe now, okay? He can't hurt us anymore."

"Killed him, killed him like it was nothing..." she whimpered.

"He hurt you. He probably would've done worse if I didn't..." he corrected himself, "if he wasn't stopped. We might both be dead or seriously hurt. But I understand why you're feeling the way you are right now. Your emotions are valid, my love."

"But the Evil, Aiden--"

"Look at me. I don't care about what you've done, who or what you've killed. None of it matters. I am meant to be by your side and take care of you, nothing will stop me from doing that. No amount of evil, no amount of blood. Nothing will keep me from loving you."

Slumping into him, she eventually nuzzled into his shoulder and chest. Remembering about the wound, he gently straightened her before pulling her shirt up. The cut wasn't too deep, but blood still gushed out. Excusing himself to the bathroom, he tore apart his backpack for a first aid kit. When he found it, he returned to patch her up. She was dead inside the entire time, still shaking ever so slightly. Once he finished bandaging the cut, he invited her to bathe with him.

During the shower, she turned away and cried. Aiden wrapped his arms around her waist. He traced letters into her stomach—*talk to me*—and she only broke down further.

"Don't know why you love me, don't know how anyone could. Kevin told me wasn't possible. Can't love Evil, can't love someone who ain't God-fearin'. That's why Anuli's gone, that's why Everlee hurt me... everything is my fault. It's all my fault, Aiden." He shook his head, the tip of his nose brushing against her spine and she persisted, "Why lie to me? What's the point? Don't get you at all, don't get why you stay after I hurt you so bad. Should've never came crawling back to you."

The words burned him, but he knew she wasn't in a good headspace. Ignoring the pangs of pain, he simply hugged her tighter. She didn't resist and he only let go to help wash her. As he ran the rag over her body, she faced him, puffy red eyes following his every movement. Once soap lathered her entire body, she spoke.

"I love you. S-Sorry for saying that," she looked down at her hands. "Did you get the blood?"

Aiden lowered her hands towards him, flipping them palms-up. He pretended to check before smiling.

"All clean."

"Thank you," she grinned in relief as her fingers curled inwards. "Thank you, Aiden."

She didn't say anything to him as they packed up their things a few minutes later. He tried not to press the situation further, yet it became increasingly difficult to keep his distance as he saw her holding back tears. Watching her mentally tear herself apart, he stood up and went to her.

"We're gonna be okay," he reassured.

"Know that. Might take some time to feel... normal again."

Tears rolled down her cheeks. Backpacks packed, she embraced him for a long time until they were ready to leave. Once they checked out from the hotel, they boarded a bus to Daytona Beach.

CHAPTER SEVENTEEN

January 1987

Another weekend night, another heaviness in bed. Masika sank into it as ten p.m. struck, waiting patiently. Waiting as her eyelids grew heavy, thoughts twisting and churning, finally finding a subject to home in on.

The person it *always* homed in on.

Aiden had already been a variable in her life. Only meaning to stop Eddie at first, the last thing she expected was a friendship to blossom; yet here she was, yearning for him.

Aiden had become incredibly bold in the last couple months, sneaking out late to spend the night. Most times, they'd spend hours snuggling in bed, not a word exchanged. Masika would wake with empty arms and a tinge of sadness. She knew she would always see him at school, but sometimes that wasn't enough.

He tried to hide the cut lips and bruises, yet Masika knew better. She knew how Dorothy Ann was. While Aiden may not have mentioned anything, Abeje often talked about her volatile nature in the class they shared without him. Learning of many incidents, the more she found out the more she feared for them both. Recalling one conversation made her particularly upset.

Masika had briefly mentioned Kevin—something she rarely did to *any-one*—and Abeje was quick to share a similar story.

"I 'member Ma left him out in the woods for a couple hours a few years back. Scared him real bad. Then, when we got home, she…" Abeje half-mumbled, fidgeting with her limbs, "D-Did what your stepdad did."

After that, Masika tried to dissuade Aiden from sneaking out and visiting. To her dismay, he resisted her attempts, showing up more than ever before. When she tried to ask him why, he simply wrote '*I can't sleep without you anymore.*'

That got her realizing she could only deny how she felt for so long. Though she knew nothing of romantic love, when Aiden wasn't around she dreamed of a life by his side. She knew that it couldn't happen, knew how unlovable she was. Their post-graduation plans were incompatible, but the closer she got to Aiden, the more she wanted to forfeit those ideas.

Realistically speaking, she had no say in the matter.

***

The new year rolled in, bringing a fresh start. Or so that's what people say. Masika found it hard to believe there was such a thing as a 'fresh start.'

To her surprise, a conversation with Dorothy Ann challenged that belief. Alone at the park one morning—her typical skipping spot—the woman approached. Wanting to flee, Masika instead stayed put on the swing set, gripping the chains tighter.

"Are you M?"

Masika avoided her gaze when she responded, "Yeah."

"I've heard a lot about you," Dorothy Ann noted matter-of-factly. "Shouldn't you be at school?"

Knowing this woman would use literally anything against her, she came up with a fib. "Old man let me stay home today. Got bored and came here."

"I don't see you at church, you ain't going to school. You must think you're too good to learn the word of God," she paused, looking down her nose at Masika. "That's besides the point. I wanted to say you're welcome to come by for dinner sometime."

The teen's eyebrows raised in shock, "Really?"

"Yeah, my kids are fond of you," Dorothy Ann moved closer, putting her hands in her skirt pockets. "And I talked to your old man at church last week."

"Ah..."

Conversation stalled when she sensed Masika's discomfort. Telling her once more that she should come by for dinner, the woman shuffled away. The interaction left her stomach in knots.

***

That Sunday after church, Dorothy Ann asked Herb if he and Masika wanted to join the family for dinner. Herb agreed on Masika's behalf, which pissed her off. The day had been spent brooding in her room, simmering in self-hatred. She didn't mind the twins, but Dorothy Ann irked her. Herb should've known that better than anyone.

Yet there Masika was, dressing her Sunday best at five-thirty p.m. Herb ran late like always, but had already phoned Dorothy Ann to let her know. Masika took her sweet time getting ready until Herb called her out.

"Now M, quit the stallin'. We have to go."

She groaned, "Hate Dorothy Ann."

"Listen kid. I ain't fond of her either, but I agreed 'cause I want you to be able to have your friend around."

Masika crossed her arms as she followed him out of the trailer and into the front yard. Going ahead to his truck, watching as he locked up, she tried to ignore what felt like a dozen pupils on her.

The whole ride proved tense. Herb did what he tended to during stressful times—whistle his favorite records—while Masika tried to think past her anger. She couldn't let Dorothy Ann know her true feelings, for Aiden's sake. In order for dinner to go smoothly, she needed to keep her head on straight and play the perfect little angel.

Herb parked behind Dorothy Ann's car ten minutes later. Helping himself to a cigarette, he told Masika to go ahead. She shifted as she unbuckled her seatbelt.

"Don't know about the charges, right?" she asked.

"Nope, not unless someone else told her." Like he sensed her dread, he let out an annoyed sigh, "M, ain't nobody out to get you, alright? Try to relax."

Masika wished she could easily do such a thing.

Heading up the driveway and to the front door, before she could knock it swung wide open. Aiden stood in the doorway, eyes flickering with delight. Instinctively reaching for a hug, he recoiled last second upon remembering their environment.

Instead, he waved Masika on in and guided her to the dining room, a rather small area. A diamond patterned rug lay under a round table and four chairs, display case off in the corner. Dorothy Ann, in the middle of setting plates, acknowledged Masika with an errant wave.

"Hi there, glad you made it. Where's your pops?"

"Having a smoke, can't eat without one," Masika answered.

"Haha, I remember those days. Though, Lord, I don't smoke no more. Have a seat, honey."

"Is M here?!" a voice boomed from the hallway. Abeje came rushing into the room, greeting Masika with a crushing hug. "Good to see you."

"Good seeing you too."

"Alright, enough. Let the kid sit please," Dorothy Ann lightly scolded before vanishing into the kitchen.

Masika left Abeje's grasp just for Aiden to embrace her right after. The difference between the exchanges were obvious to Masika. Aiden held onto her with desperation, like if he let go she would slip away forever. He held on until he heard Dorothy Ann's footsteps come towards his direction. Masika took her seat before she passed through the doorway, carrying a plate of freshly cooked ham.

"Aiden, Abeje. Get the rest for me."

The twins bowed their heads and left as Dorothy Ann put the platter in the center. Masika sat there awkwardly, waiting for some shred of nonsense. Dorothy Ann quietly eyeballed her, taking her own seat directly across from Masika. She tapped her nails against the wooden table.

"So, a little birdie told me 'M' is a nickname. Not your real one."

Masika pressed her palms together, staring at her fingertips, "That's right."

"What's your real one?"

Instinctively, Masika got defensive. Knowing exactly what the woman was trying to do, she smoothed out the wrinkles in her slacks, making hard eye contact.

"That is my real one. 'Cause it's real to me, to my family, my friends. Other name ain't me at all."

"I see..." The twins promptly returned with the remaining food but she paid them no mind, "Is there a reason I don't see you at church?"

Aiden and Abeje exchanged irritated glances, nearly making Masika snicker. She cleared her throat, "Got private tutoring on Sundays. Just doesn't work out."

"Uh huh."

Sweating bullets, Masika knew it was only a matter of time before she would run out of ways to dance around the conversation. Thankfully, Herb found his way to the dining room only moments later, right after Aiden and Abeje took their seats.

"Sorry about that, like to have a cigarette before my meals." Herb said.

"No worries, your kid already done told me."

The older adults blabbed on for a few minutes while the teenagers traded uncomfortable glance. Masika tapped her foot, doing her best to keep her head, hoping the soft sounds would somehow level her out. It was difficult to listen to Dorothy Ann's voice.

Inviting the group to self-serve, Masika waited to go last. When she did, Dorothy Ann observed. She wound up filling only half a plate, instantly earning a question from the older lady.

"That's all you're gonna get? I made plenty."

Herb answered before Masika could. "My kid don't eat much, Dorothy Ann. Take no offense."

A long-winded prayer followed, none of the teenagers engaging outside of the concluding amen, and everyone dug in. Relief washed over Masika as a comfortable silence filled the room.

Before Masika knew it, Dorothy Ann bid them farewell. Herb thanked her for the meal and she offered to let Masika come over again sometime soon.

"I'm sure M would like that, right M?"

Masika wanted to decline, not wanting to be around Dorothy Ann more than she needed to. Herb elbowed her and raised his eyebrows.

"Sure," she answered, the only one she could muster with so many eyes on her.

***

Dorothy Ann's death grip on Aiden loosened. She allowed Aiden to spend the night, so long as he slept on the couch away from Masika. Masika wasn't gonna tell her that stipulation wouldn't be met.

Aiden showed up a couple evenings after the dinner. Masika let him in upon knocking, having been lingering in the kitchen for an hour. She told him to go ahead to her room while she finished putting up cleaning supplies.

When she joined, Aiden scurried to his feet from the right side of the bed, wide-eyed. She shut the door as he smiled sheepishly.

"Everything good here?"

Aiden nodded only to trip on something. Masika rounded the corner, watching him try to kick a box under the bed. She knew exactly what it was and gently moved him aside to retrieve it. He nibbled on his nails as she sighed deeply, noticing fabric spilling out from beneath.

"Looked at it, didn't you?" Removing the lid, she freed a dress from its hiding place. Gaze running over the satin emerald cloth, she unfurled it as she sat. Aiden watched apologetically.

As Masika admired the gown, he fetched his notebook and pen. Sitting beside her, he went straight to writing. Reading what he put down—*I'm sorry, I got nosy. It's beautiful though*—she smiled.

"It's okay. My mama's before she passed. Got married in it. First in our family to do that outside a plantation. When she died, Herb tried to sell it. Took it before he could," she glanced at Aiden, downhearted. "Tried it on once. Don't fit me."

Aiden moved closer, gesturing for Masika to stand. When she did, he pressed the dress against her body. She blushed as he pinched different parts of the fabric, eyebrows raised.

"What you thinking?" she asked.

Gently folding up the dress, he returned it to the box before telling Masika he could alter the size.

"To fit me?"

Yes—he jotted down another sentence—*You would look stunning in it.*

Masika's entire face heated up and she averted her gaze, remembering how hard she cried trying it on. How it had sagged on her body, how unflattering it was. She shook her head.

"No, that's alright. Dresses look stupid on me anyway."

Despite the disagreement in Aiden's eyes, he didn't write anything else. Masika laid next to him and he touched her thigh.

"What is it?"

It took a while for Aiden to look away. They cuddled for a few hours as normal until his snores filled the room. The whole time, Masika couldn't shake the encounter. Was it possible that Aiden saw through her? She didn't try all that hard to be masculine, but she didn't think she made her gender woes that obvious. The only other person to notice them had been Teneca, yet Aiden had that flickering suspicion in his gaze.

She had no choice but to deny it.

***

Aiden wouldn't let her live in denial.

The realization came a week later when Aiden went over to study (watch movies) at a relatively low point in Masika's day. For some reason, anxiety and disgust ambushed her for hours without respite. Finding it difficult to do much of anything beside lay in bed, cycling thoughts gave way to near-panic-attacks. She was immobilized in darkness.

When Aiden showed up, seeming overtly joyful—giddy even—she was suspicious. Light blinded her vision as she sat up, shielding her eyes from the brightness. When everything finally adjusted, she found him by her side. He grinned up at her, concealing something in his grasp.

"Scared me... you okay?"

Opening his hands revealed a lipstick and eyeshadow palette. Masika flinched away as if it were forbidden to gaze upon. Flashbacks of haphazard attempts to use lipstick struck her blind. Biting down on her lip, the sound of pen on paper filled her ears shortly after. A notebook now in her lap, she glanced down.

Can I do your makeup? I've been wanting to.

She gulped, "G-Guess so."

Masika and Aiden sat crisscross on the bed together. Aiden had emptied the vanity drawer and she watched as he sorted the makeup into piles. Nervously fidgeting with her limbs as he picked up the eyeshadow palette and a couple brushes, her heart leapt. He lifted her chin. Dabbing a brush in a dark red, he motioned for her to close her eyes. Doing so, she nearly jumped when the bristles connected with skin. Aiden rested his free hand on her thigh, offering reassurance.

Masika had fully relaxed by the time both eyelids were coated. She opened them when the movements ceased. Aiden perused the lipsticks available to him. Settling for a dark brown one, he parted her lips with a thumb and applied the product.

Aiden signaled when finished, makeup covering his fingers after being used to correct any crude mistakes. Masika reluctantly got up from the bed and walked to the vanity.

It took several seconds of mustering strength to look in the mirror. When she did, she took a step away in shock. A hum of satisfaction followed. For once, her face didn't repel her. Instead, she stared right into herself, twirling a loc on her pointer. Resisting a wave of tears, she glanced back at Aiden. He gave a thumbs up, questioning eyebrows raised.

"Yes, did a great job," she told him, returning to the bed. "Barely recognize myself."

Aiden wrote down a response: *it's still you, and you're pretty either way.* Masika's heart fluttered. She tucked a hair behind her ear, fighting the urge to close the gap between their mouths. She delicately took his hand.

"Thank you," she breathed.

Aiden nuzzled his head against her shoulder in response. The two went out to the living room to watch a movie. For a while, she felt relaxed. About halfway through, paranoia became too much to ignore. She wondered if Aiden schemed against her, wanting her vulnerable and trusting of him. Maybe he planned to expose her to the whole school, to make a joke out of her. After all, there was no way in Hell he would ever accept her like this. Just like Herb wouldn't. The only person who truly did was long gone; she had to accept that.

The film ended in the blink of an eye. Masika realized she dissociated through it all and turned her head to apologize, only to find Aiden fast asleep. His drool on the armrest made her giggle as she put a hand on his shoulder.

"Hey... hey, sleepyhead," she shook him lightly until his eyes shot open. "Fell asleep on me."

Aiden yawned right as footsteps echoed from the hallway. Herb ventured into the living room, two empty beer bottles in hand. Yawning as well, he looked at the teenagers sitting on the couch.

"Hey there, Aiden. Hey M," he greeted.

"Hey Pops."

He took a long glance at Masika, raising his eyebrows. Having totally forgotten about the makeup, she clenched her jaw. Herb scratched his beard with his free hand.

"Is that your mama's makeup?"

Aiden stared at Masika with fear. She swallowed the log in her throat and nodded.

"Lipstick is."

She waited for Herb to tell her off and say she had no business wearing makeup. Yet, he simply nodded in understanding before retreating to the kitchen.

Herb ended up taking Aiden home and Masika stayed, needing alone time. Frantically scrubbing her makeup off in the bathroom, she wound up sobbing on the cold tile. She reminded herself the end neared, graduation would come and freedom with it. There would be no more hiding, no more shame. Most importantly, there would be nobody in her way. Even if it meant burning every bridge available to her. She sat up, weeping again at the thought of Aiden.

Would she truly have the heart to leave him here?

Chapter Eighteen

February 1987

Dorothy Ann arrived at church twenty minutes before the sermon as usual. She chatted up the priest while Abeje gossiped with a few older ladies. Aiden sat in the pews and drew in his weathered sketchbook.

The makings of a dress formed on the page and he wondered how easily it could be made. He spent the time before service fine-tuning details and gauging his skill level. When everyone took their seats for opening prayer, he snapped the book shut.

Everyone closed their eyes besides him. Out of curiosity, he looked to where Herb normally sat. To his surprise, a cluster of orange locs caught his attention. Masika turned her head. She waved softly in Aiden's direction as he deeply blushed.

It was only natural to follow in tow when Masika slipped away ten minutes into the preaching. Waiting a little to do the same, he wandered into the main hall towards the bathrooms. Finding no one there, he walked outside and found her sitting on a bench, smoking a cigarette.

"Why, hello there. Come here often?" she teased him.

Aiden scoffed in amusement, sitting down beside her. Scoping out his outfit—a sickly pink dress that fit too tightly—she addressed it sympathetically.

"Dorothy Ann make you wear that?" He nodded and she scratched her neck, "Doesn't really suit you, seem uncomfortable."

Aiden took out his sketchbook from his small tote, opening to a clean page. *I am, it's not me.* He paused briefly before adding another note, *it would look much better on you.*

Her grin faltered. She awkwardly took a couple puffs. Aiden thought the subject was dropped until she furrowed her eyebrows suddenly.

"Really think so?"

Aiden nodded with a smile, writing again. *It's yours if you want, I can adjust it.*

Masika waved a hand immediately upon reading the response, "N-No, appreciate it though."

Aiden frowned, deciding to change the subject. *Why are you here?*

"Wanted to see you. Was, um, was listening to some music yesterday. Thinking about you."

What music? Aiden asked.

"Uh, *Mothership Connection.* Album by Parliament."

I'll have to listen to it.

"Do it, let me know what you think."

She held his hand and sparks ignited in his stomach. Even after all these months, he had no idea how she made him feel this way. He got so relaxed that he didn't notice Dorothy Ann charging out the entrance, barreling right towards the pair. The clacking of heels alarmed Aiden, prompting him to stand up from the bench.

"What do you think you're doing?" She gawked at the cigarette in Masika's grip, "Were you smoking?!"

Aiden shook his head no but Dorothy Ann slapped him anyway. Masika shot up, tossing the cigarette and wedging herself between them. Dorothy Ann scoffed.

"Move," She demanded.

"No. Not after *that,*" Masika spat back.

Heart beating loudly in his ears, Aiden dissociated as the two argued. Masika held his hand tightly as they shuffled backward. Dorothy Ann kept getting closer and closer until they were cornered up against the bench. She screeched at the top of her lungs and he covered his ears.

"What's going on?!"

A concerned Herb joined the fiasco. While Masika was distracted, Dorothy Ann shoved her and reached for Aiden. Grabbing him by the wrist, she dragged him to her side. Herb watched in confusion and Dorothy Ann raged.

"Your child is corrupting my baby, I saw it!"

Herb stared at Masika. Aiden's head hung as he fought tears.

"I don't wanna argue with ya, ma'am, but my kid wouldn't do that," Herb said.

"Oh yeah? But your kid will set a house on fire, right? With a buncha white boys inside?" Herb's lip curled and she laughed, "That's what I thought. Did ya think I wouldn't find out?! I got ears everywhere, Herbert."

Masika looked at Aiden. That recognizable anger wracked her face. Aiden shook his head, trying to convey this wasn't worth whatever she wanted to do. Herb took a long time to answer, and when he did, he did so carefully.

"We all make mistakes, Dorothy Ann, and God forgives," Herb insisted. "M is a good kid—"

"Save it!"

Holding Aiden by the arm, Dorothy Ann rushed inside and retrieved Abeje. She questioned quietly why they were leaving as the family walked out of the main room towards the entrance. Dorothy Ann didn't answer, instead pushing Aiden towards the door.

"Go straight to the car. You so much as *look* at those two, you're in for it. Do you understand?"

Aiden tearfully nodded, opening the door and keeping his head down. He saw Herb and Masika's feet in his peripherals as he hurried to the parking lot, Dorothy Ann and Abeje in tow. Once they reached the SUV and got in, the woman continued her tangent.

"This is why I don't trust you! This is why I don't trust *anyone!* So many sinners, so many sinners..." Aiden sighed and she snapped her attention to him in the rearview. "You stay away from that kid, do you understand me? No more hangouts, no more sleepovers, *nothing.* You're grounded for a week!"

Aiden nodded, but when her eyes left him, he smirked. He could certainly wait to see Masika again. Shit, he could wait forever if he had to.

She was more than worth it.

***

Masika mulled over the confrontation that night. Knowing her impulsive decision got Aiden in trouble sickened her. A whistle crawled through her mind like a serpent. She faded away from reality, barely able to distinguish time passing.

A crack of lightning jolted her out of a trance. A trance, she quickly realized, had been slumber. Wiping drool from the corner of her lips she sat up, craving a glass of water. Trailing into the living room, Herb sat in his lazy boy, watching a movie.

She yawned, "What time is it?"

"Nearin' midnight," Herb answered, not averting his attention from the film.

Masika sat with him after she got her water. Herb took a long swig of beer before letting out a throaty chuckle. She stared hard at him.

"What?"

"Just wonderin' when you're gonna tell me." Herb said.

"Tell you what?"

"Ha! You must think I'm an old fool. I've seen how you get when he comes around."

Masika's chest tightened. She opted to deny, "Don't be ridiculous."

"Oh, M. You think I'm afraid of havin' a queer kid?"

She hugged herself, "Didn't think the church condoned that."

"The church ain't right about everything," he topped off the beer and sat the bottle on the floor, "I learned that when I met your momma."

Masika's eyes widened.

"What?"

"You heard that right," Herb slurred, hobbling to the kitchen. "It's a real funny story, honestly. Met her at a gay bar my buddy convinced me to go to. Really got me thinking, yanno? Right after, Phillis told me she plays both teams. Ha! I had no idea."

Masika, rattled by the influx of information, shrugged him off. Telling herself he was drunk and confused, she excused herself to her room. After all, he had a habit of spinning tall tales when inebriated. Second-guessing her thoughts, she remembered vague mentions of Momma's 'good lady friends' and affectionate nature with women in the past. Was Momma more like her than she realized?

Teneca entered her thoughts. Specifically, all those times she assured Masika she was not alone. Inside and outside of the prison, an entire world of queers and transsexuals moved simultaneously loud and in silence. *For all you know, your own family could be that way too.*

She had been right. Masika wondered just *how* much she was missing stuck in this tiny Alabama town.

***

Masika and Aiden had to get used to only seeing each other at school again. Both refused to let the incident snuff out their deep connection. Aiden and Abeje placated Dorothy Ann by staying on her good side, helping her forget the church scuffle quickly.

Even as months passed, Herb's drunken speech hadn't escaped Masika's mind. She once believed Herb could never accept her. Yet during that conversation, he confirmed this wasn't so. The possibility he would understand if she came out terrified her. She knew her father would welcome her; she knew Aiden would as well. Could she leave knowing she had support?

Nevertheless, Masika held on to her plans to flee up North. She would do so until a theophany provided her better horizons. If it was meant to be, another path would present itself.

Things were relatively quiet until the final week of classes. That Monday during lunch, Masika alerted the twins of Eddie's recent behavior. He'd been off the radar for an eternity, sinking into the backdrop. Last week, he started haggling her.

"Him and his groupies been following me. Stabbin' me with pencils, calling me a..." she trailed off, crumbling up a piece of trash. "Been bothering the two of you at all?"

"Nope," Abeje replied, "I'm surprised, thought he finally straightened out."

"People like that don't change easily," Masika huffed. "Think he's planning something."

Aiden and Abeje leaned in at this.

"Like what?" Abeje asked.

Masika lowered her voice, "Dunno for sure, but I got an inkling. Maybe wants senior year to go out with a bang."

Aiden shivered at the thought. Accustomed to the peace and quiet of the last few months, the idea of it being disrupted rattled him to his core. He wanted nothing more than the end to be smooth, easy sailing. His diploma was so close he could *taste* it. A hard hand clamped down on his shoulder.

"Abeje, Aiden," Masika stared at the twins intensely. "Promise not to interfere if something happens."

"Don't have to tell me twice," Abeje joked, finishing up her food with a snort.

Aiden defiantly stared at Masika. She rubbed her lips together, head tilted slightly.

"Mean it," she stated firmly. "Gotten in enough trouble 'cause of me. So, if Eddie does somethin', stay out of it."

Aiden agreed with a nod, but that wasn't enough for her. She stuck her finger out and he begrudgingly wrapped his pinky in hers.

***

A foot off the bus on Friday morning, the final bus ride of the year, Aiden knew something was terribly wrong. The passengers that day had been scarce, Aiden and Abeje being the only seniors. At first, he relished the quiet; then he worried.

That concern amplified as he looked around the bus drop-off for students. Other than underclassmen leaving the bus with him, there were none. Abeje and Aiden headed towards the main building. his anxiety rising as they grew closer and closer to the courtyard.

The underclassmen broke out into a sprint, passing the twins. Aiden slid off his headphones as he espied a massive crowd, packed together like sardines. Unintelligible yells and jeers echoed throughout the campus. Abeje briefly came to a stop.

"Oh shit! Someone's getting their ass beat," she commented.

Aiden threw his backpack to the ground, barreling towards the sea of bodies. People shoved, but he persisted to push his way through, hearing impact blows and grunts of pain ahead. He shouldered off a final pair of white students and broke into the inner circle, stumbling to his knees. Panting as he caught himself, he jerked his head up.

Rodney and Carter pinned Masika to the ground, holding her steady as Eddie brought a baseball bat down on her repeatedly. A pool of blood mixed with dirt beneath her head.

Aiden's heart wrenched in his chest, none of the boys seeming to notice his presence. He weighed different courses of action. Shakily standing, he briefly turned to the crowd. Abeje appeared then, trying to reel him in with a grab at his hand.

"Don't!" she yelled over the noise. "You promised!"

Aiden ripped his arm away from her, scooping a rock from the ground and letting out a long, whiny whistle. Eddie paused, turning his head as he threw the rock with all his strength. To his glee, it connected with the bully's jaw. Eddie stumbled a couple steps, giving Aiden a running start. Yelling as he tackled him to the ground, the onlookers roared louder as he pried the bat from his grasp.

With one powerful swing, Aiden struck Eddie smack in the middle of his face. That blow was all it took for him to slip into unconsciousness. Rodney left Carter's side to attack; Aiden dispatched him with three swings to the face, stomach, and groin. He crumpled like paper and Aiden redirected his attention to Carter, only to see Masika headbutt him.

She didn't miss the chance to pin Carter down, punching his skull until his movements faltered. Masika staggered to a stand, spitting out a wallop of blood and dirt, looking at Aiden with heavy eyes.

"Promised me…"

Aiden started towards her, only to be grabbed from behind. He kicked his legs as the individual tried to lift him. Managing to squirm out of the grip, he promptly turned around and punched the assailant. Before he could even process the man's badge and uniform, his whole body seized. Blacking out, his last sight was a taser in the resource officer's grasp.

He jolted awake to the sound of radio chatter. When he tried to flail his hands, he found them bound. His surroundings actualized, he groaned when he realized he was in the back of a cop car. Thrashing around, he tried to free himself from the cuffs.

"Calm down, not getting out of those."

The serene voice relaxed him. Masika sat right beside him, pretty wrists trapped as well. Groaning once again, he let his head hit the seat.

"You okay?"

Aiden turned to Masika, hardly recognizable under the swell of her cheeks and eyes. Aiden nodded tearfully and she grinned in relief.

"Good. In a shit ton of trouble though."

Despite everything, Aiden laughed. Protecting her gave him a rush he hadn't anticipated. The feeling of knuckles against flesh, the cries of pain beneath him, all of it kept a smile on his face. Knowing Masika was safe and relatively unharmed made it all the better.

"Promised to not get involved," she mumbled.

"Hmph," Aiden faced the window again. He had helped her, hadn't he?

The door on Aiden's side of the vehicle swung open, the resource officer ordering the two of them to exit. Aiden hobbled out first, struggling with bound hands. When he nearly fell backwards, Masika caught him with her weight. The officer took them to the principal's office. As he opened the door, a full house of adults greeted the pair. Principal Mathers sat in his chair, a look of utmost disgust on his face.

"Take off the cuffs, Bradley," he instructed. When Aiden and Masika had free hands, he continued, "Sit down, both of you."

They did so, only then recognizing some of the adults in the room: Herb, the vice principal, his wife Beatrice, and Dorothy Ann. Two women he didn't know stood in the corner, assumedly related to Rodney and Carter. Dorothy Ann avoided Aiden's gaze, similar to how Herb avoided Masika's. After a prolonged silence, Principal Mathers spoke.

"I'm disappointed. A bunch of seniors causing mayhem on the final day of class," He sighed deeply, resting a palm on his beer gut.

"Where the other three?" Masika asked.

"Got rushed to the hospital. What did you think was going to happen after you two nearly beat 'em to death?" Mathers questioned, clear annoyance in his voice. "That doesn't matter though, I need to hear your version of events."

Masika leaned in her chair, fingers trailing the arm rest. It took her a moment to speak, likely due to the adults' looming around her. When she did, she spoke incredibly fast.

"Got to school. Eddie, Rodney, and Carter were waitin' for me in the courtyard. Tried to walk away, they attacked. Friend here saved me."

"Why would those three boys attack you?"

"Hate me, hate Black folk. Don't think that's too hard to see, sir," Masika stated matter-of-factly.

Beatrice shrieked something unintelligible, earning a hush from her husband. Mathers turned to Aiden, "What about you? Why did you jump in?"

Aiden stared at him. Expecting Dorothy Ann to disclose his condition, she did nothing of the sort. It was Masika who told the principal he couldn't speak.

"Need paper and pen."

After being handed ink and a notepad, Aiden wrote down his version of the events. He'd come to school, saw Masika getting beat up, and jumped in to help. He mentioned Eddie's harassment throughout the entirety of his attendance, as well as his disdain for Masika. When Mathers read it, he occasionally paused to exchange glances with Beatrice and the vice principal.

"Well, both statements match up with underclassmen renditions of the tale," he said, pushing the paper to the side.

"Excuse me! My son would never do such things," Beatrice exclaimed.

"Respectfully, Beatrice, I have let a lot of his behaviors slide. But attacking two Black students after instigating one of them for *years*? Inexcusable. And while I understand fighting back," he pivoted, redirecting his attention to Masika and Aiden, "the two of you went *too far*."

Masika stifled a snort, Aiden resisting the urge to laugh too. Wanting to say he couldn't give less of a fuck, he didn't need to, Mathers detecting their lack of concern instantly.

"I'm glad you two find this funny, because now *none* of you are going to graduate."

The room exploded into chaos. Beatrice cursed Mathers out, Dorothy Ann sobbed; the unknown adults talked over each other. The only ones who remained neutral were Masika, Aiden, and Herb. Aiden knew he should be upset, but he was relieved he wouldn't have to set foot on campus again.

That relief didn't last long. Mathers finalized the punishment, ushering everyone out of his office. Dorothy Ann quickly pulled Aiden away from the group, grumbling to herself as she walked him to her car. When the two had privacy, she laid right in, calling him a failure and screw-up. Ignoring her tangent, he stared down at his roughed-up knuckles. He couldn't help but smile a little, recalling the violent incident with fondness. He didn't fuck up, he saved someone, someone that meant more to him than a diploma ever did.

***

A couple hours later, Abeje and Aiden locked themselves away in their bathroom. They had to wait for Dorothy Ann to pass out to do anything about Aiden's wounds. Normally, he could at least walk after. Hardly able to do that, he needed Abeje's help getting out of bed and down the hall.

Abeje gathered the scarce number of medical supplies from the bathroom cabinet as Aiden sat on the edge of the bathtub. She started patching up what she could—a few open cuts and scratches—and told him the bruises would have to heal on their own.

"Why'd you do it?" Abeje mumbled suddenly, applying a bandage to a welt. "You were so fuckin' close. *We* were so fuckin' close, and you *promised*."

Aiden, sick of being lectured and too weak to care, tuned her out completely. Only thinking of Masika, he wondered what punishment Herb had laid out for her. If he hadn't intervened, would they both be walking across the big stage? Would he be walking without her? How many times have his brothers and sisters faced the exact situation, white men reigning supreme? It's a small victory, he thought, and he'd do it again and again.

Chapter Nineteen

July 1987

As summer fell into place following Abeje's graduation, Aiden stayed holed up in his room. Dorothy Ann had grounded him shortly after the fight. Banned from leaving unless it was with her, she even began staying up late to ensure he didn't go anywhere.

He truly thought his time with Masika was over. To his surprise, when he checked the mail one day, he found a folded piece of paper. Once inside, he tossed the rest of the envelopes on the counter and opened it.

Hope you're doing well. Caught up with Abeje yesterday, told me you're grounded all summer. Real sorry. Told her I wanted to talk to you. Said since you're the one who checks the mail, I could probably write letters to you. Promised to deliver to me if you write anything back. Hopefully this isn't too much, just miss you a lot.

Aiden ran straight to his room. Stuffing the letter in an old shoe box, he got straight to writing his response to Masika. Leaving it folded neatly on his nightstand, he resumed his chores until Abeje got home.

Over the next two weeks, Aiden and Masika corresponded via letters. She told him she started a couple side jobs, he told her about new music he discovered. The longer they spent apart, the more desperate Aiden became for her presence, unable to shake the need for her.

The only way he managed to distract himself was with a new project. Sneakily requesting her measurements in one of the letters, he bought some gorgeous blue fabric from the store. Devoting all his time to sewing and sketching, he hardly took breaks to eat. When Dorothy Ann questioned him about it, he simply told her he was working on a dress for himself.

An exhausting day of sewing left his hands sore and full of nicks. Right before five, Dorothy Ann's typical arrival time, he remembered to check the mail. Returning with a hefty stack, he saw Masika's letter first thing as always. For some reason, he found himself anxious to read. He made a cup of coffee before finally picking it up.

Noticed something. Never get tired of you. Know I act like the touches and hand-holding mean little. If I told you that you meant the world to me, would you believe me? Dream of running away with you, I do. Dream of a world where you don't have to go home to tears and slamming doors. Wish you could come home to me instead. Can't help but wonder if you feel the same. Think I know the answer, though. Just too scared to admit it.

The letter slipped from his grasp. Covering his mouth, he stifled a sob. Picking it up once again, he brought it to its home amongst the other letters. He sat idle for an incredibly long time after. It was only a matter of days before the dress' completion, and he couldn't be without her much longer.

***

Masika didn't expect Aiden to invite her out to the barn. In fact, she had trouble withholding her suspicion, especially after sending him such a vulnerable and foolish confession. She had no idea why he wanted to see her in person after everything that transpired.

She had helped Herb a little with bills, but kept most of her pay-checks to herself. Doing so saved up enough for a bus ticket, food, and a couple weeks of travel.

This potential trip to the barn complicated things. For starters, she had planned on breaking the news to Aiden via letter. Short, sweet, quick, and she wouldn't have to see his reaction. Now, she struggled to decide if she wanted to tell him at all, not knowing if she could handle the heartbreak that would surely result.

A part of her wondered if he could come with. Yet she was unable to see Aiden, someone who had never once left his hometown, gung-ho about completely starting over. Aiden enjoyed familiarity and routine. She couldn't rob him of old comforts.

At first, she planned to ignore the request to meet up and leave a few days early. Every time she started packing, regret ate away at her, panic following shortly after. Wanting to see Aiden again badly, she caved into her emotions and wound up agreeing. She promised herself she would flee Alabama immediately after.

That Saturday Herb drove her to the barn, not wanting her to walk the whole way alone. Masika took comfort in knowing that Abeje would give Aiden a ride and he wouldn't have to walk either. The drive there proved awkward, she could tell Herb sensed something was off. Like usual, he said nothing. Only a quick, "love you," before she got out at the gate.

Heading up the winding path, ridden with anxiety, she ran over the plan in her head: spend time with Aiden, get her things from home, head for the bus stop. As the barn came into view, she cautiously approached, still half-expecting some horrible prank or ambush.

Not a thing out of place, she continued inside. Aiden sat by a boom-box, his back turned from the entrance. He'd made a small fire-pit, feeding it with sticks. Not hearing her come in, he was only alerted when she cleared her throat.

Leaping up, he barreled towards her, crushing her into a deep hug. She couldn't help but grin into his shoulder. When he pulled away, she swatted tears.

"Surprised you still wanna see me," she voiced.

Aiden traced a circle in the dirt with his foot, ghost of bruises still lingered on his arms and face. Masika frowned deeply as he left her side to retrieve a box. Beaming, he extended his arms towards her. Thunder shook the whole barn as she stared at what he held.

"What's this?" she took it, a nervous glint shimmering in her eyes.

As she opened it, pools of baby blue fabric spilled out the sides. Tossing the box, she unfurled a knee-cut sundress, tiny plush blueberries dotting the waist. Aiden observed her surprised reaction, smiling softly when she hugged the dress close to her chest.

"Some kind of joke?" Her words were a lot harsher than intended.

Aiden shook his head as she ran her hands all over the fabric, the seams, tracing every little detail and hiccup. A carnal part of her desired to smell it, as she knew with certainty it would smell like Aiden. Like home.

So that was the first thing she did, excusing herself to a secluded part of the barn. She buried her nose in the soft, gentle waves of the garment. Inhaled Aiden's smell, and oh, was petrichor divine as always. She found herself burrowing her face into it and had to restrain herself. *Fuck*, she thought.

Focusing instead on putting on the dress, she felt so odd without her signature blocky hoodie and baggy jeans. Keeping her head tilted upwards, she avoided looking down at her body as she pulled on the garment. Why was she so terrified to look at herself?

Masika returned to Aiden and he skipped up to her excitedly. He played with the ends of the dress briefly before crossing his arms playfully.

"Really like it," Masika said over the sound of rain pattering against the exterior of the building. Her hands twirled anxiously in front of her waist, "Made it yourself?" Aiden nodded. "That's impressive."

He drew closer and she stood her ground. Gently dusting off her shoulders, he glimpsed her exposed collarbones. Masika tore away, walking over to the boombox where her backpack sat.

"Brought some albums," she said, rummaging through her bag. "What you in the mood for?"

Aiden joined her as she lay out the cassettes in rows. After reading each title, he pointed to one towards the middle. Masika craned her neck to read it.

"'*Young, Gifted & Black.*' Don't think I've listened yet."

The cassette was swept out of her grip and put into the boombox. Aiden grinned with excitement, exchanging glances with Masika. His eyes kept falling to her limbs and muscles. She couldn't fathom why exactly, nor why she found herself doing the same. Only she admired his fat arms laden with stretch marks, peeking down at his legs; parts of him that warmed and held her on a regular basis. A sudden wave of arousal subdued her as she considered what was beneath his clothing. She imagined how his bare thighs would feel in her grasp.

When the first track began, the two moved not an inch, Aretha Franklin's vocals gracing their presence. Masika hugged her knees, left cheek falling onto them as she watched him sway his head. She too enjoyed the song, and let it be known as it ended.

"This was a good choice," she stated over the fading vocals and instruments.

Aiden's reached for her as another song began to play. *Daydreamin' and I'm thinkin' of you* rung out, airing out the pair's dirty laundry in the process. They both chuckled nervously before Aiden got to his feet, helping her stand.

Masika and Aiden shared a tiny joint, loitering in the center of the barn the whole time. Eventually, Aiden took Masika's hand as he had a couple hits. She blushed, gazing at the dirt floor beneath their feet. Right as the blunt reached its end, the next track rolled in.

Aiden ran over to crank the volume to max, drowning out the downpour and thunder. His shoulders bounced to the beat, breaking out into bigger motions. He danced over to Masika, who shyly covered her face and giggled. A grin broke out as he gently pried her limbs away, taking them into his own. The movements began slowly—arms swinging in sync and low laughs escaping their lips—but soon she got into a groove.

He was offbeat, too busy devouring her shape. Letting go of his hands and spinning, she landed facing the other direction. Her own touch roamed her shoulders, sinking to waist, then hips. Masika looked over at Aiden, beckoning him. Enticed, Aiden drew closer, hips moving once again as he wrapped his arms around her waist.

Another song, much slower, began shortly after. Masika turned around to face him. With the shyest smile, she draped her arms over his shoulders.

"Slow dance fits better."

Aiden dipped his head in agreement, gently holding her figure. Swaying side-to-side, they fell into an easy rhythm against the vocals. She wound up embracing Aiden, holding the back of his head tenderly. Right as the chorus hit, the boombox sputtered and crackled.

Aiden groaned in annoyance and peeled away from Masika, making a mad dash to it. He ejected the cassette, holding it on his fingertips and investigating for damage. While he did so, she hugged herself, lips tightening into a frown. She inhaled deeply before speaking against the pitter-patter of the rain.

"Why you entertaining me?"

Mid-switching albums, he looked over in confusion. Masika trembled as she stared, Aiden getting to his feet and steadily approaching.

"First the makeup, then Abeje gave me your old razors with your letter the other day. Now this dress... Doing this shit could get us hurt, so why? Why waste time on me? Why spend all your energy on somebody who's done nothing but get ya in trouble? Good for nothing kid, I am. Good for no one, not even you. Not even you..."

Buried beneath the thorns of each word lay panic. Aiden opted to glance at her hands. Running a lone finger down her palm lines, a droplet landed on overlapped digits. Aiden captured the tears pouring down Masika's face as he finally looked at her, gazes snapping together.

"Worth it to you? Why?" She whispered, voice fraying.

Aiden answered with a tender kiss. Noses collided for a brief second as Masika melted into it, grasping the back of his head and waist tightly. She cried with each kiss that followed until Aiden pulled away, wiping her face again and eliciting a chuckle.

Another cassette, this time *Mothership Connection*, was put in and music refilled the barn. Aiden joined Masika on a pile of blankets sitting by the fire. He kissed her a thousand more times, starting at her mouth and leading to the rest of her body. Neck, collarbones, chest, further as he lifted the dress. Noisy breaths escaped her nose as it grew harder to maintain control. His hot breaths against her thighs brought her over the brink.

The album reached the end. The two lay intertwined, Masika's head against Aiden's chest. A choir of rain and wind replaced the tunes as she held onto him tightly, believing he would slip away at any moment. Words bobbed in her throat, but nothing came out. There was nothing to say besides the one thing she was afraid to admit. She closed her eyes and let Aiden's warmth soothe all fear. When he started to snore, she silently wept.

Chapter Twenty

September 1994

Aiden craved a stargazing moment on the beach. It took Masika a week to muster the energy to oblige.

Since taking the bus to Daytona, she'd been wrapped in strings. Strings of anxiety, paranoia, and errant thoughts gradually sank deeper into her skin. Threatened to slice her up while she tried to save face for Aiden. For days she stayed cooped up in the room despite his suggestions to explore the city.

Admittedly, her dirty hands had ruined the trip for her, refusing to tell Aiden even though he saw right through. He stayed by her side the whole time, eagerly snuffing out his disappointment to ensure her comfort. She appreciated it more than she could express.

It was Friday when Masika brought up his idea. Aiden jumped at the opportunity and they headed down around eleven p.m. Fingers clasped together tightly during the promenade. She relished in the cool night breeze and, for a moment, her brain allotted her a breather. She enjoyed the warmth of Aiden's palm and grin stretched across his face. Internally fawning over his cute nose and kind eyes, she missed crossing the threshold between sand and concrete.

Without warning, Aiden broke out into a sprint towards the shore. Masika ran after him with a yelp, "Be careful, we left your cane!"

Skidding to a stop right at the edge of the water, he stumbled a bit before falling to his knees. He clutched his heart as he looked up at the vast sky. While Nevada certainly boasted more stars, the view still delighted. She trailed slowly to his side, head tilted skyward. They stood in silence until Aiden got on his feet.

"I have a couple blunts rolled," he informed, digging into his pockets.

"Didn't forget the lighter this time?" Masika teased. He flipped her off and she smirked, "Right here?"

Aiden smirked back. Blunt between his digits, he brought a lighter to it. Masika watched him inhale a hefty hit before passing it to her. Taking it from him, a jolt coursed through her body as their fingertips brushed together. With a shake of her head, she took a hit. All these years later and he could still send shocks through her whole body with a simple touch. Lost in thoughts and memories, she didn't notice Aiden waving a hand to get her attention, a muffled snap alerting her.

"Sorry."

"No worries, I have something for you."

He fished an object from his pocket as Masika put her hands on her hips in anticipation. A necklace dangled from his palm in one smooth movement.

"What's this?" she asked.

"I bought it in Jamaica while you weren't looking," he motioned for her to turn around. When she did, he put the necklace around her neck. She thumbed the red carnelian pendant laying against her chest. "Do you like it?" he asked.

"Yes," she paused, eyes full of disappointment in herself. "Sorry I'm not good at showing it."

"I know you've been really stressed. It's alright, love."

Aiden suggested they get the beach towel after finishing the blunt. Scoping out a spot a few yards away from the shoreline, Masika shouldered off her bag to retrieve the towel as Aiden waited. Right as she laid it down, he retched, making it only a couple steps before vomiting on the sand. She sprang up in concern at once.

"Holy shit, you okay?"

Aiden slowly unfolded from his crouching position and wiped his mouth.

"Yeah. Just been throwing up a lot recently," he admitted.

Her face soured, "Not stressed from dealing with me, are you?"

He shook his head with a chuckle, "Of course not. I'm okay, promise."

Hours of cuddling up under the stars passed. Before Masika knew it, the sun threatened to breach the horizon. Its blinding light illuminated Aiden's sleeping face in her lap. She'd dissociated for most of the night, but it wasn't bad like it usually was. In fact, she felt tranquil. Aiden soothed her expertly without even trying. So, despite her chaotic thoughts, she'd been able to enjoy the serenity of the beach and his company.

Another violent retch later and Aiden was vomiting in the sand again. He threw up three times and Masika was sure he'd emptied his stomach in the process. Packing up quickly, she approached to wipe his mouth with her sleeve.

"Let's go back to the room, seem really sick."

He backed away slightly, "Actually, I was gonna run to the convenience store. Grab some snacks," he responded with an unsure expression. "I'll walk you to the room, grab my cane and head out."

"You sure?"

"Yeah, let's go."

On the ride up the elevator, anxiety reclaimed Masika's body and mind. Aiden leaned against a wall, pallid and sweaty. He forced a smile.

"I'm okay," he told her.

She didn't buy it. Rather than resist his wish to journey to the store, she stayed quiet. Neither of them conversed until eight minutes later when Aiden was on his way out. She gently took him by the arm.

"Aiden, stay safe out there and don't push yourself. Come back to me unharmed," she kissed him deeply before giving him a hug. "I love you."

"I love you," he signed as he slipped out the door.

She backed up all the way onto the bed, collapsing. Her gaze roamed the beige ceiling, painting pictures of the stars from hours earlier. She saw Aiden, too, sick and heaving. Taking a deep breath, she knew he had a good head on his shoulders. If he was withholding information, it was for a reason.

Turning on the television for background noise, she got under the comforter. Underneath, she traced the lengthy scar on her torso with her index, the same finger toying with her lips. She cried, rife with worry.

Right when she numbed out and nearly fell asleep, she heard a *click*. Groggily sitting up, she watched Aiden storm towards the bed. His bleary eyes looked past her at the far wall. Masika rubbed her face in attempt to wake up, sensing his strife.

"Aiden, what's the matter? You okay?"

Not responding, he clutched something in his hands. Guilt stretched across his face, he put down what he was holding and robotically moved away.

"What—" she tried to conceal her shock, but he broke down into sobs, pacing frantically. She swallowed hard, "Aiden? Aiden, come here my love."

Aiden joined her, doubling over and devolving increasingly into hysterics. Masika picked up three positive pregnancy tests with one hand. She asked if he was okay with touch and he furiously shook his head. Opting to let him cry it out, she watched with an increasing feeling of helplessness.

After several minutes, the tears subsided and he stared emptily at the hotel television. This went on for an hour as Masika, too, stared off into space. Finally, with a serious expression on his face, he began signing.

"I know I don't seem happy. I am, but I'm also shocked," he explained.

"Me too, I'm sorry," Masika whispered.

"It's okay, love." He paused, nervously biting his lip, "Is it bad I want to try?"

"Try what?"

"Raising a kid with you. I think we could."

She stared at him, "Sure about that?"

He nodded, taking both of her hands with a sincere smile, kissing each before responding again.

"Yes. You have plenty of money, right? And I still have the apartment in Nevada with two rooms, so we can just convert the guest room into a nursery. It'll be so nice..."

"On the run though—"

"So? Does that mean we can't have a family? Or that we aren't *supposed* to?"

Aiden was right. Admittedly, the thought of starting a family with him sounded nothing short of a dream come true. She pictured a child running happily around a luscious yard and into her arms. Hugging herself, Masika softly grinned at Aiden.

"Are you sure? Up to you in the end, not just me."

"Yes, and if I change my mind? I know you have my back."

Embracing, the two cried in each other's arms. When she pulled away, she placed her hands on his belly. Beaming at her warmly, he enticed her into a long kiss.

Chapter Twenty-One

July 1989

Not much changed after Masika disappeared, if you didn't count the hole in Aiden's heart.

Abeje successfully moved out of Dorothy Ann's, leaving Aiden alone to deal with her antics. Thankfully, the woman spent most of her time black out drunk, dismissing his presence outright. Having gotten a job at a meat plant within walking distance of the barn—still abandoned—it paid decent enough money. Planning on saving up to leave just as Abeje did, the barn was his escape in the meantime.

During a particularly sweltering summer night, Aiden decided to stay later than usual. It was the two-year anniversary of Masika's disappearance and he needed to mourn in private. Rolling two blunts, he occasionally glanced at the dusty boombox, untouched after their final night together.

The morning after replayed in his mind: frantically running straight to Masika's home, hoping she was safe and sound, only finding Herb wilted and grief-stricken in his chair. Nowadays, Aiden couldn't even look at the man across church pews. He knew Herb still grieved. Knowing he wasn't the only one would just make things worse.

Smoking the blunts, he hummed to himself between hits. Masika's smile gleamed in the back of his mind, taunting him further. Allowing himself to cry, the sobs drowned out insect nightlife. Like always, he questioned why she left, why she couldn't stay after everything the two had been through. Unable to really blame her, he still longed for a reason.

He wished she had taken him with. In the wake of gentrification, the town's population had doubled in size. So did the number of cops, arrests being at an all-time high. Dorothy Ann always cracked up poking fun at mugshots in the newspaper. Aiden didn't find it remotely funny and had no clue how she did, considering her husband's fate.

Once he was high enough that everything mattered significantly less, he headed home. The five-mile stretch proved treacherous as always. Halfway along, sweat started to pour down his forehead and into his lashes.

Winding up tying his hoodie around his waist, he approached an unruly cornfield. Close to the rickety fencing sat a police car. Aiden tensed—it hadn't been there earlier—and squinted to see if anyone was inside. A chill went up his spine when he found it to be vacant and he quickly turned back the way he came.

Killing another hour in the barn before making his way back, he hoped the patrol car had vanished. The cornfield came into view, and he saw the vehicle parked in the grass, close to the edge of corn rows. The sight of a figure in the driver's seat made him backpedal. *Fuck it, I'll cut through downtown.* Feigning a calm demeanor, he began to walk towards the road, facing away as a car door slammed shut behind him.

"Hold it right there, son."

Aiden's sense of control collapsing into pieces, the man's boots crunched in the grass as he approached. He sheepishly faced the officer, careful not to look him in the eyes.

"It's awful late for a stroll, don't ya think?" the cop challenged, crossing his hairy arms over his chest.

Aiden nodded in agreement, reading the name on his badge. Dalton. Hugging himself, his mind wandered and a strange sense of deja vu washed over him in steady tides. Each word the officer spoke lured out memories he'd willingly repressed. *Could it be...?*

"Where ya headed?" He held on tight to his belt as he got closer to Aiden. "Better yet, are you even from town? Or maybe someone without a home, searchin' for a place to sleep? Hm..."

Ready to crawl out of his skin from the way the sleaze scanned him, Aiden rubbed his arm. After all, he had absolutely zero way of responding even if he wanted to. The perverse glint flickered to irritation.

"What's your name?" he tried again, stepping in time with Aiden. The man suddenly snatched his arm into a vice grip. "You're startin' to piss me off, boy! I've asked you about a dozen goddamn questions and you haven't answered a single one. I oughta slap a pair of cuffs on you right now, haul you back to the station."

Aiden tried to tear away as Dalton pulled him close, slipping a free claw under his tank strap. When he found a bra beneath, a barbarous grin sprawled across his face.

"Ah... Interestin'," he popped the strap with a snide snicker, "Tell ya what? If ya put that pretty mouth to use, I'll let ya go. Ain't nobody gotta get in trouble, ya hear?"

Mustering the strength to shove the officer off, he broke into a sprint, managing to make it a couple feet before Dalton tackled him to the ground. Screaming and kicking as the man climbed on top of him, frustration rippled across the officer's wrinkled face.

"Stay the fuck still—"

One headbutt froze Dalton in place as Aiden escaped from beneath him. The officer yelped and curled up in pain, Aiden scrambling to his backpack. Fumbling the contents, he searched for a weapon. The handle of a blade slid into his grasp as Dalton jumped on him once more. He managed to bat away his arms and remove the sheath, crying out as he thrust the weapon forward. The blade drove straight into Dalton's throat.

Blood spewed onto Aiden's face. Lips reddened as Dalton gurgled, hands clumsily attempting to remove the blade. It was no use; he fell forward with a solemn thud.

Aiden shoved him off and rose, scooping a rock from the ground. He staggered back, Dad's crumpled corpse flashing in his mind.

As he bashed the rock into the officer's head over and over again, viscera gradually blanketed his face. He didn't stop until he barely contained a wail of rage building in his lungs. *FUCK YOU! FUCK YOU! FUCK YOU!* Throwing the rock, he ripped the bloodied badge from Dalton's shirt.

Fuck you.

Holding on with a death grip, it took a full minute to actualize the gore before him. When he did, his breath hitched.

Aiden made a mad dash through the cornfield in the opposite direction. Panic plagued his senses, leaving his breaths ragged and short. An image of the officer's corpse sat pretty in his mind, unrelenting, reminding him of what he had done.

Once he exited the endless rows of stalks, he skidded to a stop. Taking a gander at the field--desolate as usual—he kept running all the way to Abeje's house. She was close, close enough he wouldn't get caught. The shroud of late-night rural countryside would leave him unbothered for the half mile he needed to travel.

Not bothering to knock upon arrival—the kitchen window had no lock after all—he approached the pane, opened it, and shimmied through. Ending up on top of the sink, he once again took a moment to catch his breath. He threw himself onto the ground, groaning upon impact and staring up at the ceiling. The adrenaline fully waned and tears slipped out.

Footsteps echoed and Abeje appeared in the doorway, pistol aimed right at the window. Flicking the light on, she saw her brother on the ground and at once lowered her weapon.

"What the hell are you doing?" Moving closer, she saw the blood coating Aiden's face and torso, "What the fuck?"

Aiden turned onto his side and sobbed. Abeje knelt, investigating his state.

"Are you hurt?" Aiden shook his head in response and she stuttered, "Then... then whose fucking blood is that?"

Aiden sat up, eyes dulled. He let go of the bloodied cop badge he'd been gripping in his hand.

"Shit..." she scrambled to her feet. "No fucking way, tell me you're joking."

His undone belt and shudders spoke plenty. Abeje swallowed hard as Aiden threw the badge across the room, muffled sobs escaping his throat. He stared at red-stained hands in disbelief and she drew closer.

"Hey, hey, it's okay," Abeje comforted him. "Come on, I'll get a shower running. We can talk after."

The spray of liquid felt wrong, undeserved. Aiden let the blood run off his skin as he stared at his feet. Once reconvened in the living room, Abeje poured two glasses of scotch. An empty notebook page implored him to explain what happened. He swiped one of the glasses off the table and downed the liquor.

Wiping his mouth with a grimace, he began to write. Fear largely worn off by this point, he wrote a flat and depersonalized account. He remembered his backpack had been left behind and lost control of the pen. He sighed, scribbled out the word and hastily finished up the story. Turning the paper to Abeje and himself away from her, she read it in less than a minute.

"Holy fuck. He didn't... y'know...? You killed him before he..." she trailed off as Aiden nodded. "Good. Fucking bastard. We gotta get your stuff, c'mon."

Even though he was terrified, he tagged along on her motorcycle. Driving to the cornfield, they parked on a levee and checked for bystanders before making their way through the thick stalks. Aiden's breath quickened the closer they drew to the scene of the crime. As the end neared, he steeled himself.

Abeje stepped out first, whisper-shouting *"Goddamn"* as she shone a flashlight. The beam irradiated Dalton's nonexistent face. Aiming it away towards her brother's items, brain matter littered the grass. Redirecting the light, she covered her mouth. Scouring the area nearby, she found a rock two-times the size of Aiden's fist. It laid a foot or two away, doused in deep red. He came forward, picking up his backpack with relief.

"You messed his ass up."

Aiden glared at her briefly before the officer's walkie roared to life. The twins jumped at the sound of a woman's voice crackling in and out.

"10-20? Officer Landon, do you copy?"

"We need to get out of here, c'mon!" Abeje exclaimed, stepping carefully over the officer's body and grabbing Aiden's arm.

The ride home blurred, Abeje grilling him the minute they re-entered her place. Aiden half-listened, still shaken. Panic rose in his sister's voice as she demanded a response.

"It's only a matter of time before someone finds him, and by extension, your Black ass. What are you gonna do?" Aiden delivered a glance of defeat. Abeje shook her head as she leaned against her fridge, "So you're just gonna give up? Let them lock you away?"

Aiden covered his face. He had no planned course of action, nothing about this night was normal. Complacence in his everyday routine made it impossible to process the entire situation. He knew only that he didn't want to go to jail. If life was difficult already, it'd be even worse locked up. Abeje allowed silence to pass, tightening her jaw.

"I might have an idea."

Aiden rose from his sunken posture. Abeje clasped her hands together and stepped towards him, suddenly radiating.

"Maybe it's as simple as a quick switch. I mean, we're identical. Why don't you become me, I become you. Take your name, take your crime. Then, you'd be free to do whatever you want!" She put her hands up at his shock, "I know it sounds crazy, okay? But seriously, do you have any better ideas?"

Aiden didn't respond. The last thing he wanted to do was put Abeje in danger. Her protective tendencies would be her downfall in this case, so he simply put his face in his palms. She stormed off when she realized he was more against the idea than for it.

As hands on the grandfather clock turned, Aiden re-evaluated the circumstances. Abeje had always been a wild card, an adrenaline junkie. Maybe this is what she needed, not a nine-to-five at the local burger joint. And where she'd find thrill, he would find peace—something he wasn't sure could exist if he landed in prison. When he settled on a decision, he found Abeje in her room, pouting.

"I know it's a crazy idea. But I honestly think you've been through enough," she began, pausing at sight of the notebook rooked under his arm. Her expression brightened with cautious optimism, "You changed your mind... There would be no turning back. You know that, don't you?"

He turned the page to face her: *Let's ditch this shit hole.*

Abeje sprung to her feet. "We're gonna have to make some changes."

She started by shaving most of her beard off and plucking her eyebrows to mimic the shape of Aiden's. When the shears were ready for him, an odd eagerness shrouded his anxiety. Abeje made him stand in front of the mirror as she investigated his hair situation. She reminded him it would need to be chopped and Aiden readily agreed. Still, he closed his eyes at the first snip, a voice in the back of his head hissing that he was making a mistake. Soon enough, no weight remained on his head. He was terrified until Abeje tapped his shoulder.

"How does that look?"

Opening his eyes, he gasped. Previously, his hair had been down to his ass, kept in a long braid to appease Dorothy Ann. Running his digits through the mere half-inch that remained on his scalp, he couldn't help but... smile? Looking so much more like Abeje, wearing her clothes granted him even more euphoria. She snickered behind him.

"By the looks of it, we shoulda done this a lot sooner," she brushed tufts of hair off his shirt. "You look happier. So will I once I pick a wig from my collection."

Aiden turned to her, eyebrows drawn inward. *Wig collection?* Abeje, sensing his shock, simply laughed.

Taking him to her 'office'—the room she usually forbade him and Dorothy Ann from—Aiden soon learned why. A wooden table spanned across three walls, covered in tools and mannequin heads. Open cabinets were stacked above it, a single rolling chair in the middle and dozens of shelves. The sheer amount of makeup containers astonished Aiden; Abeje simply threw him an amused glance.

"Once I left Mama's house, I started exploring. Drove out to the city, went to a gay club, had my whole life changed." Delicately picking up a wig, she beamed, "Been practicing makeup since, got a bunch of wigs... Dunno, being a boy never felt right, ya know?"

Aiden remembered the giddiness when Herb read her as feminine. Browsing her collection, he locked in on a dark brown afro. Looking between the mannequin head and Abeje, he tried to picture it on her frame. The texture resembled his when not styled. Abeje left the one she was messing with and took the afro off its stand.

"Think this is the one, huh? I thought so too, your hair's just like this."

Pulling it on, she adjusted it and posed. Aiden's hands clammed up—a better version of himself stood before him—and he had to shake off his plaguing fear.

What he couldn't shake was feeling the switch was inevitable. The trading of cards, so to speak, was nothing short of destiny. Soon, hope enveloped his doubts, only growing stronger the longer he and Abeje prepared. By the time she had her bag packed, certainty overwrought every other emotion.

"Alright, here's what we're gonna do. I packed you some essentials and some sentimental crap. Before you leave town, we need to get anything we need or want from Mom's, 'cause we can't come back once we go." Aiden drew in a deep breath, waiting for her to continue, "We're gonna take my motorcycle, you drive."

Aiden's jaw slacked. He had *no* clue how to drive a motorcycle. Abeje sensed his hesitation and tutted, "Sorry bro. If you take my name, you gotta take my bike too. Gonna be real suspicious otherwise. I promise you it's easy to figure out." With no choice but to concede, he let her finish, "Anyways, we'll both pack up and head out. Drop me off at a bus stop. Go anywhere you want, just... try to get out of the bible belt, will you?"

Don't have to tell me twice, he thought. They relocated to the living room where he wrote two questions.

Where will you go? Do you want to know where I'll be?

Abeje hummed in thought, "That's a good question...I dunno. Kinda wanna go to Canada, if I can. Somebody's gonna have to smuggle me up there, though. And *yeah* I wanna know where you'll be! Gonna be worrying my ass off otherwise."

With a dreamy smile, Aiden imagined icy desert winds against his scalp, paired with an unpolluted view of the endless night sky. *I need to go to where the stars are. Where would that be?* He asked her.

"Probably somewhere out West, like Nevada. Just fuckin' desert and wasteland for miles. I'm sure the stars would be gorgeous out there."

Then Nevada it is.

Much to Aiden and Abeje's delight, it took a mere fifteen minutes for him to get a handle of the motorcycle mechanics. Driving them to Dorothy Ann's, albeit slowly, he tried to ignore the faint cop sirens echoing in the distance. They were running out of time.

Pulling into the driveway, he parked and they both jumped off. Jogging to the front door, Aiden wrangled his keys out of his pocket. He was unsurprised to hear snores from the living room.

The twins snuck past Dorothy Ann, passed out cold in her favorite chair, and into Aiden's room. Abeje closed the door behind her and they sprung to action. She picked at the remnants of her belongings in boxes while Aiden wracked his brain for anything he absolutely needed.

Starting with his music collection—or rather, Masika's—he packed it along with his cassette player and headphones. He couldn't forget Mr. Snuggles, of course. He then packed his sewing kit, as well as a couple smaller projects he'd been slacking on. If he was going to be on the run he needed shit to do. Throwing in a few bras to the mix, he backtracked to the bathroom, grabbing his toothbrush and toothpaste. When he returned, he gave Abeje the thumbs up to leave. She jerked her own towards Aiden's bed.

"What about that box?" she asked quietly.

Aiden's expression softened. A tattered blue shoe box called out to him from the bottom of the bed. He shoved all emotional pain down, deciding to save it—but still wound up taking the box with him. That final item filled the backpack to capacity. Swinging it over his shoulders, he pointed his head towards the bedroom window. Abeje nodded in understanding, unlocking it.

"Good thinking, leave the keys here," she whispered, already halfway outside.

Aiden threw the house key carelessly to the floor and followed. The two tiptoed around the house, Abeje in the lead. Shushing him, she stopped at a brief flash of red and blue lights. Aiden pressed against the wall, taking her hand and squeezing it. She squeezed back until the colors vanished from the street.

"Fuck... Yeah, it's time to get the fuck out of here."

The two made a run for Abeje's bike. A mere two minutes later and Aiden was ready to go.

He drove the scarce streets of his hometown. The only place he ever knew, born and raised, gone like nothing. Scarce town lights paved way to darkness, nothing but plains and trees for almost four miles. Aiden's heartbeat against his ribcage threatened to end him, the adrenaline rush both petrifying and elating. He felt free—he felt *hunted.*

He felt terrified for his sister. Abeje talked a big game, but he didn't know if she could handle being a fugitive. Yet, she seemed serene as he pulled up to the bus stop and parked. She hopped off, taking a couple steps away to drop her backpack on the bench. As she did, the actuality of the situation hit Aiden with the weight of a train. Detecting his anxiety, Abeje brought him in for a hug.

"It's gonna be okay. I promise I'll be safe, just look out for yourself, alright?" She noticed his soft weeps and wiped his tears, "I know this is scary, but I believe in you Aiden."

The name drop sent chills down his spine, at the same time giving him resolve. He hugged Abeje again, this time significantly tighter. Moving away, he took a deep breath; there were so many things he wished to say to her, but no means. Abeje clamped a palm down on his shoulder.

"You better get out of here," she hurried, pulling out a wad of bills and handing it to him. "This should be enough money to get you where you need to go. Use it wisely."

Aiden stashed the cash away before returning to the motorcycle seat. Bringing the engine to life, he wielded Abeje's helmet as he watched her take a seat on the bench.

"Goodbye Aiden," she called.

With that, he took off into the night.

Chapter Twenty-Two

July 1989

Aiden stopped only twice for gas, tearing through Mississippi and speeding across Louisiana. The six-hour drive proved wretched on his body, but the concern of being caught kept him on the road.

A swarm of anxious thoughts never ceased to terrorize him. They drowned out pockets of noise the few times he drove through cities. He had stuck mostly to back roads, not wanting to alert any authorities on the interstate. By the time he reached Shreveport, he was practically falling off the bike from exhaustion.

A quiet, hardly occupied motel close to the main roads enticed him for a stay. He parked the bike in the back lot of the building, keeping it hidden. Hunched over, weighed down by the heaviness of his backpack, he entered the establishment. A front desk attendant greeted him.

Approaching, he shrugged off the bag so he could reach into his pockets. Fishing out Abeje's driver's license and a hundred-dollar bill, a relatively quick transaction followed. Aiden used his head and fingers to communicate that he wanted a room for the night. The receptionist booked him without a fuss and he could hardly contain his relief.

Once he had a room key in hand, Aiden went straight for the elevators. An "out of order" sign mocked him and he openly groaned. It took five minutes to find the stairs. At the bottom of the staircase, he read his room key. *Well, at least it's only two flights.*

He painstakingly conquered each stair until he reached the second floor. Debilitating pains shot through every single limb. By this point, he wanted to crawl the rest of the way. Resisting the temptation, he made his way to 204, walking agonizingly slow. By the time he reached the room, his breaths were reduced to wheezes.

A few minutes later, in safety, Aiden slumped to the floor. He sobbed from his body swelling, hot to the touch. No longer concerned about being seen, he eventually crawled into bed. Dorothy Ann's voice screamed in his head to check for bugs, but he couldn't give less of a shit given the current situation.

Abeje took his name, his place, his crime, and let him run free disguised as her old self. Why on Earth would she do such a thing? Unable to wrap his mind around it nearly eight hours later, the encounter with Officer Dalton kept replaying in snippets. He was desperate to stop crying, but he couldn't. The influx of mixed emotions—guilt, anxiety, and fear—kept the tears flowing.

He wound up crying himself to sleep, not bothering to tuck in beneath the covers.

***

Aiden departed from the hotel around seven a.m., wanting to grab breakfast and fill up the motorcycle tank. Driving to the closest gas station, a block away from the motel, he was dismayed to find all the pumps out of order.

Heading in the opposite direction, he reached the town outskirts. He stumbled upon a gas station with an adjacent diner. Stomach gnawing at him, he decided to give the restaurant a chance.

After grabbing gas, he parked at the diner. A few individuals stood beside the entrance, cigarettes in hand, chatting. Quietly walking past to go inside, he ignored the dead silence that befell the group when he did. The interior instantly overstimulated his senses, almost every chair, booth, and table filled with loud customers. Scouring for an empty seat, he found one on the left side of the bar.

As he sat, the crowd quieted. Not enough to be obvious, but enough to alert Aiden that he was being watched. Dozens of blue and green eyes locked onto him as he gripped his chest. For all he knew, *everyone* knew who he was and what he did. Bracing for trouble, he was pleasantly surprised when a young Black girl came bounding up to him from behind the bar.

"Hey love, the name's Bee. I'll be your server today," she said sweetly, handing him a paper menu. "Want anything to drink?"

Aiden glanced at her notepad before pointing to it. Their train of thoughts clicked and she handed it over, nostalgia crashing against him. It'd been a while since he used pen and paper for anyone but Abeje. Writing down both his drink and food order, he passed the notepad to Bee.

"A sweet tea, eggs, and grits? Good choices all around. I'll let the chef know," she flashed him a tiny grin and disappeared into the kitchen.

Once he had a sweet tea in hand, he spent the time it took making the food lost in thought. Absentmindedly looking at a tiny television mounted above the bar. It played a local news station, the anchors highlighting upcoming Shreveport events. Half-way through his tea, a breaking news story interrupted the program. The patrons' heads snapped to attention.

"Authorities in Pike Road, Alabama are searching for information regarding a homicide. Beloved Officer Dalton Landon was found deceased at his two-a.m. post. At this current time there are no suspects or leads. Anyone who has information regarding this homicide is encouraged to contact the Montgomery County Sheriff's Department as soon as possible. The suspect may be traveling across the country."

A steaming plate of eggs and grits was slid in front of Aiden. Blinking, he forced himself to smile at his waitress, swallowing his anxiety. Inhaling the platter, Aiden paid and hauled ass out of the building. The news had put him on edge and he needed to flee, needed to make even more distance between himself and Alabama. Louisiana wasn't enough; he wouldn't feel safe until desert sands crunched beneath his feet. One leg over the bike, a figure came running towards him.

"Wait! You forgot your stuff, sir," Bee called to him, effortlessly holding the backpack.

Aiden hopped off the bike, meeting her in the middle. Passing it to him, she chuckled a little when he nearly dropped it. "Seems like you got your whole life in there."

Little did Bee know, Aiden really did. Thanking her with a brisk nod, he didn't wait to see her go inside before speeding off.

***

Terrified of new developments on the murder, Aiden drove the next twenty-two hours of the journey straight. Even when his body threatened to shut down, he pushed on; only taking breaks to use the bathroom, eat snacks, and gas up. Twelve hours in, the motorcycle wobbled in the lane as he struggled to keep control of the vehicle. Sleep threatened to take him, but he wouldn't allow it, projecting a vision of countless stars in his brain to keep him running.

Aiden could hardly believe it when he passed the 'Welcome to Nevada' signage around seven in the morning. Time blurred, mixing in his mind. Before he knew it, he was in another motel room, limp and hurting atop a beige comforter. The fatigue and pain finally caught up to him and he slipped away without effort.

***

Following a well-needed eighteen hours of sleep, Aiden finished the final leg of his journey. He drove towards the California border, scoping out the towns adjacent to it. When he arrived in sweltering and desolate Cradyon (a puny, humdrum valley town), he knew he found his new home. As he looped the roads, he counted a fast-food restaurant, a diner, and an out-of-place Jamaican food shack. One gas station existed on the outskirts, next to the town's only grocery store. After glimpsing the neighborhoods in the area, he headed to the store, not thinking beyond more than the rumble of his stomach.

Once parked, he quickly counted his cash. He grimaced at notice of a mere one-hundred-dollar bill remaining in his wallet. His measly check and Abeje's offerings had disappeared. Stuffing it into the folds of his wallet, he headed inside. *I can panic after I eat. I need to fucking eat.*

Aiden entered the store, a mostly empty and lifeless building with a grand total of five people inside, including a lone cashier. Heading straight for the deli aisle, he grabbed chicken salad with a ham & cheese sandwich. Spending the next few minutes scanning each aisle, he wondered if there was anything else he needed. After all, he would likely have to sleep on the streets tonight.

During his perusing, he encountered an elderly woman stationed in front of various firewood packs. She anxiously reached out her hands just to reel them back. Watching with great sadness as she tried to lift the pack with the most wood, he went to her, getting her attention by tapping on one of the shelves. He motioned for her to let him try. She stepped aside, a pleased smile on her face as he loaded up the pack of wood. When he went to walk away, she gave him pause.

"Wait now... I ain't ever seen you around here before, young man."

Aiden's heart leapt into his throat. A portion of him worried she was aware of his identity and crimes, but her confident and charismatic aura dissuaded it. She seemed trustworthy, and he'd been lacking in positive human interactions. Pointing to his lips to let her know he couldn't speak, he hoped she would understand.

"Got it, you against walking with me for the rest of this trip? I could use your strength, if I'm being frank. Have a lot more heavy things that I need to get."

Politely nodding, he accompanied the woman around the grocery store; right after she insisted he add his items to her buggy.

In many of the aisles, she needed no aid, simply plucking the items from the shelf and dropping them into her cart. The whole time, she chatted about herself, telling Aiden she'd moved into town after living in Virginia for forty years. She spoke of a husband and a child, both of whom she shared a home with; her husband was a realtor, her daughter a writer. In terms of her own career, she boasted an impressive position as a principal.

When fifteen minutes passed and Aiden had not helped her even once, he realized what was actually going on. She craved a good connection and conversation just as much as he did. Aiden listened, absorbing the details she provided.

Before he knew it, the two were in line for check-out. He loaded the groceries onto the conveyor belt, earning a noisy sigh from the woman.

"Really don't have to do all that, now. I could've helped a little."

Aiden waved her off with a smile, assisting the cashier bag her items. A few minutes later, he shut the trunk to her SUV, now filled with her shopping haul.

"Why, thank you young man. I have a question for you, if I may," twirling her keys in her hand, she waited for Aiden to nod. When he did, she continued, "Something tells me you don't have a place to call home.

That maybe you're running away from a bad situation. If that's the case, I'd like to help you."

Trying to keep a neutral expression, he raised an eyebrow, requesting her to go on.

"I can do two things for you. First, my husband owns a two-bedroom apartment just a mile from here. Can't sell it for the life of him. Just sittin' there collecting dust; if you want it, it's yours. Second, if you need some income, I'm in dire need of a janitor at my school. The last guy quit 'cause he didn't realize most of the students were Black. Racist prick," she tutted and put her hands on her hips. "Point is I ain't against helping you get on your feet. You seem like a real good kid."

Aiden gave her his best smile and put up his hands as he shook his head. He couldn't involve this kind woman in his mess, no matter how good the offer seemed. She bowed.

"I understand, but listen here," digging into her purse, she fished out a bent, crinkled business card. She tapped the phone number under the words *Ruby Mae Seymour, Principal.* "Call me if you change your mind."

Heart wrenching in his chest as he walked back to his bike, he took a minute to scarf down his food items and throw away the trash.

Heading to the nearest hotel and booking a room, he took a break to sit in the lobby. His body had been pushed far beyond its limits based on the ache in his bones. He headed to the elevator at turtle speed, keeping the same pace as he headed down the hall of the third floor. This time, he went straight for the bathtub.

He felt a little more sane after the warm bath. Crawling from the bathroom into the bed, he grabbed the remote off the nightstand and tiredly flipped through channels. He craved sound, something to distract him from the anxious web of thoughts spinning in his head. Flip after flip, he found every noise he met grating and unbearable. Going through every available channel three times, halfway through the fourth run he threw the remote across the room.

Rage and frustration exploded from his throat in the form of a loud bellow. Jumping off the bed, he ripped the comforter off and tossed it to the floor. Repeatedly slamming his fists into it, hot tears poured down his face. He tore up the entire room, including his backpack, his belongings strewn about the dingy carpet. By the end of the outburst, he lay curled up in fetal position, rocking. He locked onto a singular item; that stupid, godawful shoe box.

Hours must have passed, Aiden's head empty as he resigned to staring at the baseboards of the room. At some point, he reached into his pocket and retrieved Ruby's business card. Replaying the offer in his mind over and over again until it seemed more tangible, he pictured himself sweeping a school bathroom, clad in a baggy jumpsuit. Imagined a home, not the Hell he grew up in, but a place just for him. Freedom danced on the tip of his tongue, taunting him.

Maybe, just maybe, he deserved to start over after all the fucked-up shit he'd been through.

***

Aiden didn't even wait a full twenty-four hours to contact Ruby. Not having any coins for a telephone call, he opted to find the school she worked at. This proved an easy task considering the town's size. A measly two minutes away from the hotel, Aiden discovered a square shaped building, gold plating on the front that matched the name on the card.

Everything that followed flew by. Ruby invited him over for dinner where he met her husband. Right then and there, he offered Aiden the aforementioned apartment. Ruby also re-offered the janitorial job. Despite the nausea of change trying to overtake him, he accepted both. The couple gave him some money to spend two more nights at the motel while they prepared the apartment.

Aiden spent those two days mostly in bed, giving his body a much needed rest. Not bothering to clean up the tornado of a room until the morning of check-out, he tidied up everything in about half an hour.

Ten minutes later, he rolled up to his new home, parking next to Ruby's blue car. Clean pavement led up to a set of stairs; the green, square exterior gave Aiden a cozy feeling. He headed straight inside.

Ruby's husband gave him a quick tour, guiding him through the reasonably sized living room and kitchen. Seeing the two bedrooms and bathroom upstairs last, most of the rooms boasted no furniture, which was at once addressed.

"Might need a 'lil maintenance here and there. The bedroom and guest room already got beds in them, fresh sheets 'n all," the older man informed, walking him downstairs to the main room. "You got a washing machine and dryer in the pantry. I wasn't able to furnish the rest of the place, but we can help take care of anything ya need. Don't be a stranger!"

Aiden hugged him without thinking. The man grinned into his shoulder, clapping his back. Pulling away, teary-eyed, he avoided his gaze. Feeling embarrassed, he looked at Ruby.

"We'll leave you to it, keys are on the counter," she stated. "Try and make yourself comfortable."

Once the pair left, Aiden did exactly that. Taking a hot bath, he stayed submerged for two hours, long after the water turned cold. Reality sunk in. *I have a home now.*

He thought of ways in which to decorate it, as well as the potential for a garden in the vast backyard. By the time he had a full image in his head, he scolded himself and got out of the tub. *I shouldn't get too ahead of myself.*

So he refocused his energy on unpacking his backpack. Once dried off, he sat cross-legged on his new bed and got to it. He started by emptying out the side pockets, mostly full of snacks and wadded up receipts. Then he emptied out the front, which held his cassette player, tapes, headphones, and sanitary products. As his fingers hovered over the zippers to the main compartment, he hesitated.

Rage flooded his every vein and he angrily unzipped, practically ripping the tattered shoe box out. Dalton's badge tumbled out with a thud. Slamming the box onto the bed, he stared at it with grief-stricken eyes. Conflicting emotions pooled and swirled around as he lifted the lid, a worn, yellow paper taunting him. He read the first sentence and shoved it into the bottom of the box. Wailing, he wound up curled up on the bed holding Mr. Snuggles, heart heavy yet so hollow.

***

"Mr. Aiden! Mr. Aiden!"

Aiden paused mid-task, mop in hand, to greet a little black girl tugging at his overalls. The lunch bell had just rung, signaling the children to file out of the classrooms. He had been getting ready to clean the bathrooms when the student approached, hiding something behind her back. Acknowledging her with a little wave, he let go of the mop and stepped away from the bucket.

"I drew you this!" she announced, brandishing a drawing on notebook paper and passing it to him. "Hope you like it!"

Before he could do anything else, she sprinted down the hallway. Aiden chuckled at the artwork. It depicted what he assumed was him, standing in the middle of a grassy field with a mop and broom in each limb. Neatly folding and tucking it into his pocket, he reminded himself to put it on his fridge later.

Two months into his new job, Aiden ran into no issues. He took up the janitor role with ease, attuned to a life of cleaning from his upbringing. Kids were gross, sure, but Dorothy Ann had been far worse. He had an easier job cleaning up after one-hundred kids than he ever did with that woman.

His new boss was much more than understanding of his physical limitations, too. More often than not, Ruby would scold him for pushing himself too far, forcing him to take frequent breaks at least every hour. Even sending staff to check on him, he was grateful to have such genuine care—a rare commodity these days.

To sweeten the deal, Aiden found zero trouble. He'd been following the case the best he could through news channels. It had soon run cold, Montgomery County Sheriff's Department practically begging for some kind of lead. Better yet, neither he nor Abeje had been reported missing. *That* he found to be surprising, but he assumed Dorothy Ann was probably too drunk to even notice their absence. Guess their jobs didn't give much of a fuck, either. He hoped and prayed it would stay that way.

Spending his weekdays working, he usually fell asleep around seven every night. Even with the breaks, the labor took a massive toll on his body each day. Sleep helped enough to rejuvenate him for the next workday, but on weekends he did his best to rest. Often finding himself sewing new clothes, the ones Abeje gave him now far too small for his frame; it delighted him to finally have control of his wardrobe. A sense of accomplishment each time enlightened him.

With the sense of accomplishment, grief usually followed. Every time he sewed, without fail, Masika's project overtook his thoughts. How could it not? She'd been the first person he ever made a full piece of clothing for, and he could never forget that dress, nor her shape in it as she twirled and danced.

Originally, he felt nothing but anger towards her disappearance. The longer time droned on, the longer he experienced freedom, it stung less and less. Still missing her dearly, the hope that she was alive drowned out her betrayal. Even if he never saw her again, he only wished for her safety. That's all that had ever mattered to him, really.

Every night, before bed, Masika crept into his thoughts. All the good memories flashed in bursts, leaving him emotionally vexed yet oddly tranquil. He wouldn't trade those experiences with her for the world, no matter how much it hurt to wake up all alone. No matter how much it killed him not knowing where she was, if she was safe or not. No matter how much time passed, his love never waned, not once. As he drifted to sleep, he would always imagine the warmth of her calloused yet soft hands.

There was no denying it; he would love her until his last breath.

Chapter Twenty-Three

September 1994

Ruby didn't so much as bat an eye when Aiden showed up a month into the school year. She conversed with him as if he hadn't been away at all. Once he divulged details of his vacation, he humbly requested if he could resume his stay.

"Of course. Everything is where you left it. And don't worry about comin' back to work unless you want to," she took a sip of coffee and smiled. "All I ask is you take care of yourself."

Aiden's heart warmed from Ruby's soothing words and he returned to the parking lot. As he bounded up to an older truck, Masika grinned at him from the passenger seat.

"All's well with the apartment?" Masika asked as she rolled down the window further.

"Yes, my key should still work," he told her before getting into the vehicle.

"Good," she turned to the driver, "let's go."

The driver turned the engine over as Masika gave directions, guiding him through town and to the apartment. The roads and desert sights made Aiden's heart flutter. This town had been the first proper home of his, after all, and he was excited to begin anew with Masika.

Aiden was curious about the man in the driver's seat, whom Masika referred to as an 'old friend.' This individual volunteered to be Aiden's doctor during the pregnancy, since the couple couldn't exactly pursue regular medical visits.

"Take a right onto this street, Mahpiya."

"Got it," Mahpiya acknowledged, clicking the turn signal.

Aiden's stomach surged as the apartment rolled towards him. Even though it had been less than a year, it felt like it had been eons since he waved goodbye to it. Masika got out first, opening the passenger door for him.

"Ready?" she asked.

"Yes."

Masika helped him out of the truck and up the stairs with a steady palm on his back.

Mahpiya followed in tow. Just as Ruby promised, everything was exactly how they left it. Walking into the living room, he blushed at the all too familiar staircase. Masika made tea while Mahpiya and Aiden conversed.

"It's good to finally meet you, Aiden," Mahpiya said with a firm hand-shake.

"It's nice meeting you too."

Mahpiya knew American Sign Language; in fact, he knew eight languages total. Masika told Aiden that before he picked them up. When Aiden asked Mahpiya about himself, he was surprisingly shy and humble regarding his credentials.

"I have a broad scope of work, specializing in obstetrics aided by an incredible team of midwives. I also treat sexually transmitted infections and diseases, as well as distribute hormones. Really depends on the client. In your case, I'll be focusing on your pregnancy," he told Aiden. "Do either of you know how far along you might be?"

"We have no idea," Aiden replied to him.

"Are there any guesses?"

Masika entered the room, setting cups down on the coffee table. Aiden blushed at her, "We... were too busy to pay attention."

"That's alright. As Masika already told you, I'll be staying for a week, observing you throughout. Then, I'll perform a physical exam at the end. Is that alright with you, Aiden?"

"Yes."

"Great! Congratulations, by the way."

"Thank you."

With that, Masika took the floor. While she and Mahpiya chatted, Aiden drifted away in his own head. He daydreamed about falling into a steady routine with his partner. He felt confident that everything would go smoothly.

It had to.

***

Aiden found out quickly just how little he knew about pregnancy.

Mahpiya gave him an endless list of dos and don'ts. No more alcohol or weed, and lots of dietary changes were in store. Worst of all? He couldn't go on Testosterone until well after the birth of his child. When Mahpiya told him, he cried.

He had hoped that as soon as he came back to his apartment, he could start hormones. Seeing so many people like him on the vacation excited and delighted him to the point where he got ahead of himself. He was never taught the consequences of unprotected sex. He had to wonder though—why now? Why after a year of it?

Mahpiya suggested Aiden may have fertility issues, specifically correlated to polycystic ovary syndrome. He based this theory on a history of inconsistent and painful cycles, hormonal acne, and rapid hair growth. Aiden may naturally have higher levels of Testosterone as well, all of which could explain why it took so long for conception to occur. When Aiden requested more information, Mahpiya could only give him what he knew.

"We've got a long way to go in terms of researching the condition, but I will keep looking for more information to bring to you," Mahpiya promised.

To Mahpiya's face, Aiden stayed sincere. The moment he left, abnormally high levels of animosity poisoned him. At first, he believed the emotions to be related to Mahpiya. Keeping to himself, it festered into something entirely different.

Over the first trimester, it grew harder to leave bed. He didn't know a moment without nausea or pain. Emotionally, he resembled a six-car crash. When he wasn't empty, anger infested his very being. He hated Masika for getting him pregnant, hated Mahpiya for telling him he couldn't go on Testosterone, hated himself for keeping the thing in his stomach before thinking about what it would do to his body.

Masika, now on the receiving end of constant outbursts, repeatedly told him he could stop at any point. There was no shame in needing an abortion. Aiden shot her down every time, but not due to shame or dislike of the operation.

Even though further hardships awaited, his gut told him he wanted the baby. Masika questioned his gut, as it regularly collided with spontaneous breakdowns suggesting otherwise. One evening, when his head was semi-clear, he explained his thought process.

"The breakdowns are because I wasn't prepared. I wasn't prepared and that's okay, you know why? I have you and Mahpiya, the midwives soon... so I know it'll be okay. You'll know if I truly change my mind, but if I say it while I'm having a freak out, don't listen."

"Don't wanna try again? When you're more ready?" Masika suggested.

Aiden shook his head, "You remember what Mahpiya said. If he's right about my diagnosis, that means this might be my only shot. Even this shot is a risky one, I wanna give it a fair try."

Masika, respectful of his autonomy as always, validated him. In the coming weeks, she dealt with his meltdowns and shutdowns expertly. Little did she know just how undone Aiden would become as time passed. He didn't remember to apologize when he snapped, skipped meals, and outright refused to bathe. Time smeared together, the only way he could tell any passed was by staring down at his growing belly.

His partner, through trial and error, crafted a routine for him. She knew consistency calmed him and he commended her dedication to keep him comfortable, even when treated poorly.

Accepting the routine along with a surprise package from Mahpiya—a gardener starter kit—Masika took a trip into town, getting the rest of the supplies needed for the garden. He spent the following days watching her build planters from scratch.

Soon, he fell into rhythm once again. He followed a simple routine: breakfast, nap, lunch, nap, garden, shower, transition to bed.

Masika cooked all his meals, spoon-fed him, helped him shower, and even carried him when he couldn't stand to walk. Through the endless suffering his body and mind provided, her protective nature was elating. He knew no matter what, she would take care of him.

Even if blood ended up on his hands.

Chapter Twenty-Four

August 1987

After what felt like hundreds of bus rides, dozens of hours spent hitchhiking and sleeping in desolate alleyways, Masika reached Illinois. Admittedly, she got farther than she thought she would. Yet, as she rode the bus into Chicago, she found herself grief stricken.

The whole way up North, her final glance of Aiden's sleeping face haunted her. Unable to shake the deep intuition that she made a grave mistake, by the time she reached Tennessee, she had contemplated turning back over a dozen times. The thought of him enraged by her abandonment pushed her further up the country. Cowering behind his old letters, she settled for his ghost.

Most times, the letters got her through the long bus rides—not today, though. Today she stood on an overcrowded, rancid-smelling one. People surrounded her, all standing as well, and she tried her best to ignore the suffocating sensation. To her immediate right, a woman slightly shorter than her read a magazine, pitch-black hair tied into braided pigtails. Enormous baby blues scanned words on the paper. A brutish man beside her kept sneaking glances at her body. Masika ignored it at first, but he made the mistake of opening his mouth.

"Hey girly, whatcha reading?" he slurred to the woman, vodka on his breath recognizable from a mile away.

The woman paid him no mind, but desperate for her attention, he snatched the magazine out of her grasp. Masika didn't waste a second stepping between them, having seen enough. Extending her palm, she stared right into him.

"Give it back and leave her the fuck alone," she snapped.

Instantly intimidated, he handed the magazine to her and sheepishly put his hands up, "S-Sorry."

She turned to the woman, who gazed up at her with fascination, cracking a tiny smile as she took the magazine.

"Thank you," she breathed.

"No problem," Masika mouthed back.

The remainder of the ride was uneventful, and she got off at her stop without issue. To her surprise, the stranger she assisted followed. Masika kept walking, hoping it was just coincidence, but the woman didn't let up. She called after her multiple times until finally being acknowledged.

"Can I help you?" Masika scoffed, throwing disgust in her direction.

"No, you already did," the lady responded, "I was wondering if I could help *you*."

Masika shifted her weight uncomfortably, shaking her head, "Don't need help."

"Are you sure? Don't want a hot shower? You look like you've been through Hell."

"Don't *most* homeless people? Leave me alone."

She tried to walk away as the stranger went on, "It's okay to need some help, you know. What's your name, darling?"

She squinted but relented with an answer, "Masika."

The name had come to her naturally, a mere three days after beginning her journey across the country. She remembered several months ago, Herb gave her a list of names Phillis had considered for her. Masika in particular called out to her, especially later pondering its meaning: 'born during rain.'

While her actual day of birth sported no rain, the night in the barn brought Hell from the heavens. That night she regaled as a more legitimate birthday, the full actualization of her true self. Thus, the name fit her like a prophetic glove.

"Masika," the woman said, "that's beautiful. I'm Everlee, Lee for short."

"Normally invite strangers into your home?"

"No, but there's something different about you," she smiled serenely. "I have a good feeling you should come with me."

Everlee reached out a hand and Masika finally stalled in her movements, gob smacked by the woman's audacity. Nearly all the white people she met hitchhiking from Alabama to Chicago did nothing but sneer at her; yet here Everlee was, offering a spa night.

So despite her nagging hyper-vigilance, she joined the woman on her stroll home. Or rather, a ridiculously lavish loft tucked into a five-story building. The kind of building that required six figures minimum to make rent. As the two went up the elevator, Masika wondered how she managed to get into this situation.

Everlee didn't bother with a tour, imploring Masika to take a shower. Self-conscious of her physical condition and dying for the sensation of hot water, she agreed without much fuss. Her host provided a robe, towel, and told her the rest would be in the bathroom.

"Thank you."

"Of course, I'll be in the living room."

The moment the hot water hit her skin, Masika cried in relief. Slowly but surely the grime on her body swirled down the drain. She didn't dare use the shampoo Everlee had, knowing it would only irritate her hair. Feeling clean again after a month of discomfort, she shut off the tap.

Sitting naked in the tub for five minutes, she shivered from the temperature shift, paralyzed. Only an hour ago she contemplated an easier way out than starving on the streets, an easier way to dispose of the Evil. Now, she sat in the tub of some random lady's apartment in Chicago. She knew she would need to slip away again as soon as possible.

Plotting her escape, Masika dressed herself in the velvet red robe granted to her. She managed to find her way out of the bathroom and into the living room. There, Everlee nursed a glass of wine.

"Join me if you'd like," she offered in a tantalizing tone.

Masika obliged, sitting beside her on the couch. Absentmindedly scratching the hair growing on her jaw, she watched Everlee down glass after glass of cherry wine. Despite the glamorous surroundings, Masika was too lost in her own head to admire anything. Everlee, detecting her aloofness, tilted her head.

"Where are you from?" she asked, "You aren't the typical tourist."

"Alabama."

"A fellow Southerner, huh? I'm from Virginia."

"Seems like a lot of people leave the South," Masika mumbled.

"Most of us have no choice. I didn't, get the impression that you didn't either."

Swallowing, she pictured a big red barn disappearing from her sight over the horizon.

"Had a choice. Sometimes think I made the wrong one, other times grateful I did. Feels strange."

It was odd being vulnerable with someone new. Masika kept to herself so long, it felt unnatural even speaking to another human. The last time she had been this verbal was to berate a man catcalling her across the street. She thought she may have sounded off putting, but Everlee just nodded in agreement.

"I understand that feeling. What brings you to Chicago then?"

"Been hitchhiking for a few months now, this is my last stop."

"You wanna move here?"

Masika scoffed, "If that scenario is better for you to think about, sure."

She watched the gears turn in Everlee's brain as she processed what was said. When the light bulb went off, she gave her a disapproving scowl.

"Look, I get it, but giving up isn't the answer. Maybe you should be concerned about why you're having these thoughts."

"Don't think I signed up for a therapy session—"

"Is it your body?"

Masika's entire world shattered, the rush of emotions that followed Everlee's question made her nauseous. She tried to disguise her shock at the accuracy.

"Why you say that?" she retorted.

"Because I see myself in you. The me that wanted to strip the skin and flesh off my bones every time I so much glanced in a mirror. You're just like me, Masika, and I could teach you *so* many things."

"T-Teach me?"

"Yes. I was like you just a few years ago, but I've achieved the ultimate form of womanhood, as you can see."

Masika had no idea what the 'ultimate form of womanhood' even meant. From what she observed, women varied in appearance and personality just like every other being. Was there such a thing as an ultimate form? Did she miss some kind of memo? Had Teneca been lying to her when she said it didn't matter how she presented, as long as she loved herself? While she didn't want to believe Teneca could lie to her, here Everlee was, stirring up everything she thought she knew. Would achieving what Everlee did finally allow her to love herself?

What Everlee *should* have said, she realized, is that she achieved conventional attraction standards. The woman boasted an hourglass figure with little weight on her bones, along with porcelain white skin. Plucked eyebrows, makeup; you name it, she had it. Masika couldn't help her twinge of jealousy, feeling hunky in comparison. Subconsciously reaching for her chest, Everlee raised an eyebrow.

"Let me show you something," she uttered.

Leading her to a personal bathroom, behind the mirror were three little shelves lined with dozens of vials. Masika watched as Everlee plucked one up and handed it to her. Gently taking it, she read the label: estrogen.

"Where did you get this?" she asked at once.

Everlee stepped back and crossed her arms, "A lot of places. The most recent shipment was from overseas."

Masika cradled the vial against her chest. Finally coming to the realization that Everlee was a lot more like her than she originally thought, she spoke carefully.

"Why show me?"

"Because I can tell you want it. Call it instinct," her blues twinkled with intent, "Why don't you stay with me for a little while? I'll provide everything you need. Think of it as... a mentorship!"

"No," Masika speedily responded, causing Everlee to frown. "S-Sorry, don't want to burden."

The real reason had nothing to do with being a burden. It followed more along the lines of intense mistrust. Vulnerability always led to debts, ones impossible to repay. Everlee seemed unbothered by the response.

"You wouldn't be a burden, but I understand. Can I give you money for a hotel room at least?" she offered. "I need to make sure you stay safe, this is the best way to do that."

Why does this random woman care about my safety? Masika questioned internally, trying not to rip off her own skin. She had to admit, it would be nice to have a shower and real bed to sleep in. Limbs falling to her side, she glanced at Everlee.

"Fine, can't pay you back."

"I don't care. Come on, I'll drive you to the best hotel."

Everlee led her out of the apartment. A bright pink sports car was the only vehicle currently parked in the lot. Masika was surprised she hadn't noticed it earlier. Everlee unlocked the doors and got inside as she followed suit. The interior of the car boasted leather seats, the floors so clean not even a speck of dust existed. Masika, realizing how muddy her boots were, cringed at dirt flaking off the soles and onto the floor.

"Don't worry, doll. I get it detailed every week."

The rev of the engine made Masika flinch as Everlee peeled out at alarming speed. The rush continued as she barreled down the Chicago streets, weaving in and out of traffic. Paying the various honks no mind as she sang to the radio, Masika leaned her head against the window, trying not to get dizzy. It took fifteen or so minutes to reach their destination.

"We're here." Everlee waved a thick wad of bills in her face, "Take this."

Masika scoffed when she realized there must be at least one-grand contained by a flimsy rubber band. "No, way too much."

"Take it, I *insist*," Everlee shoved the cash into her hand, clasping her fingers over it. "It'll keep you here for a week, and you'll be able to eat too. I have to make sure you're safe."

The 'here' in question was a massive ten-story building where Masika had no business being. All the cars in the parking lot were brand new and fancy. Anxiety climbed at the thought of the stares she would get. Lost in her head, she sat there frozen at the lobby entrance.

"What are you waiting for? Go on."

Masika exited, feeling Everlee's eyes on her walking inside. The air conditioning chilled her to the core as she breached through the entrance, seeing pristine quartz tile decorated in fancy patterns and big open squares. Mini tables decorated with vases sat atop intricate green rugs. A few white businessmen glowered at her from red leather seats. Ignoring them, she headed straight for the front desk. To her utmost relief, a mousy Black girl sat behind it, scribbling on a notepad. It took a full minute for her to notice Masika. When she did, she profusely apologized.

"No worries. Uh, want a room," Masika said.

"A room?" The woman folded her palms together, eyebrow cocked in confusion, "We only have suites available, honey."

Masika's lip twitched. She should've known by the sheer size and scale of the building.

"Okay, take that instead."

"Alright. May I see your ID?"

"Don't have one."

The woman played with her lower lip. Masika waited to be told to leave, but she wasn't.

"Normally, we turn away customers with no identification to avoid trouble. But I can tell you ain't gonna bring any. I just need at least a first and last name, if that's okay," the clerk compromised.

"Masika Holt."

"Perfect."

Once she paid upfront—about seven hundred dollars for a week's stay—the woman gave her the suite key. As Masika headed to the elevator, she read the number on it. Heading up to the fifth floor, she was grateful the elevator remained empty the entire way.

To say the suite was high class would be a massive understatement. Taking in the living room's freshly vacuumed carpet and brown leather chairs, she walked around an exquisite glass table. Lounge chairs and a flatscreen sat to the left of a window; single light on the far wall and nothing else. Astonished by the quality, she spent a good while afraid to touch anything in the room. Rationalizing, she eventually ventured further into the bedroom, unpacking her belongings. When she checked through everything, she kicked off her clothes and beelined for the bathroom.

She dozed off around three in the morning while submerged in the tub. Not that she needed another bath, but it helped the ache of her muscles. Awakening in a pool of cold water five hours later, she promptly rinsed off and properly put herself to bed. As she settled under the silk sheets, she wondered why exactly Everlee had been on the bus if she had her own fancy sports car. Seemed... performative.

Masika didn't linger on the thought much longer.

***

Taking the free week as a chance to properly explore Chicago, Masika found serenity in the city's lively presence. The first day, she bought herself some perishables at a local market. The next, she splurged a little on clothes. After all, she'd worn the blue dress she'd been gifted down to its last thread. That left her with only her signature hoodie, wife beater, and jeans (all of which were on their way out). Visiting a few outlets, she earned some weird looks from the women working them. Thankfully, nobody kicked her out and she was able to leave with a decent haul.

The rest of the week blurred, the most memorable instance being a quick trip to the library. The one nearest to the hotel was a masterpiece. It was a two-story marvel resembling Roman architecture, equipped with pillars and a tastefully off-white hue. Inside, dozens of book-lined shelves awaited.

Hours and hours passed as she perused the massive aisles, observing other patrons along the way. She happily bought a poetry collection from the library's book sale. On the way out, she took a backward glance, heart dropping.

Everlee peered at her over a newspaper several yards away, sitting on one of the many couches. The moment Masika detected her presence, she shifted her arms to obscure her face.

Masika fled, heading down the busy streets and trying to convince herself it was a natural encounter. Yet, a part of her worried that Everlee was stalking her.

Rushing to her suite, she locked herself away in the bathroom. Sitting on the toilet seat, she withdrew a pocketknife, aiming the blade towards the closed door. With those diabolical eyes, she doubted Everlee was even human. Surely the creature would break down the door any second, and

Masika would have to defend herself. Had this thing been following her long before the encounter on the bus, maybe all the way back to childhood? Maybe the bus ride had been pre-planned? It was the perfect scenario for Everlee to ensnare her.

Regardless, the terror of infinite possibilities kept Masika perfectly still against the bathroom tile, a pinned bug ready to sting.

Waking up on the floor in her own drool much later, she cautiously left the bathroom. Only darkness greeted her. Flipping the light on with bated breath, she triple-checked the suite for any intruders, finding none. In attempts to calm herself, she got into bed. Settling on an action movie channel as she spaced out, she half-way convinced herself Everlee wasn't after her. That the part of her suspecting foul play was wrong and she was safe.

Little did she know, that part of her had been right.

For the rest of the week, any time Masika would brave the city, she found Everlee observing in the distance. She began to feel akin to a zoo animal in its enclosure. That Friday, while she perused a park around nightfall, she felt a presence. This time, she didn't flee. Instead, she spun on her heel.

Sure enough, hardly a yard away, Everlee was reading a book on a bench, boldly staring over it as usual. She tried to hide her face again but Masika rapidly approached.

"Stop following and use your words," she snapped at the woman.

Lowering the book, Everlee unveiled a cheeky smirk. Closing it, she rose to her feet and left the bench to join her side.

"How's the suite?" she asked, swiftly changing the subject.

Masika stared at her blankly, "Good. Gave me a *lot* of cash, way too much."

"Keep it, I don't need it," Everlee replied. "It seems you put it to good use and got some new clothes."

Everlee leaned a little closer, enough for Masika to catch a whiff of her perfume. The hairs on her neck stood at the overwhelming stench of rose and ylang ylang. Scooting away to spare her nose, she played it off with obliviousness.

"Gonna give you a suggestion. Be more discreet when following people," she half-joked.

"*Following* you? Ha! I was waiting for you to notice me, to thank me for my kindness—" Uncomfortable, Masika tried to walk away. Everlee gently took her forearm, batting her eyelashes innocently. "May I give *you* a suggestion? You might want to pluck the chin hairs, sweetheart."

Masika's ears burned and she tore away, storming off into the empty street. Everlee had the nerve to give chase when she broke into a sprint. *What the fuck is this bitch's problem?* This only solidified her impression of Everlee's otherworldly and potentially Evil nature.

The whole time Masika ran, her thoughts flurried, struggling to come up with motive. At first reaching the conclusion Everlee was here to punish her, to deliver Kevin's promise of an eternal Hell, she then pondered the opposite. Did she aim to tempt Masika away from good, to steer her away from cleanliness and repentance? The bible spoke of many a succubus who preyed upon sinful humans after all. Every time she looked over her shoulder, Everlee's demonic blue orbs glowed at her. Had she made a grave mistake in pausing her prayers, relinquishing God's protection and guidance?

Everlee chased her all the way into a secluded alleyway, cornering her. She doubled over, attempting to catch her breath; Masika, on the other hand, stood her guard, preparing for a fight. Or, alternatively, to repent and beg for the Lord's mercy.

"You've got legs, I'll give you that," she straightened, wiping sweat off her forehead. "Sorry about the comment I made, I'm known to be blunt."

"Just say 'I'm an asshole.' Better than lying," Masika glowered through gritted teeth. Taking out her wallet and grabbing the remaining bills inside, she threw them at Everlee. "Fuck off and leave me alone. Mean it."

The walk back to the suite was perfectly silent. Packing up her things, she felt slightly ashamed of her behavior. But the girl had been *following* her for the entire week, so it was perfectly reasonable to be on edge. She decided she would skip town the next day and head for Wisconsin.

***

Masika rose at dawn, making sure to leave the suite in decent standing, not wanting to burden the cleaning staff with too much work. Once tidied to her liking, she headed downstairs to check out. She turned the key in and made her way to the closest bus stop. Double checking the routes, she made sure it would get her to Wisconsin, wanting to get out of Illinois as soon as possible.

Boarding a mostly empty bus a few short minutes later, she took a seat in the very back. Taking a deep sigh of relief, confident she would never see Everlee again, she decided to take a nap. After all, it would take a few hours to reach the state line.

To her utmost dismay, three stops later she was pulled from her doze at a tragic sight. A row ahead, Everlee twisted to face her. Masika had to resist the urge to fly out of her seat. Instead, she spoke her mind, chuckling in disbelief.

"Fuck's sake! The fuck you want from me?" Masika growled, "How did you know—"

"I want to tell you a story," Everlee stated.

Masika glared, watching her move to the unoccupied seat beside her. Even though she didn't agree to listen, Everlee proceeded.

"When I was a little girl, I lived on a farm with my family. Southern Baptists. I had eight siblings, a working dad, and a stay-at-home mom. We went to church every day, thought my life was normal for a very long time. But that all fell away. I had to grow up real quick, had to face the reality of what it means to live as a woman. Ever since then…" her head drifted back dramatically, "…I live to eradicate vermin."

Masika's heart-rate jumped at the last word, trying to be stoic as possible when she cooked up a response.

"Vermin? Rats?"

"Men, my dear. They should all be in landfills, I reckon, or locked deep away from the rest of us. Haven't you seen what they're capable of?"

Bethany burned in Masika's thoughts. The thrill of that night came rushing back with her view of flames ebbing away the abandoned house. She remembered Teneca, who watched her home get desecrated, only to be prosecuted for the death of the man who orchestrated everything. A knot formed in her stomach.

"Yes," Masika whispered.

"Then let me teach you."

The silver platter of an offer danced around Masika's brain, thyme garnish and all.

"Teach me what?" she asked without thought.

"How to take out the trash, and whatever else you desire. I can give you anything you want. Anything."

The bus skid to a stop. Just an hour before, Masika had settled on never seeing Everlee again. Now, she no longer feared the woman. The anxiety and paranoia from the previous days shifted to certainty, to faith. With such a powerful message and divine timing, she could only assume Teneca sent an angel to her. A guardian angel, a mentor to guide Masika as she once had. Everlee stuck out her hand for her to shake. All doubts rescinded, she took it.

After all, she'd be a fool to reject fate.

CHAPTER TWENTY-FIVE

October 1987

Masika couldn't get rooted in Everlee's lifestyle, not even after two agonizing months.

The arrangement began fine. Everlee offered her estrogen. Masika refused until she could acquire it herself, not wanting to partake in another's supply. When she told Everlee as much, she earned a scoff.

"Suit yourself. That means we have a lot more work to do, though," Everlee told her.

The 'work' in question was what it took to be fully perceived as a woman, according to Everlee at least. Masika knew from Teneca that womanhood wasn't a monolith, yet Everlee insisted otherwise. Conformity was how you earned respect. Traditionalism had value in the sense it brought safety. The more you blend in, the less of a target you are.

Everlee started her lessons with hair removal. Masika naturally lacked body hair, most of it consisting of light peach fuzz. Everlee claimed it needed to go anyways, "It doesn't matter if nobody can see it, you have to be smooth." When Masika challenged this, remembering Teneca's emphasis on only shaving when *she* wanted to, Everlee lashed out at her.

Masika ignored the tantrums, remaining resistant for days until Everlee raised her voice at her over dinner. Questioning her seriousness about being a real woman, she cruelly joked that only men liked having body hair. That's when Masika caved, allowing herself to be shaved head to toe. Unable to withhold her tears, she held the image of Teneca's gentleness with each drag of the blade.

A couple weeks later, Everlee did away with nearly all of Masika's wardrobe. She replaced the baggy jeans, tank tops, and hoodies with dresses and skirts. Masika didn't mind, at first, until she got suffocated from the lack of choices. Wanting experimentation that Everlee wouldn't allow, she didn't see an issue with wearing both masculine and feminine clothing herself. The 'one or the other' mentality, however, was posed as law and forcefully silenced her perspective.

The final straw had to be when Everlee took her to a hair salon. Buying Masika six or seven hideous wigs, she demanded her locs be cut. She quietly agreed at first. But at home, when a pair of scissors came at her head, panic wracked her entire body and mind.

"Have to?" Masika mumbled.

"Your hair is a rat's nest, dear. So yes."

She mentally slipped away as Everlee readied the cutters. Struggling not to cry as loc after loc hit the floor, her head was left barren.

"Don't be sad, sweetie. You'll look much better in the wigs I bought!"

Masika believed that for the minute it took Everlee to retrieve a wig—an atrocious hot pink bob—but had trouble once it was against her scalp. Wincing at her reflection in the mirror, Everlee only hummed in satisfaction.

"That's better... You're beautiful."

She didn't feel beautiful at all.

***

In between the tortuous adjusting to forced femininity, Masika attempted to learn more about Everlee's past. Only vague details were spared until tonight.

She'd left early that eve to go drink, giving Masika quiet time to read. Having enjoyed her brief absence, she deflated upon seeing Everlee stagger through the front door.

"Masikaaaaaa! I'm hoooome!" Everlee announced, kicking off her heels and stumbling over with open arms.

Masika closed her book and stood, "Have fun?"

"Sure did. Wish you came along..." she crumpled onto the couch, sinking into the cushions with a giggle. "Would you be a doll and get me a glass of wine?"

Even though Masika didn't think she needed any more to drink, she obliged. Slinking off into the kitchen, she poured half a glass and retraced her steps. Handing it over, she sat a couple seats away from Everlee, who downed the wine in less than five seconds.

"Today marks twenty years..." she mentioned offhandedly.

"Since what?"

"Since I escaped the farm."

Masika listened as she rambled about said escape. Not fully understanding Everlee's words, from what she gathered: Everlee's grandpa discovered her plot to leave, tried to trap her in the basement. She broke out took it upon herself to slaughter her family.

"All of 'em were crooked, complacent in their sins while preaching against them. The men couldn't keep their hands to themselves, the women turned a blind eye. I had enough, grabbed Paw's machete and hacked everyone up," she told Masika.

"Got away with it?"

"Think so, didn't stick around long enough to check. I hitchhiked all the way out here, met the sweetest girl at a bar. She was just like me at the time but... prettier. Took me to her place—this very apartment—and made love to me. Didn't know I wanted everything she had, didn't know I would take it whether she liked it or not."

Disturbed and confused, Masika nervously fiddled with her hands. The mantle of guardian angel seemed less and less appropriate the more she learned. She reminded herself even angels are capable of sin; if Everlee held remorse, God would forgive.

That logic fractured as Everlee suddenly burst into hysteric cackling, clutching her stomach and doubling over. She didn't stop until she threw herself into a coughing fit. When everything finally settled, she eased.

"I think she'd be proud of me. I made a good name for her, nobody noticed a thing either. Poor dear had no family, no friends; taking her place was easy. Ran out of money fast, but I figured it out."

"How?" Masika asked.

"I know what to sell, who to kill, who to blackmail—" she grinned thinly, "It's all a game, Masika."

It didn't feel like a game to her. Everlee had killed an innocent woman—taken her place, her home, her belongings. Fighting off the urge to comment, Masika rubbed her nicked arm hairs instead. Everlee, sensing the shift in behavior, opened her mouth to pry. Masika commanded her not to with a sour glance. She proceeded anyway.

"What's wrong? Speak your mind, you know I hate liars."

Masika deeply sighed, her gaze falling to her hands, "Must be nice to 'win' the game. Even just once."

The moment she spoke she regretted it. Everlee's posture straightened as she processed what Masika said, the corner of her mouth twitching ever so slightly.

"Excuse me? You think I'm 'winning?'"

"Look at you, straight out of a movie. Got this nice place, fine ass car. Much better than what any of my folks back home had, or ever *will* have. Last I saw my old man, he still lived in a beat-up trailer. If he saw me here... wouldn't know what to think."

"Well yeah, I may have it good compared to some, but I still struggle."

"With what?" Masika challenged, "Curious."

"Ugh, you're persistent," Everlee murmured.

Naming not a single one, she poured herself more wine.

The conversation died off, and that night on the couch felt despicably cold and eerie. Masika's dreams were bitter and ravenous as usual, brief. She kept waking up in a cold sweat, terrified of Everlee spying on her in a corner of the room. After giving the area a once over, she returned to the couch. She would entertain her thoughts until daylight, when Everlee emerged from her room in a velvety red silk robe.

"Good morning," she greeted, stopping mid-walk when she realized Masika wasn't responding. "Hello? Are you okay?"

Masika shifted her glance, "Yes."

"What were you doing?"

"Minding my business," she deadpanned.

Everlee's jaw slackened only to be wiped away with a defiant smirk.

"Guess I should be teaching you manners, huh?" She sipped from a half-empty coffee mug, "I was just checking on you, asshole."

"It's nothing, really. Nothing you can do anything about."

"Okay, *fine*. How did you sleep?"

The small talk continued for five minutes. To Masika's dismay, she found her gaze—and thoughts—distracted by Everlee's skin poking out beneath the red fabric. Burning envy poisoned her veins at sight of the paper-smooth texture, soft and feminine compared to her. Everlee noticed, giggled, and let her gaze fall to Masika's mouth.

"Alright, I'm gonna make us breakfast. Then, I think I'm going to show you how to do your makeup."

Masika's entire body tensed, "N-No, think I'm okay."

"Why not?"

"Only let one person ever do my makeup. Don't want anyone else but that person to, make sense?"

The memory floated about her mind in snippets: her dear friend's hand ever so gently guiding the makeup brush, holding her breath, the expectations, the fear, *the joy of being seen*. It was far too precious to replicate with anyone but him. She half-expected Everlee to insist, but she had already moved on to listing other ideas on what to 'teach' Masika.

"I mean, we could always go to the gun range together. All you need is a fake ID and I can get that. I know a guy."

"Sounds good," Masika agreed, trying to pretend she wasn't mentally lost in the past.

"Great! I'll go get those soon."

When Everlee left for the day, Masika allowed the memories to take rein.

***

Several evenings later, Everlee surprised her with a gift: a quarter of bud and some rolling papers. This was unexpected and Masika was certainly suspicious of it. Accepting, albeit reluctantly, Everlee noticed her hesitance.

"And here I was thinking you'd be grateful," she berated.

Masika opened her mouth to respond but shut it. Knowing there wasn't much of a point in snapping, she instead feigned a sincere smile.

"Thanks, you smoke?"

"Oh, *me?*" Everlee clutched her non-existent pearls and giggled, "Never tried it myself. I'd rather cut up, if you catch my drift."

Not catching her drift, Masika preoccupied herself with scouting the living room. Finding a jewelry tray, she stripped it of the various earrings and necklaces, bringing it with her to the recliner.

"Wanna try it, be my guest," she offered.

"I might take you up on that."

Everlee fell back to the kitchen while Masika rolled a joint. As she broke apart the bud with her fingertips, she tried to remember the last time she smoked. When she realized, her hands froze along with her brain. Over the course of her bond strengthening with Everlee, a scab gradually formed over her past. She usually thought nothing of it unless something happened to scratch it, causing it to promptly tear open. Absorbing the earthy smell led her mind towards the barn. Soon, the scent of petrichor suffocated her.

Shoving it all down, she asked Everlee where she wanted to smoke. Busy loading the dishwasher, Everlee mentally chewed on the question until she closed the door.

"How about... my room. In my bed?"

Suddenly anxiety ridden, Masika's heart skipped a beat at the last three words. She nodded in silent confirmation and headed to her room—the first time she set foot in there—with the joint in her grasp. A massive king-sized bed was pushed against a long, single panel window. Lush silk sheets and a duvet cover adorned the stretch where Everlee launched herself. Masika noticed how bland the room was aside from the bed and curtains: no decorations, no dressers, no rugs, no nothing. Just a giant walk in closet that surely was the size of the room itself. The whole interior made her feel out of place, so she stood in the corner, rubbing her arm nervously.

"Are you just gonna stand there and stare, or have a seat?"

Everlee's voice pushed her towards the bed. She laid on her stomach and pawed catlike at Masika's back. When she turned her head, Everlee patted the spot next to her. Masika swung her legs over and got a little closer.

"A light?" she requested.

"Will matches work?"

"Yup."

After retrieving a box of matches from her nightstand, Everlee struck one. Joint between lips, Masika leaned over for her to light it. Everlee ogled curiously at the other woman's mouth as a flame brought the joint to life. Masika took a few puffs and Everlee extinguished the match with a shake of her hand.

Soon smoke hung in the air, filling the entire room. At some point, Everlee waved the joint away, leaving Masika to finish up. She did so, only to find Everlee fast asleep against her shoulder. Haphazardly tossing the roach onto the nightstand, she cherished the rare delight of human warmth. Her thoughts once again drifted back to senior year.

No.

She couldn't, she refused to; yet once again she walked an overgrown path, folded notebook paper between her fingers. Then she was back at the barn, slowly dancing with her loved one. The tangling of their bodies like branches in a flood, the thrill of a brand-new dress, the confirmation of her womanhood—

What the fuck am I doing here?

Getting up to splash her face with water, she longed to return. Maybe steal Everlee's money, Hell, the bitch could lose a grand without batting an eye. That was enough to get to Alabama, to apologize. To give her friend the life he both wanted and deserved.

The life she had *promised* him.

A pair of arms slithered over her body. Everlee sleepily mumbled into her ear.

"Come back to bed."

***

The air between the odd pair changed after that night. Masika noticed Everlee treated her... differently. Having her suspicions, she didn't dare bring anything to attention. After all, this wasn't a romantic connection. As far as Masika was concerned, she was her mentor. Getting physically or romantically involved was of no interest.

Yet sultry glances and touches persisted. Masika drowned out the worry that Everlee was catching feelings with self-deprecation; there was no way in Hell she would be into her that way.

Masika read a book one evening, lounging with a glass of wine. Halfway through the fifteenth chapter, Everlee called her name from her personal bathroom. After finding a good stopping point, she followed the voice. The woman lounged in a filled bathtub, pink bubbles obscuring her body.

"Everything okay?" Masika asked, albeit uncomfortably.

"Yes, I just left my towel by the sink. Can you grab it for me?"

Masika glanced to her left, where the sink was. She found the towel on top of a hamper next to it. Water gurgled behind her which she paid no mind to, picking up the towel and turning around. When she did, her heart nearly jumped out of her chest. She instinctively looked in the other direction, but Everlee's nails gently moved her chin until their eyes met.

"I'm not shy. I *want* you to look," she told her with a smug smirk.

"Do you now?" Masika challenged, gaze withstanding.

"Yes, look and tear me apart."

"*Tear you apart?*" Masika repeated in confusion.

Everlee nodded and she swallowed the lump in her throat, eventually allowing a glimpse at her body.

"There's nothing to tear apart. You're beautiful," Masika stated, handing her what she asked for.

She tried to go out into the living room, but Everlee's touch ghosted her waist.

"You think I'm beautiful?" she teased.

"Anyone would think so."

"Aw, well I'm flattered. You will be beautiful too."

Will be.

Mood ruined, Masika fled to the guest bathroom. Remaining there for an entire hour, sitting on the floor in the dark, she half-expected Everlee to check in on her. Nothing happened, so she stayed secluded with her overactive thoughts and self-hatred. She *knew* she wasn't beautiful, but hearing it out of someone's mouth was a whole other ballpark.

Opting for a shower, before getting in, she did something she never did—glance at her naked reflection in the mirror. This proved a brutal mistake as her knuckles curled into fists. Every negative thought that could emerge about her body did, along with a tsunami of emotions. She sobbed violently, until the sobs paved way for silence as she stared blankly at herself. She tried to rinse herself of the pain to no avail. Instead, the water eroded her emotions, emptying her out. By the time she returned to her spot on the couch, all she could do was stare off into space; guardian angel nowhere to be found.

CHAPTER TWENTY-SIX

October 1994

Masika hated being a witness.

She hated seeing and knowing someone reached their limit. She specifically hated being unable to help, to offer anything to quell the pain.

Aiden told her every day it wasn't her fault; she told him she knew while not believing a word. How could she not blame herself whenever he lost it and tore up everything around them? Every time, in the heat of the moment, he claimed he wished their child was dead. Only to flip back when soothed, sobbing and begging to keep it.

Masika knew Mahpiya needed to visit soon. The routine could only work for so long, and she was starting to realize that. The garden helped, but she'd seen the tilt of several stems. Aiden neared a crash. One worse than anything either of them had yet to experience. She feared it.

She stopped sleeping, leaving Mahpiya dozens of calls despite knowing he was busy recruiting a team of midwives. Day by day, Aiden's physical condition deteriorated. He couldn't leave bed for a grueling four days, telling Masika he was better off dead. She told him that wasn't true, but that she understood how he felt.

Words weren't enough. How could they be? Aiden navigated the unimaginable and unexpected, even turning away testosterone to bear her child. The sacrifices he made to start a family shocked her—anything she did paled in comparison. After all, an inadequate, loose screw like her could never be a good companion or mother.

Fears were proven at the tail end of Aiden's first trimester. When she came to wake him for breakfast one morning, she jumped in fright. He stood facing the bedroom window, head hung. Steadying her pounding heart, she stalked towards him.

"Walking's okay today?" she asked, gently touching his shoulder.

"Yes," he replied.

"Good, made your favorite. Grits and bacon."

"Thank you."

"'Course," she began to guide him to the door, "wanna eat by the garden?"

"That sounds nice."

Calming words aside, Masika detected a false sense of security. She didn't call it out, knowing better not to. Instead, she helped him to the garden before heading to the kitchen. Once she made his plate, she returned to see him sat ankles-crossed in his lawn chair, covering his eyes. Placing the food in his lap, she stepped away.

"Bright, isn't it?"

"Yeah, I damn near forgot what it was like."

Angrily digging into his plate, Masika gave him the choice to eat alone or for her to join. He opted isolation and she obliged, eating by herself in the empty dining room. She left her helping half-finished before heading back outside. Aiden's figure stayed motionless as she waited for any sign of life.

Eventually, he put the plate down on the left side of the chair and stood, wobbling further into the garden with his cane. Watching him approach the failed pumpkin patch, Masika stifled a sigh. In between her numerous duties, she'd neglected the plants. Aiden bent down, palming the dirt with his hands. Catching the threat of tears as he grazed his fingers against the flaccid stems, she vanished inside.

Aiden watered all the plants before shutting himself in the room—this time locking it. Masika allotted him space, busying herself with cleaning the breakfast aftermath and prepping dinner. Minutes caved into hours and, before she knew it, corn, potatoes, and chicken where ready to be served.

When she called him to dinner, he didn't come out. Waiting five minutes before trying again, she still received no response. Concerned and frustrated, she went back to making their plates, deciding to wrap his for later. When she came to let him know as much, his silhouette greeted her in the hallway.

"Hey. Was just gonna let you know I made a plate, but... don't gotta eat it right now, if you ain't feeling good." Eyes crept down his shadowed body, all the way to a blade extending beyond his fingertips. Her heart raced, "Aiden?"

The knife stayed snug in his grip. Masika moved slow, trying to conceal the fear overtaking her. He stared past her and down the hall, void and vacant. She spoke his name again, taking a step forward.

"Aiden..." she rubbed her lips together, nervous as his breaths started to quicken. "Aiden, give me the knife."

Aiden's gaze fixed onto her. A blur of motion broke out as he lifted his arm, aiming the blade towards his swollen belly. Masika grabbed both his wrists and pushed him against a wall, holding them above his head as he thrashed. Tears threatened to escape as she tried her best not to be rough. He struggled until she managed to wrestle the knife out of his grasp, releasing him. Crumpling to the floor, he screamed and sobbed.

Backing up, Masika tried to remember what helped whenever he had meltdowns. This was a lot different, though, a lot scarier. The other meltdowns never worried her; this time he tried to plunge a knife straight into their unborn child.

She let the tears fall and Aiden's wails halted after a couple minutes. He defaulted to his new-normal look of emptiness. Propped against the wall, his head cocked slightly to the side as Masika failed to notice she was holding the knife by its blade. Blood trailed down onto the carpet and she debated cleaning up, but the thought of leaving Aiden alone in the hall frightened her. Shoving the injured hand behind her, she went to his side.

"Hey, must be tired. It's been a long day," she said, kneeling and moving hair out of his face. "How about you try and get some sleep? Washed your favorite pillows today, go get comfy while I get them for you."

Aiden nodded like a zombie and she walked him to their room, making sure he sat down on the bed. Hastily patching up her limb before retrieving the pillows from the dryer, she returned. Aiden hadn't moved an inch.

Placing the pillows accordingly, he laid down. Once the comforter was draped over him, she reached for the lamp sitting on the nightstand. Aiden stopped her with a gentle hand to the shoulder, squeezing his free hand into a fist and circling it around his heart. Masika softened at the apology.

"It's okay, can't really blame you. Been hurting a lot."

He moved her hold to his stomach. Masika pressed their foreheads together briefly before planting a kiss on his.

"Love you. Be back in bed soon, okay?"

She shut off the light. In the darkness, an ugly sob nearly escaped her throat. Rushing out of the room and heading for the kitchen, she picked up the landline and dialed Mahpiya's number. It went straight to an answering machine, and she trembled as she recorded a message.

"Mahpiya. Aiden's getting worse. Give me a call when you can."

She held her face in her palms, allowing herself to cry for a bit, hoping Aiden had gone to bed and wouldn't hear. Waves of relief washed over her when she later entered the bedroom to the sound of his snores. Crawling beside him, she reached for his hand and shakily took it. Guilt ate her alive as she wept once again in the darkness. It was her fault they were in this situation; none of this would be happening if she had been less reckless.

He suddenly squeezed, two digits wrapping around her thumb. Steadying her breathing, she recognized he was awake and aware of her emotions. She spoke in the pitch black of the room.

"Wish I could do more to help," she confessed.

Rolling onto his side to face her, even in the dark she could see the impression of his forlorn eyes. Stroking her arm and nuzzling his nose against it, she reached over and petted his hair. He didn't have to say a word for Masika to know what these actions meant.

You're doing all you can.

***

Mahpiya flew in from Tennessee a couple days after. Masika tried to pay him the moment he entered the house and, as usual, he shooed her dollar bills away.

"What have I told you?" he maintained in a low voice.

"Know what you told me, but you came all this way–"

"Aht aht aht, I told you I would be here to help. I meant that," clasping his hands together, he wandered the empty living room. "Where is he?"

"In the garden, only place that makes him even slightly happy anymore," Masika told him, leading down a hallway and towards an open sliding door. "Done everything you've suggested. Might be in more pain than I realized."

"He's experiencing a very high-risk pregnancy, so that assumption is a good one. I've brought some more herbs you can try."

"Thank you."

She stood in the doorway as Mahpiya stepped outside, limping down the gravel pathway leading to the garden. The chair Aiden sat upon was propped right in front of a flower bed. He held a watering can limply in his hands, hazy-eyed, staring at the clouds. Sweat poured down his forehead as Mahpiya approached.

"Hello, Aiden. It's been a couple months," Mahpiya greeted, taking a seat in the empty chair. "I see you've taken a liking to the garden, I've brought more seeds with me for Masika to plant."

Aiden nodded in thanks and Mahpiya glanced upward. The sky held no real clouds, only pathetic shreds of vapor scattered scarcely among vast blue. Aiden did not look away from it.

The questionnaire lasted for almost twenty minutes, Mahpiya asking about his emotional state as well as physical. Aiden answered with honesty–he had no reason to lie–and Mahpiya grew more and more concerned as those answers came forth. He disguised the worry with a soft, patient smile. The smile shattered when Aiden had a question for him.

"Is there something wrong with me?"

"How do you mean?"

Aiden proceeded with a lengthy response, "I wanted this. I told Masika I wanted this, but I'm struggling. Can't stand the way it's changing my body, don't look masculine anymore. I wasn't able to look into a mirror for the longest time, not until Masika and I got together again. Now I'm back to loathing my reflection."

Mahpiya responded with a hand to his shoulder, "I see what you mean. What defines 'masculine' to you? The ability to or to not carry children? I think society drilled that into you, let me show you something."

Reaching into his coat pocket, he pulled out several photographs and leaned closer for Aiden to see. The photos showcased several pregnant men and androgynous people with various body types, skin tones, and presentations. A couple of them were teary eyed and beaming down at a newborn post birth. Some boasted scars across their chests, others had tape binding theirs, and a few were unaltered. Aiden teared up; Mahpiya simply grinned.

"These are all people I've helped with their pregnancies. Many of them gave me permission to document, which is why I have these photos. I started taking them because one of the first fathers I helped was very much like you. He felt alone, and scared, because he'd never seen anyone like him. He said it seemed unnatural. I wanted to prove that there's nothing unnatural about people like us wanting to have children."

Aiden's eyebrow raised as if to ask 'us?' Mahpiya's smile returned.

"I had my own child long before I knew. It brought me great pain to see my body changed, too. I understand what you are feeling," Mahpiya assured. "I was able to persevere through the pain, but I know it's never easy for everyone."

Aiden's eyebrows pinched in the middle as he gazed upon the garden again, chuckling. "I feel like a seahorse," he informed Mahpiya, a new light in his eyes, "did the others feel that way too?"

"It's certainly a common comparison." Mahpiya's expression turned serious, "Aiden—"

"Before you ask, I want to proceed. You've given me a lot to think about. Thank you for being so kind and making sure I always have options."

Mahpiya patted his shoulder affectionately, "Of course. I'm here to help. You let Masika and I know if you need anything else, alright?"

When he trailed back inside, Masika was on his heels and eager for answers. He told her they could talk in the kitchen.

"He's dealing with dysphoria the most, it seems. As for physical ailments, I'd say the pregnancy is exacerbating his chronic pain."

"So you're saying he *is* trans?" Masika questioned.

"That's up to him, Masika. I know the answer is complicated. You told me he never considered transgenderism an option until he met you, correct?"

"Yes. Think he views the switch with his sister as less a gender thing and more for safety. Still reduces himself to his biological assignment at the end of the day, but Mahpiya..." she sighed, arms deep in dishwater, "telling you, when we were in high school, hated 'being a girl.' When I found him after the switch? Comfortable and happy, he was."

"Then I'd say it's possible, but I wouldn't push it too much. Let him discover and come out at his own pace, he's the only one who can decide his label at the end of the day."

Masika agreed, letting him stay for dinner and calling Aiden in around the time it was finished cooking. She had no idea how he could stay out there for so long in the heat.

Coming inside, Mahpiya saw his awkward, limp gait from the hallway and rushed over. Taking the brunt of Aiden's weight as they walked to the sofa, he melted into the cushions with a breath of relief.

"Thank you," he signed.

"Of course, I'll be in the kitchen."

Mahpiya aided Masika with dinner. When they went to bring Aiden a plate, they found him passed out. Sharing a chuckle, Masika asked Mahpiya if they should wake him up or not.

"Nah, just save his plate for later. I can tell he needs the rest."

With that, Mahpiya and Masika sat at the dinner table and dug in.

***

Mahpiya stayed for two weeks, taking a more hands-on approach with Aiden. Busying Aiden with low-energy gardening tasks and new sewing projects, he also developed an exercise to help whenever irrational thoughts arose.

By the time he left, Aiden seemed significantly better off. Masika showed her gratitude by sending him off with several containers of leftover food. Mahpiya promised to return closer to the final trimester, when he and the midwives would relocate to the same city.

A couple hours after, Aiden sat Masika down for a talk. She tried not to let her anxiety get the best of her as she watched him collect his thoughts. When he did, she inadvertently held her breath as he started signing.

"I think I'm more like you than I originally thought. I know I used to say the switch with Abeje was just that—a simple switch—but it's not. I've always been masculine, I think. Just didn't have the tools, the words, or the balls to admit it." He sighed deeply, "I think that's why this is so hard for me. Once the baby is here, I really want to start testosterone, maybe get my chest removed. I want to feel *happy* in my body, not miserable."

"Understandable, gonna do the best I can to help," Masika responded immediately, feeling a wave of relief wash out the anxiety. "Sure that Mahpiya can get everything you need."

"Good. I'm looking forward to it," his face softened, "I'm sorry for being such a pain."

"Who got who pregnant?" Masika retorted.

Aiden blushed, "You're right," he hugged her hard before finishing his thought. "I love you, thank you for taking care of us."

Masika beamed, this being the first time Aiden referred to himself and their unborn child as a unit. She hoped this meant good things were in store for her family.

CHAPTER TWENTY-SEVEN

November 1987

Masika stonewalled Everlee the following three weeks. She dismissed the sudden lack of interaction, acting like everything was normal when Masika didn't or hardly replied. This only further solidified that Everlee wanted her gone, wanted her dead. The facade of mentorship was nothing more than a smokescreen to get her hooks in. An effort to control another person she viewed to be weaker than herself.

The more Everlee feigned normalcy, the more Masika faded from reality. She stopped showering and couldn't eat since everything tasted of ash and burnt wood. She got up only to relieve herself, ignoring the other woman entirely. Why talk to a sniveling creature she couldn't trust?

At the three-week mark, Everlee told Masika she would spend the day out. This wasn't atypical of her, but usually she would disclose the general plans. Sparing no details, she left Masika with no idea when to expect her home. She told her leftovers were in the fridge and left right around ten a.m.

From ten to eleven, Masika tried to finish her book. She got two chapters in and threw it across the room in frustration. From eleven to eleven-thirty, she paced the apartment, trying to quell increasing paranoia regarding Everlee. She suffered from a sinking feeling her return only would bring chaos and punishment.

So she did what she did best—fled. Packed her backpack and left without so much a second thought.

Taking the bus to the library, she attempted to find another story to read. Unable to fully comprehend why, she was certain something in the catalog *must* have answers. Maybe she could find out why Everlee functioned in such an odd way, or why she fell upon this path to begin with.

She pulled five or six books, frantically skimming through them for an hour or so. She found nothing, absolutely nothing. When her focus waned and frustration took over, she resolved to requesting a study room. She needed to meditate. To her relief, the staff member she spoke with was happy to provide.

The isolation felt eerie but comfortable, the most comfort she had felt in weeks. Before she knew it, an attendant informed her she had thirty minutes until closing. Gathering up her stuff, she headed out, not knowing what her final destination would be.

Unable to sleep that night, not wanting to chance being vulnerable out in the open, she found a twenty-four-hour diner. She ordered a soda with the three remaining dollars in her wallet. As employees rotated per shift, night paving to day, Masika sat perfectly still at a booth. She stared at her hands the entire time.

***

She managed to stay away from Everlee for nearly two weeks. She did so even when she caught glimpses of her in the distance, watching. Waiting for her to crack and come crawling back. Masika acted like it wouldn't happen at first.

After falling victim to cruel stares and hostile encounters all over again, she craved the consistency Everlee provided. Trying to shake off the desire to return, she managed until a particularly bad run-in at the diner. A group of boys had thrown their sodas at her on the way out, dousing her in a sticky, overwhelming texture. As she tried to clean herself up in the bathroom, Everlee's words probed their way into her brain.

I can protect you. You'll never be safe out there without my help.

Masika punched the wall. She'd done just fine until this point, so why did she feel so vulnerable? Why was she so desperate for Everlee's validation and mentorship? She didn't fucking need it, but it drove her up a wall that she craved it.

She didn't know how long she could stay away from her.

"It's about time, I was getting worried about you."

That's the first thing Everlee voiced upon Masika's return on a rainy Wednesday evening. Only a few hours after the soda incident, Masika stood in the doorway, defeated and pissed with herself. Everlee's eyes narrowed at the sight of the ruined dress. As if she never left, she ordered her to wash up and 'fix' herself. Masika obeyed, feeling like a mangy mutt as she took a shower.

She was gonna have to get used to this. After all, there was nothing else out there for her.

***

Some days later, Everlee drove herself and Masika to a gun range.

The door to the range opened with a faint chime as they stepped inside. Gunfire echoed from further within the building, contrasted with the silent and peaceful atmosphere of the lobby. Everlee went right up to the counter, handing over two fake IDs for the attendant to check. They went over the identification before giving her two sets of ear protection and safety glasses. With a soft "thank you," Everlee took the items and guided Masika to the next room.

Masika scanned the numerous rows of targets and shooters, surprised at how busy the place was. Everlee led her to an empty lane, taking out her two personal firearms and handing over a pistol.

"You've never shot before, right?"

"That's right," Masika answered.

"I'll show you the ropes."

Everlee went over basic handgun safety for ten or so minutes. When finished, she set Masika up in the best position to shoot at the target. Standing behind her, touch ghosted her body as she adjusted her stance.

"Hold it with both hands. That makes your aim steadier," she instructed, humming in satisfaction when Masika's other hand went to the firearm. "Good. Now take the shot."

Masika lined up, thumb sliding the safety off. Pulling the trigger, a subsequent *pop* filled the air, and the bullet hit the target smack in the middle. Everlee whistled.

"You're quite the shot! Let's see if you can keep it up."

She managed a smile, this time aiming for the 'head' of the target and firing. Once again, she made a perfect shot, shooting a few more times until the clip was emptied. She stepped aside to let Everlee have her turn.

Everlee was a much messier shot, missing the target nearly four times before a successful hit. Trying to hide her self-disgust with a cocky grin, Masika easily saw right through her. Not bothering to finish emptying her clip, she put the safety on and told Masika to have another go.

Back and forth they went until Everlee claimed she needed to use the bathroom, requesting Masika tag along. Nothing could've prepared her for what happened next.

One step into the restroom, Everlee pushed Masika towards the wall. Hand wadding up her dress and pulling her close, she kissed her. The champagne on her breath sickened Masika, who stared blankly when she pulled away.

"Everlee?" she trailed off, not knowing what else to say.

The older woman dove into her neck, running her tongue along it before responding. "Fuck, I love the way you say my name..."

Everlee ran her hands over her hips and Masika stammered, "*What?*"

Then, she froze.

***

"So, did you enjoy yourself?"

Cigarette smoke permeated the entire bedroom and Masika choked on it. Already winded, this wasn't helping. So, when Everlee asked the question, she had to repeat it several times until Masika finally registered it.

"Was this part of the 'training?'" Masika questioned.

"No. That wasn't planned, but when I saw the way you held my gun? I knew I *had* to taste you," Everlee ran her fingers along Masika's arm. "There's something fascinating about you. I can't resist you, I'd be surprised if anyone could."

Getting up from the bed, Masika watched her pour a glass of wine. Her brain teemed with questions. When she met Everlee, she assumed that she must be like her in every regard, even down to intimate body parts. The encounter revealed otherwise and Masika could no longer brush off her curiosity.

"Have questions, if that's okay."

"Of course."

"Were you... born with your current equipment?" she asked, feeling childish with the phrasing.

"With my pussy?" Everlee giggled, "No. I used to have the same 'equipment' as you, but I paid a pretty penny to fix that."

"'Fix?'" she echoed.

"Yes, I considered it an error that I corrected. It is the only way anyone will take us seriously, you know."

"*Only* way? What if..." she shrugged, "What if I don't want surgery? What then?"

"Then you remain a joke to the world. To the community." Everlee gurgled down half the glass and slammed it onto the nightstand, "Does that make sense, dear?"

Masika shrunk into herself. She loved having the option and was happy such an operation existed—but she wasn't sure it was meant for her. Out of everything she disliked about her body, her genitals were not one of them. In fact, she quite enjoyed what she had. The only thing she craved was estrogen, she could happily go without surgery personally. To be told she would *have* to get it? It set her aflame in a way she hadn't anticipated.

"When the time comes for you, I'll help with the cost," Everlee droned on, impervious to Masika's hurt. "After all, we both know you couldn't afford it yourself."

Masika's waited until Everlee fell asleep by her side. Then, she fled to the bathroom and wept on the frigid tile. She couldn't cope with the expectations that supposedly came automatically with womanhood. She could handle the shaving, the fashion, the disapproving glares. What she *refused* to believe was that body modification was her only route to acceptance. Teneca always told her the opposite, she would have *never* said such things. Why doubt her over some white girl?

Yet doubt she did. She doubted obsessively, the fear of not truly knowing kicked back into full gear. Perhaps she wasn't a woman at all, maybe she'd been lying to herself her entire life. Maybe Teneca had been wrong to enable her. If Everlee was right, there was no point in even trying to transition if you didn't go 'all the way.'

But exactly how long would it take her to reach that point? And would she still be herself by then, or a shell?

***

It took four months for training to end. When it finally did, Everlee announced the pair's first goal—taking out a preacher's son.

Sitting Masika down in the living room, she showed her several photos of the man. Tall and lithe with a salt and pepper beard and hair to match, he bore a kind grin. The photos caught him in several random places: a church, a diner, the library, etc. Masika eyed the images curiously.

"What he do?" she questioned.

"Nothing. Absolutely nothing," she told Masika, "I just hate his smile, his demeanor."

"Want to kill him because of *that*?" Masika clarified, staring up at her in confusion.

"Precisely," she responded, not missing a beat, "I've spent the past two weeks learning his routine. On Sunday mornings, he always visits his favorite diner before church. We can get him there."

Everlee wanted her and Masika rolling up to the diner around eight a.m., five minutes after he typically showed up, wearing cheap Halloween masks. Everlee would manage any panic while Masika took the shot. Then, the two would flee, tossing the masks in the trash receptacle behind the diner.

"After that, we board the nearest bus and head home."

"Might get blood on my clothes."

"We can wear a jacket and toss it with the masks. There's no need to worry, we'll definitely get away with it."

Masika initially believed she could participate in Everlee's mission, but now doubt ebbed away at her. Could she really kill a man for no good reason? She falsely assumed they would *only* be eradicating vermin—genuinely vile men—not randoms whose smiles Everlee disliked. She scratched her face nervously, irritating several razor bumps in the process.

Everlee sensed the reluctance and snatched up all the photos, returning them to their envelope. "Don't tell me you're getting cold feet."

"N-No," Masika lied, forcing her hands into her lap, "just think I'm confused."

"About *what?*" Everlee got into her face, causing Masika to flinch. "I told you everything on that bus. There should be no surprises, and there's absolutely no backing down now, do you understand me?"

Heart racing, Masika nodded.

***

It was another beautiful morning in Chicago. Oswald read the newspaper at his favorite booth while waiting for his breakfast, the diner astir with its usual pre-church traffic. The aroma of various meats and food filled his nostrils as he sipped his coffee impatiently. He couldn't *wait* to eat his pancakes.

His waitress brought his food only moments later. Thanking her whole-heartedly, she smiled at him before making her way into the kitchen. He watched ten or so people leave in the following two minutes it took to eat his meal. As he slurped down his last slice of bacon, the diner doors burst open.

Having little time to react as gunfire rang out, screaming and shouting ensued, staff and customers running to take cover. Oswald covered his ringing ears.

"Nobody move!" Someone shouted over the chaos, "And stay away from the fucking phones, or else!"

A figure bounded to him, wearing a rubber face mask along with a black jacket and slacks. They pointed a handgun right at his face. He shrank into the booth with a shriek.

"No! P-Please don't!" he begged.

The stranger clicked the safety off. He waited for them to pull the trigger, but they didn't. Cowering bodies all around the diner stared at him. A second assailant stood by the entrance, wearing the same outfit and mask. Oswald looked back at the barrel in his face.

"Please don't," he uttered again, noticing their limbs tremble.

For a couple minutes, the stranger did nothing. Soon, they put the safety on. Oswald heaved in relief until the other person ran up and shoved their partner away. His mouth opened ever so slightly to speak as they aimed their own gun and pulled the trigger.

***

Gunfire, yells of agony, panic. That was all Masika remembered until her and Everlee ran out of the building, going around the back. Ripping off her mask and bloodied jacket, she tossed them both in the dumpster. Everlee mirrored her before the pair made a mad dash down some alleys in the opposite direction. Masika made sure to conceal her firearm as they got closer to the streets. About three blocks away, Everlee suddenly pushed her into a wall.

"What the fuck was that?!" she hissed, drawing in close.

Masika's brows knitted, "What you mean?"

"You didn't shoot. Not once! *I* had to do it," she spat.

Masika's head tilted to the side. She swore she had pulled the trigger. In fact, she was *certain*. She even remembered taking the safety off, so she argued.

"Did shoot, I swear. Shot him at least once."

"You *froze*. You didn't do shit, Masika. If you think you did, you must be fucking crazy—"

Set off by the term, she shoved Everlee away. "Don't call me that. Not crazy," Masika mumbled, taking a few steps forward.

Everlee glared at her, "What should I call you, then?" When Masika grimaced, her voice grew louder, "Tell me, doll. There aren't many words to describe what you are."

"Shut the fuck up!" Masika shouted, "Cops will be here any minute, need to go."

Everlee, knowing Masika was right, kicked an errant soda can before following her out of the alleyway. The two boarded a bus together. The subsequent ride home proved tense. All the passengers' eyes bore into Masika, probing and curious. Trying to ignore them by chewing away at her nails, Everlee offered no comfort. She sported a twisted and ugly expression the entire ride.

Neither exchanged a word when they reached the apartment. Floor by floor ticked by as the women stared at each other in the elevator. Before Masika could even process it, Everlee kissed her. She awkwardly kissed back.

About an hour later, Masika lay in Everlee's bed staring at the ceiling. Hollowed and empty, she allowed herself to daydream. Daydreams rudely interrupted by Everlee's authoritative voice minutes later.

"You can't make a mistake again, do you understand me?"

Masika rolled her eyes. She *didn't* make a fucking mistake! She had done exactly what was asked. Wanting to tell Everlee that she was the crazy one, not her, she had a bad feeling she would get hurt if she did. So she opted to keep her mouth shut.

The woman planted a kiss on her forehead, "Glad you understand. We start preparing for the next target tomorrow, try to listen better this time."

Once Everlee went to bed, Masika treated herself to an entire bottle of wine. She couldn't think of another way to deal with the incoming storm of nonsense.

***

Masika didn't think she would fail the second hit, but once again her version of events didn't reflect Everlee's.

She'd chosen a newcomer on the jazz scene this time, on account of his 'overly charismatic' personality. When she broke down the details of the plan, Masika once again realized how absurd a lot of her reasoning was. It was too late to complain though, she had no choice but to go along with everything. For this hit, Everlee planned to ambush the man in the privacy of his own home.

She didn't fully recall the journey to his house, nor the act of killing itself. She assumed, based on the red drenching her palms, that she participated. These gaps in her memories normally didn't bother her nor cause issues, but it was striking a nerve with Everlee. Especially when, on the drive, she was once again complaining that Masika clammed up. This time, she didn't bother arguing, not saying a word until the squealing began.

"Don't yell at me," Masika deadpanned, leaning against the window. "Know I shot him, know I helped. Got blood on my hands, didn't you see?"

Everlee groaned, tightening her grip on the wheel. "You're a filthy, lying dog. I'll tell you what. You get one last shot, or you'll be sleeping on the streets again. This is serious business and I need a partner who gives a fuck, not what you're currently providing me."

Masika didn't know how to respond to this. Whether she admitted it or not, she was terrified to be on the streets again. Her implication in Everlee's crimes prevented her from a clean escape, too. She stifled a sob.

As this arrangement stretched on, Masika increasingly struggled to view Everlee as a protector. In her mind, she gradually shifted and contorted into a demon; fallen or deceptive, she had yet to decide. Fear-stricken, it took her several minutes to respond to Everlee.

"Okay, I'm sorry," she whispered.

"Good."

CHAPTER TWENTY-EIGHT

December 1987

A week later, Everlee decided to test Masika after she messed up too many times for her liking. The announcement reeked of Kevin's rhetoric; a punishment disguised as game.

She did her usual ritual of calling a meeting in the living room, laying out the target's photos, and putting together a plan. Except she stopped at the second step this time, leaning back.

"What do you think?" she asked.

"What you mean?" Masika responded, admittedly not paying a lick of attention.

Everlee slid the images closer. The subject of the four photos was a middle-aged white man. Two of the photos painted him as painfully average. The third told another story. The man bent over a table, arm wrestling another. Without his shirt, several tattoos, including a giant swastika, could be seen. Masika squinted at recognition of other hate group symbols.

"He's a white supremacist, runs a couple groups in and around the Chicago area. Figured this kind of hit would be more up your alley," Everlee explained. "He's a regular at Oasis, a club where he's at his most vulnerable."

Masika picked up the heinous photo, fury bubbling in her stomach, "How do we get him?"

"Despite his 'ideals,' he loves Black women; caught him with quite a few prostitutes. You'll lure him out of the club and to his demise, simple as that."

"How?"

"That'll be up to you, my dear."

The last thing Masika wanted was a test. Once again, Kevin's hushed recitations poisoned her subconscious. Having little choice but to accept, she sighed.

"Need time to plan."

"Take as much time as you want, I don't think Sherman is going any-where."

For the following two hours, Masika pieced together a plan with Ever-lee's information. She decided the best option would be to go solo for most of the mission. After all, Everlee insisted she couldn't do shit without her. This was a perfect opportunity to prove her wrong.

She would dress real nice, meet Sherman at the club, invite him to 'her place.' In a taxi—Everlee posing as the driver—they would take a lovely trip to the forest. A forest she'd had her eyes on since her arrival, dying to explore it. Knowing it ran deep enough to conceal any potential screams, her and Everlee could easily do away with him there.

Breaking down the plan a couple times, she could tell there was significant doubt. Everything in Everlee's posture and expression screamed amusement, expectations to mock her inevitable failure high. Masika refused to give her that satisfaction.

She let Everlee pick out her outfit and wig, much to her excitement. She ended up choosing a burgundy tube dress, slick black heels, and a blonde wig. Masika cared for the hair the least but opted not to vocalize it.

She got dressed in privacy, only returning to Everlee to get a second opinion. Everlee circled her, tugging at the ends of the dress and dusting her off. She adjusted the wig before taking a second to ponder.

"Hmm, you're still missing something. I'll be right back."

Masika dared to look in the mirror. Surprisingly, she found a grin on her face. Though the blonde, straw-like wig didn't suit her, the dress hugged her body beautifully. Her muscles, normally a source of insecurity, filled her with confidence. Checking out how she appeared from the back, she couldn't help but giggle.

Her cheeriness shattered upon Everlee's return, carrying a pouch which she emptied onto the bed. Dozens of lipsticks, eyeshadows, eyeliners and more fell onto the sheets. Masika's heart skipped a beat as Everlee fished through the pile.

"Don't. Told you already how I feel about that," Masika said to her, leaving the mirror.

"You need *something*. Otherwise you're a bit... brutish."

The term stung but Masika concealed her emotions, putting her hands on her hips, "Never met a man into strong women? Seen plenty myself. Besides, reins are mine this time. Finished getting ready, don't need make-up." Picking up the purse atop the vanity, she swung it over her shoulder as she walked towards the door, "Be out front by midnight."

Everlee bowed her head, "Yes ma'am."

Masika smirked, quite liking the sound of that.

Catching a cab to the club—a high-class lounge in spitting distance of a suburb—she mentally prepared. She felt like a spy on a top-secret mission and constantly had to remind herself that wasn't the case. What she was *really* doing was killing a white supremacist for the approval of her partner. Her heart raced at the thought of caving the man's face in with a sleek, black stiletto heel.

It didn't take much effort to find her target. He stuck out with baggy shorts and a Hawaiian shirt against dozens of suits and ties. Sitting alone at the bar, he skulked by a collection of empty shot glasses and bottles. Perking up immediately when Masika plunked down, she ignored him practically drooling and busied herself ordering drinks. Two shots of tequila and half a beer later, he got the courage to speak to her.

"Hey gorgeous! Can I buy you a drink?" he slurred, waving around a wad of cash in front of her face.

Masika flipped her hair over her shoulder and forced herself to make eye contact. When she did, his Adam's apple jumped.

"Rather buy *you* one," she remained stoic as he blushed. "What'll it be?"

"Shot of whiskey."

She wound up ordering him five shots over the span of twenty minutes, watching him drink until he could hardly sit upright on the stool. Despite his incoherence, he rambled on and on about his wife and how beautiful Masika was by comparison. After a while she checked her watch, irritated to find she had fifteen more minutes to kill until midnight. Gritting her teeth, she did her best to tune out the man.

At eleven fifty-eight, she requested he accompany her on the cab ride home. He agreed, oblivious as ever when a black Honda pulled up front. Masika practically shoved him into the backseat. He was chortling as she entered the vehicle, gaze snapping onto Everlee in the driver's seat. Her mentor glanced at her knowingly.

"Where to?" she asked sweetly.

"My place, miss," Masika replied.

"You got it."

Masika didn't expect to hear snores only moments later. Chuckling in amusement at Sherman passed out in his seat, her eyes flitted up to the rearview.

"How far out?"

"Fifteen minutes," Everlee answered, "you're doing a good job so far. Let's see if you can finish it."

A right turn a few miles later and Everlee drove down the forest path. Masika's heart suddenly raced, actualization blindsiding her. She was about to kill this man and leave his body in the woods. A part of her didn't know if she could do it.

As Everlee parked the car, she twisted in the driver's seat, "Coast is clear. Are you ready?"

Moving as swiftly as they could, Masika aided Everlee in lifting Sherman out of the vehicle and onto the ground. From there, they dragged him through the trees. She hadn't accounted for lack of lighting, but it didn't bother her one bit, able to see well in the darkness. Everlee couldn't, cursing and muttering to herself every time she crashed into a trunk or tripped over shrubbery. Masika couldn't contain her snickers after a certain point.

"I'm glad you think this is so fucking funny," Everlee shot in a cruel tone.

That shut Masika up until her legs grew too tired to go on. Signaling for Everlee to drop him, he yelped in pain upon hitting the soil. Both ladies watched as he quickly came to, still clearly drunken out of his mind.

"Is this..." he hiccuped, lazily pointing to his surroundings, "this your place, sweetums?"

"Sure is," Masika replied, not missing a beat as she propped him up against the closest tree. "Why don't you rest?"

Stepping back, she wiped her hands on the dress. Everlee shot her a questioning look.

"Any minute now," she scoffed.

Masika nibbled on her lower lip, the only detail of the plan she left up in air was how Sherman would die. Would she waste a bullet on him? Stomp his head in with a stiletto? Both those options seemed too messy.

As she wracked her brain for more, Kevin unexpectedly breached through. Her chest grew twenty pounds heavier as his baritone yells ricocheted in her thoughts: *Evil! Evil, hideous creature! I cast damnation upon you!* Soon, she trembled, oblivious to the taste of blood in her mouth.

"I knew you couldn't do it."

Everlee's words overlapped everything else, yet Masika heard them distinctly. She hoped Everlee would stop there, but of course she didn't.

"You aren't just crazy, you're a fucking coward too. A shoddy excuse of a woman. A—"

Masika unleashed a sob of agony as she swung for Sherman's head. She struck the life out of him in one blow. Shocked at her own strength and brutality, Masika stumbled back. Covering her mouth, she fought the urge to retch as Everlee cackled and danced in celebration.

"Delightful! Oh, love, I hope that felt good," she mimicked Sherman's frozen expression briefly before breaking out into gut busting laughter once more.

It felt abysmal, like a film of pure filth over Masika's body. Slipping into a catatonic state the whole walk, she was a stark contrast to Everlee's giddy skips and chatter. Back in the car, Masika let out the breath she was holding. Everlee's hand crept to her thigh.

"You did such a good job, doll. You know that?"

Masika, mentally adrift, simply nodded. Everlee's grip stayed on her thigh the whole drive home, harsh reprimands flipping to extravagant compliments. Such sweet things were told: how lovely she was in the dress, how good she had been. Masika latched on solely to that—she had been good. She had done good and Kevin was *wrong*.

Everlee didn't disguise her intentions for the remainder of the night. Afterwards, when she lay next to her fast asleep, Masika stole a cigarette. Slipping a robe on the way, she stepped out onto the balcony, a rare enjoyment. Absorbing the cool night air on the bare parts of her skin, she gazed up at the moon.

It didn't take long for the buzz to fade. When it did, flashes of the forest came gushing. Her mind reminded her that once again, she had blood on her hands. She might as well be back at Kevin's, out by the creek hunting rodents. Everlee was a liar, she wasn't good at all; she was a killer, a hunter, a predator. Incapable of anything else.

No one had ever challenged that belief other than two people. One was dead, the other person she threw away like trash. Upsetting memories wormed their way into her brain, sending her into hysterical sobs in the pale moonlight.

Rocking herself on the cascading ledge, her life flashed before her eyes. Questioning how she even got to this point, she secretly hoped the police would come knocking the next morning to take her away. Any excuse to atone for the blood on her hands.

Any way to be profoundly good.

***

Three successful hits later, Everlee no longer had anything to complain about.

Masika's participation was satisfactory, even though it hollowed her out day by day. By the time Everlee came up with their next target, she could hardly look at the other woman's face. All she saw was Kevin, blue eyes gleaning at her, eager to mold her into God's perfect child. The two blurred together in her mind and she spent most days saying nothing, obeying Everlee's every command.

The circumstances for the next hit were strange from the get-go. Everlee wanted to travel to Iowa of all places, specifically the city of Des Moines. Unlike the previous times, she gave no name and no photos. Additionally, she requested to carry out the kill alone. These alarm bells weren't enough to deter Masika from half-heartedly agreeing to the mission.

A week later, Masika dropped Everlee off at a hotel. After procuring a parking spot, she helped herself to a bag of chips and kept watch. She still didn't understand why Everlee insisted on going inside alone. The mission seemed oddly personal compared to the last ones, but she knew better than to question Everlee's haywire logic. Instead she tried to plan ahead, figuring out what she might want for dinner after everything was said and done. Tacos sounded perfect.

After daydreaming for a few minutes about fajitas, red and blue lights flashed in her peripherals. Stuffing the mostly empty chip bag into the center console, she watched two or three patrol cars pull up. They parked right in front of the lobby and Masika's chest tightened as men exited the vehicles, bolting inside.

Checking her watch, she realized Everlee should have been out five minutes ago. She decided that without the details conveniently left out from the plan, she couldn't risk going inside. She had no idea where she was in the building, nor if they could both make it out without police involvement.

So she waited, chewing at her cuticles the whole time. A grueling eight minutes later, one of the doors to a side entrance flew open.

From her position, she espied Everlee stumbling out. Frantically waving Masika over, she held her stomach as Masika shifted into drive. Rolling up right next to the sidewalk, she unlocked the doors and Everlee practically threw herself into the passenger seat. Masika's mouth gaped at the blood pouring through her blouse.

"Go! We have to get the fuck out of here!" she exclaimed, slamming the door shut.

Masika stared at her with a terrified expression, gripping the wheel with white knuckles. "Where do we go?"

"Anywhere, just fucking drive!"

She zoomed out of the parking lot. Once on the main roads, she tried to figure out what went wrong with the mission.

"What happened?"

"Motherfucker was an undercover, I should've fucking known." Wincing, she adjusted in her seat, "The cyanide did its job... *after* he called for backup. His buddy shot me but I got away, just grazed."

"Shit, anyone see your face?"

"I don't know."

Masika weaved in and out of traffic, the engine of the rental shrieking in protest. The moment she thought she was in the clear, flashing red and blue lights appeared a few lanes behind. Slamming her foot on the gas, she did her best to avoid pedestrians and other drivers as she rubber-banded to the far-left. To her dismay, the cop caught up fast and Everlee hurriedly reloaded her pistol. Masika side-eyed her, panic dousing her entire being.

"The fuck are you doing?!"

"Buying some time—"

Masika cut her off with an abrupt turn into a narrow alley, "No! Shoot the pigs and we'll have a lot more trouble, trust me."

Patrol car trailing close behind, Masika pushed to go faster. A quick glance in the rearview mirror revealed the pursuing officer's cocky grin and focused gaze. She glanced out the front window once more. A dead-end rapidly approached and she sped up. Everlee yelled at her, but she ignored it, taking a sharp turn at the last possible second.

Expecting the car to spin out, she was pleasantly surprised to still be forward facing. Brakes squealed behind her and she didn't check to see if the cop had crashed or not, barreling out of the alley. All that mattered is that she escaped for now. Back on the streets, she forced herself to take several deep breaths.

"It's okay. We're okay," Everlee mumbled as Masika snuck a glance at her, "Watch out!"

Masika snapped her head forward, actualizing a telephone pole growing closer and closer. Then, everything went black.

***

The world returned to Masika sense by sense, starting with her hearing. Ambient city noises and traffic greeted her. Airbags deployed, she could hardly see the eviscerated front window and smashed in bumper. Ignoring the ache and burn of her body, she looked over at Everlee, head drooping but appearing relatively unscathed. Masika reached over to check her pulse, confirming she was alive.

Car door already ajar, Masika kicked it the rest of the way open. She fell out of the vehicle, coughing and hacking on her hands and knees. When the feeling in her legs returned, she got up and staggered to the passenger side, trying the handle only to find it jammed. Impatient and pressed for time, she broke the window the rest of the way and carefully hauled Everlee through the gap. A few glass shards to the flesh were better than a lost life.

Ears still ringing, Masika dragged Everlee into the nearest alleyway. Not even a second later, she heard the vehicle explode. Checking for wounds, she discovered a deep gash on her head along with various scratches. Distant sirens alerted her and she scanned her surroundings. Throwing Everlee over her shoulder, she ventured deeper, not stopping until she spotted a dumpster.

Everlee would surely rip her a new one.

Oh well.

She lifted the lid before throwing Everlee inside. She landed on the numerous trash bags with a soft groan and Masika jumped in after. The reek overloaded her senses instantly and she groaned. It wasn't ideal, but this was the best way to keep the cops off their trail.

Somehow Masika managed to slip into a slumber; one abruptly ended by a loud, obnoxious gasp for air. She wrestled Everlee atop the trash, trying to quell the noises she made.

"Stop! Gotta be quiet—"

Everlee dramatically gagged, *"Are we in a fucking dumpster?"*

The younger woman stilled, "Y-Yes. Best place after the wreck, no other choice—"

"No other choice my *ass!*" Everlee jerked one of her arms, "My clothes are going to be fucking ruined now!"

Masika snatched the limb out of Everlee's grip, lip curling into a snarl, "Rather me leave you in the rental? Would've blown up with it."

"Everything is ruined," Everlee whined, ignoring Masika's hypothetical. "Those cops saw my face, fucked up my perfect plan. It wasn't supposed to go this way!"

"Next time—"

"There won't be a next time. I'm done. That was too fucking close!" She sighed deeply, "How long are you planning on staying in here?"

"Few more hours, guarantee the cops are still looking for us."

"Fuck's sake..."

Everlee wiggled away from her, curling into the corner of the dumpster. Masika gave her space, worrying she'd made the wrong choice. Filth clogging up her nose aside, she forced herself to relax. She started with the muscles in her feet and ended with the release of her neck.

Waking up to nearby skittering, stiff and aching, she rolled onto her side and stretched.

"Shit, didn't mean to pass out on ya. Everlee, you okay?"

No answer. She called for Everlee again, crawling to the side she last saw her on. Limbs sank into the trash bags and she cursed; Everlee abandoned her.

She didn't stop to think before throwing the trash lid open and climbing out. Landing delicately on her feet, she took a moment to regain her balance. Ignoring the white man sitting on the opposite wall, staring at her with bewilderment, she hobbled down the alley and into the city streets.

By some miracle, Masika found her way back to the hotel Everlee booked. She checked her pockets for the room key, heading up to the eighth floor when found. Giving less of a rat's ass about her, Masika was dying for a scalding shower and new change of clothes. When she got to the suite, she steeled herself.

Opening the door, she found all the lights on. The room was exactly how they left it, seldom Everlee's wallet missing from the nightstand. Masika wasted no time stripping her clothes and leaving them in the corner. Going straight into the bathroom, she turned on the water.

Later, Masika investigated her naked body in the mirror. Gnarly bruising coated her thighs and arms, alongside a few cuts and gashes. She was happy to report no other injuries. Her and Everlee were incredibly lucky to leave the crash largely unscathed. Drying off, she donned her favorite satin nightgown.

Everlee wouldn't appear until hours later, arms occupied with dozens of shopping bags. She didn't say anything to Masika, who had secretly hoped she vanished forever. Disregarding one another, Everlee organized her purchases while Masika dissociated. Hours of aimless wandering later, Everlee finally settled in bed beside her. Masika didn't move an inch, not until Everlee latched onto her thigh with a bite.

"Ow!" The woman giggled at her response and Masika shoved her away, "Not funny. Knock it off."

"Aw, sour about me leaving you in the dumpster? Maybe you should've picked a better hiding spot then."

"Maybe you should've picked a better target," Masika stood from the bed. She scoffed at Everlee's look of disgust, "What? Don't enjoy playing your own game?"

"It wasn't my fault everything went to shit."

"Wasn't mine either."

"You're hopeless, you know that?" She reached for a half-full glass of water on the nightstand, "You'll be happy to know I'm leaving any future jobs to you."

Masika sat at the desk, grabbing the complimentary notepad, "Yeah right."

"I'm being serious. This is way too much for me, I think you're better suited for it. I can outsource you, too, broaden your range."

Ignoring the tangent that followed, Masika doodled, scribbling a sun, then a puppy, then a set of bones. Right as Everlee's voice resembled glass shards to the eardrum, she finished a pair of eyes. They gazed at her, hollow and vacant as rage bubbled up inside.

"Shut the fuck up," she demanded, Everlee's lips gluing together. The women stared at each other across the room as Masika gripped the chair, "Seriously? Think I wanna hear your bullshit after everything? Just want some fucking peace and quiet..."

Peace and quiet Everlee provided for the rest of the night. Masika's shock at her obedience lasted until grotesque snores filled the room. Grimacing, she shook her head and spent the next ten minutes scratching obsessively at her arms. Stopping, she stood up to discard the drawings she made. As she went to crumple one, the somber eyes made her hesitate.

A sinister change in the air made her hold her breath. Would Everlee really turn her into even *more* of puppet to orchestrate her mission? Or was she drunkenly bluffing, as she tended to do after a couple bottles of wine and a few lines of coke? Reality blurred with her busy mind as she wadded up the image of her ex-lover's eyes.

Chapter Twenty-Nine

February 1989

An eon certainly passed; one consisting of death, misfortune, and a descension into madness. It all started with a gun too big for Masika's frame. A weapon that took a special trainer to teach her how to wield. A sniper rifle for her first solo kill.

That's right, the inebriated babble wasn't just talk and empty lies. The day after the mishap, Everlee told her the mission must be continued alone. At protest, she quickly reminded Masika she had nowhere to go, nowhere else to get hormones. To sweeten the deal, she told Masika that she could keep any money made from the hits.

She wanted to slap Everlee, to scream in her face. Instead, she contemplated what the money could bring. Not only could she begin estrogen, but she could get back to Alabama. She could rescue her friend and run away for good, rectifying her mistake. She needed to get away from this wretched hellion as soon as possible.

So a week later, at the top of a skyscraper, Masika readied herself behind a scope. In a building hundreds of yards away, a strung-out man danced in his living room—visible through his open window amongst dozens of others. When he bent over to fill up his glass with vodka, she took the shot.

At least four kills followed, all within spitting distance of Chicago. Everlee never aided her, only showing up to randomly check on her progress. This time was no different.

"What are you looking at?"

Masika peeled her gaze from the window. She turned to Everlee lying on disheveled sheets, a cigarette sitting between her lips. Long blonde hair, crisp from a fresh bleach job, stuck to her sweat-ridden face. Masika took a seat on the edge of the bed.

"Nothing," she answered, "still getting used to cities. Always so much to see."

Reflecting in the glass again, her room in Louisiana stared back; nothing but fields and grass stretching beyond a decrepit fence. Everlee touched her shoulder, startling her out of the memory.

"Don't get too comfortable. This is only one of many stops on your journey, you're going to New York City next."

"Yeah..."

She wasn't thrilled to spend several hours on a crowded, stinky bus. Everlee temporarily distracted her from the anxiety surrounding the next job. Now though, her thoughts ran rampant, and Everlee's touch couldn't stop or fix anything.

"It'll go smoothly, I'm sure of it. And once it's done, I'll follow through with getting you hormones."

Great, another source of anxiety. Masika had already asked a trillion questions about Everlee's source of estrogen, and she was assured it was authentic and safe. That didn't stop her worrying though. What if it was a trick to poison her? Even if it wasn't, was she finally ready to transition? Would it help the void in her chest, fill it and make her whole?

Estrogen was the only thing that could aside from who she left behind in Alabama. Ideally she'd take it for a year and then return, rescue him from that Hell of a town. The thought of his warm hands made her close her eyes. Everlee's cold palms bedded into her hips.

"How are the changes? How long does it take?" Masika interrogated.

"It's a case-by-case basis. For some, it can take six months for noticeable effects—breast growth, weight redistribution, less hair, more—for others, it can take longer." Everlee leaned forward, "I wasn't very lucky. Took me five years. Bad genetics, maybe. I hope it's not like that for you."

Masika held no concern about the potential cards dealt to her—only that change would eventually happen. That's all that mattered. She didn't need or want to look like Everlee. Not that Everlee looked bad, just wasn't her style.

Despite Everlee's vitriol, Masika desired little change in her physical build. She simply wanted slightly bigger hips and a pair of boobs; size irrelevant. Other than that, she didn't want to lose all her muscle definition, taking great pride in being intimidating.

"Not that worried about it," Masika said to her.

"You never are. I envy you for that, you know."

"'Course you do."

Masika made a point of rushing to get dressed. Everlee openly pouted, "Where are you going?"

"Now that you're done distracting me? Got a bus to catch, job to do."

***

Blending in New York City was the easiest part of Masika's next hit. Amongst the crowds she slipped through, undetected and unbothered for most of her day. Thick black shades sat crooked on the bridge of her nose, hands tucked into her jacket pockets as she walked the city. The bus ride had been less obnoxious than she expected, so she had an extra pep in her step.

After two hours of foot travel, she arrived at a tiny corner bookstore. She strolled into the building. Amid dozens of crowded shelves and customers stood a short Black man brandishing a lavender button up and slacks. He passionately conversed with an elderly white lady about the book she held in her frail hands.

She slipped off her glasses and strode further into the building, grazing numerous book titles. Each room aside from the main room held only one or two genres. She searched for the Crime section, eventually finding it in the final room near the bathroom.

She searched for a specific title—which served as a code word—not managing to find its location right away. When she did, she brought the copy up to the front and the man from earlier gave her a kind smile.

"Hey, how may I help you?"

Masika untucked the book from under her arm and placed it down flat. Wordlessly sliding it over, his eyes flickered knowingly.

"I see. Angel, can you watch the front counter?" Shouting to an employee stocking shelves, he gestured to the door behind him, "Follow me."

Down an intimidating set of stairs, Deylin led Masika to a singular office room, imploring her to have a seat. Doing so, she did her best to mask her aloofness.

"Everlee's contact, right?" He shook her hand firmly as she nodded. "I'm Deylin, good to finally speak with you. How was the trip?"

"Was fine. Weather wasn't too miserable either."

They sat across from each other at an ivory desk with marble finish. Masika crossed her ankles, feet bouncing as Deylin picked up a manila folder next to his computer. Opening it, he removed several photographs and placed them in a row in front of her. She picked up the first one, a family photo of four consisting of two little girls, a middle-aged woman, and a man.

"The man in the photo is your target," he informed her. "His name's Christian Smith."

"Why you want him killed? Don't need a reason, of course; just curious."

Deylin pointed to a framed photo of a toddler by his computer mouse.

"This is my daughter, Nina. My wife enrolled her into daycare a few months ago. The place is run by a bunch of Catholics. They bring Good Father Chris to read bible verses every week." His knuckles tightened into fists, "The man doesn't know how to keep his hands to himself, if you catch my drift. Not remorseful about it either."

Masika's own rage brewed as she stared into Nina's innocent eyes. She briskly stood.

"Drag it out, I will. Make it nice and slow. Could castrate too, if you want."

A grin spread across Deylin's lips.

"Only if you take pictures."

***

Light flooded the room, along with Father Chris' vision.

He shuddered violently and sobbed as his assailant pocketed a camera. Putting on her gloves, she bent down to shuffle through her backpack. The Pastor's muffled begging grated her ears.

"Think whining is going to save you, Father? If you wanted your life, should have kept your hands to yourself."

Masika found her pliers quickly and returned to Father Chris. She crouched in front of him and pulled his bound wrists towards her. Delicately aligning the corner of his pinky with the pliers, she clamped down and tugged. She kept tugging until his whole nail came clean off, blood bubbling where it used to be. He wailed and she laughed in his face as she prepped for the next.

Once all his fingernails were scattered on the ground, she moved on to breaking each of his digits. The fun was near its end, Father Chris growing weaker by the moment from rapid blood loss. A strange, foreign feeling stirred in her stomach as the bones crunched beneath the weight of a hammer. Through it all, the man still managed to whimper and plead. Masika slapped him across the face, causing a delirious roll of his head. She smirked and patted his cheek.

"There we are, didn't want you to miss the best part."

***

An hour later she arrived at Deylin's book shop, just in time to catch him locking up. Nearly jumping out of his skin when she cleared her throat, he relaxed seeing it was only Masika.

"Oh, you're fast," he shifted and stared at her. She handed him the father's rosary along with the camera, "Where did you—"

"Somewhere fucker won't be found for a few days," she assured him.

"Okay, good... I-I don't have the money on me right now, it's at home. If you don't mind tagging along, I can give it to you there."

"Sounds fine."

Deylin drove her to his home—a two-bedroom duplex on the outskirts of the city—and told her to wait outside. She did so, soaking in the suburban nightscape. When Deylin returned, he did so with a hefty envelope, which was passed to her.

She accepted the cash and Deylin thanked her profusely, wishing her goodnight before vanishing into the house. Heading out onto the streets, she walked until she caught a cab to the hotel.

Shedding her backpack and clothes onto the floor the moment she locked the door, she decided a hot shower was in order. Once the hot water hit her skin, waves of relief crashed over her entire body. Father Chris' blood curdling weeps ricocheted in her head.

***

Masika returned to Chicago to formally report her success. Upon entering the apartment building, she gave the security guard a friendly wave. An uneasy feeling worked up her spine, leaving her shifting her weight between feet as she rode the elevator up. The doors opened and she headed straight for Everlee's.

She was met with pure darkness, something she found oddly comforting. It meant that either Everlee wasn't home at all, or fast asleep in a wine coma.

Navigating towards the living room, she set down her bags. Spending the next thirty minutes counting her bills, a rush of relief cooled her anxiety. This money would be more than enough to get estrogen and put aside the rest. Maybe once she started, Everlee would finally shut the fuck up about her not being woman enough.

It had been a sore subject for her, admittedly. Ever since her first solo mission, Everlee gifted her tuck wear and bra inserts; she threw them away, telling Everlee she lost them. She stopped wearing girly outfits entirely. The more she resisted Everlee's efforts to feminize her, the more hostile she got.

Once Masika had a total—roughly ten-thousand—she put half on the table and stashed the other in an envelope. She taped it to the underbelly, just as Everlee's snoring alerted her. Masika brushed off her pants and made her way to the room, standing on her side of the bed.

Not wanting to wait any longer to figure out HRT, she shook Everlee. She startled, thrashing around in the comforter violently. When she stilled and turned on the lamp to see Masika, she scoffed.

"What the fuck?! You scared me," she scratched her disheveled bed-head.

"How else supposed to tell you I'm back?"

"I don't know, maybe knock."

"Wouldn't make much sense when I have a key."

Everlee got up from the bed with annoyed grumbles. Masika followed her to the living room. Looking at the stack of cash on the coffee table, she rubbed her eyes.

"That all you got?"

"Yup," Masika crossed her arms, "Enough to get estrogen?"

"Yeah."

"When can we get it?"

Everlee threw herself onto the couch and blew a raspberry, "I gotta call the guy. It'll probably take a couple months to get here."

"Months?"

"Yeah, did you expect overnight shipping?"

Masika rubbed her arm, cursing beneath her breath as she paced. She didn't want to wait. Waiting meant a longer period of Everlee's antagonizing, meant she was further and further away from repentance. She fumbled with her lower lip in thought. Everlee, detecting her strife, chuckled.

"My offer still stands to start you with my batch. You can use it until yours comes in."

"Fine," Masika replied sharply, "Want to start now."

Everlee and Masika headed to the bathroom. Opening the cabinet behind the mirror, Everlee then crouched to grab supplies from beneath the sink. Masika stared off into space as she prepped the dose.

"Where do you want it?" Everlee asked.

"Want what?"

"The injection. Ass, thigh, stomach... which one?"

Masika thought for a millisecond before answering, "Ass is fine."

A mere five minutes later, she bent over the sink. Everlee delicately pulled down her shorts and underwear. Masika gripped the edges as she awaited the prick. The needle injected and she didn't flinch, holding her breath until withdrawal. Everlee cleaned the area with an alcohol wipe, the tiniest sting lingered as she applied a bandaid.

"All done?" Masika asked.

"All done," she slapped Masika's untouched cheek. Masika turned around, scratching her chin as she gave her a once over. "How do you feel? Any changes?"

"Trick question."

Everlee smirked, "You're catching on, doll. That's good, I just wanted to taper your expectations. I was foolish enough to believe the effects would be overnight."

"Nothing like you, just happy to start."

***

Estrogen gifted Masika more than she could've imagined in the first year. It drove Everlee up a wall.

Between her assignments, Masika celebrated the changes. Noticing her scent change first, along with less sweat, the new softness of her skin elated her. To Everlee's utmost disgust, her hips and butt filled out well too.

The further along she got, the more Everlee attempted to sabotage. Feeding Masika more false truths about womanhood, she once again persuaded her into the possibility of cosmetic surgeries. The subject came up every single day without fail, leaving her more irritated than anything. Teneca's lessons slowly coming back to her, she knew Everlee was full of shit by comparison. She'd be leaving this false 'mentor' as soon as she could.

Narrowly fleeing a difficult hit, Masika returned home one night hoping to unwind. Instead, Everlee rushed her the moment she got through the door, clearly wine drunk as usual.

"I have wonderful news for you!"

Masika kicked off her shoes, avoiding Everlee's gaze, "Hello to you too."

Everlee followed her through the foyer into the living room. Collapsing on the couch in exhaustion, Masika looked up at Everlee's barely contained excitement. A bad feeling pooled in her gut.

"Go ahead," she mumbled.

"Soooo... I talked to my surgeon. He'll have an open spot for you as soon as next March!"

Masika's expression darkened, "No."

Everlee disguised her hurt with a fake smile, "Masika. I've told you already, you're going to have to do this—"

"Don't *have* to do anything."

Getting up from the couch, she walked into the bedroom and began shedding her clothes. Everlee tailed right behind with crossed arms and furrowed eyebrows.

"I don't understand you. I give you all these resources, help you get on estrogen, yet you can't accept my offer for surgery? I find it insulting, to be frank."

"Don't give a fuck about your standards, Everlee," Masika told her, putting on a nightgown.

"You should. To me, you don't sound serious about your transition. You sound unsure, conflicted," she inched closer and tilted her head to the side. "Does that make sense?"

"Maybe stop projecting and you'll see what I see. Goals don't align with yours, never will," she stated, sitting down on her side of the bed. "Accept it."

"Then you'll *never* be what you want to be. No one will ever take you seriously. You'll be a fool, a joke, and certainly not a woman."

Masika gripped the edge of the bed; staying calm was excruciating. She knew what she was, knew what she wanted for herself, for her body. Finding this demon's excessive meddling hurtful, her insecurities invited themselves further in. She only really loathed her body when Everlee was around, insisting she needed surgical operations to finalize her 'womanhood.' Masika despised it.

"Keep talking about this and I leave," she warned her.

Everlee scoffed, "Leaving isn't going to change reality, but if you want to go? Be my guest."

Grabbing her coat off the dresser and getting her shoes on, Masika didn't acknowledge Everlee's muffled giggles. She took off to the elevator, not bothering to grab her key. Sleeping on the streets sounded more palatable than returning to Everlee's arms.

Roaming until the brink of dawn, she waited for the library to open. Sequestering herself in the restroom, she cried in a stall and wondered just how much more she could take.

A few hours of reading later, Masika headed out to get food. Stepping out the entrance, she saw Everlee leaning on a pillar. Masika spun around to storm away, but the woman ran right up to her.

"Masika," she tried.

She didn't stop, waving her away, "Fuck off Everlee."

"You know I can't let you leave, Masika," Everlee persisted, "you haven't completed our agreement."

Masika threw herself towards the fiend, stopping only inches away from her face. "Never specified how long it would take or how many kills, did you? Did that on purpose. Gonna keep me on a leash like a goddamn dog forever, aren't you?" Her chest puffed up. "All while you mold me into whatever the fuck you think womanhood is? Must be stupid if—"

"I love you."

The words left Masika speechless. Staring at Everlee for a long while, she backed up a step. "What?"

"I love you, Masika. You aren't my dog, I'm not 'molding' you into anything," she claimed in a conciliatory manner. "I just want what's best for you, but I've been putting too much pressure on you. I'm sorry, can you please forgive me?"

Masika itched to run as far as she could. Instead, she stayed rooted to her spot, lip twitching as she frowned.

"Why should I?" she challenged.

"Because who else in this world loves you? From what I know, there's nothing but a trail of ghosts behind you."

Tears burned her as Masika willed them not to fall. "N-Not true," she tried.

"Oh, but you know it is," Everlee took her hand, "and that's okay. You belong with me, no one else. Do you understand?"

Masika stared down at the concrete, hoping at any moment it would reduce to putty and she would sink far below the surface. Away from Everlee and closer to her deceased mothers. Realistically, she had to face the truth.

Everlee was right, just like Kevin was. There was absolutely nothing out there for her, she had to accept Everlee was her best option. Had to admit there would be no running back to Alabama. After all, how could her friend ever forgive her after her callous decision? Would her father even look her in the face after running away?

There was no point, none of it mattered anymore. She existed to be Everlee's perfect killing machine. Nothing more, nothing less. So she nodded.

"Understand."

"Good, let's go home. I've already got your next target."

Chapter Thirty

April 1995

Against the odds of a rocky second and third trimester, Masika and Aiden handled themselves decently. Aiden existed in constant pain. His lash-outs and shutdowns only increased in frequency. Despite this, she was almost always able to comfort him effectively, talking it through with him afterwards.

By the time his water broke, Aiden could dare say they made a little progress.

In the spinning world, Masika's disembodied voice begged for answers to unheard questions. Trying to push against the nausea rippling through his body, he leaned against the stair rail. Bracing for a fall, she was suddenly right behind him, palms steady on his back.

"Aiden? Aiden, are you okay?"

Trying to nod, a sharp pain sent him towards the ground. Catching him, her face rife with worry as she watched liquid pool at his feet. Without hesitation, she brought him over to the couch.

"Stay right here, okay? Gonna call Mahpiya," Masika said.

Promising it would only take a moment, she rushed into the other room. Holding his swollen stomach, he tried to concentrate, breathing through his nose. When she returned, her eyes were wide and concern-ridden.

"Okay, okay, gonna be here with the midwives in ten minutes. Hear me?" She touched his cheek, "Aiden?"

Nodding weakly at the information, she asked him if he thought he could make it to bed. Answering yes, he allowed her to guide him there.

Mahpiya and the midwives showed up in record time. As the group entered the bedroom, Masika anxiously approached him. The midwives circled around Aiden on the bed, encasing him as they checked his vitals and delivery progress. Mahpiya leaned close.

"How long ago did his water break?" he questioned.

"About fifteen minutes."

"Alright," he took off his backpack and began rummaging through it, "have a seat. We'll take over from here."

Fully trusting in him, Masika obeyed and took a seat at the desk. Watching helplessly as hours flew by, to her utmost worry, Aiden declined any pain medication under the assumption it wouldn't help.

Six hours turned to eight to ten. Mahpiya regularly suggested Masika go eat or have some water, but she refused. She wouldn't leave Aiden's side until the baby was in his or her arms.

A grueling twelve hours later and the midwives deemed Aiden ready for delivery. With their aid, he transferred from his back to his hands and knees. Masika tore at her nails as everyone got into place, Mahpiya smack in the middle ready to catch the baby. Arms held out, he steadied himself.

"Alright, Aiden. I need you to push as hard as you can."

Aiden gritted his teeth, unsure if he could gather the strength. Knuckles digging into the sheets, he paled as he attempted the first push. Masika expected him to scream, but nothing escaped his lips seldom muffled grunts. The midwives grounded him with soothing words and comfort as Mahpiya furrowed his eyebrows.

"You're doing great, I already see the head. Only a couple more pushes, Aiden. Push!" he encouraged.

Another push followed with a cry of agony. Masika stood, feeling help-less off to the side. A midwife named Ewahee placed a gentle yet firm hand on Aiden's shoulder. Mahpiya whispered something, but it was lost in the chaos of the room.

"One more push and you've got it," Mahpiya softened at Aiden's stifled whimper. "I know, we're almost there, I promise. One more."

With all his might, Aiden pushed with every bit of energy that remained in his body. The child shot into Mahpiya's arms, bloodied and squirming as Aiden outright collapsed on the bed. The nurses tended to him as Mahpiya snipped the umbilical cord and stepped away. Much to Masika's distress, the infant didn't make a single sound.

"That's bad, isn't it?" Her voice tinged with panic.

"Not always," he used his stethoscope to check the baby's heartbeat, then two fingers to monitor breathing. He sighed in relief, "All normal, nothing's blocking any airways. Just not much of a crier I guess."

Revi, the eldest of the midwives, suddenly alerted the two, "Placenta is on the way out. I'm going to get him some fluids and food."

Gently rocking the newborn, Mahpiya offered them to Masika. Swal-lowing hard before taking the child into her arms, their weight filled her with joy. Mahpiya noticed Aiden's hard glare and put a hand on her.

"Here, why don't we clean the baby up?" he suggested, quickly pushing her out of the room and into the hallway. He closed the door. "I could tell he's upset, I think he needs time alone with the midwives to recoup."

Mahpiya and Masika washed up the newborn in the bathroom. The infant made not a single sound, but Mahpiya insisted they were perfectly fine. He repeatedly rechecked their vitals to quell her anxieties. As she held the now clean baby swaddled in a towel, Mahpiya washed his hands in the sink.

"Has Aiden's eyes," she commented, tracing a lone finger on their fore-head. "Aiden will love that. Go back now?"

"I don't think he's ready to see the baby yet," Mahpiya deadpanned.

Masika frowned, "Why? What makes you say that?"

Mahpiya held the edges of the sink, "The pregnancy wreaked havoc on his body, he seems absolutely exhausted. Months and months of living not only with another being growing inside him, but also alongside debilitating health conditions? That would have taken a toll on anyone. He's going to need time." As if sensing her anxieties, he continued, "I assure you this isn't uncommon. There are many instances in hospitals where a parent does not see their child right away, for one reason or another. But I promise you, the midwives are going to help him and provide what's best for him in this moment."

She took a minute to process, rocking her child gently in her arms. "How long should we let him rest?"

"I think that should be up to him, not us. I'll be sure to keep checking on him and I will keep you updated. For now, you and the baby should rest too."

She retreated to the nursery for the night. It felt incredibly odd with just her, the baby, and Ehawee. Throughout, the midwives would pop in to check on her. She stayed wide awake, too anxious to sleep even when Ehawee passed out in a rocking chair. The worrisome thoughts accelerated by dawn, whites of her eyes bloodshot.

"Masika," she turned to attention at Mahpiya's voice. Walking over to her, he chuckled a bit at Ehawee snoozing with her mouth open. "How'd you sleep?"

She brought her knees to her chest, "Didn't. Worried about Aiden... doing okay?" Mahpiya hesitated, scratching at the stubble on his jaw. She detected trouble and raised an eyebrow, "What's wrong?"

"He hasn't improved. His physical condition deteriorated overnight, his body is swelling and we had to put him on fluids. Hasn't mentioned the baby, either, not once." Mahpiya rubbed his hands and sighed, "Masika, can I be frank with you?"

"Of course."

"I think he's going to need more time than I thought, which is perfectly understandable. But that means you will have to raise this baby on your own until he's ready."

She stood and moved closer to his face, "What about breastfeeding?"

"Ehawee just had a child a couple weeks ago herself. She's still producing milk, I'm sure she'd be more than willing to provide it until no longer needed."

Masika held her head in her palms. She spent so much energy caring for Aiden during the pregnancy, she hadn't prepared at all for the aftermath. Should've known better than to think Aiden could bounce back after such treachery on his body and mind.

"I'm sorry Masika, I should have prepared you for this possibility," Mahpiya said.

"No way you could've known," she wiped her eyes, moving to the doorway, "need a moment."

None of this was turning out as expected. She had hoped Aiden's pain would end with the birth, but it only brought more complications. Aiden resented their one-day-old and she had no idea what to do except blame herself. Blame herself for everything, dismissing all the glaring signs during the pregnancy that he couldn't handle it. *Maybe we were never meant to be parents*, she thought bitterly, openly weeping into her fists as she collapsed onto the kitchen floor.

Mahpiya found her in hysterics. Moving straight to her side, he sat her up against the fridge.

"Masika. I know you're blaming yourself," he told her carefully, "but this isn't your fault. It was a mutual decision. What matters now is how you proceed from here. You're going to have to step up to the plate, no matter how scary it may seem."

"Know nothing about being a mother," she whispered under her breath, "know nothing about... about *nothing*. Fucking useless, I am. Waste of human space, a fucking joke—"

"Listen, I'll be here to help. I can stay in Nevada as long as you need me to, okay? Just say the word."

Feeling cornered, Masika had no choice but to agree.

***

Full-time motherhood began as a struggle, but after four months Masika felt like a professional.

As Aiden holed himself away in the bedroom, she juggled every responsibility and task imaginable. Ehawee stuck around for the first month of the child's life to teach Masika the ropes of motherhood. Diapers, feeding, bathing, you name it. The knowledge overwhelmed her at first, but she put her anxieties aside. After all, the kid wasn't gonna take care of themself.

She learned quickly that Aiden's mental health relied on his awareness of their child. If he heard them crying, or caught even the slightest glimpse of them, a meltdown would ensue. Unable to stop him from harming himself the first couple times, she reminded herself she had no idea what he was going through. She made a vow to be constantly awake to prevent this.

One eve, no longer able to fend off sleep, she passed out. Unbeknownst to her, the baby's wailing was ceaseless around two in the morning.

In his sanctuary, Aiden tossed and turned, covering his ears. Typically, Masika would rush to comfort the child. After ten minutes of nonstop crying, he forced himself out of the room to check on her.

Two steps into the living room and he found the cause of the issue; Masika slept upright in the recliner, headphones on full blast. Aiden smiled softly at her, interrupted by the shrill cries of an infant. He forced himself to take a couple deep breaths. The intrusive thoughts were already barking at him, displaying images of the unspeakable.

Shoving them down, he flooded his mind with reassurances instead. After grounding himself, he tracked down the hall to the nursery. The door was cracked and terror cascaded down his spine. Staring down at his hands, then at the low blue light spilling into the hallway, he took a deep breath.

Pushing the door open, the yellow walls within taunted Aiden. The crying stopped as he stepped through the doorway. The sandy, striped wallpaper around the blueberry-colored furniture brought him to tears. The baby lay in the crib by a table. Passing the changing table by the door and rocking chair to the left, he walked up to the crib and placed both hands on the rails.

Big browns stared at up at him, curious and lost. To Aiden's shock, the sight didn't outright provoke or disgust him. Testing his limits, he lowered his limb slightly in front of the baby's face. The tiniest little hand reached for it, latching onto the ends of Aiden's fingers. Tears poured down his face, refreshed at the feeling of relief instead of torment.

Reaching both arms to pick them up, a thunderous panic gutted his body and mind. What if he dropped them? Killed them? Threw them against the wall? Masika would never forgive him, and he wouldn't blame her.

Taking a couple steps, anxiously fidgeting, he reasoned with himself. *I would never hurt my child. I'm not my mother.* After repeating the words like a mantra, he drew close to the crib again.

This time when he reached, he remembered the words coupled with determination to be a better father, to be *present*. It granted him the ability to pick the baby up, to cradle them against his chest and sob with elation. Swaying side to side, running his palm over the child's head, he took in their appearance for the very first time.

Frantic footsteps echoed through the hallway. When Aiden turned to the door, Masika skirted into view, resembling a startled cat with bed head and wild stare to match.

"Aiden? Everything okay?" she took a couple steps forward and Aiden gave her a genuine smile. The surprise on her face fell away bit by bit, caving into delight.

In her eyes, father and child stood frozen in time, bathed in soft golden light. At that exact moment, everything fell into place. All the unease from the past few months sank deep into the recesses of her mind. Surely, this was a sign. Whatever existed in the heavens above, beyond her reach, carved this path just for her. All her trials and tribulations were predetermined, simply serving as steppingstones to a greater future. Everything would work out in the end, and she had nothing to worry about. How could such a beautiful moment not be a gift from the Gods above?

Masika clutched her chest and let out a deep exhale, "S-Sorry. Didn't mean to fall asleep."

The baby sprung to life, resuming their tears. The wail resulted in a sour face from Aiden, prompting Masika to sweep them away. Aiden's expression changed to self-disappointment, but she was quick to comfort.

"Hey, hey, it's okay. One step at a time," Masika soothed him with a kiss to the forehead, "Proud of you, know that?"

Drawing closer, he laid his head on her shoulder. *One step at a time.*

Chapter Thirty-One

March 1990

Another night spent struggling to sleep, another opportunity to hit up a bar for half-off drafts. At least, that's how Anuli viewed the occurrence.

Snaking through empty alleyways and streets, they couldn't shake the sensation of being hunted. For nearly a week now, they swore someone was following them. As if a wolf lurked in shadows, waiting to gobble them up. They hoped the hairs standing up on their neck wouldn't give their insight away.

Anuli sped up as discreetly as they could, rushing into a shoddy, dude-bro bar. Taking the sole empty barstool between two men twice their size, both grumbled discontentedly in response. Ignoring the pair, they patiently waited for the bartender to finish a round of dishes as a TV played a campaign ad. Patrons gestured to the screen, muttering their allegiance to the candidate. Anuli sighed noisily from their nose.

When able, they ordered a beer and two whiskey shots, straight up. While they waited, they soaked up the crowded interior. Being at a sports bar during a major game night meant little feminine presence, but they searched for it like always. Never feeling safe without at least a semblance of femininity, they almost stood.

That was until their eyes landed on the opposing wall, where two-seat tables were lined up. Past a couple thick heads, Anuli caught glimpse of a figure leaning back in one of the chairs. Orange locs spilled over the individual's shoulder. Even though Anuli couldn't see pupils beyond black sunglasses, they felt watched.

They sat up to get a better look, but the frat boys moved, completely blocking their view. They scoffed, rushing the two shots down as they waited for their line of sight to clear. When it did, the stranger was gone and a shiver drove down their spine.

They didn't linger long, already having an idea of what to expect upon leaving the bar and braving the streets. Finishing their beer, they watched a little bit of the game before heading out. The whole time, that feeling of being preyed upon never subsided. As they exited, they decided to take a detour. They headed deeper into the city, towards the French Quarter.

Ten minutes into the stroll, Anuli swore they heard footsteps in tandem with theirs. They grasped their 'umbrella' in a death grip, not daring to address their stalker. If the motherfucker tried anything, they'd be met with a blade.

Anuli took a left turn—leading to a dead end—and stopped. Right as they did, the attacker ambushed them from behind. Spinning around, they dodged a few messy swipes of a pocketknife. Although the person moved fast, Anuli registered the locs from earlier. They side stepped, taking her loss of balance as an opportunity to shove her to the ground.

They unsheathed their katana. Aiming it towards the stranger, they backed her up towards the dead-end wall. Shoulders hitting the brick, they pressed the tip of the blade against her Adam's apple.

***

Fear did not overtake Masika as she held a smitten gaze towards the stranger. The grainy pictures she'd been shown didn't do them justice. Upturned, large chestnut eyes sung irritation, their stout nose turned up at her. Belly drooping over belt loops, she admired it alongside various stretch marks. Hair ending right at the neck, the lilac and ruby ombré complimented their brown skin.

The fierceness in Anuli's eyes—heavy with knowledge that one slice would end Masika's pitiful life—captivated her. If this was how she'd be struck down, she'd gladly take it.

"That all you got? You let me disarm you and now you're surrendering?" Anuli asked, holding the weapon steady.

Masika smirked, "Go ahead, cut me up. Couldn't ask for a better final sight."

The tip of the blade trembled, "Answer me this. Who the fuck are you and why have you been following me?"

"Got a hit on you. Been a hard target to follow until tonight." She told them.

"So you *were* trying to kill me."

"Yes."

A motion broke out and Masika expected pain. Instead, they clicked the katana into its sheath. Anuli breathed heavily out of their nose, glaring down at her.

"Who hired you?"

"Man named Arnold Sikes, recommended by my mentor. Told me all about you, he did."

Anuli whistled, "You're way too pretty to be taking hits from politicians."

Masika's eyes widened, had Everlee lied to her? She blinked and leaned forward. Anuli sensed the confusion and gestured to a poster plastered to the alley wall, faded and covered in graffiti. Beneath the insults and obscenities was a picture of the very man she had met with seven days prior.

The one who insisted he needed Anuli deader than dead, deal sweetened with the shiny promise of ten grand. The one Everlee said to be a good man. A wave of sickness crashed over her and she held her head in her palms.

"You know what he's trying to do, right? Take us straight back to the sixties, undo everything our parents worked their entire lives for. You are actively fighting for the people who put us in chains."

"I'm sorry," with trembling breath, she wiped her nose. "Kill me if you want."

Anuli studied her defeated posture and shook their head. "No. When did you tell him you'd be reporting back?"

"A week from now."

"Come to my apartment, lay low. We'll find a way out of this, but it ain't safe out here."

Bewildered by Anuli's blind trust, she frowned. "Are you serious?"

"I am," Anuli gave her their hand. Tenderly taking it, they pulled her to her feet and patted her shoulder. "Come on, it's about five minutes away."

The duo navigated the French Quarter at two a.m., cobbled streets underfoot. Street-lamps painted shadows on aged building walls. The distant sound of a saxophone lingered in the air, a soulful serenade from a nearby jazz club. Neon signs illuminated their path, highlighting businesses still praying for attention. Anuli passed an indigenous man sitting at a booth, offering readings and crochet blankets. Masika trailed close behind.

"Ain't nothin' like New Orleans nightlife," Anuli commented, taking Masika's hand as they ducked into another area. "First time here?"

"Yes, but I was raised in Shreveport."

"Ah, what was it like?"

Heart clenching in her chest, memories overcame her—overlapped bellows of angry white men, blades of grass slicing at her ankles, a fox bone crunching in half, bible verses spouted forth like curses, the crack of a belt against her hide, stolen lighters, moonlit abductions, burning houses—and she sighed.

"Mostly tragic. A little ethereal," she answered.

"Like most of the South, I suppose. We're here."

Checking into reality as Anuli unlocked the door, they went in first, vanishing. Masika stepped inside, not having time to adjust to the darkness when light blinded her vision. After briefly covering her eyes, she found herself facing the tip of a katana once more.

Anuli stared at her, "I need to see if you have any more weapons, or a mic."

Masika bowed her head, compliant as she stripped every layer starting with her fuzzy jacket. Tossing each article until only her undergarments remained, Anuli held the weapon steady as they crouched to check each item. Eye level with her crotch, they blushed before returning to their task.

"Sorry. Didn't tuck today," Masika joked.

"I don't give a shit about that," they replied with a barely concealed laugh.

Anuli gathered up her clothes, handing them back. They immediately turned towards the living room and sheathed their katana.

"This is my place. Not my favorite, but it gets the job done," they stated, sitting on a plaid-patterned sofa as Masika got dressed. They kicked up their feet on a coffee table in front of it.

"Insistent on me staying here, aren't you? What if I kill you in your sleep?" Masika asked, sitting beside them.

"What if? I'd die in my home, away from the cold streets. That's better than how most folk go around here," they crossed their arms. "Besides, you won't. I'll be missed, and surely my friends would come right after you."

"Your friends?"

"The group of people your client is trying to eradicate. People like you and I."

"Transgender people?"

"Yeah, anyone who's not heteronormative and white."

'I'm sorry for not fighting the oppressor' didn't seem appropriate, so Masika opted for silence. Anuli, sensing the discomfort, offered her a cup of tea. Even though she didn't respond, they got up and made it anyway. While they did, her thoughts circled to Everlee, cruel nature shining through significantly more now. Why the Hell would she want to help a corrupt politician?

Everlee wasn't against punishing her, and Masika wouldn't be surprised if this was such a case. Either way, the betrayal burned her stomach and mind. Regretting not leaving the night they argued at the library, she tried not to think too much, dissociating until Anuli returned with a hot mug of tea.

"Thank you."

"No problem," they sat on the couch, smoothing out their pants. "So... you're a hitwoman, so to speak."

"Could say that."

The conversation dawdled for a while. Anuli resigned themself to reading on the couch while Masika sat opposite. Zoning out, she couldn't talk even if she wanted, her mind preoccupied with concern. This was her first failed hit in years and she knew Everlee's reaction would be bad. Flying through scenarios in her head, she came to the realization that she couldn't avoid Everlee for the entire week. She would have to go to her hotel sooner rather than later.

Anuli, satisfied with the progress of their book, got up and returned it to its place. They yawned dramatically, stepping in front of Masika.

"Alright, I'm calling it a night. Where do you wanna crash?"

"Have a guest room?"

"Nope, it's either with me or on the couch."

"Can stay out here, guard the door for you," she offered.

Anuli lifted their hoodie, revealing a gat tucked into their boxers. Masika's heart fluttered.

"Cute, but I don't need a guard dog," they approached their room with a soft chuckle. As they turned the knob, they blessed Masika with a final glance, "Goodnight. See you tomorrow."

"Goodnight."

Tranquility brought on by the gentle lighting of Anuli's apartment advanced her exhaustion. She hadn't slept in four days. Shedding her shoes and curling onto the sofa, she closed her eyes. Releasing the tension in her neck, she attempted an exercise she stopped doing long ago. In...

She thought of lipstick running over her lips, guided by a hand of the Divine.

Out... In...

The grin on his face in the police car, blood streaked across his teeth. The bruises on his knuckles, dotted with crimson.

Out...

***

As per usual, she tossed and turned throughout the night. By four a.m. she was wide awake, smoking a cigarette in the kitchen. She gazed out of the open window, lounging in front of it. The structure of the room was strange. Four lone counters sat against one wall; fridge and sink on the other. Patchy beige wallpaper hid behind posters and photos. It was a good thing Anuli knew how to decorate. After putting the cigarette out on the windowsill, she got ready to return to the couch. Blue orbs greeted her in the darkness.

"Getting comfortable?" Anuli spoke to her.

"Sorry," she mumbled instinctively.

Masika soon slithered onto the couch. She turned a lamp on and picked up the book Anuli had been reading.

***

"Hey, wakey wakey."

Masika rolled onto her side and shook her head. Anuli gently nudged her again and she caved, sitting up slowly. They stood in front of her, hands on their hips. Anuli looked at her lap, where their book sat.

"I see you picked up what I was reading yesterday."

"Was having trouble sleeping. Reading always helps," she responded. "Hope I didn't wake you last night."

Anuli scratched their head, "Uh... I don't think you did. I sleep like the dead. Still okay with spending some time here?"

"Yeah, just have to get belongings from my hotel room."

"I see. Well, I think I'll tag back in case any other attractive assassins try to murder me."

The corner of Masika's lip lifted, "Attractive?"

"There's no point in lying. Let me know if it makes you uncomfortable and I'll stop."

"Will do. Just... not used to hearing that."

She retrieved her jacket before checking to see if the room key remained in its pockets. Sighing in relief when her fingers brushed against plastic, Anuli offered to make her something for breakfast. Normally, she would decline, but she couldn't remember the last time she had eaten.

Squatting down in the living room as Anuli made her a batch of toast, Masika held her head. She had a sinking feeling Everlee awaited her. The last thing she wanted was scrutiny and disapproval. When Anuli placed a plate on her lap, she forced a smile.

"You okay?" they asked, lightly grazing her shoulder with a thumb.

Masika's eyes fell upon the interaction. Usually, she hated it when people touched her. Yet she felt unfazed as she perused the downward curve of two lips unevenly glued together. They were gritting their teeth in worry. She got up quickly, picking up both pieces of toast and heading for the door.

"Taking this to go. Sorry, need to get this over with."

Turning briefly mid-bite, Anuli was right behind her. "You expecting someone?" they questioned in a suspecting tone.

"Boss who sent me to Arnold will drop in," she resisted the urge to shudder as she opened the door. "Don't worry, already know what I'm gonna say. Be back soon."

"Alright. Here," they grabbed a key dangling from a nearby coat hook and handed it to her, "lock up behind, will you?"

"No problem."

With that, she left Anuli in the apartment. Walking at first, she opted to take a carriage ride when her legs started to ache. The driver dropped her off right in front of the hotel entrance. Bypassing the lobby and going straight to the elevator, she braced herself to see Everlee. Masika took a few deep breaths as she reached the eighth floor. Trudging down the hall, a couple turns later she found her room and fished the key from her pocket.

Sure enough, Everlee greeted her from the interior.

"There you are, doll!" Masika shut the door and approached. Laying on the bed, fiddling with her pager, Everlee glanced upwards with annoyance. "You didn't answer my messages. Where were you? What happened to the overnight flight, hm?"

"Slow down please."

"Then *explain*—"

"Then *let* me explain," Masika, briefly taken aback by her gall, paused and swallowed. "Made a mistake. Getting my things and going to another hotel until it blows over."

"A mistake? So unlike you, just like leaving the pager," Everlee deadpanned.

"They put up a hell of a fight. Messy, harder to conceal. Need a little more time, already let Sikes know." Masika tried not to fidget, barely finding her own words believable as she spoke, "Be in contact soon, I promise."

"I see," Everlee rolled onto her feet, gesturing to a wine bottle sitting on the nightstand. "Well, you should have a toast with me before you go. I bought some delicious wine from a market nearby."

"Don't have time," Masika mumbled after gathering her belongings.

When touched, Masika nearly flew halfway across the room. Everlee gauged the gap she created between them and crossed her arms.

"Really?"

"Sorry, don't feel well." Masika slung the two backpacks over her shoulders. "Turn the room keys in, will you?"

She didn't let her get a word in before slipping out the door.

***

When she got back, Anuli was tending to a few plants sitting in their bedroom. They told her to come in and Masika did so, arms full of her belongings. Anuli tilted their head to a shoddy wooden dresser.

"You can put those there for now," they instructed.

"Okay," Masika said, piling them atop. "Turned in the hotel keys. As far as anyone knows, I'm hiding or on the run."

"Nice job, douchebag Sikes can't contact you?"

"Sure can't."

Anuli waved a hand towards the empty side of the windowsill, "Sit with me."

Masika joined them. Hugging her legs, she looked at the three potted plants between their forms. One was certainly a berry plant, the others unknown to her. The berries had been recently plucked, she'd seen them in a jar sat inside the kitchen. Anuli watched her admire the leaves.

"I wanna hear more about you," they stated.

"What about exactly?"

"Like what were you doing before you got hired to kill me?"

She grimaced, "Long story."

"We have time. A whole week, in fact, where we should pop a squat and do a whole lotta nothin'," they leaned forward. "So tell me, unless it's genuinely too much."

"More like..." Masika shifted, gazing out the window, "where to start?"

"How long have you been a hitwoman?"

"About two years now, you're the first hit I've failed."

Anuli smirked, "You surrendered, remember?"

"Yeah, really thought you would kill me."

The conversation stalled. Anuli got up and walked over to the bed. They ran a palm over the comforter, stared at Masika with an ambiguous thirst.

"I'm glad I didn't." They paused and briefly smiled, "You can sleep in the bed with me if it gets too lonely out there."

They were still so confident Masika wouldn't blindside them. Their boldness surprised her and she crossed her arms.

"Toss and turn. That bother you?"

"Nope. Sleep like the dead, already told you."

"Then might take you up on that, just don't want to take up your personal space."

Anuli assured it wasn't a bother. Masika would spend the rest of the evening on the living room couch, reading the book she had eyeballed the previous night. They cooked dinner—a meaty stew—while they listened to music blaring through headphones. She would see them occasionally wiggle their hips or make a sassy gesture in between stirring. She chuckled behind the book, concealing her amusement.

They brought two steaming bowls to the couch forty minutes later, telling Masika to scoot. Ceasing her lounging position, she sat upright, closing the book and accepting a bowl. While waiting for it to cool, she decided it was her turn to be nosey.

"Why would Arnold Sikes put a hit on you?" she brought up.

"Heh, no idea. All I did was shoot him with a paintball gun during a speech. Got arrested, friends bailed me out. Then we all shit on his doorstep a few nights later. Maybe he's worried we'll assassinate him next."

"Will you?"

They gave her a tempted smirk, "Would you? If someone paid you enough?"

"Wouldn't have to pay me if he's as bad as you say."

"I feel the same."

The pair quietly ate dinner after that. Once finished, Anuli collected the plates and excused themself to clean.

Once they were in bed, Masika borrowed the key and walked a few blocks. Finding a hefty dumpster behind a cluster of restaurants, a deep sigh left her body as she stared at the pager. The last link to Everlee. Fear burned her insides; would she dare leave her behind for good? They were never officially involved anyway. No business contract either.

Masika threw the device onto the ground. She stomped on it until it caved to her heel, picking up its remains and throwing it into the dumpster.

Once back at the apartment, unharmed with the door locked, she melted into Anuli's bed. After a few hours of tossing and turning, her body caved to sleep.

CHAPTER THIRTY-TWO

March 1990

"So, what do you call yourself?"

It was Thursday, four days into hiding. Masika and Anuli conversed on the couch, bouncing from topic to topic. The days went by faster and better than she originally assumed they would, Anuli beaming brightly through her cloud of misery. They didn't stop it, but they made it bearable through constant comfort. Usually Anuli's questions were straightforward, but this one wasn't.

"Meaning?"

"Well, are you into other women? Or feminine leaning people in general?" Anuli clarified.

"Never really thought about it too hard. No preference, I think."

"I see."

Their thighs brushed against her legs. Masika's heart fluttered. Anuli's shape, especially in satin green shorts and an oversized t-shirt, enticed her. They tossed a knowing glance in her direction.

"I see you checking me out, you know," they teased, smirking at Masika's blushing. "I don't mind, can't say my eyes haven't been roaming too."

Just like that, Masika couldn't breathe. Her gaze crept up Anuli's body.

"Still think I'm attractive?" she asked, trying to sound justified.

"Yeah, can you blame me? You're beautiful, Masika."

Masika wanted to believe them. After all, they were significantly more genuine in their compliments than Everlee. Yet, she stayed shrouded in fear of not being feminine enough.

"Not sure how you could find me beautiful when I look this way," she admitted.

Their lips turned downward into a frown, "What do you mean by that?"

"Boss—or partner—well, actually…" Masika sighed. "Nevermind what she is to me. Just hear a lot about how there's more work to be done before anyone will see a woman. Looking this way, well…"

"That's bullshit, first of all. Secondly, what does she mean by 'work?'"

"Surgeries. To get bigger breasts and get rid of my…" she trailed off. "You know."

"Do *you* want those surgeries?"

"Maybe, if it means not being a joke to people."

Anuli sighed and shifted forward. "Let me tell you something. It sounds like your boss or whatever thinks conforming to the male gaze is the safest way to be a woman. To avoid becoming a target. She's wrong, women don't need to do that to claim femininity, to *be* a woman. If you feel like a woman, Masika, then you are one. If you're fine with what you have and don't want it to change, you're still a woman. I'm sorry she told you otherwise."

Masika, emotional and rushed with a wave of Déjà vu, excused herself to the kitchen. Finding something to do—settling on the dishes—she started reassuring herself under her breath. Anuli came to the doorway, seeing her anxious attempt at cleaning a load of dishware. Walking up to her side, they gave her a foot or so of distance.

"I'm sorry, I know that might've been hard to hear. Do you need to talk about anything?"

"What's to talk about? Last two years of my life been a goddamn lie. So much fucking blood on my hands, Kevin wouldn't believe it. No…" she stalled, soapy hands hovering over the sink. "Kevin would believe, call me a sinnin' bitch. Don't think I really meant to let it go on so long, but it did. So many people dead. Blood... blood on my hands, on my face, my clothes. The stench... insufferable. All I wanted was a chance to be a woman. Everlee promised she'd help me, but lied. Lied to me."

She bit down on her lips, Anuli inching forward ever so slightly. "You *are* a woman. And honestly, this 'Everlee' is a royal cunt."

"Need space right now." Masika cleared her throat, "Sorry."

"Don't be sorry for needing space. I'll be in bed, reading."

They left her alone in the kitchen. Taking her time, she left Anuli a clean, empty sink. Masika stared into the silver material, reflection taunting her. She closed her eyes and gripped the edge, steadying herself.

Knowing deep down Everlee had been full of shit, she had ignored it for convenience. For safety, she pretended to believe Everlee's quixotic tirades about 'real beauty.' To have confirmation she lied still agonized Masika somehow. Perhaps another layer of betrayal kickstarted a rage within her, one that'd been brewing steady over the years. Either way, she couldn't help but sob. Between catharsis and misery, she found a focal point.

If Everlee's soap opera apology meant nothing, then it was truly time to go on the run again. She knew she had at least thirty grand in cash stored away, unbeknownst to Everlee. She could get out of the city and find a place to put her head on straight. There, she could make a long-term plan.

On Sunday, she would make her way to Chicago. Hoping Anuli would be understanding of her decision, she decided to inform them once morning breached.

***

Announcement getting cut short by a suggestion from Anuli to celebrate the weekend, Masika couldn't resist the stoned grin on their face.

"Want to celebrate?" she asked.

"Sure do. 'Cause, despite the circumstances, I've been having a great time getting to know you. Figured I'd get a bottle or two of my favorite tequila to share."

"Didn't know any better, would think you're asking me on a date."

"It's only a date if you want it to be."

She fell silent at that. A couple minutes later, Anuli headed off to the store. While they got drinks, Masika habitually cleaned up the living room and kitchen. When Anuli came back, they playfully scolded her.

"Didn't have to do all that now," they said, putting the bottles on the kitchen counters as Masika wiped the sink.

"Force of habit, least I could do for you," Masika responded without looking. "Trip good?"

"Yup, nice and quick. You let me know when you're ready for the first shot."

Masika finished her task, signaling Anuli to grab the shot glasses. They poured themself and her a shot of tequila.

"To thwarted assassinations and surprise companionship!" they cheered, raising their glass.

Clink. Masika drank, not batting an eye in comparison to Anuli, who gagged after their shot. Wiping their mouth in embarrassment, they gave her a silly grin.

"I can hold my liquor, getting it down is the problem."

"See that."

Shot after shot the pair took. Anuli suggested going to their bedroom, ending up lounging on the yellow sheets together. For a while, neither said a thing. Masika and Anuli simply sat, eyes roaming in quiet adoration.

"Do you know what it's like?" Anuli suddenly asked.

"What what's like?"

"To have unconditional love from someone?"

The kindest smile she'd ever seen flashed in Masika's head. She nodded somberly, "I think I did, long time ago."

"Seems you struggle to accept you deserve something like that. You should tell me about them."

"There's not much to say; ran away and never saw them again. Ran all the way into trouble. Haven't found my way out yet, I suppose."

Anuli put out their cigarette before drawing closer to Masika. She naturally tensed but relaxed when they rested their head on their arms. Peering up at her curiously, they sprung another question.

"Has anyone told you a lip piercing would be awesome on you?"

"Nope. Which one? Or any?"

Anuli sat up, pressing a fingertip against the center of their bottom lip.

"Right here—I can see it clear as day in my mind," they said, a playful smirk on their face.

They went to say something else but were entranced by Masika's mouth. Eyes leaving her lips, climbing up her nose, gazes met. Her heart twisted in her chest as Anuli reached for her face, granting her a single, timid kiss. She flushed as they cradled her cheeks. When she fully realized what happened, she tore to the bathroom.

A million racing thoughts was enough to make her stomach feel sick. She regained control by splashing water on her face and focusing on the ice-cold liquid. It really wouldn't have been a big deal if she didn't want to kiss them back, but she did.

Oh, she wanted that and much more.

She reminded herself what happened when she acted on impulse. Shortly after, Anuli entered the room, eyebrows scrunched in the middle of their forehead. They stuck a couple of their knuckles between their teeth, nervously watching Masika.

"I'm sorry, I shouldn't have done that," they apologized, wringing their hands together. "I don't want to make things weird between us."

"Didn't do a thing," Masika replied, turning to them. "Wanted to kiss you back, maybe more... Instinct just says run like Hell."

Anuli's expression changed from worry to intrigue. They approached and rubbed her shoulder.

"I understand. You're safe here though, you can do whatever makes you happiest. It doesn't have to involve me whatsoever."

Masika appreciated the option to choose—a decision so rarely granted to her nowadays. As she looked at Anuli, she pinned her attraction as a good thing. Something to indulge, to covet. A soft smirk lifted the corner of her mouth.

"Then let me worship you."

Anuli's touch ghosted her waist, "By all means."

They opened their legs as she kissed them, fingers traveling towards the center of their boxers. Anuli gasped and Masika suckled on their neck, teasing touches turning into a full-scale romp against the bathroom sink.

She gripped their hips as they sat on the edge, legs spread as they took her length. Gasping in ecstasy, they stroked themself to the sight of her rutting into them. Masika moaned into their mouth, a firm hand cradling their neck. She wouldn't last long, but she knew the fun would be far from over once she finished. Anuli tightened around her as she released into them, running a digit down Masika's face as her lips parted with theirs.

"That was quick," Anuli teased.

Masika gently caught their wrist, "Not finished with you yet."

She feared it came out too harshly, but they only smirked back. Helping herself to the mess between Anuli's legs, their hips bucked towards her, desperate and needy for her tongue. Focusing on their clit, the moans that ensued were a delight to her ears, quiet and mousy in nature. As Anuli shyly covered their face, she couldn't help but smile.

When they came their thighs convulsed, rattling Masika's shoulders, neck, and head. Her grin that followed feigned innocence.

"Oh my, looks like I'm making a mess out of you." She didn't bother to wipe the slop on her mouth and chin. "Keep going?"

Anuli, chest still rising and falling rapidly, stared hazily down at her.

"Yes," they spoke between breaths, "until I can't walk anymore."

An hour later, the pair lay tangled atop messy sheets. Unlike her most recent sexual experiences, post coitus didn't consist of dissociation. In fact, the clarity and contentment of her mind astonished her. She didn't experience this level of intimacy with Everlee either; it felt nice to be vulnerable with someone that didn't view her as prey.

Anuli ran their fingers along Masika's scalp, luring her out of her thoughts. "Can I ask a potentially dumb question?"

"Sure."

"How'd you get so ripped?"

She shrugged, "Always been a bit on the muscular side. Taught myself some ballet, probably helped."

"Ballet! That explains it," Anuli tapped her cheek. "You know, I used to dance as a kid."

"Bet you were great."

"Thanks."

Anuli leaned over her and felt a bicep, Masika's muscles still glistening with sweat. They kissed her neck, a mischievous grin dancing on their face.

"How lucky am I..." they started, moving their lips to her ear, "...to have you try to kill me?"

Both erupted into laughter as Masika playfully shoved Anuli away. Picking up a half-full beer can on the nightstand, she smirked.

"Wouldn't call it lucky," she replied sarcastically, having a sip.

"Why not? Are you still lying to yourself about being a bad person?" Masika's smirk faded and they sighed, "Sorry, told you I'm blunt."

"Not far off," she admitted.

"I know, I see it every night. You're terrified of your 'sins.' Weighed down by them."

Masika was speechless. Finishing the drink and returning it to the nightstand, she sat up in the process. Staring at a cluster of faded posters on one of the bedroom walls, her vision blurred and her thoughts vanished. Anuli started speaking again, but it fell ineligible on her ears. This went on only for a few seconds until Anuli noticed the vacancy in her eyes.

"Hey, are you okay?"

"Of course."

"You don't have to be you know. You've been through unfathomable things," Anuli tried.

"Everything was my own doing, by my own hands. Don't know the half of it, Anuli."

"I don't have to know. Nothing you tell me could make me hate you or think you're a monster. None of it could make me believe you deserved the things you've been through, do you understand?"

Masika, drunk off the strange mix of comfort and terror, melted into their chest.

***

Waking up tangled in Anuli's arms felt like a distant dream. Nuzzling her nose into their bare chest, she inhaled the scent of cigarette smoke and raspberries. Anuli's digits met her scalp, holding on tightly and grinning sleepily into her hair. Masika pulled away just enough to kiss them. The kiss lasted until Anuli left to make breakfast, insisting she stay resting in bed.

"Let me take care of you," they whispered.

She pulled the comforter over her body, dozing off until the smell of bacon and eggs filled the room. Anuli was at her side, holding a steaming hot plate.

"Here you go, I'll be right back."

Admiring their naked figure as it vanished through the doorway, Masika nibbled on her bacon. The moment the meat hit her tongue, she gagged. Spitting it out, the taste of blood was undeniable. With an onset of fear, she leered at the plate's contents. Knowing it was futile but not wanting Anuli's efforts wasted, she tried the eggs. Once again the food fell from her mouth. She couldn't bear it.

Anuli returned with their own plate, seeing Masika scrubbing her tongue. She was quick to reply, "S-Sorry, tasted weird to me."

"Let me see," Anuli grabbed a piece of bacon and chewed it carefully. "What does it taste like to you?"

Normally, Masika would not say a word, but Anuli's worried expression lowered her guard.

"Blood. Tasted like blood," she wiped the grease off her mouth. Her fingers curled and Anuli delicately took them, "Sorry, can keep trying—"

"No, please don't put yourself through that. Would making something different help?"

"Don't hurt to try," she lied, doubling down when Anuli gave her a skeptical look. "Promise it's fine."

She grimaced as they walked away, not sure why she felt the need to fib. She tried to be hopeful at the sight of a new offering in Anuli's grip. That false hope dwindled when the bowl traded hands, actualization binding her thoughts. Everlee must've been lurking in the shadows of the apartment, tampering with the food. She clutched the bowl tightly, staring into it. How'd Everlee get inside the house? Through the unlocked window in the kitchen? Had she been hiding under the bed, waiting to strike? Surely Anuli would've seen her, considering their perceptive nature.

Unless, she thought, terror building in her belly, only *she* could see Everlee. The revelation rang clear as day as she reminisced on the past couple years. She couldn't remember a single instance of another human acknowledging Everlee. Frantically scanning memories for proof, she froze. Anuli tried to get her attention to no avail. She soon took a running start for the kitchen, leaving the dish behind.

She glimpsed every corner, enraged to find absolutely nothing. No trace or evidence of another presence existed. It took all her might not to punch a wall; how *dare* Everlee terrorize her this way. How dare that demon loom in Anuli's sanctuary, putting them in direct danger. The bitch loved to taunt her, and this was no exception. Pissed off and perturbed, she broke down on the floor. Anuli stood in the doorway, watching her with solicitude.

"Masika?"

"Dammit! Has to be here, I know it! Fucking with my food, she is. Fucking with my head, trying to fuck with you," she rambled on as she peered up at Anuli. "Can't see her, can you? Nobody can, nobody but me. Must be a demon, a creature sent to punish me. Believed her to be an angel, I did. How foolish. 'And no wonder, for Satan himself masquerades as an angel of light.' 2 Corinthians 11:14. Doomed, I am. Dooming you with my presence... have to leave *now*."

"Whoa... hey, let's slow down a little bit," Anuli suggested, plunking down. "Where did this come from?"

"Think I'm crazy, you will."

"No, I won't. I promise."

Masika explained her thought process—the best she could with a jumbled psyche. The whole time, Anuli listened with slow, understanding nods. They didn't diminish her feelings whatsoever, waiting until she finished speaking her mind to respond.

"Do you want me to go get something fresh from the store? Something we know she hasn't tampered with?" they tried.

"No. Just... maybe need a distraction, is all."

Anuli offered to roll up and watch TV together. Masika accepted, knowing a blunt would have calming effects. Following them into the living room, they hunkered down on the couch and started flipping channels.

Masika stood behind at first, only sitting when her nerves felt less on fire. Still trying to get her mind off the terrible taste coating her mouth, she focused on Anuli's facial expressions. Making jabs at the mediocre soaps they skimmed by, they eventually reached a news channel. At first they skipped it, then their eyes lit with curiosity. Backtracking, they leaned against the cushions and crossed their arms.

Three news anchors discussed the predicted outcome of the election. The odds were in favor for Sikes. At first, Masika tuned it out; when the broadcast cut to footage of the man himself, her chest tightened.

"I guarantee to scrub our streets clean. There will be an increased police presence in the city to get rid of the filth. If you want to see true change, you know what to do. There's nothing they can do to stop us; they will have no choice but to obey."

Her knuckles clenched into a fist. "Why hasn't somebody killed this fucker yet?" she seethed openly.

"No idea. He has no security, so it'd be pretty easy."

Masika detected their intent in an instant. She scooted closer, mouths inches apart.

"How would *you* do it?" she questioned.

Irises flickered with admiration.

"Any way you wanted it," they breathed.

Taken aback by the response, Masika swallowed a lump in her throat, "Saying you'd kill him with me?"

Anuli nodded, curling their head onto her shoulder. Their touch roamed down Masika's bicep as they bit down on her neck. Masika moaned, head reeling from the warmth of their tongue mixed with the idea of their meddling scheme. The chaos and freedom that would erupt from Sikes' absence, all the doing of her and her lover's delicate hands.

How could she resist?

Chapter Thirty-Three

April 1990

Following a frankly hellacious day, Arnold was grateful to be home. Sprawled out on the couch, he phoned his favorite escort service. Needing a way to vent his frustrations, what's better for that than a disposable prostitute? He scheduled the visit for around ten-thirty p.m., giving him plenty of time to shower and unwind.

Leaving the couch and heading for his bathroom, he undressed quickly and turned on the water. Grumbling to himself about his annoyance regarding the day's events, he scratched his scrotum mindlessly. Watching the water escape into the drain, he realized he neglected to grab a towel.

Right as he turned on his heel, he gasped. A woman stood before him, giggling mockingly at his naked body. She adorned a simple black bra-and-panty combo. Fear crossed his eyes at full recognition of the individual.

One slice to the chest was all it took to send Arnold backwards into the bathtub. A shrill scream left his body as he frantically clutched at the open wound. Masika's thumb ran across the smooth sides of the blade, aiming it at him while he struggled to get up.

"Don't fucking move," she commanded.

As he cried, Anuli entered the room. Upon seeing them, Arnold grew frantic, diving out of the tub and flopping onto the hard tile. When he crawled to the entrance, Anuli blocking it, Masika stomped down on his neck. Arnold looked up at Anuli pitifully, choking, and earned a smirk from them.

"Remember us?" they spoke.

Wheezing, he started blabbering about a safe in the garage, at least ninety thousand dollars in cash stuffed inside. He gave the code without a second thought.

"Just let me go! Let me go, please..."

"You know we can't do that, Sikes. We can't let you win," Anuli chuckled darkly in amusement. "Masika, step aside."

Masika obeyed, taking great amusement and pleasure watching Anuli kick the shit out of the man. When that method didn't satisfy them, they rolled him and climbed atop. Expert blows landed on his face, him begging for mercy until blood flooded his mouth and he couldn't any longer. Anuli didn't stop until the man became unrecognizable, a pulp of brain mass and broken skull remained. When he took his last breath, Anuli finally ceased. Masika eyed them as they got to their feet.

"You okay?"

"Yeah," Anuli answered, closing their knuckles into fists. "Better than okay. Glad he's fucking dead."

"Get the sheet now?"

Anuli nodded and Masika headed to Arnold's bedroom, pulling a black sheet off the mattress. The couple wrapped his body in it, transporting him onto his bed. While Anuli scrubbed the bathroom clean, Masika wiped all the door handles. Once everything was said and done, the clock nearly reached ten-twenty. They both stripped down their blood-covered undergarments and hopped into the still running shower.

What happened next blurred in Masika's mind, vaguely remembering getting dressed and shoving bloodied clothes into a trashbag. Now she sat with Anuli on a loveseat, garbed in a jumpsuit and thick rubber gloves. They stared at the front door in anticipation.

"What's happening?" Masika asked them.

Before Anuli could say a word, there was a knock at the front door. They got up to answer it and a mild-mannered, short Black girl stood, anxiously clutching her purse.

"Is this the Sikes residence?" she asked.

"Sure is, come on in."

The girl trailed behind Anuli, eyebrows raising at Masika's presence in the living room. "My booking agent didn't say anything about other people. Where's my client?"

Anuli sat down, granting the girl an innocent smile. "Go check the bedroom."

Masika wanted to ask what the hell they were doing, but she trusted Anuli. The escort walked to Arnold's room, hinges of the door creaking as she opened it. Two footsteps were followed by a retch, then a shriek of terror. She came running back down the hall. Despite her horrified expression, the following question was asked in a shockingly calm voice.

"Are you gonna hurt me? What the fuck is this?"

"No, we won't hurt you. And this? It's way above your pay grade. Which is why I want you to have something." They gestured to a suitcase on the table, "There's forty-thousand dollars in here. You're gonna let us walk out the front door, using your hand to open it. Keep the money for yourself, hide it, then call the cops and tell them you found him alone. No signs of a break in, say nothing about us or the money. Do you understand?"

The girl rubbed her arms, "I-If I listen to you, promise you won't hurt me?"Anuli and Masika both nodded in response. "Okay, we have a deal."

With that, she opened the front door for the partners in crime. Anuli and Masika left as if nothing happened.

***

Hectic packing ensued at the apartment. Masika's belongings didn't take long to gather, but Anuli had an entire home to pilfer through. Joking about their foresight to not deck the place out, it still took nearly an hour to get everything they needed.

Anuli requested Masika step outside with their stuff. She obliged, carrying all the luggage out and quietly admiring the apartment's exterior.

They joined her at the front door, panting. They reeked of gasoline and the two exchanged glances. A matchbox emerged from their hands.

"Step back, way back. This is gonna be messy."

Masika moved a yard away, watching Anuli light a match and toss it into the entryway. They scrambled to her side, observing a line of flickering light dance atop the wood. She watched in awe as the apartment gradually went up in flames. The gentle crackles whispered to her, emboldened. When a window shattered, Anuli grabbed her hand.

"C'mon, we gotta get out of here." When she didn't move, they squeezed, "Masika?"

"Sorry. Love watching the embers." She tore her eyes away, "Let's go."

Booking it to the closest bus stop, both ignored the distant sirens. As they sat down on a bench, Masika tried to conceal her trembling limbs. She couldn't help but feel anxious about Arnold, about the corpse of an apartment they left behind. She had no idea where to go from here.

"Where are we gonna go? Any ideas?" Anuli asked, as if reading her mind, "You mentioned your high school friends and your old man, maybe we can head that way?"

"Would like that."

***

The bus rolled into Pike Road, Alabama around seven forty-five a.m. Anuli and Masika ventured to the cheapest motel they could find, buying a room.

She found the lower quality to be quite refreshing. Anuli got comfortable watching the news while Masika excused herself to shower.

Stepping into the bathroom, Masika admired the subtle curves of her hips and butt, running over them with her hands. The same hands reached up to her chest. To her surprise, she found herself beaming at her reflection. If she didn't know any better, she would thank a higher power for crafting her in such a way; but she knew it had been herself aiming the syringe. No Gods, no unknown force. Only the workings of her own hands. Anuli appeared behind her, wrapping their arms around her abdomen.

"This is the first time I've seen you look at yourself."

Masika toyed with the grip clasped around her stomach, "Yeah... been a long time."

"Are you happy?"

She turned to face them, taking their face into her palms. Anuli giggled as she kissed them in response.

"Gonna check the news soon, gotta make sure nobody's on our trail," they said.

"Hopefully our friend followed your instructions."

"I have a feeling she did," Anuli ran their thumb along Masika's arm, "but we'll know for sure soon. Is there anything else you want to do beside visit your old man? Maybe see your friend?"

"Don't think I'm ready to talk to them yet. Don't know where they are either."

"Can I help you find them? I would love to meet them, too, if you're okay with that."

"Yeah. Two of you would be good friends, I think, but have no idea if they'll forgive me."

"Forgive you for what?"

Masika looked at them sadly, "Abandoned them. Right after we slept together."

"Ouch. That's..."

"Fucked up, I know... Was scared, but that's no excuse."

"Are you going to apologize?"

She nodded, "Gonna try. Wouldn't blame them if they decide not to forgive me."

The news broadcast suddenly shifted to a breaking story, alerting the two. The pair rushed out of the bathroom to watch, news anchor flashing onscreen.

"Political candidate Arnold Sikes was found dead in his home last night after an anonymous report was filed with the New Orleans Police Department. The investigation is ongoing."

"Yes! I knew that girl would have our back!"

Anuli bounced around the room like a hyperactive cat. Kissing their forehead in celebration, Masika retreated to the bathroom.

A rather long victory shower later, Masika entered the main room to find Anuli sprawled on the bed. Clad in nothing but their underwear, she joined. Nuzzling into their belly and wrapping her arms around their waist, they pet her head.

"Everything okay?"

"Yeah. Trying to muster the courage to see my old man," she responded into their tummy.

"Do you want me to come with you?"

Masika sat up and shook her head immediately. "No, should probably talk to him alone. Might be pissed at me for leaving, don't want you dealing with that."

"Ah, that makes sense. No worries," Anuli kissed Masika before taking her face into their hands. "I'll be right here when you get back, okay? Then, maybe we can go see your friend."

"Good idea," Masika stated with a tiny grin.

She hugged them crushingly tight, holding their head against her own. Once she had cuddled enough to be satisfied, she dressed herself and bid them farewell.

"See you," she said.

"See you soon. Don't keep me waiting too long," Anuli teased.

"Won't."

With that, she slipped out the door.

***

Herb's neighborhood was a merciful ten-minute walk. Upon reaching his dilapidated trailer, Masika's nerves shredded to bits. She clasped a hand over her chest to steady her beating heart. All of a sudden, she held no desire to speak with her father. Instead, she longed for her mother's wedding dress. She decided to break in, take the dress, and leave. Rounding the side of the house to her bedroom, she checked the window to find it unlocked.

Climbing through, she gently closed it before jumping onto the floor. Waves of Déjà vu entombed her; her room hadn't changed. The same bedding was there from the night she left town. She had somehow expected the room to be turned into storage, but no. Here it was, just as she left it.

Approaching the door, she pressed her ear against it to it to see if she could hear the living room TV. Silence. Opening it, she headed down the long, dark hallway. She made it only a handful of steps when a voice chilled her to the core.

"M? Is that you?"

Masika stopped, sucking in a sharp breath. Uneven footfalls echoed behind her. Her father repeated the question, voice shakier than before. She bit her lip before daring to respond.

"Yes," she answered.

"My God, I've been worried sick. Thought you was dead."

"Well, not dead," she stated gruffly, only slightly turning her head, "so quit worryin'."

Masika went to leave, but he rushed towards her. She whirled around as he touched her shoulder. The moonlight filtering through shoddy curtains unveiled a new sight to him. He paused, absorbing the details of her face. Masika instinctively flinched away in shame. She didn't expect Herb to cup her chin and force their eyes to meet. His filled with tears.

"You look like Phillis," he stammered, now holding both of Masika's cheeks in his weathered palms. "Golly, it's…"

"Disgusting?"

His hands dropped. Herb scowled at his daughter and savagely shook his head.

"You ran away with no note, no trace. The cops didn't wanna help me search on account of yer ass causin' so much trouble. The town was happy to be rid of ya, but I kept on worryin' anyway. I thought you was dead, or worse." He inhaled loudly as tears fell down his face, "So to see my baby here, right now, alive and well? I don't give a damn about anything else. What made you come back?"

"Mom's dress," she lied.

"Figures, you were always attached to that thing. I'll grab it for you."

Masika lingered in the hallway until he returned with a paper tote, passing it off to her. She peered in, saw the emerald green fabric inside, and lowered the bag to her hip. She thanked him before leaving the hall once more. He followed her into the kitchen, insistent.

"Where you runnin' off to? Don't have even five minutes for your old man?"

"Have nothing to say to you," she replied, tight-lipped.

"We both know that's a lie, girl."

Clenching her fists, she paused at the front door. He was right, damn near always was. She hated that about him. He was the only wise man she had ever known; could read people like the back of his hand, especially her. She wanted nothing more than to tell him everything, yet she couldn't reveal her pain.

Masika couldn't tell him that she never forgave him for leaving her with Gram and Kevin. Couldn't breathe a word about the animals who would never find proper graves, undone piece-by-piece via a child's clumsy hands. Nor about all the fires that perpetually burned in her head.

Or could she? A part of herself asked if it would hurt to try. By this point, she couldn't contain her emotions. Tears poured down her face as she trembled, rooted to her spot. Bracing her head with her hands, she tried to crush her skull in her palms.

"No! Can't... Can't do it..."

"M? Come here."

She glanced over her shoulder to see Herb, arms outstretched and ready to provide comfort. She did something she had never done before, and accepted the offer. When he wrapped her into a hug, her silent tears transformed into wails. Anguished, she balled both her hands into fists as she shook her head. He only held her tighter.

"I've got you. I've always got you, M. You know that," he spoke, holding her head. "I love you, I'm sorry I never said it enough. If you must go, I won't be upset."

Masika contemplated his words as she wept. By the end she was dangling off him, head limp against his chest as he rocked her side to side. She eventually peeled away.

"Can stay for one hour. No more," she uttered.

"Ya sure?"

"Yes, Pops. C'mon, sit on the couch 'fore your knees snap in half."

He chuckled, letting her lead them into the living room, "Never lost your smart mouth, huh?"

Father and daughter conversed for thirty minutes. Herb asked mostly of her travels, how she got out of Alabama in the first place. She spoke the truth, mostly, leaving out her and Everlee's escapades of course. Asking what he'd been up to, the answer was the same as always: working himself to death. She questioned his decision to still be working well past retirement age.

"Well, how else bills gonna get paid? Gotta keep the lights on somehow."

"Walking much worse than the last time I saw you. Need to be in a wheelchair, Dad."

"Maybe you're right, when pigs fly."

And that was that. She couldn't talk him out of capitalism no matter how much she tried. She decided at once she would leave him some money, cover three months of rent at least. Another subject crossed her mind. If the town was running Herb this ragged, how were the twins faring?

"Twins still live here? Thought about going by Dorothy Ann's, but—"

Herb scoffed, "Glad you didn't, she woulda ripped you a new one. They've both been missing for a good while now. Dorothy Ann don't leave the house no more, either. She might as well be dead, for all we know."

She straightened. Bringing a palm over her mouth, she blinked a few times. *You idiot. You should've expected this*, she thought to herself. She needed more details.

"Missing? Like... kidnapped?"

"Nope, one of 'em killed a cop and fled. Guess the other didn't want to deal with that either, ditched town around the same time. Nobody knows for sure, the details are vague. Tell you what though? I think they were both in on it. They was always smart, the two of 'em, especially that boy you liked."

She longed for more details but could tell her father had none to spare. It was midnight, and he was exhausted by the way he kept rubbing his face.

"So did you decide M would be your full name, or...?"

"Masika's my name, but M works fine too."

Herb repeated the name aloud five times, getting a grasp on it. This made Masika smile. He then checked the time on his watch, saw only fifteen minutes remained, and fetched two beers.

"To celebrate the daughter I didn't know I had," he started with a grin. "To celebrate your womanhood—"

"Okay, okay can stop there," she stifled a snort as she opened a bottle. "Appreciate it, Dad. Really do."

They drank their beers in silence. Herb was awkward, but he always meant well. She took the last sip and he voiced something unexpected.

"I shoulda never sent you to live with Kevin, Masika."

She looked at him, disheveled, "What?"

"I know he tortured you. Prolly tortured you like he used to torture me. That stupid fucking belt—" he choked up, "Parents should never hurt their children like that. He hurt me, I let him hurt you, and my momma didn't give a rat's ass about either of us; only that white man's approval. I left you there for so many years. When you'd call, you always sounded so damn scared. Until you didn't. After a while, you sounded like an adult. That terrified me and I still didn't have the courage to bring you home. I'm sorry, I'm so fuckin sorry."

She put a hand upon his shoulder. An apology was unexpected, yet welcome. She didn't know how to respond, though. At a loss for words, another silence fell between them.

"You grew up too fast. I should have protected you," he muttered.

"Dad... what's done is done," she said plaintively, "don't get me wrong, appreciate this. But can't change the past, can we?"

"Doesn't mean it won't haunt me. Not nearly as much as it haunts you, I'm sure. I've accepted I can't change it, just wish you didn't have to carry that pain for the rest of your life. Is there anything I can do?"

"No, not an overnight thing. But this chat certainly helps, I think."

The two quietly wept, Masika's cries lasting until her father had dozed off. Sat beside him, she watched him fuss in his sleep. She did so until exhaustion tugged at her body.

A sudden dread filled her entire being, snapping her out of the drowsy state. She got off the couch, trying to detect the origin. When she did—a instinctual concern regarding Anuli—she kissed Herb on the forehead. She made sure to leave him some money before fleeing through the bedroom window.

CHAPTER THIRTY-FOUR

April 1996

Any of Aiden's attempts to rush the process of cohabitating backfired, leaving him no choice but to take things slow. He began with spending the mornings with Masika and the baby, tending to be calmer and more relaxed then. He did this for a month, soon joining in for breakfast and lunch too.

At this point, Aiden freely roamed the house, holding his kid like it was second nature. The remaining hurdles related to helping Masika with childcare. She insisted she could do it alone, but he knew motherhood was far from easy. He refused to throw her to the wolves while he did fuck-all. The best place for him to start was changing diapers; a task he failed spectacularly at.

Plenty more he did in the coming weeks, taking over feeding and bath time. He started to assist Masika in teaching ASL as well. She told him that he could take the reins once the child learned how to walk (which, with their fast-learning skills, didn't seem very long from then). Cleaning responsibilities other than diaper changes being his until further notice also allowed Masika great relief. She displayed elation—and slight solace—at his further involvement.

Perhaps the most pleasant surprise regarded Aiden and Masika's agreement on parenting methods. Their child's upbringing would not mirror the horrific physical or mental abuse they once endured. If either of them accidentally lashed out at the child, they would do their best to comfort and hold accountability. Many long-winded discussions followed over the months, reaping improvement and fostering patience.

A more recent conversation occurred when Aiden asked what gender the kid was. He didn't know why it took him so long to even *think* of the question. As he had with Masika during senior year, he'd easily defaulted to referring to the infant as 'they' for now. She told him she wasn't going to force their child in any specific direction. The couple decided to let them choose what they wanted for themself, whenever they were ready.

The family fell into routine. Before Aiden and Masika knew it, their child turned a year old. On that sweltering spring day, the three played in the garden for hours on end. Since mastering the ability to walk, the child took great interest in the various flora and fauna, wanting to poke and touch every leaf and petal. They especially loved the vegetable patch.

At that very patch, while Masika and Aiden chatted, a butterfly floated in the baby's direction. When Aiden turned his head, he didn't expect to see it atop his child's hair. He tapped Masika, who glanced over and beamed.

"Aw, have a little friend."

"Two friends," Aiden replied, pointing to a second, smaller critter on the infant's hand. "Bugs really love them."

"Noticed that too."

Over the next few days, several incidents led Aiden to an idea. All aforementioned incidents involved bugs—even poisonous ones—crawling or interacting with the infant without any repercussions. When two wasps landed on them and didn't sting, Aiden's mind couldn't help but wonder. He brought it up to Masika one quaint afternoon spent in their garden.

"Name..." he began before his hands fell into his lap as he pondered.

"Who's name?" She asked.

Aiden gestured to the toddler, squashing fallen petals with their feet. Masika slumped against the rocking chair and blew a raspberry.

"Never talked about a name, did we? Too focused on other stuff I guess."

Aiden flushed and signed an apology, not believing how much he glazed over during his haze. She nudged him, reminding it was nobody's fault. The two resumed observing their child run rampant, excitedly squealing every time they came across an unknown plant.

Somewhere along the way, both Aiden and Masika zoned out. Aiden bounced back at the tug of his sleeve, their child standing beside him with a hand closed into a gentle fist. He touched Masika's arm, gifting them both their attentions.

"Whatcha got there?" Masika asked.

They proudly stretched out their hand, revealing a ladybug in their palm. They babbled in joy as it crawled onto the other side of their limb. It launched off and away into the sky, and the toddler scurried to the plants. Aiden couldn't help but smile.

"What's on your mind?"

"You're gonna think it's dumb," he responded.

"No way, go ahead."

"I think we should name them Bug."

A large grin spread across her face. The child launched themself into her arms. She repeated the name over and over as she wiped dirt off the infant's face. They giggled and reached for her hands as she looked into Aiden's eyes.

"Sounds good to me."

Aiden's heart melted.

***

Aiden's bedroom was akin to a doctor's office as Masika stretched a pair of sterile gloves over her hands. She prepared a syringe and he stared intently at the vial on his nightstand. Despite knowing the first shot wouldn't magically change everything, he still itched his arms in anticipation. He daydreamed about his eventual hair thickness, the sharpening of his jaw, and everything else Masika spoke of. He would not mourn his current body, the one Dorothy Ann never found to be satisfactory. Testosterone would save him, gift him with confidence only Gods could bestow. He wished for nothing more.

Masika was at his side in a flash, holding the now filled syringe. "Do you want your legs, stomach, or butt for the injection site?"

He gestured to his belly and she made quick work of sterilizing the area. An agonizing thirty seconds passed as she uncapped the needle, "Are you ready?"

Aiden took a deep breath, staring down. Not a shroud of doubt existed as he nodded.

"Alright, on the count of three," she aimed the sharp end towards the fat, pinching it with her left hand. "One..."

He closed his eyes. Dorothy Ann's disapproving finger wagged in his mind.

"Two..."

He forced himself to breathe. *No, this moment won't be ruined. This is my body, my decision.*

"Three."

At the sharp penetration of his skin, he felt no fear.

***

Beneath clear skies, Masika and Bug chased after one another in the backyard. From the screened in porch, Aiden observed peacefully. Just having come home from work, he had detoured from his usual path to their living room. He chuckled as neither Masika nor Bug noticed his return.

Today marked his third year on testosterone. Some changes took longer than others; jawline delayed while his body hair developed in less than two months. By year two he resembled a bear, his beard cascading down to the beginning of his chest. A chest now flattened and adorned with floral tattoos sitting atop faded scars. He'd gotten top surgery to celebrate his second year, something he was surprised he waited so long to do. The healing process was nothing compared to the years of binding. He'd finally made his body a home, and any short-term immobility was worth that.

Aiden started working for Ruby again the year Bug turned five. Masika took care of them during the weekdays, but he always made sure to do his part when he returned home.

He'd implore Bug to tell him about their day, to which Bug would happily oblige. The child never ran short of imagination, spinning tales of fairy madness and dragons bursting through clouds. Bug talked a lot about Masika, too, holding a fondness for her that Aiden could relate to. He knew they loved him, but he couldn't blame them for preferring Mom. Mom who—despite her chiseled and often intimidating appearance—always offered good advice and tender affection when needed. Her comfort was often warranted in those early years especially.

Bug carried similar needs and behaviors to their parents. Something the couple noticed right off the bat were meltdowns. From toddler age, Masika told Aiden of her suspicions. She told him the meltdowns Bug had were identical to his, seldom the fact the child preferred physical comfort. Aiden, being at work most times, didn't see any for over two years.

The first instance he witnessed had been recently during a rough night of sleep. Bug kept waking him up, leading him to get overstimulated and demand they stay in their room. This triggered a full-scale meltdown, complete with ear piercing shrieks and tears. This triggered him—it was much like seeing himself—and he apologized without hesitation. He let Bug sleep in their room, and let Masika know about the incident. Since that point, more similarities continued to surface.

After researching similar traits and behaviors, Aiden came to a conclusion. He suspected all three of them were autistic. It would explain his own struggles to fit in, as well as his disdain for change and numerous other things. Masika agreed she had a lot of similar experiences, and so did Bug. It bothered the couple none—in fact, it did the opposite. The revelation provided much needed clarity and closure, as well as the ability to support Bug in ways they weren't growing up.

Lost in his thoughts, he didn't see Masika enter the porch. Slick with sweat, she released her locs from the bun atop her head. Hair falling upon her shoulders, she reached for a water bottle and chugged. Crushing the plastic, she peered over at Aiden; he gazed with sleepy awe.

"When did you get home? Would've started dinner by now," she spoke.

"It's okay," Aiden signed, standing up to give her a deep kiss. When he pulled away, he nudged her shoulder, "Bug good?"

"Yes, been really good. Just a lot more energy than usual. Haven't forgotten what day it is, have you?"

He shook his head and she kissed him once more. Bug came barreling onto the porch, tackling Aiden's hip in a hug. He wished he could pick Bug up and spin them around. Instead, he pet their head and they stepped away to anxiously tug at his shirt. When he realized they were trying to get him to go inside, he followed them to the screen door. Masika, the last to enter, shut it behind her as Bug ran to the fridge. Aiden watched, Masika capturing his hand as she joined his side.

"Made a surprise for you," she told him, looking at Bug as they opened the fridge. "Be careful when you take it out, Bug."

"I will!" Bug replied, pulling something from the middle rack.

Aiden's heart leapt at a small, star-shaped cake sat upon a sheet pan. He accepted it from Bug, who began to jump up and down excitedly. Three candles nestled around the words 'Hapy Jooce Day!' Aiden chuckled as Masika pointed to the lettering.

"Did the decorations all by themself, isn't that right?" she cooed.

"Yes! Did I do good?" Bug signed before tugging at Aiden's work pants.

He nodded, bringing the cake over to the dining room table. Masika fetched a knife and cut three slices, distributing each to a paper plate. As she went to grab silverware, Aiden admired the fluidity of her movements. The flexing of her arm and back muscles, enticing as always. When her eyes met his, they reflected equal adoration. Setting the table, Aiden thanked her as Bug patiently waited in their seat.

"Daddy gets the first slice!" they declared, excitedly clapping their hands.

Aiden grinned at them, "Okay, here goes," he took his first bite. The taste of chocolate and strawberry combined pleasantly on his tongue, and he gave Bug a thumbs up as he finished chewing. "Wow, that was amazing."

"Really?" Bug beamed.

"Yes really, did Mommy help you make it?"

"Yeah!"

"You two did a great job."

Aiden helped himself to another slice before assisting Masika in clean up, putting the rest of the cake away. Bug ran circles in the kitchen, singing loudly. Right as Aiden stepped from the fridge, Bug latched onto him for a hug. Carrying them hurriedly into the living room, he showered them in kisses before settling down on the couch.

"Are we gonna watch a movie?"

"We sure can," Aiden replied, picking out a cartoon from his VHS collection. He popped Bug's favorite into the television.

He could hear utensils and pans clacking in the other room as the movie played. He decided fifteen minutes into the film to go help Masika finish cleaning. When he entered the other room, he detected her chaotic mental state almost immediately. She sporadically tried to organize an overflowing sink, jumping when he tapped her on the shoulder.

"Sorry," she mumbled, "in my head."

"It's alright. Do you want some help?"

"Won't be a problem?"

"Of course not."

He separated the dishes into piles as Masika swept the floors. Washing and hand-drying several loads, he left only an empty basin in his wake. When he turned around, Masika sat at the table, utterly exhausted. She apologized again.

"Earlier tired me out more than I thought," she admitted.

"Why don't you go watch the movie with Bug? I'll finish up."

"Sure about that?"

"Of course, go," he playfully shooed.

Aiden wrapped up kitchen duty in twenty minutes, body aching by the time he finished. He retired to the living room, a happy sigh escaping his lips; Masika and Bug were fast asleep on the couch. Aiden got comfortable in his reclining chair, admiring his family.

Chapter Thirty-Five

April 1990

Slamming the taxi door shut behind her, Masika tore through the lobby and straight for the hotel elevator. Her heart threatened to burst through her ribcage as she took deep, messy breaths. The ding upon passing each floor disrupted her nerves further. When it reached eight, she broke into a sprint towards the room. Fumbling the key from her pocket, she unlocked the door.

Swinging open with a creak, only darkness awaited her. She gnawed on her nails, trying to remember where the light switches were.

"Anuli?" she tried, "You here?"

Her hands groped at the walls around her until her fingers met plastic. Flicking it, light flooded the room and blinded her briefly. What she assumed was the bed swirled and warped in her vision as it adjusted. She swore she saw... red?

The confusion shattered into pieces when her vision finally functioned. A howl of pain nearly escaped her throat, but she was able to deter it by covering her agape lips. Trembling, she shrunk towards the dresser.

"No! Nononono—"

Retching, vomit doused the carpet as she fell to her knees. Her sobs were ceaseless even upon collecting herself enough to stand. She faced the beheaded corpse on the bed, the viscera and gore on the white sheets.

Their name tumbled from her, over and over again; apologizing, flustered, begging for it to not be true.

Hands extended in front, palms upwards, they clutched their 'umbrella'. An envelope lay on the nightstand closest to her. Masika took the letter, which was addressed in her least favorite handwriting. She tore it open. When she saw the hotel notepad paper, she nearly threw it. It took all her strength to read the sprawling words.

You know better than to disobey me, Masika. I am so disappointed in you. You were supposed to come right home after killing the target. You chose to frolic instead, to try and run. Did you really think you could get away from me? I hope you've learned your lesson. It's time to come home to me.

Masika spent hours holding the remains. She cried for the first two, dissociated for the final three. Briefly taking to their echo, their ghost, she promised she would carry out their wishes. Then, she spoke the words Everlee robbed her of.

"I love you, Anuli. I'm so, so fucking sorry."

For the first time, witnessing death made her violently ill. She threw up twice more in the sink before forcing herself into the shower, needing to process Everlee's request. She needed to figure out if the goal was to lure her back. Killing her most recent lover seemed like it would do the opposite. The act must've been out of jealousy, or some kind of hatred for them. Hatred for everything Anuli represented. It would be on brand for her.

The remainder of the shower, Masika sat in the tub. The last few weeks with Anuli flashed before her eyes. It started with a blade against her throat, recalling all the shared joints in the kitchenette; every kiss, laugh, and sob. Every layer had finally peeled by the time Everlee killed them. The bitch had immaculate timing, damn her. Masika only wished she never left Anuli's side.

She knew, deep down, Anuli wouldn't want her blaming herself. In fact, they would have wanted her to grant herself kindness. The woman had a knack for stalking, unpredictability always in her favor. She certainly couldn't have predicted Everlee would *kill* Anuli out of possessiveness.

Thinking quickly, Masika wrapped their body in the bed sheets after storing the weapon away. Not wanting to look more suspicious than she already would, a second layer was added using clean sheets in the linen closet. Taking a gander at the blood splatter, there was no way in Hell she would be able to clean it up. The best course of action would be to take Anuli's body somewhere and dip.

And there was only one person in town that could help her.

When Masika showed up on Herb's doorstep, he was shocked. He blinked, making sure he wasn't dreaming.

"Thought you was busy."

"Change of plans, Dad. Need to borrow your truck."

"For what?"

Masika tensed, "Have to take a trip to the forest. Bring it right back, promise."

Herb yawned, "Alright. Let me get the keys. Need anything else?"

"Shovel."

"Alright— Hey, are you okay?"

She didn't notice the influx of tears at first. Shuddering, she pushed the sobs down her throat and nodded robotically, forcing a smile.

"Everything's fine Dad."

Already knowing not to press, Herb vanished momentarily to grab his keys. He passed them off to Masika, who ran straight for the truck.

The five-minute drive to the hotel only drained her sanity further. In the absence of radio, she wept all the way there. She parked as close as she could to an exit. The lobby would be a bad place to drag a dead body through, but she might be able to risk the halls.

On the way up the elevator, flashes of Anuli's corpse plagued her thoughts. She tried to shove them away but failed. Instead, she focused on forming a plan past leaving the hotel with a cadaver in her backseat. It being two a.m. did her little favors, since the pigs were especially active around this time. What would she do if someone approached her? With the final ding, she cursed Everlee under her breath.

To her assuagement, Masika spotted an abandoned hamper on the eighth floor. She peered inside, noting it was half-full of dirty rags and towels. Waiting a few minutes, she idled long enough to check if anyone would come for it. When nobody showed, she got behind the handle and pushed it towards her room.

Once she squeezed the cart inside, she emptied its contents onto the floor. From there, she hoisted Anuli's body into it. They fit perfectly at the bottom, and she sighed in relief, piling dirty laundry over them. Checking her work, she packed her and Anuli's bags and threw them on top. One more walk around later, she departed with the disguised body bag.

Blood pounded in her ears as she pushed, hoping not to run into whoever she stole the cart from. Thankfully, the halls remained dead as she called the elevator. Waiting, surges of anxiety threatened to cripple her. Grief paved way for rage, slowly swirling within and ready to burst.

The overlapping thoughts almost made her miss the elevator opening in front of her. A scrawny, elderly white man stood inside, looking at her with confusion. Mumbling "'scuse me," she put herself and the cart in the elevator. The man eyed her suspiciously. She briefly worried he may cause trouble. Thankfully, he got off on the third floor, leaving Masika alone.

Arriving, she took a sharp left into the first-floor hallways, pointedly avoiding the lobby. Her teeth dug into her lip as she navigated the maze, trying to locate the exit she parked near. When she found it, adrenaline coursed through her, and it was a fight not to break into a sprint. She didn't know if the establishment had any cameras. By the time she reached the exit, blood dotted on her lower lip.

As she burst through the doors, the wind whipped her hair around her face. Herb's truck only a couple yards away steadied her hopes *just* enough. Throwing the backpacks through the open doors, she lifted Anuli's corpse from the bottom of the parked cart. Rags spilled over the edges and onto the gravel below. Hastily shoving Anuli into the seat, she inadvertently unraveled the sheets, leaving their arms hanging out. She covered her mouth before slamming the door shut.

Hurriedly returning the rags to the cart, she glanced around to double-check for witnesses. The parking lot was desolate to her relief, so she went directly to the lobby. She brought the hamper right up to the front desk, where a petite white girl smacking gum sat. Alerted to Masika's presence, she blew a giant bubble and popped it with a smile.

"How can I help ya, darling?"

"Left this," Masika mumbled, running her hands over the handle.

"Excuse me?" The girl cupped her ear and turned it towards her, "Can't really understand you."

Masika furiously scratched her arms, "Someone left this. Returning it. Goodnight."

She said nothing more and left. Once outside again, she exhaled loudly with reprieve. Now that the hard part was through, she knew exactly where to go next.

Heading straight for the woods, she was driven by a one-off conversation Anuli started while alive. They had informed her of their desire to be returned to the earth upon passing—"put me anywhere near nature, just not in a goddamn casket"—making the forest a perfect place. Once parked, she hauled the body deep into the trees, until Herb's truck vanished entirely from view.

Masika dug a makeshift grave for an hour. Once the hole was more than deep enough, she unwrapped Anuli from the sheet. She recoiled at the lack of head on their shoulders, biting into her palm. Ever so gently, Masika lowered them into the ground. She took a last glance at their corpse with a heavy heart.

"So sorry. Fuck..."

Making quick work to conceal the body, she buried them in twenty minutes. She stared at the dirt until the sun rose, the light seeping through the dense trees. She got to her feet, knowing she needed to make her way to Herb.

Upon arriving, she spotted him smoking a cigarette in front of the trailer. He got up from a rickety beach chair and met Masika halfway. She abruptly handed him the keys and tried to walk away without so much another word. Herb wouldn't allow it.

"Where ya going now, kid?"

"Chicago."

"Let me take you to the bus stop, least I can do."

Masika, too emotionally wrecked to decline, accepted the offer. Riding in his truck with him at the wheel should've felt positively nostalgic, but Masika could feel nothing besides loss. Grief and rage simmered ever so slowly in her gut and brain. Herb sensed her strife.

"You know you can always come back if you need to, right?" he tried.

"Can't. Got unfinished business," Masika deadpanned.

As he rolled up to the stop, she unbuckled her seatbelt. Before she could get out of the truck, Herb stopped her with a hand to the shoulder.

"Good luck. Stay safe out there, Masika."

"Will try."

"Try not to kill anybody," he added.

She couldn't help but laugh at that.

***

The trip ahead didn't give Masika nearly enough time to grieve. The first bus she boarded proved cumbersome, the commotion in her brain withstanding. She could only stare blankly at her hands.

For the following fourteen hours, Masika let her imagination run wild. Each scenario began how the trouble had in real life—with Everlee smiling sweetly. The smile never reached her cheeks. Not during the first daydream, where Masika pressed her thumbs right into her eyes. Nor the next, where she meticulously sewed the bitch's lips shut. She killed Everlee hundreds of times, every way she could—baseball bat to the head, a slice across the throat, dozens of stabs until she had to blink blood out of her eyes—all while staring absentmindedly out the windows.

The last vision, two stops before her destination, revolved her palm over Everlee's mouth. She pushed her into a wall and screamed for her to shut up, to do *anything* but talk. As she watched her inner self struggle, tears welled. She never should have let it get this bad. She should have seen Everlee's intentions from a mile away, yet she hadn't. She fell so perfectly into her trap, and now Anuli was dead.

Thinking of Anuli brought her over the brink. She sobbed quietly, hoping not to alert any of the other riders. Not even two days ago, Anuli was alive, smiling and thriving alongside her. She vowed to do good by them, to prove they were right about Everlee's true colors. She was nothing short of a predatory scumbag abuser, and Masika had to make sure she would never hurt another soul again.

She wouldn't kill her. She wasn't capable of that, no matter how much her thoughts argued otherwise. What she *could* do, however, was punish Everlee. And punish she would.

First, Masika had to run a couple of errands.

***

In the back seat of a cab, Masika soaked up Chicago's bustling scenery. The longer the ride went on, the more anguish infiltrated her very being. Only a few minutes from having to confront Everlee, she found herself in a state of heightened senses. The city's noises blared like they were playing on overhead speakers. Even worse, everything stank of urine and copper. She did her best to not get overstimulated, reciting the plan to herself over and over again.

It worked just long enough for the taxi to roll up to the entrance of Everlee's building. Masika called the elevator, walking past the snoozing security guard at the front desk.

Soon, she stepped out of the metal shutters, hands slowly falling to her sides. Her mind roared in protest with each step towards the entrance. She quelled the panic, insisting to herself that she needed to do this. She needed to rectify her fatal error of tangling with Evil.

So she knocked. The first time, she received nothing in response. The second, same thing. Growing impatient, she resorted to a series of sharp cop knocks. She jumped hearing the lock unlatch from the other side. Bracing herself, the door handle turned.

"You're finally home!"

Being swept into a tight hug, Masika forced herself not to instinctively jerk away. She faked a grin at Everlee.

"It's so nice to see you've finally come to your senses," Everlee said, lightly tapping her cheek. "Just in time for dinner, come in!"

As she stepped over the threshold, sudden as a gut punch, paralysis overwrought her entire body and mind. The apartment hadn't changed at all since she left. She shut memories out with Anuli's headless corpse in a shallow grave. This was not the time to fawn and give Everlee the upper hand. She had to play it cool until the right opportunity struck.

She took a seat on the couch and helped herself to a wine bottle on the coffee table. Chugging about half the contents until her raucous thinking ceased, simmering rage became her only emotion. Everlee pranced over.

"What's wrong? You seem tense," Everlee sat beside her. "Is it because I killed your little friend?"

Masika's heart accelerated. She cleared a rush of impulsive thoughts by finishing the bottle. Everlee waited for her to respond. Masika didn't. Instead, she redirected and asked what was for dinner.

"Shrimp alfredo."

"Sounds good," Masika lied, fully aware of Everlee's horrible cooking skills. She told herself not to flinch as her mentor's demeanor shifted.

"Seems you know I did it for your own good," Everlee said. "Now all your ties to Sikes' murder have been severed!"

"Thank you so much," another fake smile paired with Masika's words, "really. Made a mistake."

Everlee kissed her cheek before returning to the kitchen. Masika eyed her backpack sitting next to the empty wine bottle. Listening closely for footsteps, she decided to go ahead and arm herself. She quickly withdrew a syringe from her first aid kit, stashing it in her pocket. The dust had just settled around her repacked bag when Everlee returned to check on her. Masika only looked at her innocently. Just like she thought, Everlee anticipated sabotage. She'd have to butter her up.

"Seem worried," Masika stated.

"You ran off on me. I never thought you'd come willingly after that," an unsettling grin fell on her lips. "I was ready to follow you to the ends of the Earth, though. Love you that much."

A wet, sloshing *thwap* alerted Masika, coinciding with the unmistakable sound of bones snapping. She moved her head at a snail's pace, heart racing.

Everlee's form split at the seams before her very eyes. Human skin shed, the thing that remained proved nothing short of a nightmare. A beastly creature loomed on all fours, sniffing the air. It had no face, but dozens of blue eyes littered its entire body, unblinking and oozing. Overtly perky breasts sporadically covered any eyeless space, taking up the rest of her skin. She reeked of ylang ylang and blood.

Masika wouldn't let this devil deter her from enacting justice. Anuli's soul wouldn't be free until she purged the Evil. She pushed the fear all the way down her throat and into the pit of her stomach. *Gonna get her, Anuli. Don't you worry. Gonna find your head so you can finally rest.*

Everlee woke Masika up by touching her lower thigh. She came to life, albeit barely, having underestimated the amount of wine she'd consumed. Thankfully, a remedy for that was sure to be in the apartment. Sitting up, she rubbed her eyes.

"Food's ready. I've just got to set the table," Everlee told her.

"Let me do it," Masika replied firmly, running a knuckle down Everlee's lips. "Take a seat. Rest."

Obliging, Everlee sat down at the head of the dining table. Masika went to the kitchen. Sickly yellow slop sat in a skillet. She pulled a plate from the cabinet and filled it with the revolting pasta.

Everlee sat pretty and watched as Masika set silverware. She noticed a shift in her stalker's posture. Her defenses were lowering, if her dreamy state was anything to go by. Masika came up behind her and rubbed her shoulders.

"Want more wine?"

"Yes."

Masika fetched a glass and handed it to Everlee, who kissed her knuckles in return.

"Thank you."

Everlee delicately drank, the veins on her exposed neck seducing Masika into action. With a free hand, she brushed her shoulder. Everlee's eyebrows drooped.

"Where's your plate, darling? You only brought one," she asked. When receiving no response, a hint of panic tinged her voice. "Masika?"

By the time she stood and twisted to face her, Masika had retrieved and uncapped the syringe. She quickly grabbed a fistful of Everlee's hair and jammed the needle into her neck. Everlee tried to resist, but Masika headbutted her and she went limp. Removing the needle, she set it on the table.

"Aw... A little late, doll," Masika whispered sarcastically, brushing Everlee's hair out of her face. She dropped her to the floor, observing with amusement the attempts to wriggle around, "Not going any-where, Everlee. Be surprised if you can even talk."

Everlee's lips twitched, only air being pushed out from her lungs. Masika left her on the floor as she began her search for Anuli's head. No luck in the kitchen, she only discovered a cocaine bump. Snorting it without thinking, she wandered into the office next. Instantly, she was drawn to a mini fridge in the corner. Sure enough, when Masika opened it, half-closed brown eyes greeted her.

She slammed the door shut and kicked the desk chair across the room. Throwing a mostly empty wine glass against the wall, it shat-tered and left a splatter of red on the dark wood. That image of blood among dark tree roots was enough for her to trash the whole place. She left only a small pathway to the fridge in her wake.

When she came back, foam poured out of Everlee's mouth. She wasn't seizing, however, and Masika was thankful for that. She needed her conscious, or semi-aware, at the very least. Bending down and lifting Everlee's head, she wiped the drool from her face.

"Could've left us alone, Everlee," she stated. "They would be alive and you wouldn't have to suffer. Could have forged separate paths, but just had to have your hooks in me, didn't you?"

The malice on Everlee's face made her crack up. She wrapped her fingers around her throat. In the couple of minutes Everlee fought for breath, Masika found herself lost in not only her rage, but also in the prospect of taking a life. Could she really stoop right down to the level of her oppressors? Could she ever forgive herself if she took revenge like Everlee, Eddie, or Kevin would surely do in her place?

Yelling at the top of her lungs, right as Everlee became blue in the face, Masika let go. She stood up and stumbled backwards, sobbing and yelling incoherently in an outburst of trapped emotions. She scurried to a corner, sinking to her knees.

I can't kill her, I can't. She thought as she cradled herself. *But she can't go unpunished.*

Masika got one final sip of wine. Drinking it, she smashed the glass on the kitchen floor, picking up the biggest sliver that remained. Returning, she found Everlee able to move her head and face. The drugs were wearing off fast, of course they would with her tolerance. Everlee smirked at her weakly.

"Can't finish the job?" she croaked out.

"No," Masika admitted.

"Because you love me."

"'Cause I'm not you." She paused, a slow grin forming on her face, "But you *will* be punished."

Everlee mocked her at first, mouthing off as Masika drew closer. She panicked, however, when she fell on top of her. Raising the shard of glass above her head, Masika aimed straight for Everlee's right eye.

CHAPTER THIRTY-SIX

April 1990

A trip to the local beach proved serene. In Everlee's car, Masika drove with an extra bag in the front seat. She conversed with its contents the entire drive.

"Bitch always told me my boobs were too small. Too unnoticeable. So cut hers off. Cut hers off, I did. Least didn't kill her. At least didn't kill her... Should have killed her? Or taking her eye and tits considered worse?" She stopped briefly to chew off a couple of her nails before laughing dryly, "Don't gotta worry about surgery now. Only gotta worry about purging the Evil. Only way to redemption, Kevin said. Purge myself, purge the Evil, make it right..."

Anuli looked peaceful drifting away in the ocean. Masika had closed their open, empty eyes prior. It revolted her knowing that Everlee was their final sight. She tried not to think too hard about it as she sat, waiting until she could no longer see the head in the water. When they finally vanished, she returned to Everlee's car.

She got a hotel within walking distance of that beach, hoping to visit and reflect later. She dropped her and Anuli's belongings off in the room before setting out. Before she could rest, she needed to get rid of Everlee's car.

Following the road signs to get a few towns over, she settled for a city called Peoria. She crawled the streets until she scoped out a warehouse with an empty parking lot. Well, mostly empty besides a patrol car hidden nearly out of view. She drove around in circles until the vehicle vanished. Pulling in, she squinted and checked for cameras on the exterior.

When she found none, she got right out. Grabbing a petrol can, lighter, and Molotov from the trunk, Masika doused the car with fuel. Once efficiently coated, she took a couple steps back. She lit the cloth end of the bomb, watching it catch aflame.

As she stared into the flicker, the reality of her life hit like a truck. She'd spent most of her life in prison and, when she had finally been freed, she used her freedom to abandon someone dear to her. Only to find her hands once again stained crimson, foolishly following the Devil's every whim. Masika got away, but not without a price. She lost yet another lover, this time finitely.

Her hand trembled. Was this all she was meant for? To lose loved ones? To kill? To burn anything and everything that stood in her way? Had Kevin been right about her? Tears fell down her face, and the words that came to her mind next were a surprise.

You must accept your nature. Even if it's not what everyone else wants.

With that, she cranked her arm and threw the Molotov. Upon impact, the Porsche burst into flames. She wished to watch it succumb to the fire, but knew it wouldn't be wise to stick around. She trusted the embers to do their due diligence.

So, she turned her back, exiting the parking lot as quickly as possible. She wiped her face, navigating the desolate streets until reaching a bus stop. Joining a couple of individuals, she waited on the bench.

The bus ride flew by, Masika's reality warping and twisting. She was convinced the other riders were a danger. Even with her eyes downcast to her shoes, the metal underneath blurred. Sounds of the bus muffled, she zoned out, thinking of little other than Anuli's head floating out to sea.

Masika blinked, registering the sudden jump from riding the bus to being in the hotel room. She startled at her reflection. Tearing away from the mirror, she took notice of water running in the tub. Assuming she was about to take a shower, she switched it to the overhead sprayer. Climbing inside, the icy tap lapped at her flesh just as it had Anuli's rotting skull.

She broke down in grotesque wails. Anuli was fucking dead. She left Everlee tied up, down her left eye and a pair of breasts. Cleansed of the evidence, now she was where she started—completely and utterly alone.

Masika hardly slept that night, tossing and turning. She threw around several plans in her head. Wanting to go home to Herb, to get back that same joy and comfort she shortly grasped, she realistically knew that wasn't possible. She couldn't put him in danger, and she couldn't return to the past. Having to remain solo and on the run, she would need to make a few arrangements.

***

"How long would you like your stay?"

In the crowded, bustling lobby of a hostel, Masika anxiously stood at the front counter. She shuffled a wad of Canadian dollars in her grip, trying to avoid the receptionist's gaze.

"Let's do two months," she responded.

After check in, she headed into her new home. A white room with yellow lines by the baseboards greeted her. Three bunk beds diagonal of each other, framed in solid black, stood and took up much of the room. Each had luggage space beneath. Upon entering, two girls in the room beamed. Sheepishly waving before approaching them, she clutched her backpack straps with a death grip.

"Kamau and I got the first row. The others are free right now," one of the girls told her.

Masika nodded, laying her belongings on the lower bunk of the second row. She sat down with a soft exhale.

She'd spent the last six months in North Dakota, gathering money to flee. Mahpiya hosted her the entire time. Even though she appreciated his hospitality, she felt grossly misplaced. It felt wrong eating with Teneca's son; it felt wrong having no missions, no guidance.

Mahpiya didn't bar her from leaving, in fact, he encouraged it. Even with all his hyping up, she couldn't bear to leave his home. Other than absolutely necessary outings, such as when she picked up estrogen, she stayed closed off in his guest room.

He forged a couple documents, a relatively easy task considering Everlee already created a fake driver's license for her. He gave her a lot of advice and a way to get across the border undetected. She accepted his help, and he requested nothing in return. This didn't stop Masika from keeping his house clean and taking care of his animals while he worked.

Even though she dissociated during the entire stay, immense sadness swallowed her the day she departed. Mahpiya drove her to Seattle, where the two met up with his contact: a boat owner named Tiffany. She told Masika she could get her across the border with ease. The goodbye with Mahpiya that followed proved bittersweet.

Before she boarded the boat, he pulled her into a deep embrace and thanked her for all the help. She thanked him, too, not bothering to hide her tears. She promised she would be in contact as soon as she felt safe in the states again.

"You better. Don't be a stranger, call me if you need anything at all."

With that, Masika retreated to the cargo hold. A trap door in the floor led to a small, cubby-like room where she would stay during the ride. Tiffany warned her of the temperature, as well as to be quiet when customs checked at the border. Masika minded none of it, finding sleep hard to ignore the minute she curled up inside the tight space.

Now, she relaxed in bed. Listening to the women whispering to each other, she sat up and opened her backpack. Retrieving a folder from the depths, despite its bent corners, she found the letters intact and legible. She buried her nose into the paper without thinking.

***

Masika struggled to create a routine for herself the next few months. Too busy worrying about Everlee on her trail, she didn't bother touring the city. She stayed in the hostel and hardly ate, save the free breakfast offered. Roommates came and went—all except Kamau.

Kamau proved to be an interesting character. The woman largely kept to herself. Masika would occasionally get trapped in her big, round eyes from across the room, but nothing more. Kamau never stuck around during the day, only lounging in the evenings. At that point, she would typically be reading in her upper bunk.

One eve, Masika got up to shower. She'd fallen out of consistent cleaning habits since Everlee, but tried to remember to bathe herself when she could. She would always do so during wee hours of the morning when the showers were empty, afraid of detection and outing.

As Masika lathered her skin with body wash, she hummed under her breath. A song had wormed its way into her head, although she barely recalled anything but the beat and a handful of lines. Her head moved side to side as more details surfaced, and she smiled. She pictured her friend from high school's spinning and twirling, shaking his hips to the music. Singing aloud, she began to rinse off.

Right as she turned the spout, she moved her head and was met with a fright. Kamau stood in the center of the room, beet red from her cheeks to her ears. Her gaze was locked on Masika's lower half. When she got caught staring, she bolted out of the room without a word.

Aggravated and worried, Masika dried off. Once her teeth were clean, she slipped into bed. Using the lamp to provide light, she dove into a book she had recently started. A mousy voice breached the silence merely five minutes later.

"I'm sorry for earlier, I didn't know anyone would be in there."

Masika turned her head. Kamau stood at her bedside, rubbing her arm shyly. She looked adorable in a silken navy-blue nightgown, her hair concealed by a bonnet.

"It's alright," Masika replied, "hope that didn't startle you."

"It didn't. In fact, my sister is trans. She fled to America recently."

A little shocked by the response, Masika leaned back. "Where you from?"

"Kenya."

"How's it over there?"

"Very different than here and the states. Some ways good, some ways bad."

Masika normally hated conversations with borderline strangers, yet Kamau intrigued her. She asked to sit down. Masika obliged, scooting over to make room.

"I want to get strong like you," Kamau stated, "I could use a few muscles."

She slapped her forearm and Masika chuckled quietly, "Wouldn't say I'm that strong. Thank you, though."

Chatting ensued until She wished Masika a good night. An odd feeling stirred in her stomach as she watched Kamau walk off. Getting right back to reading her book, she shooed it away.

***

A few nights later, Kamau worked up the nerve to ask her out for drinks.

Masika wasn't oblivious to the glances that lasted far too long, or how she began checking in on her more frequently. Yet, she didn't expect this. She decided it was time to finally venture out into the city. Before she agreed, she asked a question.

"Friend date? Or something more?"

Kamau's ears reddened as she shoved her hands into her pockets, "W-Well, I think it can start friendly. But if you're open to more... I am too."

"Noted."

At eight p.m., Kamau led her out of the hostel and into the Vancouver streets. Despite never setting foot into the city, Masika held no curiosity. Her attention belonged to Kamau, who spoke of her home in Kenya during the short fifteen-minute walk. She asked where Masika was from at some point.

"Alabama."

"That's in the states, yeah?"

"Yup, Bible Belt."

Kamau's expression softened to concern. "Ah, I'm sorry. I've heard a lot of bad things about that part of America."

"All of it's bad," Masika mumbled.

"I can only imagine."

Kamau held the door to a pub open for her. The two went inside, pushing through bodies before sitting at the bar. Kamau ordered a double of tequila, while Masika stuck with her traditional order of two beers. She downed the first, falling much easier into conversation. They discussed books, their strongest mutual interest. Kamau enjoyed reading crime thrillers, while Masika had always been a sucker for romance. She gave her a few recommendations as they each ordered another round of drinks.

Four orders later, Kamau drunkenly told Masika she couldn't handle the noise. The two headed outside and to the right of the building, where

Kamau got out a pack of cigarettes. Masika, despite dying for one, ignored the urge as she lit up. Instead, she admired Kamau's appearance. She wore a dark green tank top and low-rise blue jeans. Tattoos, mostly floral, covered her entire arms. Creamy brown, almond shaped eyes reflected beautifully in the moonlight. Her full lips flattened into a smile.

"Whatcha thinking about?"

Masika blinked away, "N-Nothing. Look nice is all."

Kamau moved a bit closer and Masika, not thinking, closed the gap between them. Kamau kissed back, draping her arms over her shoulders. Taking hold of her hips, Masika guided her towards the wall. Kamau tossed away the cigarette, moaning softly at her purposeful touches and strokes.

As they made out, footsteps grew closer. Masika's teeth sank gently into Kamau's lower lip as a distorted voice called out. She tried to ignore the noise, but it grew louder and closer. Halfway through another kiss, a hand reached for her shoulder. She grabbed it before it made contact.

Scrubbing. Scrubbing is what Masika saw when she came to. She gasped, jerking away from the pair of hands cleaning hers. She actualized her surroundings—the hostel showers—and immediately panicked. The washcloth against her ruddy skin steadied her.

When she saw who held it, her anxiety eased only a little. That was until she saw the blood caking Kamau's face. She noticed the red on her own arms and hands, starting to hyperventilate. Kamau frantically scrubbed harder.

"It's alright, it was a mistake," Kamau tried to soothe her.

"What did I do?" Masika shook her head, "Kamau?"

"Some asshole tried to hurt you. So I..." her gaze fell to the shower floor. "*We* kicked his ass. Got messier than I think either of us wanted."

"Killed him, didn't I?" she asked.

Kamau's eyebrows furrowed as she stared at Masika's hands, "W-What?"

"Did the final blow, always do. Can't just leave it at a beating, always have to finish the job, right?"

Kamau didn't say a word until the water spilling off Masika's hands ran clear.

"Hey, it's okay. That was a stressful situation, wasn't it?" she tried. "The best we can do is rest and get ready for tomorrow. Does that sound good?"

Even though Masika disliked her condescending tone, she nodded along nonetheless. Kamau may have conviction, but she knew better. Masika wasn't capable of much beyond stone-cold-killing, a craft she'd fully perfected under Everlee's influence. She couldn't let Kamau take the blame for a murder she wasn't responsible for; she would have to leave.

So, she said nothing, allowing Kamau to help her get the rest of the blood off. Masika did the same for her, an incredible wave of guilt all-consuming. Here she was, running away again.

Once Kamau fell asleep beside her, she stealthily packed up her belongings and slipped away into the night.

***

Masika spent another three years bouncing from hostel to hostel, area to area, until she landed in Calgary.

They came and went. Iron pervaded her tongue. Long sleepless nights bled together. She itched for cigarettes, itched for positive interactions. Her dirty hands brought no respite, only extrapolating the Evil. No matter how much she begged for forgiveness, another corpse always found its way to her feet.

CHAPTER THIRTY-SEVEN

March 1993

After dropping off enough meth to kill a herd of horses, Abeje made her way home. She took the usual route of alleys instead of the main streets. Stopping to smoke a cigarette, she reached the halfway point—the back of a teriyaki restaurant.

Light rainfall threatened her treat. She grimaced and tried to shield the cigarette from extinction. She only managed three more puffs before it went out completely. As she cursed beneath her breath, three individuals approached.

"Are you Abeje?" one of the two men asked.

She said nothing. Trying to scan their outfits for any mics or concealed weapons, she flicked her cigarette towards the man. He glared menacingly at her.

"I'll ask again. Are you Abeje Zetrenne?"

She shook her head and tried to leave, but the circle around her tightened. Dashing forward to break through, the trio captured her by her limbs. Violent thrashes ensued as they attempted to keep her steady. She headbutted one man, earning a punch to the head. The blow wrecked her vision and her knees buckled. Kick after kick landed on her body and she struggled to shield herself from the damage. Internally, she berated herself. After all this time on the run, *this* couldn't be the end.

She was right. In a blink, the attackers dropped. When Abeje uncurled herself, she first saw the boots of a stranger. As her eyes climbed up their body, she stifled a gasp.

***

Abeje looked nothing like she had several years ago. She was a little rounder in the face now and boasted snake bites. Lengthy locs obscured the right side of her face, reaching past her shoulders.

The change didn't shock Masika. In fact, she only cared that she was standing before her, alive and well. Without thinking, she embraced her. A hard slap to the face followed. She staggered back.

"How *dare* you," Abeje snarled at her.

Masika's eyebrows raised. Confusion scrambled her thoughts and Abeje covered her mouth guiltily. She crossed her arms.

"Since *when* can you talk?"

"Fuck. FUCK!" Abeje paced briefly before wagging a finger in Masika's face. "Of all the fucking people, you had to be the one to save my ass! What the actual fuck are you doing in Canada?"

"Could ask you the same question. Answer mine first."

Abeje didn't have to. At the slight turn of her head, Masika searched for the burn scar on her neck. There was none. The pieces slowly clicked together as Abeje deeply sighed.

"I can't explain it here," she conceded, leaning down and pilfering through the attackers' pockets. She fished out a badge and scoffed, "Fucking hell! They were FBI. Let's get the fuck out of here before their friends figure out they're dead."

Abeje led her to a rundown long-term care facility, overgrown in moss and vines. The minute Abeje and Masika burst through the front door, two individuals greeted them.

"Who the hell is this? We don't have room for—" one of them started, only for Abeje to pat their shoulder.

"She's an old friend of mine. We just need a safe place to chat," she promised.

"She's gonna have to get pat down. We can't have another leak," the other stated.

"I know, I know. My friend here will comply."

The pair stepped towards Masika and she gave them a nod of confirmation. She received a thorough pat down, where the taller person found all her weapons—three knives and a pistol—and put them aside while the other checked for wires. When she came out clean, the shorter gave Abeje a thumbs up.

"She's clear. You can have those when ya leave, sweetheart."

"Thank you."

"Alright, follow me," Abeje said.

Abeje took her through the lobby, marked by a large, round ebony desk where a few people stood behind. Masika rode with her to the third floor. Abeje led down a corridor, stopping at room 303. She opened the door for Masika and told her to go inside, have a seat. She obliged, finding a beanbag chair and sitting in it.

"What do you go by now? Unless it's still 'M.'" Abeje asked, turning on a set of string lights.

"Masika."

"Nice, nice. Do you want anything to drink?

"What you got?"

"We're a little low on options, think all we got is beer."

"Sounds good."

While Abeje ran to get beer, Masika absorbed the room. A twin bed with messy, dispelled polka-dot sheets sat in the middle of the room, slanting crooked. A small television resided in the corner atop a two-drawer dresser. Clothes, beer bottles, wigs, and lipsticks littered the floor. Tacky beige walls had been garnished with pinup posters and magazine clippings. One contained dozens upon dozens of newspaper articles. She got up to read them just as Abeje returned. Being passed an ice-cold can stopped her from moving forward. Masika accepted it, thanking her with a nod. Abeje then sat down on her bed, wasting no time getting to the point.

"You abandoned my brother."

Masika shifted her weight as she awkwardly stood in the middle of the room, "Thought I abandoned *you*, but the person I knew couldn't speak. Can your brother?"

Abeje swallowed before answering, "No."

"So switched places. What for?"

"It's not really my story to tell."

"Then why am I here exactly?"

"Whoa, slow the fuck down," Abeje spat. "Nobody said you had to be here! I just don't think you deserve to hear my brother's trauma after you slept with him and fucking left the state the next morning."

She tensed at that. Abeje was justified in her anger. Masika was still mad at herself for making that piss poor decision in the first place. The other woman detected her regret and huffed through her nose.

"Tell me why you left, and *maybe* I'll be willing to talk." She gestured to the beanbag chair again, "Go on. Sit."

Abeje watched as Masika did so, melting into the cushion. She clasped her beer tightly before speaking, "Thought it was the best option. Wanted more. Not more than your brother, just... more from life. Wanted to be myself. Alabama wasn't right for me."

"Then why not take him with?"

"Was too scared to ask. Was a coward."

"Is that the truth?"

"Swear it. Wouldn't lie to you, Abeje."

Abeje chugged the beer and crushed it in her palms. She tossed it in the garbage can, deeply exhaling.

"Do you really wanna know what happened? You're not gonna be happy."

"Happiness doesn't matter to me. Want the truth."

Abeje got up, walking over to the sole window in her room. Her demeanor shifted into one of deep pain and fury, filling the air with tension.

"It was two years after you left. Aiden got off work, decided to mourn the night you ditched town. On his way back home, a cop stopped him," Masika's eyes suffused with dread and she continued. "tried to force himself on Aiden. So Aiden stabbed the fuckwad in the throat, bashed his brains in, and came running to me."

Masika flew out of the chair, an onslaught of rage drowning her. Imagination painting pictures she scorned to see, her breathing quickened. She faced the corner, hovering a hand over gritted teeth. No matter how hard she tried, her fingers wouldn't stop shaking.

"Pissed, aren't you? Imagine how my brother feels," Abeje said coldly.

"Didn't mean—" Masika sucked in a sharp breath. "Right, you are... Seem so willing to switch places. Why?"

"I was tired of that white ass town too. And I wasn't who I wanted to be. Aiden and I always joked about being each other, so when he killed that pig... I figured why the hell not? Let him go hunker down and find a peaceful life, give myself a chance to transition and live on the wild side."

"Are you taking estrogen?"

"Fuck yeah I am. Been on and off it 'cause of relocating, but it's been about three years or so. How long have you been on it?"

"Four years."

"You seem a lot more sane."

Masika chuckled, "Is that supposed to be a compliment?"

"However you wanna take it," Abeje waved her off with a grin. "It's true though, trust me. There was a reason everybody at school was fucking terrified of you."

"Reason besides trying to kill seven white boys and nearly succeeding?"

"Touché. You know what? I don't think I ever knew it was seven. That's a lucky number, you know... Anyways, enough of this small talk bullshit. You probably wanna know where my brother is." Masika went quiet and Abeje continued, "No? Got cold feet?"

"What would I say? What you said earlier is completely true. Abandoned someone who loved me more than I ever deserved, couldn't forgive me and he shouldn't."

"You should still apologize," Abeje pushed. "Who gives a fuck what you get out of it? So long as he gets some godamn closure."

"True..."

"You've got about a three day trip ahead of you, so there's plenty of time to think on how to say it."

"Where is he?"

"Nevada. Before we split up, he wanted to know the best place to see the stars. I said probably somewhere in the desert, far the fuck away from the South. No mountains, no hills, no greens. Just the fucking sky and a wasteland for miles."

"Doing okay there?" Masika asked.

"Oh yeah. He's a janitor for a mostly Black school. From what I know, he's okay. Maybe a little lonely."

"No friends?"

"Hard to have friends when your twin sister might be on FBI's Most Wanted." Abeje joked.

"Very true."

Masika chewed on her lower lip. She imagined Aiden, terrified, running frantic through their hometown. If she had stayed, she could have protected him from that piece of shit officer. But she knew better than to dwell on lost chances. Abeje was right—the least she could do was give him an apology.

"Better go then, gotta make arrangements to get over the border."

"Ayce could probably help you with that. They run things around here and know a whole lot about border patrol."

"Only if they're sure."

Abeje smirked, "Wouldn't hurt to ask. Let me go get them."

About fifteen minutes later, Abeje returned with Ayce. The first thing Masika noticed was their stance; a chill posture with shoulders slumped forward and head slightly cocked. She could hardly see their face behind a mess of black curls, akin to a mushroom. A single bleached stripe existed on the left side—all of which swiped back by their hand as it pulled the mop of hair into a messy bun. Calm, curious black eyes homed in on Masika. They shook her hand firmly before everyone took a seat.

"So, you need help getting across the border?" Masika nodded and they folded their limbs together. "Well, you're in good hands. I'm taking a brief trip to the states myself, you're welcome to tag along."

"Sure about that?"

"Damn sure. Any friend of Abeje's is a friend of mine," they replied cooly. "We'll leave at dawn to get your things."

Masika agreed, profusely thanking Ayce before they left the room. Abeje got up from her desk and headed for her disheveled bed. Tossing several items aside, she jokingly bowed at her.

"All ready, my liege."

"Lord... Please don't call me that again," Masika said crawling onto the side of the bed closest to the wall. "Don't mind sharing?"

"Of course not. I won't be asleep until later though, so it's all yours for now."

Abeje left the room. All alone, the chaos of the past few years dissipated. Masika felt more hopeful than she had in eons.

CHAPTER THIRTY-EIGHT

February 2003

Masika's mental health had improved significantly over the years. With the help of a supportive husband and child, she found it easy to be vulnerable. Aiden helped her tackle her delusions, something she never thought could improve. Bug and Aiden's presences comforted her enough to finally face them.

In private, she and Aiden rationalized together, and she slowly realized there was much less blood on her hands than previously believed. More epiphanies followed and, for a while, stability knew her better than instability. Her psychotic episodes were easier to manage and lasted significantly less time than before. She was proud of her progress.

It was a shame it only took one catastrophic event to bring her world crashing down.

The morning had been normal, serene even. Masika told Bug to play outside while she cooked up breakfast. She tried a new French toast recipe, eager to hear her kiddo's thoughts. When she finished and made their plate, she headed into the backyard.

"Hey sweetheart, made breakfast."

Bug sat on the garden pathway, turned away from her. She approached and they glanced over their shoulder. The tray immediately slipped from her fingers, creating a mess of food and glass on the ground. Blood smeared across their face, coating their cheeks and nose.

"Bug! Bug, are you—" she began, rushing to their side. Stopping dead in her tracks, she saw what laid out in front of them. "Bug…"

Sprawled by their feet, the remains of a squirrel stained the sand with blood. At sight of the body, dissonance ravaged her mind. All at once, the bones and corpses of Masika's past—nonhuman and human alike—flashed in her head. Without thinking, she yanked Bug up by the arm.

"What did you do?" she asked, her entire body shaking. "Bug, what did you do?!"

They said nothing, terrifying her more in the process. She dragged them inside at once, straight into the bathroom, where she demanded they clean up. Bug, frightened by her behavior, was quick to undress and hop in the tub. She filled it with water, the sound of it running being the only thing keeping her breathing calm. She beat herself up over her outburst, hoping no wounds existed beneath the layer of blood. A few minutes later, she took a rag to Bug's face.

"Are you mad at me?" Bug signed.

"N-Not mad. Sorry for reacting that way," she forced a smile before dropping it. "Can you tell Mommy what happened?

"I found it in the garden crying. It hurt its leg," they wiggled their toes in the water. "I made it stop crying."

"How?"

Bug looked away guiltily. "Hit it with a rock."

She tore her eyes away from them, stifling a gasp. All she could see was her younger self. She covered her mouth briefly before returning her gaze to Bug.

"Am I bad?" they asked.

"Did you mean to do it?"

"Do what? Make the squirrel go to sleep?"

Masika glanced up at the ceiling. There was no way she was about to have this conversation. She thought it would be years from now, not today. Why today of all days? She sucked a sharp breath through her teeth and set down the rag.

"Bug... the squirrel wasn't asleep after that. It was dead," she slowly informed.

"Dead?"

Masika rested her arms on the edge of the tub, "Think of it as a forever sleep you don't come back from. All living creatures, squirrel or human, end up dead. Make sense?"

Oblivious to her trembling, they tilted their head to the side, "So I'm going to die?"

"Eventually. But not anytime soon, okay?" She pulled the plug, "C'mon, let's get you dried off."

After sending them to their room to get dressed, she sat on the toilet lid for a long time. She stared at the tub, still draining. The crimson tinged water permeated her with anguish. So did Bug's bloody dress on the floor. She rocked, trying her best to calm herself down. She was no service to anyone like this, and it would be several hours before Aiden returned from work.

Once she regained her composure, she searched for Bug. She found them in the backyard, staring hard at the corpse. This time, they sobbed. Masika leaned down and planted a long kiss on their forehead.

"I didn't mean to, I'm sorry," they signed between ugly cries.

She brought their head into her chest, cradling it. "Didn't know what you were doing. It's alright. It's resting now," she moved away and ruffled their hair. "How about we bury it?"

"Bury?"

After explaining the process, Masika assisted Bug in digging a shallow coffin for the critter. Together, mother and child gathered the corpse and lowered it into the ground. Bug did the honors of filling the hole with sand, sealing the creature away into the darkness. After, Bug kissed their palm before placing it atop the grave. She smiled weakly.

The rest of the day unfolded as usual, besides the eerie sensation that troubling tides were ahead.

***

Bug killed a squirrel. Because Bug killed an animal just as she had as a child, that meant Evil was afoot. And if Evil was afoot, it meant her dirty past was about to rear its ugly head.

If that was the case, Everlee must certainly be after her and her family.

Obsessing over the fear of pursuit, Masika forced herself to have training lessons. After all, she'd grown rusty in combat over the years of early motherhood. So, every morning around six a.m., right after Aiden woke up to get ready for work, she'd head straight outside with Anuli's katana. She alternated between reteaching herself combat skills and brushing up on wielding a sword.

A couple of weeks into the routine, unbeknownst to her, Bug began to observe. They got away with several peeks before accidentally giving themself away. Mid swing on a Tuesday morning, she noticed movement in the corner of her eye.

"Bug, can see you," Masika wiped sweat off her brow as her child stepped into view. "How long were you watching?"

"A while," they admitted, eyes full of ripe curiosity. "You looked like you were in a movie, Mommy."

A breathless chuckle left her lips, "Really now?" Picking up the katana, she sheathed it and lifted an eyebrow. "Think I'm the good guy or the bad guy?"

She cast the blade aside. They erupted into giggle-squeals as she charged and snatched them up into a big hug. She spun them around, then briefly hung them upside down by their legs and did her best villainous cackle. She lowered them to the ground as they started to squirm, sensing they had enough.

"When did you get the sword?"

"Thirteen years ago," she replied without hesitation, "belonged to a good partner, I deeply cherished them."

"A gift?"

"Yes... could call it a gift. Been through a lot, but the blade never dulled."

"Can I get one?"

"Not anytime soon."

"Awww, why not?"

They pouted as they followed her back inside the house. She went straight for her bedroom, where she put the weapon away. Facing Bug, she tousled their hair.

"Using, even holding a weapon, brings consequences. Especially for people like us. Consequences you're far too young to understand. Make sense?"

"Yeah..." They paused before their face renewed with joy, "Can you teach me how to fight?"

"Maybe, but don't think Dad would want that."

"Why not? Means I could protect us if something bad happens."

Masika's posture deflated at those words. She wondered if Bug was able to sense her anxieties from the past month, the ones going unnoticed by her overworked partner. Did they see her frequent window checks? The constant glancing over the shoulder, the need to keep busy with chores and exercise? And most importantly, the instance they freshly witnessed––her touching up her combat skills in the backyard. She lowered herself to Bug's level and held both their shoulders.

"Nothing bad's going to happen." Bug signed 'lie' and she tightened her grip, "No, not a lie. Nothing bad's going to happen. Safe here. And, if something *does* happen, I'll protect you. That's my job, Bug. Understand?"

Bug nodded and she hugged them.

When Aiden came home that evening, he slumped into his ragged lazy-boy as usual. Masika was prepping vegetables for dinner, unaware of his presence until she went to wake Bug up from an afternoon nap. She passed him on the way upstairs, skirting to a stop.

"Shit, didn't hear you come in."

Aiden apologized and got to his feet. He greeted her properly with a kiss as she put a hand on his waist. She softened at his exhausted expression.

"Extra hours are kicking your ass."

"I know," he signed to her, eyebrows pinched in the middle of his forehead.

"Don't know why you put yourself through this. Both know I have more than enough money for everything."

"You know I love working at that school."

Masika sighed and opened her lips to lecture him further when Aiden looked away. On the last stair stood Bug, flapping their hands. Aiden waved them over and they wedged themself into the hug. Both parents stroked their hair and beamed down at them.

"Someone's happy that everyone's home," Masika teased.

Aiden pulled away and asked Bug how their day was. As the two conversed, Masika resumed her work in the kitchen. She sliced onions at an alarming rate and threw the pieces into a bowl. Thirty or so minutes passed and she was about to put a stir fry together. Footsteps greeted her ears, and she looked over to see an agitated Aiden.

"Yes my love?"

"Were you practicing in the backyard again?"

Masika almost froze but collected herself. She nodded.

"Been a while. Just wanted to make sure I still got it I guess," she tossed him an irresistible smirk as she turned the stovetop on. "Why you ask?"

Aiden stepped out of the archway to reveal Bug in the living room. They darted around with a cardboard tube, wielding it as a sword and roaring battle cries. Masika stifled a snort, trying not to irk her partner further.

"Sorry. To be fair, they were asleep when I first went out. Snuck up on me, they did."

"The weapon's locked away, right?"

"'Course. Keys always on me, love."

Aiden sighed through his nose, "I guess it's alright. I think they just want to be like you, nothing wrong with that."

Masika's stomach fluttered at that last sentence. He smooched her cheek before retiring to his lazyboy.

***

The following morning, she got up an hour early, around when Aiden left. She crept outside with her katana as silently as she could, starting her warmup. By the time the sun had fully risen, she heard crackling in the grass nearby. She sighed in annoyance.

"Bug?"

They ashamedly crawled into her view. She sheathed the katana and threw them a slightly disapproving glare.

"I just wanna watch," they exclaimed, "I'm sorry."

"It's alright," she calmed, tapping the handle as she internally questioned their fascination. "Guess if my mom had a katana, I'd be curious about it too."

She withdrew the weapon once more, aiming it towards the ground. Bug crept closer and flopped onto their belly, hands nestled beneath their chin as they gazed up at her. Distancing herself a bit, she executed a few swift swings.

Bug shifted as they observed, smile not wavering the slightest. They got up and mimicked her movements, stumbling at first before finding their footing. Masika considered buying them a play sword the next time she was out.

She finished out the display with a spin jump, landing with her knee in the dirt and blade sunk into the sand. Bug tried to do the same and fell straight onto their face. She was quick to leave the weapon aside and pick up her child gently. Face covered in sand, they trembled and struggled not to cry. Wiping what she could with her shirt, she walked them to the hose. Turning it on low pressure, she picked it up.

"Keep your eyes closed. Gonna rinse the rest off, okay?" They stood still as a statue as she held the hose over their forehead, letting the water cascade down their face. "Good job, Bug."

Salty hot tears combined with the cool water; Bug was overwhelmed by the unwelcome sensation of sand. She kissed both their cheeks before giving them a tight hug.

"It's okay. Let it out, sweetheart, Mommy's right here."

Once the droplets ceased, the two sat across from each other. Bug stared intently at her, something she still wasn't used to. Unlike her and Aiden, the child was rarely put off by eye contact. They sat wordlessly for several minutes.

"I wanna learn how to fight," they finally signed.

Masika's eyebrows furrowed, "No."

"Please?"

"Bug... Didn't learn for fun. Do it to keep everyone I love safe," she told them.

"That's why I want to learn too!"

It was obvious Bug couldn't comprehend what she was saying. They were, at times, annoyingly innocent. Masika had to remind herself that this was normal. This was how kids were supposed to be. They aren't supposed to know dread or fear. She took a deep breath and ruffled their hair.

"Let me think about it, okay?"

So, she did, late that night next to Aiden in bed. It kept her up for several hours. Thoughts disjointed and erratic as usual, she struggled to list the pros and cons. When she got close, the voices would overlap and swell into a cacophony of yelling. She eventually got out of bed to clear her head. A bowl or two of weed later, she was able to almost think.

Her main issue was she didn't want Bug growing up too fast. She didn't want their childhood to reflect hers or Aiden's. A small part of her believed teaching them violence would lead them to corruption. That their innocence would fracture and dissipate. That, like her, they would wind up taking out their emotions in blood. She reasoned with herself. She knew she was capable of showing Bug self-defense without encouraging legitimate harm. It would simply be a matter of how.

She drew up a rough lesson plan. It made sense to her—ballet, hand-to-hand combat, then weapons—so she continued the line of thinking. She stayed up the entire night writing down ideas and brainstorming. When Aiden woke up, he tapped her shoulder. She turned to face him in the desk chair.

"Yes?"

"Have you been up all night?"

She blinked, glancing at the alarm clock on their nightstand. "Guess I was."

"What's all this?" Aiden asked before picking up a paper. When he read her writing, he frowned.

"Won't leave me alone about it, and maybe it's a good idea for them to know how to defend themself. This world is cruel, Aiden. Both know that..." she trailed off and gently set down her pencil. "Need to make sure they would be safe if something happened to us. Think that's reasonable, don't you?"

Aiden visibly relaxed, returning the sheet to her. He brought his lips to her forehead before pulling away.

"I trust you," he breathed.

"Thank you."

"...As long as they don't get hurt."

"Have a feeling I'm the only one who's gonna get hurt. Don't worry, my love."

CHAPTER THIRTY-NINE

March 2003

When Masika finally caved into lessons, elation filled Bug's very being. In the days leading up, they were unable to sit still much longer than a minute. They wore themselves out running around the house, pretending to chase and apprehend imaginary enemies. Masika advised them to save their energy, but the child paid her no mind.

On the first day of training, she woke them up at eight a.m. sharp. She provided a hearty breakfast, as always, and announced that she bought a barre.

"What's that?" Bug asked, mouth full of pancakes.

"Use it to warm up in the mornings, think of it as a tool."

"Tool. Tool. Tool..." they repeated.

Once both had full stomachs, she taught them the first three ballet positions, of which they caught on quickly. A glimpse of impatience flickered in their eyes as she showed them relevé.

"Will I dance like you soon?"

"Takes time and patience, but yes. One day you will."

Once they grew bored of dancing, Masika transitioned to the backyard. She'd set up a couple training dummies made of sticks and fabric while Bug slept. They ran circles around the objects before Masika called for their attention. They bounded up eagerly as she shrugged off her jacket, tying it around her waist.

"Alright Bug. Want you to hit me as hard as you can." Their face paled and she shrugged, "Can't teach you otherwise."

"Why can't I hit the scarecrows?" they questioned.

Amused by Bug thinking the dummies were 'scarecrows,' she stifled a chuckle before responding. "For later, when you're stronger. For now, want you to use me as a target. So go on. Hit me as hard as you can."

With all the strength they could muster, Bug slapped her stomach. The guffaw that followed made them turn red all the way to their ears. Masika quelled her laughter as she knelt and patted their shoulder.

"Sorry, didn't mean to laugh. Gonna have to hit a lot harder than that, okay?" She stood up, "Again. This time, punch me."

"Punch?"

Masika molded their knuckles into a fist. "Put your thumb on the outside of your fingers. Then swing," she showed with her own punch to the air. "Try it."

Bug threw several haphazard ones. Masika observed, taking note of posture issues. She corrected them, and they stood up straighter for the next few swings. Once she was satisfied, she brought the focus onto herself.

"Good, now punch me."

Bug punched her square in the stomach. Masika yelped, not expecting the impact to be as strong as it was. Bug apologized profusely, but she simply beamed at them.

"That's the spirit!"

Substituting as a training dummy for the day, she let Bug practice for a while longer before shifting to kicks. They carried a natural strength, easily leaving marks and bruises behind with every blow. The kid was a natural, and she partially wanted to take the credit for it.

Once Bug got too winded, she introduced them to several play weapons she'd crafted out of foam and cardboard, a sneak peek for the next lesson. Bug picked up each faux weapon from the porch workbench, inspecting.

"Gonna use these to prepare you for real weapons," she explained.

"What about the pew pew ones?" they rotated a fake dagger in their grip.

Masika's eyebrows furrowed, "What?" They aimed the dagger as if it were a gun. She shook her head, "Absolutely not."

"Why not?"

"Not a fair way to fight by any means."

Bug briefly pouted, only to bounce right back when she declared the first lesson to be over. She offered to watch cartoons with them until lunch. Bug giddily agreed, flying into the apartment at record speed. She followed in tow with a slight limp. *Damn, that kid punches harder than I thought.*

Once together on the couch, Bug rambled on and on about the princess in the cartoon. Masika did her best to listen, but she started to slip away. Flashbacks riddled her brain, rapid-fire, and she subsequently zoned out. Bug sensed the shift in her demeanor instantly.

They curled into her and lightly tugged at her dress. "Mommy? Are you okay?"

It took her a couple minutes to respond, but when she did, it was with the warmest smile. She ruffled their hair.

"Yes, enjoying my time with you."

"Then why are you sad?"

"Well..." she paused, choosing her words carefully. "Have a lot on my mind, that's all. Promise I'm okay."

In reality, she knew of no such concept.

***

Before Masika knew it, April had reared its ugly head. The training sessions were becoming hellacious under the pounding Nevada sun. At the end of them, Masika and Bug would lay on the cold living room tile in front of a large box fan.

Bug's strength increased steadily. She'd noticed the tiniest bit of muscle stacking onto their frame. By week three, she felt comfortable enough equipping them with a small, dull butterfly knife. However, it wasn't strength or weapons that Bug excelled in—it was the art of escaping.

Their size gave them an advantage against grown folk. She taught them how to evade and get out of any position with increasing difficulty. They were always able to wriggle out of her grasp with ease. It impressed her more than she could admit.

April's focus, she decided, would be honing their combat skills. Slippery limbs could only do so much, after all, especially if the opponent had insurmountable strength. She encouraged them to punch, kick, and slap harder. With more intent. With the intent to...

"Kill?"

She stopped, staring at them blankly. This day the session had begun late, she'd been dissociating once again and lost track of time. Now they were out in the yard, practicing blows on the training dummies. Bug sighed in agitation at her withdrawn state.

"Sorry, lost my train of thought. What we doing?" Masika asked them, scratching her neck.

"You said I have to punch harder and I wanna know if that means kill."

"Never kill unless you have no other choice. For now, aim to knock them out and get away."

Bug spent twenty more minutes practicing on the dummies. Once satiated by their progress, she challenged them to attack her instead.

"Take me down, or hurt me enough, you can consider yourself graduated," she promised them.

Bug lit up as they repeatedly jumped, "Really?!"

"Yes, but only if you injure me or get me on the ground. Are you ready?"

"Mhm!!"

"Go ahead."

Bug launched themself off the ground and grabbed onto her torso. She grabbed a fistful of their dress and peeled them off. They swung and kicked violently in her direction, so she chuckled. She threw them to the ground as gently as she could, but enough to leave a sting on their backside. They groaned on impact, rolling on their side to look up at her.

"Try again, find another attack point."

They howled and barreled towards her once more. This time they didn't jump, staying on her level to deliver a few punches to the gut. She blocked each before pushing them to the ground once more. A fierceness manifested as they glared at her from below.

"Again, get up faster next time."

Over and over Bug tried to complete their task and she swiftly defeated them each time. She could sense the restlessness bubbling within, slowly subsiding for rage.

At one point she tackled them to the ground before scampering to her feet. This time, they didn't get up. They breathed heavily out their nose, face in the sand. They glanced at her and her chest tightened. Terror greeted her and she wouldn't let it deter.

"Get up," she spoke. They stifled a sob and her voice turned to a command, "Get up, Bug. A real enemy wouldn't hesitate. Get up!"

Masika didn't anticipate the war cry that followed, nor a fist full of sand to her face. She sputtered and frantically tried to wipe her eyes, easily taken down by her child. She fell onto her back, where she pathetically tried to cover her face from several sporadic punches. Her blocking did not work, and their fist connected with her left cheek.

She managed to shove Bug off and roll onto her knees. She wiped the sand off her face before spitting up a wallop of blood. In the puddle sat a tooth.

Bug recovered and stood, taking in their work. Before she could react, they burst into tears and profusely apologized. A laugh traveled up Masika's throat and startled them. She rubbed the blood off her mouth and beamed widely.

"Now that's how you punch. Good job!" She realized their concern and softened, "Aw, honey. Honey, it's okay, I'm not hurt."

They tearfully nodded as she picked them up, cradling their head as she walked them inside.

Later that night, as her and Aiden got ready for bed, she tapped his shoulder. He turned to her and she bared her teeth, showing a gap where one of her molars had been. Aiden gasped.

"What happened?!" he questioned, holding his toothbrush between his own teeth.

"Bug finally learned how to throw a proper punch."

"Holy shit. They really are just like you, aren't they?" Aiden responded with an amused expression.

"Maybe," Masika admitted, shy but proud.

"Was that the final lesson?"

Masika finished brushing her teeth and spat in the sink. "In terms of fighting, yes, but gonna have a few more about some other stuff."

She knew she couldn't go without teaching Bug about sympathy and boundaries; something her family never taught her.

So, over the following week, she traded combat training for meditation. Self-actualization and reflection were vital tools Teneca had given her; now she would pass it on to her offspring. To her amazement, Bug received the information equally well. This temporarily subdued her concerns of Bug transforming into a cold-blooded killer.

Key word, 'temporarily.'

***

It took all of three days to slip into psychosis. Memories of Everlee's reign of terror broiled as always, and by extension, the fear her family was being hunted. She wasn't even sure what triggered the episode, as everything had been going smoothly. In attempts to save them from her volatile state, she limited her verbal interactions with Bug. She refused to lash out at them like Kevin used to lash out at her.

When she and Aiden were alone Thursday night, she fractured in a way that could not be hidden. As she stared at her reflection in the bathroom mirror, she mumbled beneath her breath. The words were ones she rarely spoke anymore, taken straight from the Bible or Everlee's mouth. Aiden heard her from the bedroom and joined her side.

"Masika, what's wrong?" he asked.

"Sometimes wish you and Bug hated me."

Aiden frowned, "What have you done to deserve our hatred?"

"Sinned. Or..." she swallowed and turned to face him, "don't know, most of it Everlee told me to do. Sprinkled murder into her guide on 'womanhood', tested me. Maybe it wasn't my fault... No. No, was my fault—"

"She treated you horribly, love. It definitely wasn't your fault."

"Even though I slept with her?"

He drew closer, "You make it sound like you made the first move. But that's not true, is it? You said she kissed you randomly at the gun range."

"She did," Masika confirmed.

"She told you she would be your mentor. Mentors don't sleep with their students, do they?"

"M-Maybe led her to believe I liked her that way. Maybe gave the wrong impression. But don't know, thought it would be professional. Told myself it would be strictly professional. Don't think ever gave off the vibe I wanted more..."

"I don't think you did, either. Masika, can I be frank?" When she nodded, his eyebrows upturned, "It sounds like she coerced you in the same way she coerced you into killing for her. She's a monster, her actions are inexcusable. I know it's hard to believe, my love, but you didn't do anything wrong. I promise."

"Think you're right. Nothing I can do about it now."

"What do you mean?"

"Gotta get over it."

"Masika... We both know 'getting over it' does nothing but cause grief. Did you tell me to 'get over it' when I was having issues during the pregnancy?"

"No..."

"Then you shouldn't tell yourself that. You're allowed to mourn and process how you feel, you know? I'll be here to help if you want me to." He paused, leaning against the bathroom sink, "What else is on your mind? You look frightened."

"Didn't finish her off. Can't believe I fucked up so bad, should've finished the job. Never was a problem before," she scratched her neck. "Now must face the chance she'll take you and Bug away from me. That fucking terrifies me, Aiden."

Aiden straightened. "There's no way in Hell I'm letting that bitch hurt *any* of us, especially Bug. If she has the balls to show up here, she'll have Hell to pay."

Masika furiously shook her head, "No. Don't understand, she'll *kill* you and Bug."

Aiden gently took hold of her face and pressed their foreheads together. The action sent Masika straight into hysterics, eventually collapsing into his arms. He rubbed her back for a few minutes before she stood.

"We'll protect each other if something happens," he paused at the sight of her gritted teeth, a sign she didn't buy it. "How about we prepare to move? I mean, we've been in this apartment for over a decade and I'm sure Bug would love the change of scenery. Sound good?"

She nodded, sliding her hands down her tear-stained face, "Think so."

"How about tomorrow when I'm off from work, we go ahead and plan? We can go anywhere you want."

"Sounds nice," she took in a sharp breath. "What if she gets to us before we can move away?"

"We can protect each other. I'm not letting anyone take this life from us, Masika. I don't think Bug would let anyone, either. If we are together, we will be okay." Masika, exhausted by the ill pairing of her brain and the conversation, simply nodded. "I love you."

"I love you too."

Aiden returned to bed, leaving Masika staring at the mirror. Her body and face warped into a blur as white noise blacked out her thoughts. For a singular minute, her head went silent, seldom one phrase: *You won't take my family away from me.*

Chapter Forty

April 24th, 2003

By Bug's eighth birthday, most of the apartment was in boxes. In two short days, the family was slated to move to Maryland with the help of Mahpiya, who graciously returned to town to assist. Aiden had already told Ruby and her students goodbye.

He and Masika planned to celebrate with a trip to the movies; their last hurrah before bidding the town farewell. All she had to do was wait until Aiden got off from work.

As Bug busied themself in the living room, Masika prepared dinner. In less than an hour Aiden would return, and the food would finish cooking shortly after. The three would happily enjoy their meals, then head to the theater. Knowing what to expect out of the evening should have granted her comfort.

Yet Everlee burned brightly in her thoughts, causing Masika to struggle concentrating on her task. She kept fumbling, forgetting the ingredients she needed or the order in which everything was to be prepped. She had spent *at least* twenty minutes staring blankly into the fridge and pantry. She didn't wind up starting until long after she had planned. Swallowing her self-inflicted disappointment, she tried to persevere through the normally simple process.

After a while of letting autopilot guide her, Bug was at her side tugging at her skirt. She put on her best smile.

"Yes, Bug?"

"Help?" they signed and vocalized.

The fake smile became real in an instant, "Wanna help again?"

"Yes! Yes yes yes yes!" they beamed, jumping up and down.

Washing and drying her hands, she reserved her laughter and watched them run circles in the kitchen.

"Alright, you're in charge of washing the veggies. Let me get your stool."

She fetched the stool from the bathroom to place it in front of the counter. She chopped up peppers while Bug stood on their toes to rinse lettuce in the sink. Each slice she made was uneven and more frantic than the last. She could feel Bug's eyes on her as they continued their task.

"Mommy? Are you okay?"

She nodded instinctively and did her best parental grin, boasting certainty and security. Bug frowned and shut off the faucet, calling her bluff in an instant.

"What are you thinking about?" they asked.

"Just... thinking about people."

"Bad people?"

Masika cast the knife aside and placed both palms on the counter. *I swear they're psychic.*

"Maybe. A little mind reader, you are." Both of them laughed and the edge wore off some. She cleared her throat before proceeding, "Maybe just a bit, but I'm not scared. Know we're safe. Besides, Dad will be home very soon."

Bug accepted this answer, not pressing further. Once they rinsed all the vegetables, Masika suggested they resume playing in the living room. She told them she'd join as soon as the stew was cooking. Transferring the vegetables to the pot, she was lost in her thoughts once again. Right before she put the lid on, a loud thud from the other room startled her.

Rushing to make sure Bug wasn't hurt, she found them on the floor in front of the couch, clutching their head. She asked if they were okay as she brought them to their feet. They gestured to the window behind the furniture.

"Bright," they signed.

With raised eyebrows, she noticed yellow seeping through the blinds. She climbed up onto the couch, pushing one down with her pinky. LEDS rendered her blind for several seconds, clearing up to reveal an SUV in the driveway. Before Bug could do anything else, she yanked them from the floor and ran into the kitchen.

"Mommy, what are you doing—"

She hushed as she plopped them onto the floor, ordering them to stay put. Sharp knocks rang out on the front door. Electing to ignore them, she trailed through the house, checking every room. No intruders yet. On her final stop, the bedroom, she retrieved Anuli's katana. She stared down at it for a moment, gripping the handle and sheath tightly. *Please protect us, Anuli.*

The knocks grew increasingly violent, and she hurried back to Bug. They trembled and hugged their knees. Masika knelt down, setting the weapon aside as she held them by both shoulders.

"Bug, baby, look at Mommy. Look at me," she spoke, barely masking the panic rising within. Bug wriggled in her grip, but she steadied them, "Gonna play a game, okay?"

They shook their head profusely, "Don't wanna play a game, I'm scared!"

"Know that, baby, it'll be over before you know it. Remember your favorite hiding spot?"

They vaguely gestured to the cupboard behind them. Before Masika could affirm, a thunderous crack resounded from the living room. She glanced over her shoulder, where she could make out the door slowly splintering from repeated kicks. She opened the cupboard and guided

Bug into the cramped space. They hugged their legs and wriggled around, trying to get comfortable. Masika's hand ghosted the katana sitting on her hip.

"Here's the rules. Stay here, nice and quiet, 'til the coast is clear. No matter what you hear, do NOT move. Not until I come get you. Do you understand?" She caught them drifting away and repeated herself, "Do you understand?"

Bug answered with a tearful nod. Masika ran her thumb along their cheek and planted a kiss on their forehead.

"Promise it'll be okay."

Masika closed the cupboard, listening as the front door began to cave against the assailants. She made a few guesses about the number of people awaiting her and opted to grab a knife from the kitchen. Before making a stand in the living room, she paged Aiden.

Don't come home until I say. We have company. I love you.

Once she hid the pager, she stood in the middle of the room. The door flew off its hinges, splitting in half and landing on the ground. A quartet of ski-mask wearing individuals stormed in. She took a couple steps back before throwing the cleaver at one of them. It landed straight in the middle of their throat, and they crumpled to the ground as their comrades ran over. Masika elbowed one in the nose, hard enough to break it and send them to the floor with an outcry.

Two of the assailants down, she turned her attention to the remaining pair. Unsheathing her katana with one swift motion, she distanced herself enough to deliver a slice to the neck. It left another attacker's head half-hanging off as he keeled over. A man remained, eyes widening in fright. Masika spun the sword in her hand with a smirk.

"What's wrong? Don't wanna end up like your friends?" She lunged towards him, cackling when he leapt away, "Too late now."

She drove the blade straight through his heart, sending it poking out of his back. Waiting for him to still, she withdrew. He rag-dolled to his knees, landing face-first on the carpet. Masika looked at the four bodies on the floor, along with the sheer amount of crimson. She sighed. Trailing to the one still-twitching, she sent them to their grave with a stomp of her boot.

As she turned to face the entrance, a blast blew her into a wall. She howled in agony at pain shooting through her side. Vision fuzzy and ears ringing, she struggled to decipher what had just occurred. She glanced down at the blood pouring between the fingertips ghosting her hip. She grunted and tried to stand back up, only to find her legs to be gelatin. Through the blur, she recognized the woman standing in the doorway.

"Quite a lovely home you have here, Masika."

That voice.

She had been right.

Everlee paced with a shotgun filling both hands. Her hair was black once more, and she brandished an eyepatch over the socket Masika stole from. A long, dark grey trench coat obscured most of her figure. Masika spat a wallop of blood at her feet. Everlee laughed cruelly.

"Your defiance is charming as always. I don't know why you're surprised, I told you I would find you. No matter how far you ran from me."

Masika prayed that Bug still hid in the cupboard, not risking a glance in their direction. She pursed her lips.

"Just fucking finish me already," she demanded. "That's what you want, ain't it?"

Everlee's eyes twinkled with amusement, "Aw, Masika. That would be no fun. Besides, I know about your little family. I'm going to take care of them first."

"Like hell you will."

Using the adrenaline slowly leaving her, she tried to stand. Do anything except sit there. But she couldn't, the ichor draining from her paling form. Everlee taunted her with each attempt, only fueling her anger more. The anger, however, was not enough to push her to her feet as she succumbed to the shotgun wound.

Everlee cooed, "Aw, giving up so easily? That's sad... I wanted you to be here when I—"

She was interrupted by a blow to the head. Aiden, teeming with resolve, held his cane as a weapon behind her. He tossed it aside to wrestle the shotgun from her arms. It misfired once before he was able to throw it across the room, out of her reach.

Hope filled Masika, albeit only for a moment. Everlee punched him in the throat, rolling on top of Aiden as he gagged. He slapped away the appendages attempting to strike him, but she pinned his wrists with one hand and began pummeling his face with the other. Masika couldn't contain her screams of terror anymore. Breathless, Everlee stopped.

"So this is who you threw your life away for?" A cruel grin stretched across her face as she struck him again, "I'll give it to you, pretty boy. You've got determination."

Blood flew as Masika begged for her to stop, pleading to leave Aiden out of this. To just kill her and let him go. *Anything* but this. Everlee paid her no mind, taking great elation in beating Aiden to a pulp. As Masika's thoughts began to melt and dissolve, she knew the fear wasn't enough to keep her awake. She released the pressure she'd put on the wound as tears poured down her face.

Don't let this be the end, something in her trembled. *Please.*

As if summoned by the final plea, Bug emerged from the kitchen. Oh so quiet as they tiptoed into the room, eyes locked on Everlee's skull. Sight fading, Masika struggled to see what they were holding until they got close enough. Every part of her wailed in horror as she made out the cast iron skillet in their tiny hands. Masika mumbled incoherently as she weakly reached her hand out to them. Everlee noticed her movement and smirked.

"Don't worry, he'll be gone soon. Surprised he isn't already," she chided, still unaware of Bug's presence behind her.

Masika's jaw slackened as Bug raised the skillet above their head.

About The Author

Micah Flowers is a Black writer and artist born in humble Abington, Virginia. They began writing when they were five years old. At the age of nineteen, they came out as nonbinary and genderfluid. Independent of creative pursuits they enjoy watching films, playing video games, studying psychology, and spending time with their many cats.

Micah's debut novel, Where The Stars Are, perfectly encapsulates their dedication to continuously challenging systematic oppression. They aim to boost understanding of intersectionality and normalize heavily stigmatized mental disorders through their works. They believe it is never too late to uplift and amplify BIPOC trans narratives and voices.

Visit their website at www.authormicahflowers.com for writing updates and information.

www.ingramcontent.com/pod-product-compliance
Lightning Source LLC
Chambersburg PA
CBHW020521110726
47899CB00004B/1199